Off
for the
Sweet
Hereafter

A NOVEL BY

T. R. PEARSON

LINDEN PRESS / SIMON & SCHUSTER
NEW YORK 1986

6/1988
an Lit

This novel is a work of fiction. Names, characters, places and
incidents are either the product of the author's imagination or are used
fictitiously. Any resemblance to actual events or locales or persons,
living or dead, is entirely coincidental.

Copyright © 1986 by T. R. Pearson
All rights reserved
including the right of reproduction
in whole or in part in any form
Published by Linden Press/Simon & Schuster
A Division of Simon & Schuster, Inc.
Simon & Schuster Building
Rockefeller Center
1230 Avenue of the Americas
New York, New York 10020
LINDEN PRESS/SIMON & SCHUSTER and colophon are trademarks of
Simon & Schuster, Inc.
Designed by Eve Kirch
Manufactured in the United States of America

1   3   5   7   9   10   8   6   4   2

Library of Congress Cataloging-in-Publication Data

Pearson, T. R., DATE–
Off for the sweet hereafter.

I. Title.
PS3566.E235O34   1985   813'.54   85-30027
ISBN 0-671-61437-1

For
J. Nelson Hathcock
himself

One

THAT WAS THE SUMMER we lost the bald Jeeter who was not even mostly Jeeter anymore but was probably mostly Throckmorton or anyway was probably considered mostly Throckmorton which was an appreciable step up from being considered mostly Jeeter since Jeeters hadn't ever been anything much while Throckmortons had in fact been something once previously before the money got gone and the prestige fell away leaving merely the bluster and the taint and the general Throckmorton aroma all of which taken together hardly made for a legacy worth getting stirred up over but any one of which taken singly still outstripped the entire bulk of advancements ever attempted and realized by Jeeters who had scratched around in the dirt but were not much accomplished at farming and who had speculated in herds of cattle but were not much accomplished at speculating either and who at last had turned their energies to the construction of a henhouse which commenced ramshackle and got worse but became nonetheless the chief Jeeter advancement along with the hens and the little speckled brown eggs and the localized ammonia cloud which was itself most probably the primary Jeeter success though no particular Jeeter or group of Jeeters together actually contributed to it or could prevent it either and so when the bald Jeeter, with the fat Jeeter as her maid of honor, exchanged vows with Braxton Porter Throckmorton III in the sanctuary of the Methodist church on Saturday June the twelfth, 1942, and afterwards set up house in Neely proper she got away from the hens and the henhouse and out from under the ammonia cloud which was most likely beginning to expand in June of 1942 since it set in to expanding most every June and swelled straight through August and on into September, especially this past

August and especially this past September when it was bearing down on the town limits and posing some threat to the icehouse which was regular and ordinary for the season, particularly in August and particularly in September, so we were having what had come to be our usual summer straight up to the moment Mr. Derwood Bridger laid his ladder against the Throckmorton clapboard and climbed to the upper story where he pressed his nose to the bedroom windowscreen and shaded his eyes and called and hollered and shrieked at the bald Jeeter until he was satisfied that she was gone from us for good.

Mrs. Askew's front gutter had been troubling her some of late. It was not living up to its responsibilities as far as Mrs. Askew was concerned, and though she did not to any degree consider herself an authority on guttering she did hold to her personal conviction that downspouts were intended to serve more than a purely ornamental function which Mrs. Askew believed to be the solitary function her downspouts were serving since they did not seem to get involved much with rainwater when the opportunity presented itself. Instead whatever the front gutter happened to catch off the roof did not flow to the right or the left but proceeded direct over the lip into Mrs. Askew's jonquil bed and onto her front stoop where it puddled up nicely for the newsboy, Bill Ed Myrick jr., who could throw a *Chronicle* most anywhere that was wet or out of reach or otherwise excessively inconvenient and what part of the puddle the paper didn't sop up eventually seeped off through the foundation to Mrs. Askew's cellar floor where it did what it could to contribute to the mustiness roundabout. Of course Mrs. Askew's downspouts had lapsed into obsolescence long before Mrs. Askew got sufficiently worked up to cure them of it. Ever since Mr. Askew passed away in 1967 the dilapidation of the Askew house had proceeded unchecked and with some serious velocity since Mrs. Askew was not nearly so adroit and handy as Mr. Askew who had not in any real sense been adroit and handy himself but ever could successfully manipulate the telephone so as to introduce a proper expert into whatever situation might be ripe for one; as a rule Mr. Askew, who prepared the weekly payroll at the cotton mill, did not take a personal interest in any manner of degenerated household item unless it could be added, subtracted, multiplied, or divided into good repair. But Mr. Askew had not put his dialing finger to much use or even wiggled it for that matter since October of 1967 and Mrs. Askew had never come to develop any sort of purposeful relationship with the Neely yellow pages, so season in and season out for very likely a half dozen years or more rainwater dripped off the roof and overflowed the front gutter into the jonquil bed and onto the stoop without ever venturing towards the downspout to the left or the one to the right either, each of which hung at an opposite corner of the house and both of which together enlivened the general aspect with their presence.

There's no reason to believe Mrs. Askew would have ever repaired, replaced, or otherwise unduly bothered herself with the front gutter if Bill Ed Myrick jr. had not landed Mrs. Askew's brother's child full into the heart of a fully developed stoop puddle. Mrs. Askew's niece, Miss Belinda Heather Sewell, had come out at the country club on a Friday evening in late July and a picture of her and her father was to appear in the Saturday *Chronicle*, a picture Mrs. Askew intended to clip and hold for a keepsake since what girls got the chance to come out were not generally allowed to do it more than once. However, along about two o'clock Saturday afternoon a tremendous rainstorm kicked up out of the southeast and while Mrs. Askew's runoff was still beating back the jonquils and pooling up against the threshold Bill Ed Myrick jr. came round with the paper and delivered Mrs. Askew's copy by way of a sharp overhand toss from the curbing. Bill Ed did not see it necessary or fitting to squander the time it would take to walk the twenty-five feet up to Mrs. Askew's door and back again or up to anybody else's door and back again either since Bill Ed was not one to meander until he got onto the boulevard where he could do some meaningful loitering under Marcia Satterwhite's bedroom window. So Bill Ed threw Mrs. Askew's *Chronicle* from the curbing, with his wrist mostly, and like usual fired it square against the bottom portion of Mrs. Askew's aluminum stormdoor and thereby produced a severe dose of flutters and palpitations in Mrs. Askew who was momentarily too preoccupied with regulating her breathing to figure out that the racket had to be made by what it was made by. Consequently, Mrs. Askew could not manage to fetch in the paper until it had already sopped up all the stoop puddle it could hold, and even though she peeled the society page off from the rest and dried it in the oven the photograph of Mrs. Askew's brother and Mrs. Askew's brother's daughter had bled into and been ruined by a sizable rectangular advertisement for Dr. Norman Talton's Clinic of Chiropractic on the Richardson Road. And in a fit of matchless and highly uncharacteristic pique, and with Bill Ed Myrick jr. already gone off down the boulevard to Marcia Satterwhite's bedroom window, Mrs. Askew snatched up the phone and more than held up her end of a passionate exchange with a gentleman at Sears and Roebuck.

They sent Mr. Mountcastle on the Wednesday following the Saturday of the photograph of Mrs. Askew's brother and Mrs. Askew's brother's daughter at the Friday night coming out. Mr. Mountcastle was one of the Eden Mountcastles and though he had his own business he did most all the Sears and Roebuck gutter work roundabout. As a rule, Mountcastles are by nature excruciatingly conscientious and Mr. Mountcastle the gutterman was not any exception. In fact not any of all the dozens of Eden Mountcastles was any exception except for one, that being Watt Mountcastle of the homeplace who had somehow or another got burdened with all of the sloth and sorriness that the rest of the Mountcastles had neglected to take on for themselves. But even Watt Mountcastle was a joy to the family and all of the rest of the Mountcastles clamored to do for him because, with the exception of Watt himself, Mountcastles are excruciatingly considerate also, and Mrs. Askew's Mr. Mountcastle was probably one of the most excruciating Mountcastles to be had anywhere. Mr. Mountcastle told Mrs. Askew that he would come by at ten o'clock on Wednesday and he did which should have given Mrs. Askew some indication of what she was in for. Then he climbed up on the roof straightaway and studied Mrs. Askew's front gutter from all over and poked at it and tapped at it and scrutinized the downspouts with a flashlight, and the thing of it was Mrs. Askew did not want him to study the front gutter or poke it or tap it or even begin to scrutinize the downspouts. She simply wanted him to take the whole business down off the house and replace it with some of Sears's best seamless aluminum guttering which she knew to be on sale on account of the most recent of the supplementary catalogs which still came to Mr. Askew through the mail though he was not inclined to do much shopping any longer. But after Mr. Mountcastle had concluded his studying and poking and tapping and scrutinizing and had come down off the roof, he did not find himself disposed to sell Mrs. Askew even the first seamless foot of Sears's best aluminum guttering because he had brought all his native excruciatingness to bear on the subject and could not get comfortable with the notion that seamless aluminum guttering was what the situation called for. And Mr. Mountcastle screwed the toe of his right shoe into Mrs. Askew's front lawn as he commenced to endeavor to make an observation which he persisted in commencing to endeavor to make for a measurable span of time, since Eden Mountcastles are extraordinarily slow-tongued on top of everything else, until at last he did manage to say, "Ma'm, have you tended to your guttering lately? Cleaned it, I mean, cleared it of leaves and pine needles and such rubbish as that?"

And Mrs. Askew, who figured herself to be slam in the middle of tending to her guttering, crossed her arms over her chest and told Mr. Mountcastle she'd had no occasion to be up on the roof anytime lately, to which Mr. Mountcastle did not reply and did not screw his toe into the lawn either but instead simply smiled much like the way Jesus smiles in those pictures of him on the walls of the Methodist fellowship hall.

"Let's just you and me tidy this thing up some," Mr. Mountcastle said and helped himself to Mrs. Askew's garden hose which was rolled up behind a camellia bush at the corner of the house. He hauled it up onto the roof with him, squatted on the shingles, and told Mrs. Askew if she'd just step over to the faucet and give it a turn he'd wash her gutter down for her.

But Mrs. Askew did not want her gutter washed down or tended to or tidied up or otherwise fooled with. She wanted it hauled off. So Mrs. Askew did not leap directly into the shrubbery to the watertap, did not go much of anywhere at all, but instead stayed where she was, laid her head back a little, and aired out some rather emphatic sentiments on the subject of seamless aluminum guttering which was a rare display for Mrs. Askew since neither Askews nor Sewells either are known to be particularly emphatic people by nature.

From where she was there on the front lawn Mrs. Askew probably could not see that Mr. Mountcastle was smiling like Jesus again. She watched him stick the nozzle of the hose into the near downspout, descend the ladder, cross into the shrubbery to the watertap and back out again, and then up towards the roof once more, and though she did not ever not watch him from the time he came down off the house to the time he went back up onto it, Mrs. Askew still probably did not notice that Mr. Mountcastle was smiling like Jesus since she seemed to be looking at him a little too hard to actually be seeing anything. And Mr. Mountcastle sat on his heels all the way across the roof and plucked the serious debris out from the gutter and tossed it onto the lawn and washed most everything else into the downspouts until at last he was satisfied that the water was going where it ought to or anyway that most all of the water was going where it ought to except for the drips and droplets that fell through the various rust holes in the galvanized metal, holes which Mr. Mountcastle told Mrs. Askew he could patch as good as ever.

But Mrs. Askew had not wanted her gutter washed out or tidied up or tended to and did not care to have it patched either. She wanted it hauled off. So before Mr. Mountcastle could begin to spread his lips even a quarter of the way out across his face, Mrs. Askew said to him, "I do believe aluminum gutters would be the thing," and while she remained excessively emphatic for an Askew or a Sewell, she had fallen off some from her previous showing.

"Yes ma'm," Mr. Mountcastle said and swung around onto the ladder.

"I mean I do believe they are just what I need," Mrs. Askew told Mr. Mountcastle, told his backside mostly.

And Mr. Mountcastle paused in front of Mrs. Askew and replied, "Yes ma'm," before continuing on across the lawn to his truck and fetching from it a tube of plumber's dope.

"They would be a refreshing change," Mrs. Askew insisted.

"Yes ma'm," Mr. Mountcastle said, "they probably would," and back up the ladder he went with his tube of plumber's dope and squatted all across the roof dabbing a little of it into each of the rust holes. And when he'd replaced the cap on the tube and when he'd removed the tube to his pocket, Mr. Mountcastle stood stark upright and asked Mrs. Askew, "What about the backside?"

"Everything's fine there," Mrs. Askew told him, "no trouble at all, not a leak or a drip or a puddle anywhere ever."

"Yes ma'm," Mr. Mountcastle said, and then him and the nozzle end of the hose disappeared over the rooftop.

Mr. Mountcastle suggested that Mrs. Askew have the insides of her gutters painted with a sealer within the month and he wrote down Mr. Derwood Bridger's name and number on the back of the bill, for all of which Mrs. Askew did not exactly let on to be so exceedingly grateful but earned herself one of Mr. Mountcastle's most accomplished Nazarene grins anyway. And in fact Mrs. Askew intended to follow Mr. Mountcastle's advice and call Mr. Bridger straight off. She intended to call him directly after Mr. Mountcastle departed but somehow she only continued to intend to call Mr. Bridger on through the third week in July and the fourth week and the first and second weeks in August and into the middle of the third one simply because it was far more convenient for Mrs. Askew to perpetually intend to do a thing than it was for her to actually set out and do it. Any way after Mr. Mountcastle brought the garden hose down off the roof and carried his ladder to his truck Mrs. Askew discovered she was not plagued with a runoff problem anymore or a stoop puddle either and could not convince herself to feel plagued or troubled or even the slightest bit bothered by the insides of her gutters since that was not anything she could stand on the front lawn and get annoyed over. So Mrs. Askew could not seem to get beyond intending to call Mr. Bridger until midmorning of Friday August the eighteenth which was significant to Mrs. Askew only because it followed the afternoon of Thursday August the seventeenth which was truly the crucial time on account of it was Thursday the seventeenth previous to Friday the eighteenth that Bill Ed Myrick jr. cocked his wrist from the curbing and launched Mrs. Askew's afternoon *Chronicle* clean up onto the roof where it settled against the toilet vent, and while Mrs. Askew believed herself a touch niggardly for leaving her gutter troughs unpainted she could not begin to abide the sight of a newspaper on the roof of her house since of all the things a woman who can stand most anything cannot stand, trashiness is probably at the top of the pile. So Mrs. Askew slipped the Sears and Roebuck bill out from under the magnet on the refrigerator door, snatched up the telephone, and became somewhat passionately emphatic all over again.

Mr. Bridger could not possibly come by on Friday the nineteenth or Saturday the twentieth or Sunday the twenty-first or Monday the twenty-second and Wednesday was more likely than Tuesday though Thursday was probably the best he could do unless it rained. As a primary occupation Mr. Bridger drove the backend of the hook and ladder out of the Omega firehouse and he was on four days and off three days during the weeks he was not on three days and off four days. As it turned out, Mr. Bridger had duty from Friday the nineteenth through Monday the twenty-second and he figured he would need Tuesday the twenty-third to rest himself from the rigors of his occupation which in Neely consisted of eating and playing ping pong and eating and playing canasta and eating and watching television and eating and sleeping in the upstairs barracks so as to slide down the pole hungry again. There was not much call for firefighting roundabout and there was not any call for a hook and ladder or a driver of the backend of it or the frontend either unless in some unlikely happenstance the topnotch of a yellow pine managed to burst into flames on its own. So Mr. Bridger did not do much of anything in the way of work on his on days and he let himself out as a housepainter and general fixit man on his off days when he did not do much of anything in the way of work also. Not that Mr. Bridger was a lazy man or a slackard, he was just what people call steady and earnest, like a glacier is steady and earnest. Consequently, when Mr. Bridger told Mrs. Askew he'd come by on Thursday if it didn't rain and then it didn't rain and he came by on Friday, Mrs. Askew did not lay any particular blame with Mr. Bridger because she understood that Mr. Bridger had in fact been coming on Thursday but simply had never arrived. It was like the world spun around faster than Mr. Bridger could bring himself to spin with it.

But he did come by on Friday along about the middle of the afternoon and that was only one full day and four hours later than he'd said he would come which would have been unforgivable in most people but was very nearly early for Mr. Bridger. However, even on Friday and even four hours later on Friday than he'd promised to come on Thursday, Mr. Bridger did not make anything in the way of feverish progress on Mrs. Askew's gutters. Initially, him and Mrs. Askew stood together on the front lawn and considered the gutter and considered the downspouts and considered the Thursday *Chronicle* next to the toilet vent, and then Mr. Bridger asked after Mrs. Askew's well-being and Mrs. Askew obliged him with a fairly interminable and lamentatious account of her lack thereof, and Mrs. Askew, being as she was a widowwoman of considerable complaints with no regular ear to pour them into, did not leave off lamentating or contemplate leaving off lamentating until she had run up a sizable catalog of annoyances, afflictions, and general torments. Mr. Bridger, through no particular fault of his own in this instance, lagged near about twenty-five years behind Mrs. Askew and so had become only partially as annoyed and afflicted and tormented as Mrs. Askew was, but Mr. Bridger did recollect he had an aunt down with the piles and since Mr. Askew had been a pile sufferer, Mr. Bridger and Mrs. Askew landed upon some common territory and carried on from there for an appreciable spell. They did get on to the topic of gutters eventually, not because the topic of piles wore out but mostly on account of Mrs. Askew who felt that the discussion was heading in an indelicate direction and who believed that there were some things a woman of standing did not speak of with her gutterpainter. However, even once they left off with the piles and set in with the gutters, Mrs. Askew and Mr. Bridger did not go to the trouble at hand straightaway but instead commenced with gutters as a general item and wandered some to the theory of the downspout before coming full around to Mrs. Askew's specific run of freshly cleaned, plumber's doped, galvanized trough. And Mr. Bridger took ahold of his chin and surveyed the underside of Mrs. Askew's front guttering and Mrs. Askew surveyed it along with him until she finally suggested that Mr. Bridger would probably have to get his ladder and climb up onto the roof since it was not the underside of the gutter that needed any attention, and Mr. Bridger blew a breath overtop of his knuckles and told Mrs. Askew he did not see any way around it himself.

So Mr. Bridger unstrapped his aluminum extension ladder from off the top of his Country Squire station wagon, ran it up several rungs past the front guttering, and climbed onto Mrs. Askew's roof. Now Mrs. Askew's neighbors all roundabout had been watching through their windowsheers Mrs. Askew and Mr. Bridger on Mrs. Askew's front lawn discussing whatever it was they were discussing which not any one of them even remotely imagined had anything whatsoever to do with piles but which they had each speculated upon and wondered at until they were all fairly much thoroughly eaten up with curiosity. But while peeking through sheer draperies had developed locally into a kind of sport on a par with bowling or miniature golf so that hardly a prominent windowlight in the town limits did not bear a noseprint on some part or another of it, outright gawking in the open air was not nearly so stylish unless of course the outright gawkee could be construed to be engaged in some form of active labor which automatically forgave any onlookers since watching other people work enjoyed considerable favor throughout the county and on into the far reaches of the state. So Mr. Bridger had not put shoeleather to shingle when the clatter and rattle of deadbolts and screendoor hooks kicked up around him like a hailstorm. One house down the street the widow Mrs. Jennings W. Hayes stepped out onto her frontporch blinking in the sun and one house up the street the bald Jeeter Throckmorton make a great show of peering into her mailbox before hooting at Mrs. Askew as if she was verily astounded to see her. Across the way Miss Bernice Fay Frazier and her sister, Mrs. Estelle Frazier Singletary, left off haggling with and snapping at each other long enough to poke their heads out the sidedoor, and Mr. Tiny Aaron enjoyed the great good fortune of having turned off the boulevard onto Mrs. Askew's street in his stark white Impala just as Mr. Bridger was hunkering down into his initial squat on the roof, and Mr. Aaron brought his car very nearly off the road and to the curbing in front of Mrs. Askew's house but not quite and he laid himself full out the sidewindow from the chest up.

Mr. Bridger's labor took the form mainly of some serious peering, but serious peering, especially from a rooftop, can stir people appreciably and soon enough Mrs. Askew found herself in the company of the widow Mrs. Jennings W. Hayes and the bald Jeeter Throckmorton and Miss Bernice Fay Frazier and her sister, Mrs. Estelle Frazier Singletary, who lived across town on the ninth fairway with Mr. Estelle Singletary but had happily timed her visit. Mrs. Askew introduced the ladies to Mr. Bridger and introduced Mr. Bridger to the ladies, and then attempted to explain the nature of her gutter dilemma breaking off from time to time to field inquiries from Mr.

Aaron down on the street. Of course at length the topic of gutters lost the majority of its appeal, and because the issue was still much on her mind Mrs. Askew touched briefly upon the delicate subject of piles and made mention of Mr. Bridger's suffering aunt which generated noticeable feeling among the ladies who all laid their heads back and openly expressed their deep regret and sympathy for which Mr. Bridger said, "Thank you," from the roof.

On several occasions Mrs. Askew reminded Mr. Bridger to fetch down the Thursday *Chronicle* from beside the toilet vent and invariably Mr. Bridger would stand up from his squat long enough to re-hike his pants and tell her, "Yes ma'm," but chiefly Mrs. Askew found herself engaged in a lively exchange of pleasantries with her neighbors and Mrs. Estelle Singletary which were punctuated every now and again by questions from Mr. Tiny Aaron down on the road in his Impala who had dropped off the pace some and was just getting up to the piles. Mrs. Askew and her neighbors had plenty to talk about since even though they all lived within plain sight of each other not one of them ever went much of anywhere outside except to church on Sundays and while Mrs. Askew attended the Methodist church on Harker Avenue, the widow Mrs. Jennings W. Hayes gathered with the dissenting Presbyterians on the by-pass, and the bald Jeeter Throckmorton and Miss Bernice Fay Frazier both took themselves off to separate Baptist services, the bald Jeeter being a First Baptist Church of Neely Baptist and Miss Frazier, along with her sister, Mrs. Estelle Singletary, a Calgary Free Will Baptist Church Baptist, the two of which were possibly the same species but were not hardly the same animal. From all reports Mr. Tiny Aaron was generally taken to be a regular heathen. So the ladies did not run together much of a Sunday and did not run together much any other time either mostly because the weather did not ever seem to suit them. In summertime the air was far too still and hot to be ventured into while in wintertime the days were entirely too short and cold. Autumn provided occasional pleasant afternoons, but the ladies did not care for the northerly breezes, and though springtime held considerable appeal the days were altogether far too changeable to be relied upon. Consequently, Mrs. Askew and the widow Mrs. Jennings W. Hayes and the bald Jeeter Throckmorton and Miss Bernice Fay Frazier all watched their stories on television

most all afternoon most every afternoon except for Miss Bernice Fay
Frazier who was visited by her sister each Friday at 2:00 p.m. and so
got the opportunity to haggle with and snap at somebody on a regular basis.

The ladies were understandably all astir with news once the guttering and the piles gave way to let them air it, and the widow Mrs.
Jennings W. Hayes commenced the proceedings by announcing that
her daughter, not the oldest daughter Jonellen Marie Hayes but her
next oldest daughter Rachel Suzanne Hayes, had formed an attachment with a gentleman of the law in Raleigh who was, the widow
Mrs. Jennings W. Hayes said, going places. Mrs. Estelle Singletary
told Mrs. Hayes she had a nephew that was a lawyer in Americus,
Georgia, and her and her sister, Miss Bernice Fay Frazier, both expressed their belief that he was going places also. Then Mrs. Askew
wondered did anybody know just what Tuttle it was that had died in
Yanceyville, and the bald Jeeter said she'd heard it wasn't a native
Yanceyville Tuttle but some sort of imported and naturalized Tuttle
instead, and the widow Mrs. Jennings W. Hayes, who had gotten the
same story from a cousin of hers in Wentworth, threw in with the
bald Jeeter on the Tuttle matter while Mrs. Estelle Singletary made a
point to say that she herself did not associate with Tuttles as a rule.
Subsequently, Miss Bernice Fay Frazier recollected that on the previous Tuesday whole fryers had been on sale at the Big Apple for 47¢ a
pound and she said she'd bought one but wished she'd bought two,
and Mrs. Askew asked were they meaty to which Miss Bernice Fay
Frazier replied yes they were and Mrs. Estelle Singletary said she'd
bought three herself which prompted Miss Bernice Fay Frazier to re-
consider and announce that she wished she'd bought three also. Mrs.
Askew had not bought any chickens and though she wished she had
also she did not set her desires at any particular number of whole
fryers but instead persevered with the topic of edibles and was fixing
to relate the main details of a magazine article she'd read on the uses
of ornamental kale when Mr. Tiny Aaron from out the sidewindow of
his stark white Impala down on the road set in to telling how he'd
had a pilectomy himself in 1962, news of which somehow jarred Mrs.
Askew back to the business at hand and she made a point of remind-
ing Mr. Bridger to fetch down the *Chronicle* from beside the toilet

vent, so naturally Mr. Bridger stood up from his squat, rehiked his pants, and told her, "Yes ma'm."

While the ladies discussed garden vegetables which led to produce in general and culminated in a lively debate on the value of roughage so as to tie back in with the pilectomy that Mr. Tiny Aaron was describing from down on the road with both hands and his mouth too, Mr. Bridger squatted across the front pitch of Mrs. Askew's roof and tested Mr. Mountcastle's plumber's dope patching with his finger. Once he'd satisfied himself that all the gutter holes were properly filled or once he'd grown suitably weary of squatting, whichever came first, Mr. Bridger climbed to the peak of the house and stretched and straightened and worked his back, taking particular care to massage the pelvic bone he had fractured in the spring of 1977 when he fell off his ladder with his scraper and his putty knife and his softball-sized lump of window glazing direct into Mrs. Zeno Stiers's forsythia bush. But he did not linger unduly on the point of the roof and was just proceeding to vanish by degrees down the far slope when Mrs. Askew hollered up to him that everything was fine back there, that there was no trouble at all, that there wasn't a leak or a drip or a puddle anywhere ever, to all of which Mr. Bridger waved his hand back over his head before disappearing down to the far gutter where, presumably, he squatted and tested and grew weary all over again.

Mrs. Askew and the bald Jeeter Throckmorton and Miss Bernice Fay Frazier and her sister, Mrs. Estelle Frazier Singletary, were all analyzing the contents of the widow Mrs. Jennings W. Hayes's special garden salad dressing recipe and Mr. Tiny Aaron was just getting around to the virtues of proctology when Mr. Bridger climbed down off the roof and approached Mrs. Askew with his findings. He said he did believe he could clear up Mrs. Askew's troubles with a solitary coat of sealer and Mrs. Askew replied that she was pleased to hear it and Mrs. Estelle Singletary told the widow Mrs. Hayes she did not see any call for sesame since it didn't seem much of a compliment to the remaining spices and the widow Mrs. Hayes objected and became peevish. Mr. Bridger estimated he could finish the job in no more than a couple of hours which Mrs. Askew replied was agreeable to her and the bald Jeeter ventured to say the sesame struck her as particularly appealing which stirred the widow Mrs. Hayes to theorize it was the sesame that enhanced the parsley flakes so enormously and down on the road Mr. Tiny Aaron set in to describing something with his hands which did not appear quite so large as a breadbox but very nearly. Then Mr. Bridger removed a small pad of white paper and a stubby pencil from his shirt pocket, scribbled a figure on the top sheet, and tore it loose and handed it to Mrs. Askew who immediately and utterly usurped the prominence the widow Mrs. Jennings W. Hayes's garden salad dressing had enjoyed for such a considerable spell. And although Mrs. Askew dodged and twisted and maneuvered extensively, they all saw it anyway except for the bald Jeeter who got told what it was by Mrs. Estelle Singletary who decided straight off she would not pay it if it was her. Miss Bernice Fay Frazier, in an exceptional lapse in haggling and snapping, threw in with her sister and condemned the figure as unreasonable, but the widow Mrs. Jennings W. Hayes who had had a plumber in to replace her kitchen taps in 1975 took a more moderate view, and the bald Jeeter Throckmorton said it did not seem to her such an awful lot of money either. So Mrs. Askew weighed off the various opinions and just prior to settling her own mind asked Mr. Bridger when he could possibly do the work, and Mr. Bridger told her first thing Monday morning which very likely meant Monday afternoon and could even be construed as Tuesday, but since Mrs. Askew did not believe she could get anybody else before then and since Mrs. Askew held the recommendation of an Eden Mountcastle in extraordinarily high regard she told Mr. Bridger to come ahead Monday morning which would certainly not be Monday morning at all but maybe Monday afternoon and probably Tuesday with Wednesday not entirely out of the realm of possibility. And then Mrs. Askew laid her head back momentarily and said she did wish Mr. Bridger had recollected to fetch down the Thursday *Chronicle* from beside the toilet vent to which Mr. Bridger responded by sucking a dab of saliva between his front teeth.

He did in fact come back on the actual Monday after the Friday of his estimate when he said he would in fact come back and which happened to be the particular bald Jeeter Throckmorton Monday in August though nobody knew it was or even would be when Mr. Bridger brought his Country Squire wagon up the concrete runners Mrs. Askew called her driveway. He arrived in the middle of the afternoon and had full well intended to arrive in the middle of the morning but along about lunchtime Mr. Bridger discovered the middle of the morning was not around to arrive in anymore and so settled for the middle of the afternoon instead. Mrs. Askew had not expected him until along about Tuesday evening and consequently was not looking for Mr. Bridger and did not know he had returned until she heard something on the roof that she hoped was not a squirrel and in her great hurry to get out the front door, off the stoop, and into the yard, Mrs. Askew very nearly ran down Miss Bernice Fay Frazier who was standing on the walk with the widow Mrs. Jennings W. Hayes and the widow Mrs. Jennings W. Hayes's cleaning woman Shareena Moncrief of the Macedonia Avenue Moncriefs. They were all three looking at the front gutter or at the shingles or at the chimney stack, Mrs. Askew could not determine which though she was certain they were not looking at Mr. Bridger who had crossed over the peak of the house so as to commence his work on the backside. Mrs. Askew said she had not expected him to arrive so soon, and Miss Bernice Fay Frazier admitted she had not expected him to arrive so soon either which prompted the widow Mrs. Jennings W. Hayes to observe that she had not expected him to arrive so soon herself while Shareena Moncrief, who had not had any expectation to speak of, said nothing whatsoever.

As Mrs. Askew figured, they could all walk around to the backyard and watch Mr. Bridger from there or they could not walk around to the backyard and wait for him where they were, and Shareena Moncrief wanted to know just what she'd see if she took the trouble to walk around to the backyard, so Mrs. Askew, who did not understand much of what Mr. Bridger was up to, explained the entire process to Shareena Moncrief with the aid and assistance of Miss Bernice Fay Frazier and the widow Mrs. Jennings W. Hayes, who did not understand any of what Mr. Bridger was up to. As a result Shareena Moncrief decided not to circle around to Mrs. Askew's backyard and chose not to linger in Mrs. Askew's frontyard either but returned to the widow Mrs. Jennings W. Hayes's house so as to sanitize the upstairs toilet bowl which seemed to her altogether more promising than the prospect of watching Mr. Bridger do to a gutter what Mrs. Askew and Miss Bernice Fay Frazier and the widow Mrs. Jennings W. Hayes insisted he was going to do to a gutter. And when there were three of them not counting Mr. Bridger instead of four of them not counting Mr. Bridger, Miss Bernice Fay Frazier said out loud but to the widow Mrs. Jennings W. Hayes mostly, "I do believe the colored are entirely beyond me. Entirely," and near about the middle of the widow Mrs. Jennings W. Hayes's admitting that the colored were entirely beyond her also, except for Shareena Moncrief who was only partially beyond her, Mrs. Askew stepped backwards so as to glance full onto the bald Jeeter Throckmorton's frontporch and said, "Where is she, I wonder?"

Miss Bernice Fay Frazier wanted to know just who George Washington Carver was anyway, and so the widow Mrs. Jennings W. Hayes, whose partial comprehension of negrodom seemed to encompass the George Washington Carver question also, at least partially, set about with a few prefatory remarks on the significance of the peanut before addressing herself full onto the matter of Mr. Carver proper who proved to be considerably more elusive and mysterious than the peanut and who the widow Mrs. Jennings W. Hayes at last identified, following an extended bout of pondering and finger biting, as a small, curly-headed man.

"Do you think she's sick?" Mrs. Askew said.

"Who?" Miss Frazier asked her.

And Mrs. Askew stepped backwards again so as to look full onto the bald Jeeter Throckmorton's front porch.

"She's likely out to town," Miss Frazier said. "Don't you suspect?"

"I suppose," Mrs. Askew told her and lay back on her heels so as to peer around the porch stanchions.

The widow Mrs. Jennings W. Hayes decided Mr. Carver had most resembled snuff in color. "Like Tube Rose," she said. "Like Tube Rose in a can."

But Miss Bernice Fay Frazier grew testy and told the widow Mrs. Hayes the comparison was utterly lost on her since she did not and had never dipped herself and could not tolerate anyone who did dip. It seems snuff users were near about as far beyond Miss Frazier as negroes were. She said she could not ever hope to comprehend how people could befoul their mouths so with snuff or plug chew or even the buttends of cigarettes and cigars. Miss Frazier said she'd just as soon eat dirt as use tobacco which reminded the widow Mrs. Jennings W. Hayes that she'd seen pickaninnies eat dirt out of a clay bank across the road from her brother's house and Miss Frazier recollected she'd heard tell of such a thing before. "I wonder why it is?" Miss Frazier said, and since the widow Mrs. Jennings W. Hayes could not get a handle on it herself, they put it down as just one more item that was entirely beyond them.

Mrs. Askew had slipped off in the midsts of Miss Bernice Fay Frazier's snuff tirade, or anyway it appeared to Miss Frazier and it appeared to the widow Mrs. Hayes that Mrs. Askew had slipped off though actually she had walked direct across her sideyard to the Throckmorton flagstones and up the steps onto the front porch but had gone unnoticed by Miss Frazier and the widow Mrs. Hayes who had been blinded by quandaries at the time. Because the front screen was latched shut, Mrs. Askew could not get at the Throckmorton brass doorknocker and instead beat on the doorframe with her knuckles and called out to the bald Jeeter in an extraordinarily shrill and altogether arresting voice that surely penetrated the frame walls of the Throckmorton house and very probably got into the block cellar also. But nonetheless Mrs. Askew could not seem to raise the bald Jeeter no matter how she screeched and no matter how she banged and she could not seem to see the bald Jeeter either once she had left off screeching and had left off banging and had instead laid her face first against the windowglass to the left of the door and then against the windowglass to the right of the door. In fact, the sum total and accumulation of Mrs. Askew's various activities, that would be the screeching and the banging and the glaring, did not gain her an iota of satisfaction until she augmented them with some momentary peeping, mostly into the bald Jeeter's black metal postbox where Mrs. Askew discovered a water bill and a Value Days leaflet from the downtown Rose's which she dropped her chin and looked at like they were a pair of garden slugs. Then she hooted and waved the bald Jeeter's mail at Miss Bernice Fay Frazier and the widow Mrs. Jennings W. Hayes who watched the display briefly before exchanging observations and concluding that Mrs. Askew's intentions, though not entirely beyond them, were very nearly entirely beyond them.

With the water bill and the leaflet too still in hand, Mrs. Askew scooted off the porch and around the far side of the house to the back door, or anyway she produced the illusion of scooting without bothering to produce the velocity scooting generally calls for. She worked her arms and her legs and wagged her head and puffed and blew most furiously and thereby exhibited all of the trappings of highspeed locomotion while remaining almost utterly speedless and quite thoroughly unlocomoted. So Mrs. Askew cleared the porch and rounded the far corner of the house with considerable vigor but hardly any momentum to speak of. She tried to search out a trace of the bald Jeeter in the side windows as she passed them by but scooting and glaring, even the illusion of scooting in combination with actual glaring, did not much compliment each other, so after she flashed on by the dining room Mrs. Askew completely devoted her energies and attention to working her arms and her legs and wagging her head and puffing and blowing until at last she arrived at the backporch, yanked on the screendoor, and found it also to be latched from the inside. Naturally she lit out around the near corner towards the door off the mudroom and tried it as a last resort but the bolt held fast and Mrs. Askew could only peer in through the doorlight at the washer and the dryer and the bald Jeeter's straw sunhat hanging on a peg.

Miss Bernice Fay Frazier and the widow Mrs. Jennings W. Hayes still could not between them comprehend the significance of a water bill and a Rose's Value Days leaflet even once Miss Frazier had held the leaflet and eyed it while the widow Mrs. Hayes held and eyed the water bill after which they exchanged correspondences and held and eyed the item they had not held and eyed previously. For her part Mrs. Askew grabbed onto her knees and attempted to draw a full and regular breath and consequently was of little aid to Miss Frazier and the widow Mrs. Hayes who had discarded the water bill completely and were together perusing the Value Days leaflet and discussing the merits of panty hose when Mrs. Askew finally mustered enough wind to suggest that one or the other or both of them call Mr. Bridger down off the roof which Miss Frazier obliged her in primarily though the widow Mrs. Hayes attempted to oblige her in it also but could not manage much more than a squeak and it was not the squeak from the widow Mrs. Hayes but was instead the full-fledged invitation from Miss Bernice Fay Frazier that fetched Mr. Bridger up to the peak of

the house and away from whatever it was he had been doing to the
back gutter which not Miss Frazier or the widow Mrs. Hayes or Mrs.
Askew either had much of a grip on or could even convince Miss
Shareena Moncrief to look at and once Mr. Bridger arrived at the peak
of the roof he figured immediately that Miss Bernice Fay Frazier and
the widow Mrs. Jennings W. Hayes required his prompt assistance in
treating what appeared to be Mrs. Askew's coronary, so Mr. Bridger
scampered on down the rise to his ladder in as much as Mr. Bridger
could scamper anywhere and he actually gave the impression of haste
as he proceeded to the ground where he suggested to Mrs. Askew that
she stretch out on the grass which Mrs. Askew did not much appreciate coming from her gutterpainter.

She got her breath back presently, or anyway got part of her breath
back, enough of her breath back that is to tell Miss Bernice Fay Frazier
and the widow Mrs. Hayes and Mr. Derwood Bridger what she suspected had went with the bald Jeeter Throckmorton, but even with
the latched doors and the water bill and the Rose's Value Days leaflet
Miss Bernice Fay Frazier and the widow Mrs. Jennings W. Hayes continued to imagine that the bald Jeeter was only out to town for the
afternoon and Mr. Derwood Bridger, when called upon for his opinion, wanted to know was the bald Jeeter Throckmorton the one with
the hooked nose or the other one, and Miss Bernice Fay Frazier told
him the one with the hooked nose had been Mrs. Estelle Singletary
and it wasn't a hooked nose anyway, it was an aquiline nose, her
daddy's aquiline nose. She said the bald Jeeter had been the bald one.

"Bald where?" Mr. Bridger asked her.

"All up underneath her wig," Miss Frazier said.

"Was that a wig?" Mr. Bridger asked her.

"Pure horsehair," Miss Frazier said.

"Well I'll be," Mr. Bridger exclaimed. "I'd never have known it."

"Her grandmother stitched it off a chestnut mare," the widow
Mrs. Jennings W. Hayes said. "The thing must be fifty years old and
when it gets wet you can still get a whiff of the stable every now and
again."

"Well I'll be," Mr. Bridger exclaimed. "Isn't that the most peculiar thing?" and he looked direct at Mrs. Askew so as to allow her the
chance to agree that the bald Jeeter Throckmorton's chestnut wig was

in fact a most peculiar thing but Mrs. Askew did not seem to have any opinion on the matter and instead told Mr. Bridger and told Miss Bernice Fay Frazier and told the widow Mrs. Jennings W. Hayes, "The woman could be expiring this very minute."

"Oh, come now!" Miss Frazier said.

"Yes, really!" the widow Mrs. Hayes added.

"Expiring?" Mr. Bridger wanted to know, and Mrs. Askew told him about the latched doors and the screeching and the banging and the water bill and the Rose's Value Days leaflet and just talking about all the scooting she did took Mrs. Askew's breath all over again and even stirred Mr. Bridger up some which in turn affected Miss Frazier and the widow Mrs. Hayes who had not previously thought Mr. Bridger capable of being stirred up so they became a little agitated themselves and soon enough the four of them together were scooting across Mrs. Askew's sideyard toward the bald Jeeter Throckmorton's house, the ladies toting with them their heightened anxiety and Mr. Bridger toting with him his thirty-foot aluminum extension ladder.

Mrs. Askew screeched and banged at the front door and Miss Bernice Fay Frazier and the widow Mrs. Jennings W. Hayes each took a front window to screech and bang at while Mr. Bridger stood on the lawn with his ladder and bellowed towards the upstairs, but the bald Jeeter did not answer to the screeching and the banging and did not answer to the bellowing either so Mrs. Askew and Miss Bernice Fay Frazier and the widow Mrs. Hayes along with Mr. Bridger and his aluminum extension ladder all circled round to the back of the house and set up a clamor there which proved equally fruitless and left them only the mudroom door to cause an uproar at and after an especially violent outburst did not draw the bald Jeeter, Miss Bernice Fay Frazier and the widow Mrs. Hayes and Mr. Bridger all put their faces to the doorlight and Mrs. Askew directed them towards the bald Jeeter's sunhat hanging on a peg which seemed a particularly forlorn sight under the circumstances.

The ladies decided Mr. Bridger should climb up to the bedroom window and look in but they could not decide between them which window exactly was the bedroom window since the windows did not look the same on the outside as they did on the inside but they did all agree that the little window was the bathroom window and they did all agree it would not be seemly for Mr. Bridger to look in it. So they debated as to a proper choice for a bedroom window and all landed upon the same one eventually and Mr. Bridger extended his ladder, laid the ends of it against the clapboard, and climbed on up to the sill of what turned out to be the sewing room window and he verified to the ladies that the bald Jeeter was not sewing presently and apparently had not expired sewing, so Mrs. Askew and Miss Frazier and the widow Mrs. Hayes agreed straightaway that the remaining upper window was in fact the bedroom window and they each in turn suggested they had felt it was the bedroom window all along. Miss Frazier went so far as to wonder out loud what business Mr. Bridger had looking into the bald Jeeter's sewing room anyway and her and Mrs. Askew and the widow Mrs. Hayes all encouraged Mr. Bridger to slide his ladder on down to where he should have put it in the first place which Mr. Bridger promptly obliged them in doing and up he went again, this time past the genuine bedroom windowsill and to the genuine bedroom window. The bottom sash was partway up and Mr. Bridger put his nose against the screen, laid his hand across his forehead, and called out, "Mrs. Jeeter, Mrs. Jeeter," which Miss Frazier and the widow Mrs. Hayes neither one could stand for and together they shrieked, "Throckmorton!" just in time for Mr. Bridger to leave off clean after the initial pair of Jeeters and pick up with Throckmorton directly. And he called out again and yelled and hollered and shrieked some himself but didn't seem to get any return from it and at last he did not say anything more but simply peered in through the screen for a spell and then he left off peering also so as to look down at Mrs. Askew and Miss Bernice Fay Frazier and the widow Mrs. Jennings W. Hayes and tell them, "She's gone."

"You see," Miss Frazier said, "probably to town."

"No ma'm," Mr. Bridger told her. "I mean she's gone and I don't mean to town. She's Gone."

And Mrs. Askew looked up at Mr. Bridger in sheer undisguised puzzlement and dismay. "Do you mean?" Mrs. Askew said and left off talking but persisted in moving her mouth.

"Yes ma'm," Mr. Bridger told her. "Gone."

"This breaks my heart," Mrs. Askew said to Mr. Bridger. "This just breaks my heart," Mrs. Askew said to Miss Frazier and the widow

Mrs. Hayes who concluded it just broke their hearts also and told Mrs. Askew as much while Mr. Bridger looked through the screen again to confirm his diagnosis and saw precisely what he had seen before which was the bald Jeeter Throckmorton lying on her side partway under the bedclothes and seeming for all the world very much asleep.

"Why I just saw her on Friday," Mrs. Askew said. "Don't you recall we were all out on the walk and I showed her the gutter estimate and she said to me, 'It's not such an awful lot of money.' Those were her very words. 'It's not such an awful lot of money,' she said."

"She did, she surely did," the widow Mrs. Hayes added. "I heard her myself."

"She had a way with figures," Mrs. Askew said, "always did have a way with figures."

"She did, she surely did," the widow Mrs. Hayes added.

"Saturday, Saturday I saw her," Miss Frazier started in. "I saw her in the sideyard with the water sprinkler. She set it in her azalea bed." And Miss Frazier paused to draw up her lips into an ever so slight and bittersweet smile. "Do you recollect the way she had of stooping over so as not to dump her wig off?"

"I do," the widow Mrs. Hayes said. "I surely do."

"She was a fine woman," Mrs. Askew added.

"She was," the widow Mrs. Hayes said. "She surely was."

"A fine woman indeed," Miss Frazier said. "We were like this."

"So were we," Mrs. Askew announced.

"We were too," the widow Mrs. Hayes added. "We surely were." And the ladies all held up their fingers towards Mr. Bridger who had backed down the ladder three rungs before advancing two rungs up it again to peek through the window screen and satisfy himself altogether. "Like sisters," the widow Mrs. Hayes said.

"The same as," Mrs. Askew added.

"Precisely like sisters," Miss Frazier agreed.

And Mr. Bridger wrapped his hands around the nearest rung, laid his nose atop his knuckles, and said to himself, "Lord, the woman's bald as an egg."

Mrs. Askew called the sheriff because she had experience in calling the sheriff since she had done it before in 1967 when Mr. Askew had his stroke though that was Sheriff Carl Benjamin Browner who drowned himself in the bathtub in 1974 and so had surrendered the office, in a manner of speaking, to deputy Burton who took over the desk and the paraphernalia and the title and instituted his own manner of bluster and blow but still could not get anybody much to call him sheriff and say it the way that everybody everywhere had said it to Mr. Browner. Sheriff Burton came himself because he was not doing anything otherwise and out of reflex he backed up the ladies and backed up Mr. Bridger off and away from the scene of the investigation and straightaway proceeded up the ladder without any forethought to speak of so it was not until he reached the windowsill and prepared himself to look through it that he realized how uncommonly high off the ground he had come to be, and almost simultaneously he realized how thoroughly frightful it was to him to find himself so uncommonly high off the ground so he snatched at the ladder with every attachment he had to snatch with and him and the ladder together lurched and rattled and hooted and generally made as much fuss as a cat in a treetop.

Mr. Bridger, who was professionally acquainted with the sheriff, threw his arms across his chest and called out in an especially sweet voice, "You all right up there?" to which Sheriff Burton attempted to make prompt reply but he could not seem to bring his head around to the left and he could not seem to bring his head around to the right though he appeared inclined to do one or the other or both but was prevented from any of it by the realization of his uncommon height which appeared to be running through his body like an electric charge. Consequently, Sheriff Burton addressed the windowsill directly beneath his nose and told it of the serious misgivings his present predicament had inspired in him. He said, mostly to the windowsill but somewhat to the window casing also, he would be pleased to be fetched straightaway into the bedroom. He said he would be highly gratified to whoever might fetch him. He said he would be most highly gratified. So Mr. Bridger commenced to cast around for a way into the house, not that he desired any special gratification but more because he preferred his ladder without any sort of terrified public official clinging to the top of it. He was able to get himself in through an unlatched back window and proceeded on upstairs to the bald Jeeter Throckmorton's bedroom where he removed the screen and brought the sheriff on into the house mostly by way of the back of his pants. But even once Sheriff Burton found himself safe on the hardwood he did not seem especially highly gratified unless a quick nod of the head can be construed as a gesture of heartfelt thanksgiving. Chiefly the sheriff had his hat to worry with. It had gone awry in all of the excitement so he crossed over to the bald Jeeter's vanity and put it to rights. Then of course there was the bald Jeeter to see to and the sheriff checked her pulse at her neck and checked her pulse at her wrist and laid his hand on her forehead prior to checking her pulse at her neck again. Then he stood up from the bed, took his hat entirely off his head, and fingered the brim of it as he announced to Mr. Bridger, "This woman's deceased."

"Well I'll be goddamned," Mr. Bridger shot back at him, "and I thought she was only bald."

Sheriff Burton's patrol car out by the curb in front of the bald Jeeter Throckmorton's house had attracted an appreciable crowd in the way of most official vehicles and Mrs. Askew and Miss Bernice Fay Frazier and widow Mrs. Hayes, who were all three together narrating and enacting the bald Jeeter Throckmorton story, had just raised their fingers prefatory to waving them at the crowd when the number one hearse from Commander Avery Tuttle's Heavenly Rest turned off the boulevard and glided on up the street in that way hearses have of gliding. Mr. Dunn slipped it in behind the sheriff's car without ever accelerating without ever seeming to brake either and him and Mr. Hazlip did not exactly climb out the side doors like you would from a Rambler but fairly much emerged fullblown into the sunlight looking suitably somber and grim. They removed a collapsible chrome gurney from the back compartment and toted it on into the house, and all of the residents roundabout who had not seen fit to venture out on account of a patrol car alone could not stay away from a patrol car in combination with Commander Avery's number one hearse so the crowd expanded and swelled and Mrs. Askew and Miss Frazier and the widow Mrs. Hayes felt obliged to backtrack some for the benefit of the latecomers which left the earlycomers to dawdle and chat and peer in through the tinted glass at the insides of the hearse. Mrs. Askew had just arrived at not such an awful lot of money when Mr. Hazlip passed through the Throckmorton front doorway hindquarters foremost with the collapsible chrome gurney entirely uncollapsed and in tow, and since circumstances seemed to call for an intermission Mrs. Askew left off talking and not Miss Frazier or the widow Mrs. Hayes either one set in and together the three of them joined with the rest of the crowd in watching the progress of the corpse.

Now there had been comparable excitement only two weeks previous when Mr. Peterson from up the street got taken off in an ambulance to the Annie Gattis Memorial Hospital, but it had not been the same sort of excitement exactly on account of how Mr. Peterson had been down with the yellow jaundice for several weeks and had openly contemplated going to the hospital and had discussed the possibility with Mrs. Peterson who had in turn discussed it with several of her close acquaintances and even a neighbor or two. So when the ambulance finally did come for Mr. Peterson and the attendants carted him out into the afternoon looking for all the world like a summer squash in pajamas nobody much among the onlookers was especially agitated by the proceedings since most everybody had expected Mr. Peterson to look how he looked and had figured he would eventually go where he went. But not anybody really had anticipated that when next the bald Jeeter Throckmorton ventured out into her frontyard she would venture out into it dead, so this was probably one of what the Presbyterian Reverend Mr. Holroyd calls those sheer unforeseen vicissitudes of this our life on His planet and as such took a thoroughgoing hold of the neighbors roundabout or more likely it was just the sheer unforeseenness of this particular vicissitude that got a grip on people since most everybody was usually on the lookout for a vicissitude where they could find one, but there were vicissitudes and then there were vicissitudes and the bald Jeeter Throckmorton vicissitude seemed especially sheer and excessively unforeseen mostly because the bald Jeeter had not been sick or ailing or in the least way afflicted, only bald.

Mr. Hazlip and Mr. Dunn carried the gurney down the front steps and commenced to rolling it again once they got onto the sidewalk but the collapsible chrome gurney did not glide quite like the hearse did and every three or four paces Mr. Hazlip had to stoop and attend to the front left wheel which insisted on whirling around and rattling and skidding and generally doing most every ungrim and unsomber thing it could manage. Consequently the onlookers got an extended opportunity to view the corpse or anyway to view the bulk of the corpse since the bulk of the corpse was all they could view on account of how the actual corpse itself had been covered over with a thin green blanket, but in the course of his nearly incessant stooping and rising Mr. Hazlip accidentally uncovered a piece of the bald Jeeter so partway down the sidewalk the plain bulk got complimented with an actual naked elbow which proved immeasurably satisfying to the crowd collected roundabout who had expected bulk alone and so took the naked elbow as good fortune.

Sheriff Burton, who along with Mr. Bridger had departed from the house near about when the corpse did, opened the back hearse door for Mr. Hazlip and Mr. Dunn who slid the collapsible chrome gurney on inside where it did in fact collapse, and Mr. Hazlip and Mr. Dunn, without the front left wheel to hinder them any, became suitably grim and somber all over again while Sheriff Burton commenced to forage among the onlookers for details and came across Mrs. Askew who had left off at not such an awful lot of money and so picked up from that very spot. Mr. Dunn started the hearse and brought it away from the curbing slow and stately so as to allow the onlookers to gape in through the tinted glass and pay their respects to the bulk and naked elbow of the bald Jeeter Throckmorton, and folks generally told each other what a shame it was and told each other what a surprise it was and told each other what a downright shock it was except for Miss Bernice Fay Frazier who waved her fingers at the gentleman next to her and told him, "We were like this."

"Yes ma'm," Mr. Bridger said, "I've heard."

And then it was the summer we lost the bald Jeeter which we figured to be enough for any one season out of any one year and so we did not imagine it would become the summer of anything else, did not suspect it would become worse or not worse really but more so that it was not just the summer we lost the bald Jeeter but was that too, was that on top of and along with everything else. Once Mr. Hazlip and Mr. Dunn carted the bald Jeeter out the front door and down the steps there was not anybody of the home remaining, so at the suggestion of Sheriff Burton, who did not ever only suggest anything but instead usually ordered and proclaimed what he had started out suggesting, Mrs. Askew and Miss Bernice Fay Frazier and the widow Mrs. Jennings W. Hayes retired to Mrs. Askew's kitchen where Mrs. Askew's black telephone hung on the wall and they took turns calling the near relations. Since it was after all Mrs. Askew's kitchen and Mrs. Askew's telephone Mrs. Askew got to call the bald Jeeter's only daughter little Ivy Jeeter Throckmorton Lanier who had married an insurance agent from Greensboro and together they lived there behind the Friendly Shopping Center along with three children, a cat, two painted turtles, a halfdozen tropical fish—give or take your occasional floater—and one Lhasa Apso complete with an assortment of forelock ribbons. According to Miss Frazier and the widow Mrs. Hayes, Mrs. Askew proved delicate and tactful in her grievious capacity, especially in such a "time of crisis," Miss Frazier added, but Mrs. Askew and the widow Mrs. Hayes took issue with Miss Frazier's assessment of the predicament and persuaded her towards the viewpoint that the crisis part of the thing had ended along about when the bald Jeeter did. Now they were full well into the tragic end of it, as far as Mrs. Askew and the widow Mrs. Hayes could tell, which they figured was the place all crises got to if they didn't somehow resolve themselves otherwise. So Miss Frazier stood corrected, which was near about her least favorite way to stand, and to relieve the agony of it some she took it upon herself to call the bald Jeeter's only sister the fat Jeeter in Oregon Hill even though the widow Mrs. Hayes had previously expressed her desire to call the fat Jeeter, but Miss Frazier was considerably taller and stouter and altogether bigger than the widow Mrs. Hayes which counted for something even among old ladies, so when Miss Frazier took ahold of the receiver the widow Mrs. Hayes let her.

Once the bald Jeeter's crisis resolved itself direct into a tragedy there were not any genuine Jeeters left but for the fat Jeeter who counted as one Jeeter only but possessed the volume for several. The momma Jeeter and the daddy Jeeter had both passed on in 1963, one at the first of year and the other at the end of it, which left only three actual Jeeters including the bald Jeeter and the fat Jeeter and their grandmomma Jeeter who was actually not an actual Jeeter but had

married into Jeeterdom and through the years had assumed, assimi-
lated and otherwise sopped up everything it was to be a Jeeter and so
had become one as far as anybody that mattered was concerned.
Grandmomma Jeeter lived very nearly forever or anyway to the closest
approximation of forever that anyone anywhere around could come
up with, even the clergy who generally paid some attention to the
subject by occupation. She celebrated her one hundredth birthday
three years running just so as to hit it once since she did not own the
proper documents or suitable memory to verify the where and the
when of her coming about. So one year in Oregon Hill and the next
year in Neely and the next year in Leaksville Grandmomma Jeeter got
a party first in a Baptist and then a Presbyterian and then a Methodist
fellowship hall, and hordes of people she was not well acquainted
with made her speeches and gave her presents and cooked her dinner
and for her part Grandmomma Jeeter told them all to go straight to
perdition which not any of them were offended by, not even those
people who were usually offended by everything, since Grandmomma
Jeeter had survived to ninety-nine or one hundred or one hundred and
one and so could not manage an utterance that wasn't sagacious or
amusing or at least excusable. Nobody much ever seemed to want to
know anything from her except how she'd gotten to be as old as she'd
gotten to be and when she told them they didn't want to know that
either because Grandmomma Jeeter smoked Pall Mall cigarettes out
of the maroon pack and daily drank the whiskey her grandnephew
made in a ravine behind the chickenhouse which anyway he called
whiskey and she called whiskey but was more in the line of a petro-
leum product and she chewed plug tobacco and swore in a most profane and accomplished manner and on Labor Day of her eighty-second
year she had had relations with a man from Danville and at Christ-
mastime had announced her pregnancy which turned out to be gas,
and while all of this was very fine news for the ilk that smoked and
drank and chewed and swore and fornicated it did not much comfort
the sorts of people who collected at Baptist and Presbyterian and
Methodist fellowship halls and who generally liked to figure the Lord
did not reward the brand of living that Grandmomma Jeeter had been
rewarded for.

She did die at last, however, but not until the June of the summer before the summer we lost the bald Jeeter when she was nearly done her one hundred and tenth or one hundred and ninth or one hundred and eleventh year. A cold which settled in her chest had turned into pneumonia and strangled her and we were all very sorry to see her go. The people that smoked and drank and chewed and swore and fornicated said she'd had a full and useful life and the people that didn't said she'd probably still be with us if not for the smoking and the drinking and the chewing and the swearing and the fornicating while the remaining Jeeters themselves did not say much of anything partly because Jeeters by nature did not ever have much of anything to say and partly because there weren't but two Jeeters remaining, them of course being the bald and the fat.

So the death of the bald Jeeter just over a year after the death of Grandmomma Jeeter left the fat Jeeter all by herself as far as Jeeters went but not entirely all by herself otherwise since the fat Jeeter had managed to hook a Lynch early on and had gotten a pair of Jeeter Lynches by him in the course of the years. The fat Jeeter's Lynch, who was Raeford Lynch, did not come direct from Oregon Hill Lynches but derived mostly from Stacy Lynches or anyway from a combination of Stacy Lynches and Oregon Hill Lynches who themselves were part diluted with Ruffin Lynches which was not a pure sort of Lynch but was a Lynch descended from a pair of Mebane Lynches who had in fact been Stacy Lynches until they moved to Mebane. Raeford Lynch had three verifiable brothers in Benton, Jip, and Harland Lynch and one verifiable sister in Vergie Lynch and then there was William Petworth Lynch the lastborn who Raeford's momma named out of a magazine and raised close in to home which left William Petworth unverifiable as a brother and unverifiable as a sister but more along the lines of a form of brother who should have been a sister. Benton, Jip, and Harland Lynch all married prior to Raeford and produced between them seventeen children which was not in any way excessive or out of the ordinary since their gender of Stacy Lynch generally took wives about as fertile as compost, but Raeford could never seem to manage more than his meager pair mostly on account of the fat Jeeter who was plenty fat enough to say no and mean it. As for Vergie Lynch, she had triplets by a jackleg pentecostal preacher and then took William Petworth in once her mother died since William Petworth did not seem to have use enough for women to marry one and since William Petworth's daddy did not seem to have use enough for William Petworth to abide the sight of him.

The Lynch boys all brought their wives to Oregon Hill and farmed for a living on the land their daddy had parceled out to them, that is all the Lynch boys except for Raeford who cultivated chickens and cultivated speckled eggs instead in the dilapidated henhouse with the localized ammonia cloud that he got when he got the fat Jeeter. The momma Jeeter and the daddy Jeeter, who could never seem to make a go of it with the chickens or the speckled eggs either, figured a Lynch might possibly possess the wherewithal to rejuvenate what they themselves had not ever threatened to juvenate in the first place. So there was a general optimism and rosiness in Jeeterdom once the fat Jeeter hooked a Lynch since the bald Jeeter before her had only managed to land a Throckmorton who was from notoriously worthless stock and consequently did not give much rise to cheeriness or rosiness or general optimism. And in a surge of high spirits and good will the momma Jeeter and the daddy Jeeter bought for Raeford Lynch and for the fat Jeeter Lynch a brand new never before lived in mobile home which arrived behind the truck cab complete with curtains and carpet and doormats and coathangers and appliances and Mediterranean furniture and plates and glasses and ashtrays and coasters and silverware and two oven mitts and a halfdozen floorlamps and bedlinen and a toilet bowl brush and a New Testament in each nightstand and a complimentary bathmat and shower cap along with a bound up roll of shiny silver aluminum skirting that would run round the outside to hide the block pylons. The daddy Jeeter had the thing parked next to the henhouse but upwind from it which was a fine enough gesture but a fairly empty one on account of how the chicken smell did not blow so much as radiate, and accordingly a housetrailer next to the henhouse, even next to the upwind side of the henhouse, was still atop the meaty part of ground zero.

Raeford Lynch set in straightaway to put the chicken and speckled egg business to rights while the fat Jeeter set in just as straightaway to whatever it was she did which did not seem at all connected with chickens or speckled eggs but had instead some attachment to red nail lacquer and honey grahams by the box. But if the fat Jeeter attempted less she accomplished more mostly because her husband had waded into the middle of some serious and headlong dilapidation and dilapidation is simply one of those things that cannot be properly halted or excised once it has become serious and once it has become headlong. So the fat Jeeter Lynch passed her days painting all eight of her nails—she did not have enough of a sliver on each little toe to lay a brush to—and devouring graham crackers direct from the wax paper wrappers along with the odd boxful of vanilla wafers while her husband went over to the henhouse every morning and endeavored to flag down the ongoing destruction. He hammered and sawed and drilled and stapled and tacked and taped and tied and beat and banged and did in fact manage a partial and temporary rejuvenation but the chickens pecked away indiscriminately at the rejuvenated items as well as the dilapidated ones and so persisted in unrejuvenating and redilapidating every little repair and improvement Raeford Lynch bothered to make, so he rehammered and resawed and redrilled and restapled and tacked and taped and tied and beat and banged all over again while his energy and drive lasted, but of course the chickens won outright in the end, or the dilapidation won, or maybe it was the combination of chickens and dilapidation along with a touch of flat-out Jeeter destiny that vanquished Raeford Lynch in the end because in the end vanquished is certainly exactly what he got. He still passed his days in the chickenhouse and left the fat Jeeter to do what she did in the trailer, but anymore Mr. Lynch did not hammer or saw or drill or staple or tack or tape or tie or beat or bang but mostly sat in a metal chair canted up against a roof stanchion and watched the speckled eggs roll out of the roosting boxes and down the wooden troughs as any number of unoccupied hens untied his shoes for him and frayed the laces until they decided all at once and together to flap and squawk and pick themselves up off the dirt floor so as to land somewhere else.

Each evening in the Jeeter Lynch trailer was generally very nearly identical to all the other evenings in the Jeeter Lynch trailer. Raeford Lynch would sit on the sofa with his second third fourth or fifth beer in hand and tell the fat Jeeter what the chickens had done in the course of the day which usually ranged from eggs to shoelaces to the manufacture of chickenshit since chickens do not lead lives of extraor-

dinary diversity, and the fat Jeeter would blow on her fingers and ponder over what she might thaw or open or send Raeford down the road
to fetch for supper. And once the fat Jeeter had fried or unwrapped or
heated in a pot whatever it was she had decided on and once she had
piled the supper dishes in the sink on top of the lunch dishes and the
breakfast dishes so they could all ferment together, there was the radio
to listen to for entertainment and the chickens to smell and the scintillating banter to partake of and for Mr. Raeford Lynch some earnest
urinating to engage in and for the fat Jeeter Lynch some extensive
foraging to see after straight up until bedtime when the fat Jeeter
would retire and Mr. Raeford Lynch would retire just behind her and
plead and beg and moan and set up the most terrible lament imagin-
able. But there was quite sufficiently enough of the fat Jeeter hanging
out of her nightgown to make up two Raeford Lynches, so when the
pleading and the begging and the moaning and the terrible lamenting
proved ineffective and prompted Mr. Lynch to a hands-on assault the
fat Jeeter would fling him against the far wall where Mr. Raeford
Lynch and his bladder and his libido would all slide down the paneling and pile up on the carpet. From there on the floor Mr. Lynch
would make himself pathetic and plead and beg and moan and commence to lament all over again, but he could never seem to get pathetic enough to persuade the fat Jeeter to say yes since she invariably
said "No," or almost invariably anyway except maybe for twice when
she did in fact say yes or possibly did not say no with the proper authority or perhaps was even asleep.

Most of the Jeeters and a majority of Lynches did not expect a
baby to arrive when it did arrive primarily because the fat Jeeter did
not appear to be expecting one herself. She failed to do any additional
swelling so as to be noticeable and initially she figured the twitching
and the stomping and the rolling around in her belly for a honey graham affliction, but the pharmacist at the Rexall set her straight
directly and she brought the happy news on home to Mr. Raeford
who got thrashed all throughout the trailer and managed to pile up in
a great variety of locations. The baby itself arrived along about the fat
Jeeter and Mr. Raeford Lynch's first wedding anniversary and at the
time Mr. Raeford Lynch was feeling especially warm towards his
brother Benton who had made the Jeeter Lynches a gift of four bias

belted truck tires to lay on the trailer roof against strong winds, so he named his boy Raeford Benton Lynch partly on account of his brother's generosity and partly on account of his own derring-do and perilous exploits. They called the boy Benton so as to keep things uncomplicated around the trailer, and he stayed inside with his momma and wailed at her while she painted her nails until he was big enough to accompany his daddy down to the chickenhouse and screech at the chickens. He did not much resemble a Jeeter and did not much resemble a Lynch and did not much resemble any logical combination of Jeeters and Lynches either but showed a most remarkable likeness to Mrs. Phillip J. King's sister-in-law's mother who lived in Pittsboro but came through Neely every now and again on her way to somewhere else. She was a gangly woman with pointy elbows and an equally pointy Adam's apple and a face all hollowed and carved out and a prominent chin and a prominent nose and a mouth full of big square teeth and just the kind of aspect in general that made you want to saddle her up and ride her around the block, and even when he was only two feet tall Benton Lynch was just as gangly and pointy and carved out and prominent and toothsome himself which was not in the way of Lynches and was not in the way of Jeeters either and was truly not much in the way of Mrs. Phillip J. King's sister-in-law's mother who started out as a regular girlchild and got homely later when she blossomed.

So the fat Jeeter told everybody he had mostly Lynch to him and Raeford Lynch told everybody he was primarily Jeeter and all the non-Lynches and non-Jeeters roundabout debated as to whether it was a mule or a jackass in the woodpile while Benton Lynch himself grew increasingly ganglier and pointier and more carved out and prominent and toothsome. He was not an extraordinarily bright child, was not even intelligent in any sort of ordinary way—which could have been Jeeter, Lynch, mule, or jackass—and when at last he turned seven and went into the first grade at the primary school in Ruffin he did not graduate up a level until six months after his ninth birthday on account of some general difficulties with shoe-tying and the alphabet and numbers and everything else otherwise except for lunch. By the time he did reach the second grade, the fat Jeeter had said yes on the only other occasion she would say yes or had not said no anyway or maybe even had slept through it and Benton Lynch found himself with a little brother that he did not get the opportunity to expect or anticipate since his momma did not ever swell or bloat up sufficiently to stir his interest, did not really do anything unusual in the course of her nine months except throw his daddy against the paneling most evenings. The fat Jeeter named this one herself without any assistance whatsoever from Raeford Lynch or his brothers or their truck tires and she called him Otway Burns Lynch which was not from any Jeeters and was not from any Lynches and was not from any combination thereof but came direct off the "points of interest" portion of a state road map. Otway Burns Lynch did not start out gangly or pointy or carved out or prominent or toothsome but was a fairly regular baby and looked a little bit like his momma and a little bit like his daddy and a little bit like a week-old shoat. He did not wail like Benton Lynch had wailed and he did not screech like Benton Lynch had screeched and when he was old enough to walk with Benton and his daddy out to Mr. Newsome's store on the highway he did not get fed sugarcubes out of Mr. Newsome's coatpocket like Benton Lynch had been fed sugarcubes.

Otway Burns Lynch did not turn out to be such an extraordinarily bright child himself but appeared very nearly incandescent next to his brother who in five years of schooling had advanced to the third grade and who worked at his lessons and paid some considerable attention to his teachers but could not seem to keep whatever went in through his ears from running out the bottoms of his feet. Otway Burns Lynch caught Benton in the fifth grade and left him there, and once his own brother passed him up Benton seemed to lose his enthusiasm for schoolwork which did not matter much since he'd lacked the aptitude for it all along and so two weeks into the sixth grade he quit on account of what most folks said was the Lynch in him and what other folks said was the Jeeter in him and what some folks said was the combination of mule and jackass. Of course he set out on a career in chickens directly or anyway set down on one with his daddy who gave Benton his own folding metal chair and his own roof stanchion to lay it up against, while for his part Otway Burns Lynch persisted in his schoolwork and continued at the end of every quarter to bring home average marks which Jeeters and Lynches and Jeeter-Lynches and neighbors of Jeeters and Lynches and Jeeter-Lynches and even people who'd only heard tell of Jeeters and Lynches and Jeeter-Lynches all took to be a phenomenal accomplishment coming as it did from Otway Burns who had no call to be phenomenal or accomplished either since he was not purely Jeeter and was not purely Lynch but had distillated and precipitated from a mixture of Jeeters and Lynches who were not hardly anything pure and should have been less than anything diluted. But Otway Burns Lynch became something nonetheless and the theory roundabout had it that Otway Burns had gotten what he was supposed to get at birth and had somehow also managed to collect what Benton Lynch had neglected to pick up for himself, and so with perseverance and the sweat of his brow Otway Burns Lynch became quite capable and mediocre and Benton Lynch, who persevered and sweated some himself, could not ever rise much above cipherdom.

He was not blatantly stupid or outright idiotic. There was not anything blatant or outright about him, not anything at all. He mostly simply was not. Of course there was the pointiness and the gangliness and the square teeth but there did not seem to be any of him otherwise, certainly not anything blatant or outright and really not anything measurably stupid or idiotic, simply not anything. He wasn't. He had no personality to speak of, no distinguishing mannerisms, no funny little nervous cough, no particular way of standing or of leaning or of sitting, no special laugh, no favorite turn of phrase, no pants or shoes or shirt or hat he was partial to, and no Jeeter accent or Lynch accent or Jeeter-Lynch accent that was detectable since he did not ever ask any whys or wherefores, did not wonder or speculate or declare or reckon or wish or hope or imagine, did not ever say anything much except for yes and except for no. He had only his prominent features and his general angularity, which birth itself had put him in possession of, and had bothered to accumulate nothing otherwise. He was not his daddy's son, was not his momma's boy, and did not favor his brother or his grandparents or his aunts or his uncles or any strain of family on one side or the other that did not reside in the barnyard. He had not grown to be a Lynch and had not grown to be a Jeeter and had not grown to be a Jeeter-Lynch, had become nothing really from the moment he was named and designated except taller and pointier and more extraordinarily hollowed out on the outside and maybe extraordinarily hollowed out on the inside too or primarily vacant anyway which could have been how he started but certainly was how he ended up because even by the time he quit school for the chickenhouse he already mostly wasn't. Mostly he simply was not. His daddy laid back against his stanchion in his chair and made exaggerated claims about this and exaggerated claims about that and Benton Lynch sat and the chickens laid and squawked and pecked at his shoelaces and Benton Lynch sat and the chickenhouse dilapidated and fell away all around him amid the feathers and the ammonia and the uproar and Benton Lynch sat and when his daddy spied a particularly comely bird and left off soliloquizing long enough to say to his boy, "You think I can spit on that hen yonder?" Benton Lynch sat and eyed his daddy and eyed the chicken in question and sometimes he said, "Yes," and sometimes he said, "No."

Otway Burns graduated high school, which no Lynch or Jeeter before him had ever succeeded at, and his average marks and ordinary capabilities got him a diploma which indicated and duly certified the exact level of mediocrity he had risen to, a level of course unparalleled among Jeeters and unparalleled among Lynches, and the diploma in turn got him a position at the American Tobacco plant between Oregon Hill and Neely where Otway Burns pushed cigarettes around all day on a cart and received along with his weekly paycheck a promise of advancement if not the actual advancement itself. And even if it was only cigarettes and even if it was only a cart to push them around on, Otway Burns Lynch had in fact succeeded and had in fact advanced because it was not sweetpotatoes or alfalfa or corn or short grain or beef cows or manure or chickens or eggs or feathers or ammonia or any other item that Jeeters and Lynches tended to grow or rear or market or just be blessed with. Once he'd accumulated three months' worth of pay, Otway Burns Lynch moved out of the trailer and took a room on the north end of Neely with the second Mrs. Cummings who had been the first Mrs. Tadlock before she became the second Mrs. Cummings and who had commenced to rent out the various parts of the late Mr. Cummings's house almost before they could put the dirt on top of him. So the remaining Jeeter-Lynches expanded some in the trailer once Otway Burns Lynch vacated his part of it, or anyway two of the three remaining Jeeter-Lynches expanded some since the fat Jeeter was always about as expanded as she could get, and then Benton Lynch did a little vacating on his own and left more room than Mr. Raeford by himself could expand into. He did not announce his departure and did not seem to prepare or plan for it but just stuffed two shirts into a paper sack and went, and for a month and a half, nearly two months, he stayed gone and Mr. Raeford Lynch wondered where he was from the chickenhouse while the fat Jeeter wondered where he was from the dinette in the trailer and then in the evenings they would get together over something thawed or fried or sent out for and wonder out loud at each other until at last after his nearly two months Benton Lynch just showed up one night, came direct into the trailer, and sat down on the Mediterranean sofa beside Mr. Raeford Lynch who dropped his mouth open and said, "You're back."

And Benton Lynch looked at him with that pointy, prominent, carved and hollowed out face and told him, "Yes," by way of explanation.

He stayed on after that, stayed on right up to the summer we lost the bald Jeeter or anyway right up to the May just prior to the summer we lost the bald Jeeter, and then he up and went again not even with shirts this time or a sack to put them in but just up and went and stayed gone through Independence Day and almost until August before he came home in the very middle of the afternoon and proceeded direct to the chickenhouse where his daddy brushed the chickens and the feathers and the hardened chickenshit off Benton's chairseat and told him he was back again, told him he certainly was back indeed, which Benton Lynch agreed with twice prior to canting himself against his stanchion so as to watch the speckled eggs roll out of the roosting boxes and down the wooden troughs while the chickens pecked at his shoestrings and squawked and flapped and rose off of and settled onto the dirt floor. And then we lost the bald Jeeter which transformed a regular June and a regular July and the better part of a regular August into the summer we lost the bald Jeeter and that was sufficiently lamentable for one season out of one year as far as most of us were concerned and so we did not imagine it would become the summer of anything else, did not suspect it would become worse or more or be compounded by anybody anyhow especially by Benton Lynch who nobody much had ever seen or even heard of or could have recollected anyway. But it did get worse and more and compounded and Benton Lynch got himself thoroughly recollected, all of it commencing together on the afternoon of Monday August the twenty-ninth when the fat Jeeter picked up her phone receiver and said, "Whut?" into it.

She did not know Miss Bernice Fay Frazier from Harry's fuzzy cat and could not at all make out Miss Frazier's business on account of the excessive tact and delicacy Miss Frazier's grievious capacity had inspired in her. But at length once she'd made two or three dozen laps all roundabout the dilemma, Miss Frazier set onto the crisis and tragedy part of the matter and managed to refer specifically to the individual in question any number of times until she got a legitimate shriek out of the fat Jeeter and gauged her success accordingly. Miss Frazier set about explaining the details and circumstances of the afternoon but the fat Jeeter had thrown down the phone receiver on the dinette table after her initial shriek and so Miss Frazier squandered the best part of her tact and delicacy primarily on a half-eaten Little Debbie fudge twirl. The fat Jeeter shrieked again once she got outside on the trailer steps and when she hit the ground she attempted to shriek all the way down to the chickenhouse but did not have the wind for more than an extended whimper and consequently not the hens or Mr. Raeford Lynch or Benton Lynch either heard her coming and so levitated together when the fat Jeeter burst in through the chickenhouse door and cut loose with some genuine anguish.

She could not be consoled, could not at first be comprehended. "Deaddeaddead," the fat Jeeter wailed.

"Who?" Mr. Lynch asked her. "Dead where from what?"

"Gonegonegone," the fat Jeeter wailed. "Deaddeaddead."

"Where? Who?" Mr. Lynch asked her. "Dead how?"

"Gone and dead," the fat Jeeter cried. "Deaddeaddead and gonegonegone." And the fat Jeeter raised her hands and covered her face with her ten fleshy fingers and she said, "Oooohhh," and shook and sobbed and dropped to the floor full on top of one hen and partway on top of another and together the three of them moaned and shrieked and squawked and lamented until Mr. Raeford Lynch and

Mr. Benton Lynch each took the fat Jeeter under an arm and managed to hoist her.

"Who is it, momma?" Mr. Raeford demanded.

And the fat Jeeter turned her head sideways and looked at Mr. Raeford like he'd just crawled up out of a hole in the ground.

"Momma, who is it that's dead and gone?" Mr. Raeford wanted to know.

And the fat Jeeter cried, "Ooohhh," and stretched and worked her face until her eyes just up and disappeared in the folds of it. "Dead-deaddead," she said. "Gonegonegone," and then she spun around and scampered on out the chickenhouse door in as much as the fat Jeeter could spin and in as much as she could scamper.

Mr. Raeford caught up with her midway between the chicken-house and the trailer and got from her what he'd been after all along, but she still could not be consoled even once she got comprehended and the fat Jeeter worked her way loose from Mr. Raeford and proceeded on back to the trailer all wild and incoherent with grief while Mr. Raeford returned to the chickenhouse and vented himself. "God-damn it all," he said and beat the doorjamb as he passed by it. "She was a fine woman, a fine woman. Goddamn it all." And Mr. Raeford stomped around the perimeters of the chickenhouse kicking at the hens and swearing and flailing his arms in the air and generally putting on a regular pageant for Benton Lynch who watched overtop his pointy nose from his chair against his roof stanchion. "It ain't fair," Mr. Raeford said, "it ain't never fair but this time it ain't fair especial. Shit." And he kicked at a convenient collection of chickens which mostly got clear of his foot except for one particularly sluggish animal that had been sat on previously and now got booted too. "A fine woman," Mr. Raeford said, "such a fine woman," and he threw him-self into his chair and launched his chair back against his stanchion in one reckless burst of blasphemous energy which he terminated and punctuated with a "Shitfuckitshitshit." And Mr. Raeford did commence to settle down once he got seated but he spat out his vexation at intervals for an extended spell and went through a dozen shits, five or six goddamn it alls, and a couple of fuck its until he slipped finally into a kind of even tempered silence that did not get interrupted by anything more savage and offensive than a grunt every now and again.

Then he made several demonstrative exhalations so as to illustrate precisely how put out he was and after that commenced to chew his fingernails and ponder a batch of chickens off to his left which he paid impressive and grave attention to right up to the moment he opened his mouth and said, "You think I can spit on that hen yonder?"

And Benton Lynch looked from his daddy to the chicken in question and then back to his daddy again and told him, "No."

Mrs. Askew and the widow Mrs. Hayes and Miss Bernice Fay Frazier along with her sister, Mrs. Estelle Frazier Singletary, set up vigil in the bald Jeeter Throckmorton house along about suppertime black Monday, they called it, and right off went all throughout the premises making ready for the family and the anticipated horde of unattached but equally bereaved acquaintances. Mrs. Askew and Miss Bernice Fay Frazier changed the linen on the deathbed and made it up and Miss Frazier said just the sight of the old fitted sheet and topsheet and pillowcase balled up in the corner by the dresser sent shivers up and down her backbone and Mrs. Askew said it gave her the chills too and she said, as far as she could figure, it must be awful to die and Miss Frazier said she believed it probably was. Mrs. Estelle Singletary vacuumed and dusted in the downstairs and every ten or twelve minutes interrupted herself and hunted up the widow Mrs. Hayes so as to openly express her surprise that the bald Jeeter had not been a tidier woman which was, the widow Mrs. Hayes agreed, a sad truth and together they would commiserate over several of the bald Jeeter's more noticeable failings until Mrs. Singletary decided to go back to the Electrolux and seek out some new and disturbing untidiness.

Little Ivy Jeeter Throckmorton Lanier and her husband and her two boys and one girl and her Lhasa Apso with its black forelock ribbon all arrived at the bald Jeeter Throckmorton house just as Mrs. Askew and Miss Bernice Fay Frazier and Mrs. Estelle Frazier Singletary and the widow Mrs. Hayes were fishing through some personal items in a highboy that they had not really intended to fish through but did anyway once the straightening and dusting and vacuuming gave out. In the course of the trip from Greensboro to Neely little Ivy had managed to work herself full into the throes of hysteria and so did not notice straight off that she had caught Mrs. Askew and Miss Frazier and Mrs. Frazier Singletary and the widow Mrs. Hayes in the middle of anything which gave them the opportunity to stick the report cards and the photographs and the old yellowed letters down between the sofa cushions while little Ivy paced and fretted and her husband took the Lhasa Apso into the shrubbery to evacuate itself. She could not believe her mother was gone even once she had visited the deathbed and had sat through a complete performance of the bald Jeeter Throckmorton story, she simply could not believe it even once Mrs. Askew and Miss Frazier and the widow Mrs. Hayes all assured her that the bald Jeeter was indeed gone, that they had seen her go themselves or the bulk and naked elbow of her anyway. But still she could not believe it, or would not believe it, and threw herself onto the sofa and commenced to blubber into her hands until her husband returned from the shrubbery with the dog and then she blubbered on him instead.

The fat Jeeter and Mr. Raeford Lynch and their boy Benton arrived considerably later than little Ivy and her family mostly on account of the fat Jeeter herself who could not leave off shrieking long enough to put a dress on, and little Ivy and the fat Jeeter fell into each other's arms right off and the one of them blubbered while the other wheezed and moaned until they dropped onto the sofa together and became uniformly hysterical. Mr. Raeford got treated to his own personal three-part reenactment of the bald Jeeter Throckmorton story which vexed him afresh and he spiced the narrative with several goddamn it alls for each of which he begged pardon and received it while Benton Lynch stood with his back to the front doorframe and got talked at by little Ivy Jeeter Throckmorton Lanier's husband which was not a pretty sight seeing as how a man with only a "yes" and a "no" in his entire arsenal is hardly a match for a bona fide insurance agent. So Benton Lynch sometimes said, "Yes," and sometimes said, "No," as Mr. Lanier told him every tellable item concerning the bald Jeeter's coverage and Mr. Raeford occasionally let out a goddamn it all and the accompanying excuse me as the ladies told him all about the bulk and naked elbow and little Ivy blubbered and wheezed and the fat Jeeter wheezed and blubbered as they sat on the sofa holding each other in their arms.

Otway Burns Lynch got to the house shortly after his momma and daddy and brother did and wearing a new blue suit he'd paid on and a necktie he'd bought outright which in combination with his black oxfords and his dire expression made him the picture of proper and comely grieviousness unlike his daddy and unlike his brother who did not own blue suits but wore instead identical ditchwater brown suits and starched white shirts buttoned up to the chin and no neckties whatsoever and not oxfords either but brogans brushed up and done over a little all of which failed to suggest anything proper and comely, especially grieviousness. Otway Burns took Mr. Lanier's hand, shook it, and bowed like a Chinaman and told him how distressed and saddened he was over the news of Mrs. Bald Jeeter Throckmorton's untimely death and then he advanced on to the sofa and dipped towards little Ivy Jeeter and told her and his momma much the same thing after which he greeted Mrs. Askew and Miss Frazier and Mrs. Frazier Singletary and the widow Mrs. Hayes each in turn and took them all fairly much by surprise since they had not expected any natural manners in a Jeeter-Lynch and had not anticipated that Otway Burns could develop any pushing cigarettes around on a cart, so they watched him and waited for him to show the Jeeter in him or at least a touch of the Lynch but instead he struck up a policy discussion with Mr. Lanier and appeared actively interested in the progress of it.

Along about seven o'clock the first casserole showed up in the company of a dozen deviled eggs and shortly afterwards the initial chicken pieces arrived followed close behind by a yokeless layer cake and some manner of waldorf salad in a punchbowl. Mrs. Lassister of Draper carried over a platterful of Mr. Lassister's hot dry-cured sausage sliced up and skewered on toothpicks and the firechief Mr. Pipkin's wife, Louise, brought by a tin box full of after dinner mints, mostly pink ones. Fresh potato salad came up the walk every quarter hour or so and consequently outdid every form of chicken—baked, fried, barbecued, and stewed—which arrived about as frequently but not quite. Mrs. Phillip J. King stopped in with a devil's food cake that she'd bought at the Big Apple and put on a legitimate cake plate but could not disguise anyway and a Mrs. Hastings of the Leaksville Vernell Hastingses brought by the only pigs-in-a-blanket of the evening. Inez Benfield carried over several biscuits and her own variety of waldorf salad which far more resembled the genuine article than what had previously arrived in the punchbowl, and the Drumm twins, May and Halley Verna, both came in with custard pies although and maybe because they had not consulted on the matter. Mr. Emmet Dabb brought the beverage in a five gallon bucket and it was lemonade with gingerale in it or gingerale with lemonade in it or maybe limeade with Seven-Up in it, nobody could determine which and Mr. Dabb wasn't talking, and once the kitchen counter and the hutchtop and the dining room table were all covered over with trays and saucers and platters and serving bowls the Reverend Mr. Lynwood Wilkerson showed up with his appetite and paid his condolences to the daughter and paid his condolences to the sister and then blessed the food and went ahead and had some straightaway since he was so close to it anyhow.

Everybody told little Ivy and told the fat Jeeter what a shame it was and what a surprise it was and what a downright shock it was and then told each other much the same thing, and for the benefit of those people who did not witness the initial performance or any subsequent performance thereof, Mrs. Askew and Miss Frazier and the widow Mrs. Hayes staged a fairly elaborate and painfully detailed production of the bald Jeeter Throckmorton story which concluded with the traditional waving of fingers. There was not much talk of the bald Jeeter after that and folks generally ate some of everything and a lot of some things and attempted to break Mr. Dabb's punch down into its various components. Little Ivy and the fat Jeeter circulated and endeavored to be pleasant but were not entirely successful mostly on account of their bereavement though the fat Jeeter had never been blessed with a native pleasantness anyway. Otway Burns traveled roundabout the living room and the dining room and the kitchen bobbing like a coolie and his daddy exhibited his vexation to whoever appeared able to stand still for it. As for Benton Lynch, he got put on the sofa by Mr. Tiny Aaron who sat down with him and talked at him in a most steadfast and earnest sort of way, and Mr. Aaron seemed particularly animated and worked his arms and laughed and slapped himself on the leg and slapped Benton Lynch on the leg and howled a time or two, but even when he got slapped and pounded and had his face laughed into and his whole self howled at Benton Lynch did not seem anything in return but pointy and prominent and hollowed out and very much absent otherwise, and only once when Tiny Aaron set in with his hands describing an item that was near about exactly the size of a bread box did Benton Lynch say something back that was not just yes and not just no but very much resembled half of a conversation and rendered Benton Lynch something other than just pointy and prominent and hollowed out if only for the time being. And then Tiny Aaron laughed again and slapped himself again and slapped Benton Lynch again and howled once more before he slipped his fingers down between two of the sofa cushions where he discovered little Ivy Jeeter Throckmorton Lanier's third-grade report card and brought it out into the lamplight to peruse it.

Commander Avery Tuttle had laid out the bald Jeeter in a lustrous mahogany casket with antique brass attachments and little Ivy and the fat Jeeter had personally seen to her apparel. Now on several occasions the bald Jeeter had requested to be buried in her blue cotton suit and her matching white blouse with the geraniums on it and her navy pumps and the brunette horsehair wig, but when the time came to actually do the burying little Ivy and the fat Jeeter found they objected to the suit and the blouse and the pumps and the brunette wig and they figured the bald Jeeter would have objected to them also if she could have ever seen for herself exactly how little they did for her. So they substituted the chestnut wig for the brunette wig on account of how it brought out the color in the bald Jeeter's eyes, which did not seem much of a consideration in this particular case but got by anyhow, and they replaced the blue suit and the geraniumed blouse and the navy pumps with a gauzy brown dress and a pair of oxblood heels, and then they stood off across the parlor and assessed the improvement which little Ivy and the fat Jeeter both considered to be appreciable. Of course they called in Commander Avery to verify their opinion in the matter with his own official opinion in the matter and the commander stuck the first two fingers of his right hand into his fob pocket and circled the casket at close range prior to pacing all throughout the room so as to get the fullest picture of the situation, and when he had formulated his official opinion he addressed himself to little Ivy and to the fat Jeeter and told them exactly what it was they had wanted him to tell them which was about all the commander was good for since he did not ever have an official opinion but the right one.

The bald Jeeter got viewed from seven o'clock to nine o'clock on the Tuesday evening following black Monday and the people who viewed her were most generally the people who had gorged themselves in her honor the night previous except for the addition of little Buford Needham and his son Paul and Paul's wife Mary Margaret Vance Needham and of course the bald Jeeter herself who added a kind of gravity to the proceedings that had been absent from the potato salad and the chicken pieces and the rest of the buffet. Little Ivy and the fat Jeeter had perched themselves together on a Duncan Phyfe settee by the main parlor door so as to receive the mourners and Otway Burns Lynch and Mr. Raeford Lynch circulated as a team with one bowing and the other swearing. Mrs. Askew and Miss Frazier and the widow Mrs. Hayes lingered by the casket and intermittently gave command performances of the bald Jeeter Throckmorton story which did not differ substantially from any of their earlier performances except for the not such an awful lot of money passage immediately after which Mrs. Askew and Miss Frazier and the widow Mrs. Hayes would all three gaze rather longingly at the bald Jeeter's earthly remains and so inflate the drama some. Benton Lynch did not ever enter into the parlor proper but slipped off to one side of the porch in the shadows and did not have anything to do with anybody—not even so much as a solitary yes or a solitary no—until Mr. Tiny Aaron brought his stark white Impala up to the curbing and Benton went down to the street to meet him. They talked at the back bumper for a spell, or anyway Tiny Aaron talked and indicated and laughed and hooted and slapped himself and eventually turned the key in the trunklid so as to open it and he fetched from the trunk a particular item which he examined briefly prior to handing it over to Benton Lynch who examined it a little less briefly for himself. Mrs. Harold McKinney of the block and mortar McKinneys said later she had been suspicious, said later she had been highly suspicious when she passed the stark white Impala with the open trunklid on her way into the Heavenly Rest. She told everybody she had figured they were transacting. She told everybody she had suspected they were up to exactly what it turned out they were up to. But that was after he had done what he did, and that was after we'd all found out for ourselves precisely what Mrs. McKinney insisted she'd figured and suspected and been most highly suspicious of all along.

Benton Lynch did not make for one of your more eminent pall bearers. His daddy and his brother and little Ivy's husband and Mr. Pittman from the icehouse all served well enough and carried out their business in a stately and altogether acceptable manner but Benton was just bones and joints and pointy outcroppings and appeared to have attached himself to the coffin like a spiny burr to a pantleg. He did not mar the proceedings much however since once the time came for the coffin to leave the premises the congregation had already been near about eulogized and brethrened to death by the Reverend Mr. Lynwood Wilkerson who had a way with words if sheer bulk and volume counted for anything. Mrs. Edith Sudwick Hargrave capped off the eulogy with a recitation of her poetical tribute to the bald Jeeter that did not have much of a nugget but would have been fine to waltz to, and eventually when she did surrender the floor she surrendered it to Mr. Tupperman who claimed to be a tenor and who collaborated with Miss Frankie Dull, who claimed to be an organist, on a version of "Up a Lazy River" that they both alleged to be music. To close out the whole business the Reverend Mr. Wilkerson benedicted at the foot of the altar for a full quarter hour and thereby thoroughly numbed anybody who might have avoided stupefication earlier, so consequently Benton Lynch went fairly unnoticed as he clung to the side of the casket all thorny and inappropriate down the aisle and out the chapel doors.

Commander Avery had scheduled the funeral service for two o'clock the Wednesday after black Monday which seemed to the family and the mourning party too an altogether convenient and agreeable time for the proceedings for as long as the proceedings confined themselves to the commander's air-cooled chapel, but once the bald Jeeter had been thoroughly eulogized and tributized and passably serenaded under the air-cooled chapel roof she got hauled on out to the hearse and carted off to the cemetery which was not air-cooled exactly and was hardly a desirable place to spend the shank of the afternoon on the thirty-first of August. There was not much relief from the sun within the cemetery except for a row of cedars of Lebanon just above the Pettigrews but the underside of a cedar of Lebanon is generally about as cool and shady as the hilt of a cornstalk, so there was really not any relief within the cemetery aside, of course, from Commander Avery's green canvas awning over the gravesite which looked cool and inviting enough but was in actuality a kind of open-air oven.

The family got seated in metal chairs next to the dirtpile next to the open grave where they all broasted together and the unrelated mourners collected along the perimeters of the awning where they dabbed at themselves with Kleenexes and handkerchiefs and bandannas and waved off the sweatbees and the gnats and the green-headed flies. The Reverend Mr. Wilkerson had unaccountably retained a good degree of his vigor and proved to be the windiest item roundabout. He prayed and re-eulogized and generally carried on for the most unbearable span of time interrupting himself only on one occasion when the widow Mrs. Jennings W. Hayes fell out in a faint on account of what she claimed later was excessive grief but got caught by Mr. Pittman who laid her down against a headstone so she could be attended to by Mrs. Askew and Miss Bernice Fay Frazier who said they felt a little weak in the knees themselves but held up nonetheless. Eventually the ceremony did in fact conclude when the Reverend Mr. Wilkerson lowered the bald Jeeter on into the ground next to her husband, Mr. Braxton Porter Throckmorton the third, and then tossed a little dirt in after her and benedicted briefly, or anyway the official religious part of the ceremony ended with the lowering and the praying and the benedicting but nobody moved to go anywhere until Mrs. Jack Vestal, a self-avowed funeral enthusiast who had very nearly been acquainted with the bald Jeeter, stepped forward from out of the crowd, wailed, "Farewell, brave soul!" and flung her good linen handkerchief on in after the coffin thereby punctuating and finalizing what the reverend had previously sanctified. And then and only then did the mourners and the family and the clergy and the funeral home personnel commence to agitate and disperse since anymore Mrs. Jack Vestal's good linen handkerchief was about as significant to a Neely funeral as the corpse itself.

Seeing as how little Ivy's husband had elected to tend to the children, Otway Burns Lynch put one arm around little Ivy and laid as much of the other as he could manage around his mother and ushered the ladies off to the family limousine. Mr. Raeford Lynch followed close behind them all vexed afresh and kicking at the ground to show it, and Benton Lynch came along somewhere afterwards putting on his usual display which was not a display really but more along the lines of a vanishing act, so likely as not nobody much noticed Benton as he progressed from the canopy across the slope to the limousine but most everybody recollected having noticed him once he did what he would do, most everybody recollected every little thing about him once he had rendered himself so entirely and utterly recollectable, but nobody much noticed him climb into the back of the car beside his daddy and nobody much said poor Benton Lynch like they said poor little Ivy and poor fat Jeeter and poor Raeford and poor Otway Burns, but Benton Lynch was still not anything when we laid the bald Jeeter under the headstone and the red clay and left her behind the iron cemetery fence, was not anything at all really and would not become a man of consequence for a spell yet.

Twelve days later, twelve days to the hour exactly later outside of Draper on the Wentworth road it all commenced, all got thoroughly under way at Mr. J. Earl Busick's place of business which was part service station part store part social hall and part living tribute and monument to grime and neglect. Mr. Busick sold Sunoco gasoline and diesel fuel and kerosene and potted meat and fishing floats and hinged Barlows and loafbread and combs and two dollar pocket watches and camphorated liniment and Pepsi-Cola and cigarettes mostly. His opinions he gave away, and in the middle of the afternoon of Friday September the twelfth he was treating Mr. Tommy Winn and Mr. C. W. Bobbit to his viewpoint on the federal tobacco subsidy program which was quite possibly the freest and most strident opinion in Mr. Busick's entire repertoire. Mr. Tommy Winn, who was of a mind with Mr. Busick on the topic, spat periodically into a soup can and volunteered a yes sir and sometimes a yes sir indeed whenever Mr. Busick paused to draw breath, while Mr. C. W. Bobbit, who did not have any of one arm and only part of the other ever since he plowed up a nest of yellowjackets and bailed under the tractor to get clear of them, held a cigarette between his lips and squinted through the rising smoke.

They all three heard the spring on the door draw out and heard it draw in again and they all three looked around to see the who of it, so they all three saw him, or anyway saw the side of his head and the sharp tip of his nose as he bent over the drinkbox but they did not to a man find him extraordinarily riveting and so returned their attention to the tobacco subsidy matter and Mr. Busick skewered his congressmen and basted his senators and got yes sired and yes sir indeeded by Mr. Winn and squinted at by Mr. Bobbit. And then he came away from the drinkbox and set his Pepsi-Cola and his sack of salted nuts down on the counter by the cash register and leaned there on the heels of his hands so as to display the other side of his head and give a fresh perspective on the sharp tip of his nose, and only Mr. Busick, who was very nearly looking at him anyway, looked at him this time and he told him, "Be right there, buddy," but did not stir himself noticeably and persisted in his accusations and his complaints and his general indignation until it suited him to break off and cross around behind the counter where he rang up the Pepsi-Cola and rang up the sack of nuts and stopped the cash drawer with his stomach. "Sixty-three cents," he said and looked full and front on at both sides of the head and all of the nose and the rest of the face in general no single part of which twitched or moved or seemed at all lively, and when neither hand went up to a pocket, when neither hand went anywhere at all, Mr. Busick said, "Sixty-three cents," one more time and waited with the cash drawer against his stomach.

And though the hands still did not go anywhere in particular, the mouth gathered itself up and said, "You know who I am?"

And Mr. Busick turned his bottom lip partway inside out and pondered the face briefly. "Tommy, C. W., you know this boy here?" he said, still pondering but not so earnestly as before.

"No sir," Mr. Winn told him and Mr. Bobbit shook his head no.

"Might pass for a Littlejohn," Mr. Busick said, "might pass for a Ralph Littlejohn Littlejohn."

"No sir," Mr. Winn told him, "Littlejohns ain't got them teeth," and Mr. Bobbit shook his head no.

"You ain't a Holloway are you?" Mr. Busick wondered. "Holloways got them teeth." But the pointy nose wagged ever so slightly from side to side and Mr. Busick blew out a breath and said, "Well I don't know what you are. I don't believe I've ever laid eyes on you."

"You don't know who I am?"

"Shit, buddy," Mr. Busick said, "I ain't got no idea."

"I'll tell you then." And the right hand left the counter slow and deliberate and proceeded upwards to the button of a jacket which Mr. Busick had not paid much mind to previously but which he recollected struck him at that moment as the nearest thing to turd colored he'd ever seen in an article of clothing with turd colored buttons to match it, and the fingers unfastened first one turd colored button and then the other one so as to allow the hand to proceed on inside the jacket folds from which it returned presently in the company of what Mr. Busick identified later as a regular cannon and which in fact turned out to be a Harrington and Richardson Buntline revolver of extraordinarily high caliber, sufficiently high anyway to have made a sizable hole in Mr. Busick, probably near about the girth of a bathtub drain.

They all heard him draw the hammer back, even Mr. Winn and Mr. Bobbit who had not seen the artillery previously heard the first click and the second right behind it and the third right behind that and Mr. Winn said, "Oh Jesus," and stood up out of his chair and Mr. Bobbit who did not ever say much of anything stood up out of his chair without saying much of anything and they watched him draw a bead along about Mr. Busick's midsection and they heard him tell Mr. Busick, "If you don't give me what's in that drawer there, I'm the man's gonna blow your balls clean to Fuquay-Varina."

And Mr. Busick, who had raised his hands high over his head and backed up against the cigarette rack, labored to get up some spit and said, "Where's that?"

Two

H E WAS AN OVERHILL, not one of the banking Overhills or one of the milling Overhills, not even one of the feed and grain Overhill-Dexters, but an Overhill nonetheless, a foreign and maybe even exotic strain of Overhill who had no connections in Neely or Leaksville or Spray or Draper or Yanceyville or even Greensboro or Winston-Salem or Raleigh or Charlotte but who instead hailed absolutely and completely from a place called Altoona which did not seem to be anywhere anybody knew about. He was standing by the counter in Mr. Newsome's store on the highway eating candied corn out of his fist and talking to Mr. Newsome with his foot resting atop the hand-woven seat of one of Mr. Newsome's ladderback chairs which was not a place Mr. Newsome generally allowed a foot to rest but he was a large Overhill, a very broad and sturdy Overhill and Mr. Newsome did not come from valiant or otherwise distinguished stock himself. So Mr. Overhill talked at Mr. Newsome with his mouth always at least partly full of candied corn and his foot a little burdensome on the webbing and Mr. Newsome listened to Mr. Overhill and made himself most thoroughly agreeable and very nearly pleasant.

The fat Jeeter had run out of graham crackers, had even turned up the wax paper and run out of crumbs and broken corners and was commencing to make trouble with the vanilla wafers when she gave Benton Lynch a dollar and sent him up the road with it. Mr. Overhill had some firm ideas on the subject of nuclear energy and he was just setting out to expand upon them as Benton Lynch stepped through Mr. Newsome's doorway and proceeded on to the back of the store where Mr. Newsome kept his dried beans and his cookies and his unplugged pinball machine. Mr. Overhill said he had seen some pluto-

nium once, said he had held a lump of it in the very palm of his hand
and Mr. Newsome made an altogether pleasant and agreeable excla-
mation of wonderment and awe that Mr. Overhill paused to allow for
prior to expanding still further which he managed with considerable
ease and grace since he was a highly expansive individual by nature.
Benton Lynch stood and waited behind Mr. Overhill and off to one
side of him a little with his momma's dollar and his momma's box of
graham crackers while Mr. Overhill explained to Mr. Newsome the
principles of megatonnage and kilowattage and Mr. Newsome whistled between his teeth when there seemed a call for it and Benton
Lynch just stood and just waited and did not look anywhere and did
not say anything until Mr. Overhill tossed his head back and laid in a
new supply of candied corn when Mr. Newsome waved Benton Lynch
and his dollar and his crackerbox flush up to the counter.

"Hello boy," Mr. Overhill said and eyed Benton Lynch sideways
and at a slant, and he chewed and swallowed and cleaned out a hollow
with the tip of his tongue. "Tell me something," and he knocked
down a few more kernels prefatory to expanding clear off the nuclear
energy issue and onto another item entirely, which was a particular
talent with him, "you like money, son?" he said.

Mr. Newsome took the fat Jeeter's dollar out of Benton's hand
and put the fat Jeeter's nickel and two pennies back into it and Benton Lynch closed his fingers around the coins and looked full at Mr.
Overhill who had run the most of his right hand into his mouth clear
up to the knuckles, or along about his adenoids anyway, and was
doing some serious excavation which he interrupted and departed
from long enough to say, "Huh?" when it did not appear that Benton
Lynch had an opinion on money one way or the other. "I mean can
you use some cash?" Mr. Overhill asked once he'd unstuck whatever
he unstuck and swallowed it.

"Yes," Benton Lynch said.

"You know how to dig a hole, boy?" Mr. Overhill asked.

"Yes," Benton Lynch said.

"Ain't much to you. Bones mostly," Mr. Overhill said, and Mr.
Newsome blew through his nose and told him, "Lynches."

"But you ain't scared of work are you boy? You ain't scared of a
shovel and a pick are you?"

"No," Benton Lynch said.

"Then why don't you come along and dig some holes with us," Mr. Overhill suggested.

"Where?" Benton Lynch said.

"In the ground, boy," Mr. Overhill told him and Mr. Overhill and Mr. Newsome showed each other their teeth. "Seventeen dollars a hole," Mr. Overhill added, "cash money on the spot. Truck's around back, be here till nightfall. You just give it a little attention."

And Benton Lynch did not say he would and did not say he wouldn't but left with his momma's crackers and his momma's seven cents.

"Fine sort," Mr. Overhill observed, and Mr. Newsome said, "Shit," in a manner that was not especially pleasant or particularly agreeable.

It was a Dodge truck, a faded red Dodge halfton pickup with an aluminum cap on the bed and near about a full load what with the two negroes, a fat one and a paltry one, and a wiry tattooed white boy and some other additional manner of being squatted against the fender well who was too black to be white and too white to be black. Mr. Overhill stirred up a place for Benton Lynch who climbed in over the tailgate with his paper sack and lowered himself between the tattooed white boy and the thickest part of a pick handle and then the truck lurched and sputtered and gradually wound out through the gears as Mr. Overhill headed south down the 29 highway towards Greensboro. The air in the bed was hot and close and foul-smelling even though the louvered side windows were standing straight out and the back glass had been tied open against the ceiling. They were all stretched across the same blanket, or anyway three of them were— the fat negro and the paltry negro and the wiry tattooed white boy— laying uniformly on their sides with their heads in the crooks of their arms. Benton Lynch sat with his back against the left fender well and opposite him whatever it was crouched like a toad against the right fender well and picked at his cheek and jittered and jerked in a quick, nervy, almost reptilian fashion.

At Greensboro Mr. Overhill got on the interstate and the wiry tattooed white boy woke up and crawled across the fat negro and the paltry negro who cursed him and swore him and threatened him prior to joining him at the tailgate where they all three pissed onto the highway and spat and coughed and then crawled back to where they'd come from and laid down on their sides with their heads in the crooks of their arms. Benton Lynch dozed off along about Colfax and slept entirely through Winston-Salem and near about to Clemmons when he woke up of a sudden and shook his head and blinked and squinted until he could make out the tattooed white boy and the two negroes and the vacant fender well across the way, and he squinted again and blinked again and shook his head again and still could only see the tattooed white boy and the two negroes and the vacant fender well until a voice said, "Hey," so close into his ear that he could feel the breath and then "Hey" again, and like as not Benton Lynch would have leapt over the tailgate and out into the road but for the hand on his arm that held him, squeezed him, pulled at him in nervous fits and snatches.

It was squatting there at his shoulder with its face in his face and it said, "Hey, listen listen," in a sharp airy whisper. "We stepped in some shit, stepped in some big, big shit. There wasn't nothing we could do, wasn't no place we could go. We was pinned in a stinking mudhole and him in the trees and the bushes all roundabout just shooting and shooting and shooting and shooting. Greased two of us straight off, just blown right the fuck up. Got that cocksucker Drexler in the throat, blood running down his arms and dripping off his fingers, and wasn't nothing we could do, wasn't no place we could go, just squirm around in the mud and try to sink clean outta sight. Then we heard them coming, heard them way off even with the guns and the bullets and the screaming we heard them coming, and the mud commenced to shake and the water commenced to pitch and every loose piece of shit just picked up and left. They was two of them and they was bringing it, bringing it, raining it all over him. Rockets, flex guns, fifties in the door pissing full into the trees and into the bushes bringing it, bringing it, raining it all over him. Then the one came down and picked up some of us and the other came down and picked up the rest of us and we was at sixty, seventy-five, maybe eighty feet when he got the door gunner, got him clean and rolled him on out the door but he hung up on a sled—an arm, a leg, the rest of him just dangling—and he shot him to pieces, shot him the fuck up,

killed him and killed him and killed him, and I grabbed onto the fifties and pissed it all over him, rained it, brought it, shot up the whole
goddamn jungle, just cut it to little fucking bits, and when we got
clear, when we got out, when we got clean gone the captain up on the
stick said to me, 'Outstanding, son. Outstanding,' he said, and me
and this guy we untangled the door gunner and dropped him into the
treetops."

Benton Lynch had backed up the fender well and was sitting on
top of it. "Big shit," it said. "Big, big shit," it said, and it twitched in
a half dozen different places all at once, or at least almost all at once,
and it laughed not like Mr. Newsome's petty nosetooting or Mr.
Overhill's deep, jolly HawHaw and not as flat and unfunny as what
passed for laughter in Mr. Raeford Lynch and very nearly only louder
and wilder and more mean-spirited. And it shook and flinched and
jerked and bobbed until the fat negro lifted his head off the crook of
his arm and swung his foot a hard, vicious kick that hit it across the
shoulder and partway onto the chest. "Get away from him," he said.
"Get on away." And it laughed again, louder and wilder and even
more mean-spirited and got kicked twice more by the fat negro and
threatened and cursed at by the paltry negro and the wiry tattooed
white boy and then it slipped away, slipped on back to where it came
from, and the fat negro told Benton Lynch, "Don't listen to him. He
ain't never killed nobody. He ain't never been nowhere."

By morning they were beyond Asheville, beyond Gatlinburg even
and had come into a place that was not a place really, not a civilized
place anyway or not a civilized place any longer but merely an interruption in the vines and the brambles and the laurel thickets and not
truly a full-fledged interruption either but just a distraction from the
undergrowth in the form of a block grocery, two green metal trash
bins, and several dozen unpainted, untended to, entirely unlivable,
and fully inhabited houses all of which taken together constituted the
township of Lemly as had once been designated and certified by a rectangular white sign with black lettering beside the grocery but the
honeysuckle had long since come up out of the ditch to strangle it
off. Lemly was situated in what some residents called a creek bottom
and other residents called a ravine and what the majority of the seasonal Floridians roundabout referred to as a valley but which was ac-

tually a deep and sunless hole in the ground flanked to the north and the east by one ridge and flanked to the south and the west by another. Lemly had no industry whatsoever and little agriculture to speak of unless mildew counted for something, did not have anything really, not even any Lemlys any longer in the very place founded and originated by a pair of Lemly brothers and their wives who had settled on the creekbank and thrived there but whose sons and daughters and grandchildren and greatgrandchildren had attempted to move up the slope onto the land they beat back the forest to possess and inhabit and live from but never could really possess, never could actually live from, and could only fully inhabit for that briefest of moments between the beating back and the first new sprouts and shoots and vines which spread down the mountainside across the pastures and beanfields and up to the very houses and outbuildings which had commenced to sag and rot and fall away almost before the sound of the hammers and the saws had died off entirely. So Lemly had been abandoned by virtually all of its willful natives which meant actual and full-blooded Lemlys mostly since actual and full-blooded Lemlys were generally driven to seek the sort of success and satisfaction their creek bottom refused them, and the block store and the trash bins and the ruinous houses and the overgrown pastures and garden plots had been left to Dinkinses and Greers and McDonalds and Earps and Donahoos and Rawlses and McCoys who apparently had not inherited any appreciable gumption and determination and had failed to cultivate any on their own and so were content with the underbrush and the mildew and the general dilapidation roundabout. Only Mr. Raymond Dance Greer who owned the block store made anything in the way of a living while two McDonalds and an Earp collected and sold mayapple and ginseng root as a diversion of sorts. Otherwise Lemlyites by and large got their livelihood signing checks at the first of each month and applying for supplements in the middle of each month and they occupied themselves watching what traffic passed through Lemly from day to day which didn't ever amount to much since Lemly was not on the way to anywhere in particular.

Consequently Mr. Overhill's red Dodge pickup truck got noticed and observed straight off even though it arrived early on in the day before Lemly was fully astir which it would not be until at least midmorning since there was not much in Lemly to get astir over. And Mr. Overhill compounded his impact some by delivering four short blasts on his truckhorn as he rolled to a stop in front of the block grocery just like he always did when he got to where he was going since with the absence of trumpets it was the closest thing to a fanfare he could muster. He stepped out of the cab and stretched himself and then went on into the store where he purchased a half dozen cellophane packets of candied corn and engaged Mr. Raymond Dance Greer in a varied and far-reaching conversation which commenced with a dual analysis of the localized cloud formations, fell off some midway as Mr. Greer drew Mr. Overhill a roadmap on the detached end panel of a cigarette carton, and then picked up again and carried on in a most lively and energetic fashion to an ever so boisterous climax which saw Mr. Overhill recite to Mr. Greer a snatch of poetry he had read over a urinal in Charlotte.

Occasionally consulting the end panel of the cigarette carton, Mr. Overhill drove back out of Lemly the way he had come in and turned off the main road onto a secondary one that proceeded paved for a half mile or so and then went to gravel and curled down the mountainside towards the creek bottom where it straightened out and followed the bank of what was known locally as Little Roaring Fork which came off of Big Roaring Fork to the north which itself originated just above the confluence of the French Broad River and Flatwoods Creek. Mr. Overhill kept to the creekbank for a considerable ways, several miles anyhow, and when he did eventually pull the truck off the side of the road and beat out a salute on the horn it did not appear he had come to a place worth stopping and beeping over but he left the cab with his usual resolve and after casting around for a break in the underbrush struck out between a pair of locust trees up a fairly well-trod footpath. The paltry negro lowered the tailgate and rolled out into the road followed by the fat negro and the wiry tattooed white boy who was ever excruciatingly attentive to his bladder and straightaway waded on into the weeds to relieve himself where he was joined by the fat negro who near about filled up the wiry tattooed white boy's left shoe and so got chased up the slope and into the woods and back out again to the great amusement of the paltry negro who had taken up a position directly in the middle of the gravel road where he figured no snakes could slip up on him. Benton Lynch brought himself and his paper sack out of the truckbed and stood by the left rear tire doing nothing in particular and lastly it came away from the fender well and onto the tailgate where it squatted and picked at itself. They called it the critter, the fat negro and the paltry negro and the wiry tattooed white boy did anyhow, while Mr. Overhill insisted on referring to it as Dwight, and it was not a negro as Benton Lynch had suspected right off, not by race anyway, but it was black enough what with the grit and the grime and the dust and the general filth that had collected and caked up on its face and on its neck and on its forearms and on the backs and fronts of its hands and on its ankles and all throughout its trousers and its button-up shirt and on into the hair on its head which did not lay down anywhere but stood up in the knots and mats and greasy swirls all over, and it raked out its ears with a fingernail and then without even bothering to stand up urinated off the end of the tailgate and into the road or primarily into the road but partly onto the tailgate itself so that a slight but measurable puddle formed under its haunches and around its feet and the paltry negro said, "You nasty motherfucker, you," and tried to appear thoroughly disgusted but could not.

Mr. Overhill hooted from up the slope and the fat negro and the wiry tattooed white boy and the paltry negro scanned the hillside but couldn't find him out amid the trees and the brambles and the leafy bushes so he hooted again and waved his arms over his head and the wiry tattooed white boy spotted him under a cucumber tree and hooted back.

"Come ahead," Mr. Overhill hollered.

And the wiry tattooed white boy yelled, "Awright," and the fat negro yelled, "Awright," just behind him and the paltry negro said, "Sho nuff, asshole," with no considerable volume to speak of and the fat negro fetched the picks and shovels and distributed them all around so everybody got one of each except for the critter who brought a garden trowel out from a corner of the truckbed and stuck the handle of it in his back pocket and then lit out between the locust trees and up the footpath. The paltry negro did not wish to walk in front of the fat negro and the wiry tattooed white boy and Benton Lynch and did not wish to come along behind them but desired to

climb the trail somewhere in the midsts of the three of them so as to
be suitably insulated from the wildlife roundabout. However, he
could not decide if he wanted to go second behind the fat negro or
third behind the wiry tattooed white boy and when he was at last
pressed to choose he settled on third but reconsidered partway
through the weeds and fairly much scaled the wiry tattooed white
boy's backside in an effort to jump ahead a spot but the wiry tattooed
white boy resisted and the two of them got all tangled up together on
the trail and pushed each other and swore each other and yanked each
other around and when the paltry negro had gotten where he wanted
to get he swung his pick and his shovel up onto his shoulder and
called the wiry tattooed white boy a sorry motherfucker and called the
fat negro a stupid motherfucker and turned all the way around to
Benton Lynch to tell him what a homely motherfucker he was which
was only the second thing he'd had yet to say to Benton Lynch the
first having come somewhere along about Statesville sometime along
about the middle of the night when Mr. Overhill had stopped for gas
and the paltry negro had noticed Benton Lynch against the fender
well and had raised his head up off the crook of his arm and said,
"Damn boy, ain't you ugly."

The trail cut back and forth across the hillside and eventually gave
out on a grassy plateau where Mr. Overhill waited to direct the four
of them around the rotted and tumbled down remains of a Baptist
sanctuary on the far side of which lay a modest graveyard bordered
round by an iron fence, and though it was small and sparsely popu-
lated as graveyards go it was nonetheless an extraordinary sight there
in the middle of the woods beside an abandoned and collapsed church
because it was so utterly and absolutely well tended to in a run of
country where everything else was going to ruin unchecked. The grass
around the headstones and on the mounded graves themselves had
been clipped and weeded and throughout the plots were decorated
with flowers in foil-wrapped vases and ribbons and flags and a varied
assortment of personal effects and mementos, or the majority of them
were decorated anyway except for that of Mr. Robert Earl Earp
1897–1956 Asleep in the Redeemer's Arms whose plot was as neat and
scrupulously tended to as any of the others but was entirely un-
adorned and colorless and so somehow suggested that Mr. Robert Earl

Earp was more frankly dead and perished than his neighbors, especially his neighbor to his immediate left, Mrs. Ida Dinkins McCoy 1904–1967 Gone to God who had plastic jonquils and bows at her feet and a gilt-framed picture of herself embedded in her headstone. Apparently Mrs. Ida Dinkins McCoy had not made her way in the world on account of her good looks.

Mr. Overhill stepped aside at the gate and the fat negro and the paltry negro and the wiry tattooed white boy and Benton Lynch filed past him into the cemetery. The critter was on his knees astride Mrs. Emma Vance Lemly 1821–1889 Loving Wife and Mother. He had already taken the sod off and was commencing to break up the underlying earth with the point of his trowel. The wiry tattooed white boy dropped his pick and shovel down across her husband, Colonel George Fentress Lemly 1819–1863 Brave and Just—Peace Be His Reward, and removed the flags and the vase of zinnias and tossed aside the shovel and raised the pick and said, "Probe that thing, you greasy bastard," to which the critter bared his teeth and wiped his forehead on his shirtsleeve. Benton Lynch did not go anywhere much once he got inside the cemetery gate but just stood for a spell in between a row of graves with his shovel handle against his chest and his pick handle against his beltbuckle. The paltry negro had settled on a Greer, a fairly recent Greer, and the fat negro had laid claim to yet another Lemly, William George Lemly 1859–1928 From His Labors Delivered, and the fat negro was removing some of the greenery from roundabout Mr. Lemly's midsection when he noticed Benton Lynch standing there between a Dinkins and a Donahoo not seeming inclined to go anywhere much and not seeming inclined to commence anything hardly, and maybe it was the hollowed out and prominent features and maybe it was the general pointiness and maybe it was the usual vacant expression in combination with the hollowed out and prominent features and the general pointiness all of which together suggested perplexity to the fat negro who figured perplexity was what it had to be and so left off with Mr. William George Lemly momentarily and explained to Benton Lynch, "They's a dam going up somewhere, somewhere up on the creek, up on the river, somewhere," and he jerked his head in what he figured for a likely direction. "Put all this under water, all these trees and this mess here, these dead folks and some of these live ones too, and it ain't no matter much to cover up all these trees and all these live folks round here and all their mess, but cain't cover up these dead folks, cain't cover up the first one of them. Just cain't. So ain't nothing to do but take them up from this place and put them some place else, ain't nothing to do otherwise. Dam folks paying him, he paying us, ain't nothing to do otherwise," and the fat negro tossed his pick aside and set about scraping the sod off Mr. Lemly while Benton Lynch stood as he had stood previously in all of his angularity and his pointiness which somehow suggested to the fat negro a greatly diminished perplexity and he pointed to the nearest Dinkins with the end of his shovel handle, a Mr. Robert Loyd Dinkins 1917–1972 Sleep Everlasting, and said, "Start on that one there. He ain't been dead long, probably still in the box."

Benton Lynch was up to his shins when the first pair of Lemlys climbed the trail from the creekbottom and joined Mr. Overhill at the cemetery gate. They had received their due notification, Mr. Overhill called it, back in March and so had set aside the entire morning and part of the afternoon to cross the border from Ashe county and fetch their daddy and their granddaddy and their grandmomma and their grandmomma's sister Heloise Simpkins Vance McCoy. They were clean and neat and somber and favored remarkably, appeared in fact to be two different stages of the same existence. They shared the Lemly nose and the broad Lemly brow and the red Lemly ears with the dainty Lemly earlobes and when they leaned against the fence with Mr. Overhill they both crossed their arms over their chests and inclined their heads in precisely the same fashion. Of course Mr. Overhill engaged them in conversation straightaway and whenever it seemed that one Lemly or the other or both were paying inordinate attention to the activity around them he started in afresh on an untried topic so as to divert the pair of them some mostly on account of the critter who was not especially clean or neat or somber and who was just before bringing Grandmother Lemly up out of the ground. He had put the trowel aside and was digging with his bare hands, throwing the dirt up between his legs like a dog and grunting and dripping sweat and making for his usual unseemly spectacle which Mr. Overhill did not believe was the kind of thing a person should see in conjunction with his dead relations so he developed a sudden and burning curiosity as to the indigenous foliage, especially as to the indigenous foliage down around the collapsed sanctuary and he led both the Lemlys out of the cemetery and down the hill, told them they needed to identify an item or two for him, told them they simply had to put his mind at ease.

The critter struck pure grandmother soon after Mr. Overhill and the Lemlys had dropped over the rise and out of sight or anyway the general consensus was that the critter had struck relatively pure grandmother since once he held up a trowelful of the substance in question for a ruling he got an "Uh huh" from the fat negro and an "Uh huh" from the wiry tattooed white boy and a "That's the bitch" from the paltry negro who was the one this time to notice the hollowed out and prominent features and the general pointiness and the usual vacant expression which he did not take for perplexity exactly but which instead suggested to him a kind of thoroughgoing idiocy and he rested the point of his shovel on his shoetop and turned his head sideways and very nearly addressed Benton Lynch with "Black dirt's dirt. Yellow dirt's clay. Gray dirt's folks. Ain't a goddamn thing to it."

The critter put Mrs. Emma Vance Lemly 1821–1889 Loving Wife and Mother into one of the Ziploc plastic bags Mr. Overhill had piled up at the cemetery gate. She was damp and coarse and a little lumpy and bony and splintery every now and again, and he burped the air off of her and sealed her up and dropped her behind her headstone prior to taking himself and his trowel off a plot to the left so as to commence work on Mrs. Heloise Simpkins Vance McCoy 1825–1887 Beloved and Cherished Wife of Jackson Caswell McCoy with whom she shared her granite marker. The wiry tattooed white boy hit a vein of fairly dense and incontestable Colonel Lemly just after the critter had bagged up the Mrs. and just prior to the return of Mr. Overhill and the only live Lemlys roundabout who had fairly much exhausted themselves with identifying half of the forest and speculating over the rest of it. Like his wife the colonel was gray and damp and coarse and lumpy with bone and with splinters but lumpy as well with a good half dozen extremely well-preserved brass coatbuttons and one gold matchsafe which the Lemlys arrived in time to retrieve before it got burped and Ziplocked. The paltry negro interrupted the surfacing of

Lemlys with his recent Greer whose hardwood casket he inadvertently punctured with his pick but who otherwise did not appear excessively damaged or decayed or deteriorated and who in fact had retained sufficient bulk to call for the paltry negro and the fat negro and the wiry tattooed white boy along with Mr. Overhill himself to fetch him up out of his hole in the ground, and as a favor to the living Lemlys Mr. Overhill lifted the casket lid to expose the paltry negro's recent Greer who one of the Lemlys believed he had fished with on three different occasions and him and his brother peered in at the Greer in question, who was not in any way hideous or frightening but whose mouth had opened up some and whose skin had tightened up some and who did appear in general most convincingly deceased, and after the pair of Lemlys had consulted on the matter the Lemly that had been fishing with a Greer decided it had not been this particular Greer.

A Dinkins, two Earps, and a vagrant strain of Jemison who had some Earp to him but not a good deal of Earp showed up at the cemetery just as Mr. Overhill was letting the lid back down on the paltry negro's Greer. They had not come up the trail from the creekbottom but had stepped out from the undergrowth above the ruined church and the cemetery where no trail or footpath or even deer run appeared to be. The four of them jerked their heads at the Lemlys and the Lemlys jerked their heads in return as the Dinkins and the two Earps along with the diluted Jemison took up positions against the high side of the fence opposite the gate and proceeded to ponder over the ongoing excavation, proceeded to ponder without any talk and without much interruption except for some spitting on the part of the Earps who chewed and some drooling on the part of the Dinkins who dipped and some general fidgeting on the part of the Jemison who fidgeted. As a group they were not nearly so pink and robust as the Lemlys, did not possess the broad Lemly brow or the fleshy Lemly ears or the straight and proper Lemly nose but were instead slight and drawn and waxen and predominantly eye sockets, deep and near about purple eye sockets which the Earps had the deepest and purplest of followed by the Dinkins and concluding with the Jemison who appeared as if he had slept once maybe.

Mr. Overhill crossed the cemetery and met them all hail and forthrightly but did not generate any considerable enthusiasm and so carried the bulk of the conversation himself which was not in fact a conversation really but more truly took the form of an extemporaneous panegyric on the local countryside delivered by Mr. Overhill with much energy and some highly dramatic gesticulation but received with only the usual spitting and the usual drooling and an altogether unextraordinary display of fidgeting. The Dinkins and the shorter of the two Earps did not seem inclined or able to speak and the remaining Earp would not speak until Mr. Overhill insisted on knowing who they had come to fetch away, if that was their purpose, to which the remaining Earp wiped his mouth with the back of his hand and said, "Daddy."

"Daddy who?" Mr. Overhill asked him.

"Earp," the remaining Earp said, and though he got probed and examined and prodded he could not be made to elaborate on or embellish his answer any further, could not be made to do anything really but spit on the iron cemetery fence and could not be kept from that. The Jemison did volunteer that he had a cousin across the way in the far corner and he pointed out the headstone to Mr. Overhill, the headstone of his cousin, his second cousin on his mother's side which would be his mother's sister's daughter's child, but he had not come to fetch away his cousin, had not been well acquainted with him actually on account of a rift between his mother and his mother's sister which had developed during a land dispute upon the death of his granddaddy who fell off the listening rock in March of 1935 and got broke all to pieces. The Jemison decided his was strictly a social call and told Mr. Overhill as much and fidgeted and finally shut up.

Mr. Overhill left the fence and wandered throughout the cemetery in search of all the resident Earps and pointed to each one he came across and judged the reaction on the taller Earp and the shorter Earp also who between them did not show much sign of life until Mr. Overhill arrived at and indicated Mr. Phillip Reid Earp 1902–1965 Jesus Called upon which the shorter Earp glanced at the taller Earp who managed an ever so slight nod of the head in between two exceedingly demonstrative expectorations. So Mr. Overhill put the wiry tattooed white boy on the appropriate Earp straightaway or almost straightaway anyhow once he had handed the deceased and bagged up Lemlys over the fence to the pair of live Lemlys who had decided to unseal their granddaddy and separate him from his brass coatbuttons which they set about directly. The fat negro had partly uncovered William George Lemly when Benton Lynch finally struck his Dinkins or struck the laminated coffinlid of his Dinkins which was still firm and solid and so did not give way to the tipend of the shovel. The fat negro's Lemly, however, did not have much box left and had predominantly come to pieces himself except from the knees down where he had retained the cuffs of his pants and the entire of his shoes, and there was so much corpse and so little coffin that after the digging and the sorting and the burping and the Ziplocking the fat negro ended up with a three bag Lemly. Benton Lynch scraped the dirt off his Dinkins's coffinlid and attempted to prize the box up some with his shovel but could not and so was assisted by the fat negro and the paltry negro along with Mr. Overhill and four equal lengths of rope which the paltry negro tied to the casket handles once he took them from Benton Lynch who had been handed them by Mr. Overhill but had only eyed them there across his palm with his usual angularity and pointiness and general vacancy, and the four of them together along with their rope and aided by a touch of scorching profanity from the paltry negro brought Mr. Robert Loyd Dinkins up into the sunlight which made for five empty holes in the cemetery and in keeping with his usual practice Mr. Overhill went round to each fresh mound of dirt and dropped upon it a ten, a five, and two one dollar bills.

By the top of the noon hour the critter had already bagged up the live Lemlys' grandmomma's sister who proved to be extraordinarily powdery considering her depth and the wiry tattooed white boy had sunk himself about halfway to his Earp when Mr. Overhill called for lunch. He apologized to the Dinkins and the Earps and the Jemison for the delay and they drooled and spat and fidgeted respectively, and him and the fat negro and the paltry negro tried to hand the three bag Lemly over the cemetery fence to the live Lemlys thinking it was their daddy and would thereby fill the Lemly order, but it was not their daddy after all and turned out to be their daddy's oldest brother who the live Lemlys had known as children but had not ever cherished much and did not want to carry home with them, so Mr. Overhill apologized to the Lemlys for the delay just as he had apologized to the

Dinkins and the Earps and the Jemison and they told him not to fret over it and went back to stirring their grandmomma's sister with a stick.

They had lunch at the block grocery, rode there on the open tailgate except for Mr. Overhill who drove and except for the critter who squatted beside the fender well. Mr. Overhill bought Pepsi-Colas and saltines and potted meat and fig newtons and he distributed the drinks himself but gave over the food sack to the fat negro who set aside an entire sleeve of crackers and two cans of potted meat and a dozen fig newtons before throwing the bag at the paltry negro and hitting him square in the head with it which touched off a full-fledged invective festival with the paltry negro and the fat negro as the prime participants but with meaningful contributions from the wiry tattooed white boy who got the bag himself eventually, mostly in the neck and shoulders, and then got relieved of it from behind by the critter who pilfered through it prior to dropping it in Benton Lynch's lap. Mr. Overhill ate in the store, candied corn primarily, and told Mr. Greer about a woman he'd known in Clarksburg, West Virginia, and the fat negro got choked on a saltine and coughed some Pepsi up through his nose which the paltry negro found exceedingly satisfying and to celebrate raised his left haunch up off the tailgate and farted in one brief resounding pop which prompted several strident and near about violent objections from the wiry tattooed white boy who held bodily functions in the highest regard and took an especially dim view on all recreational farting and burping and told the paltry negro as much in the strongest and gravest language he could manage and then got burped at by both the negroes together and farted on by the critter and so stormed off around the block store in a fit of pique and urinated into Mr. Greer's trashcan to relieve his agitation some.

By the time Mr. Overhill returned to the cemetery with his charges, the Lemlys and the Dinkins and the Earps and the Jemison had been joined by a McCoy, two Donahoos and a Kemp. The Kemp's dead relations were all in South Carolina and he had come primarily to see the Donahoos' uncle but perused the bagged-up Lemlys with considerable interest and helped himself to a peek at the paltry negro's Greer. The Donahoos had come primarily to see their uncle also but did not have any plans for him past the seeing of him and so volunteered their assistance and volunteered the assistance of the Kemp, who was not ever very quick to volunteer it on his own, in the eventual hauling off of the McCoy's sister-in-law, Ida Dinkins McCoy of the embedded portrait. The actual upright McCoy was Miss Vera Jane McCoy from Flatwoods who did not have an actual upright sister and had always considered Mrs. Ida Dinkins McCoy the closest thing to one when she was actual and upright herself, and Miss Vera Jane McCoy from Flatwoods took ahold of Mr. Overhill's elbow from the underside once Mr. Overhill reached the cemetery and she led him round to her sister-in-law's plot as she told him all about the funeral and all about the mourners and all about the eulogy and all about the preacher who delivered it and all about the preacher's youngest daughter that had gotten herself pregnant by a Lutheran. Then she gazed upon the plastic jonquils and the bows and the gilt-framed photograph and said, "Lord, she was a handsome woman."

And Mr. Overhill told her, "Yes," told her, "Lord," told her, "Well now."

Benton Lynch got put on the actual upright McCoy's sister-in-law and the fat negro set in on the Donahoos' uncle while the paltry negro commenced with the true and verifiable Lemly daddy and the wiry tattooed white boy persisted with his Earp. Mr. Overhill put the critter to work on a Rawls once he determined there were not any Rawlses present and then he visited with the Lemlys who had successfully fished a gold pendant out from their grandmomma's sister. Mrs. Ida Dinkins McCoy did not appear very pleased with Benton Lynch from her gilt frame and he took off his shirt and covered her up with it but could not forget she was behind his shirttail looking at him and so remained uneasy. He was blistered already underneath his fingers or underneath six of his fingers anyway and consequently he could not effectively shovel with the shovel and could not effectively pick with the pick and thereby fell off the pace of the others which he had never really been up to in the first place. If anything the critter troweled up his Rawls with a kind of velocity he had not even approached on either one of his Lemlys and the wiry tattooed white boy and the paltry negro dug with appreciable energy and rhythm themselves while the fat negro, who was a little too fat and just a touch too sorry to put in an entire day's worth of hard and honest labor, dwindled some but hardly like Benton Lynch had dwindled and was continuing to dwindle on account of his general weariness and on account of his six blisters two of which had popped open and four more of which were about to.

The critter had his Rawls sifted out, bagged, and Ziplocked before Benton Lynch was even halfway down to Mrs. Ida Dinkins McCoy who continued to glare at him from underneath his shirttail, and as much as Mr. Overhill had resisted it, as much as he had wished to avoid it altogether, he directed the critter to assist Benton Lynch so as to expedite matters and Mr. Overhill himself took charge of Miss Vera Jane McCoy by offering her his elbow and strolling with her down to the collapsed sanctuary where he initiated a discussion of Lutherans about whom Miss McCoy held some exceptionally emphatic opinions. The critter was not extraordinarily fond of sharing his hole even if it wasn't his hole in the first place and he fairly much moved Benton Lynch clean up out of it and troweled and grunted and sweated and wheezed and sprayed dirt like a hound down to the casketlid while Benton Lynch squatted on the lip of the grave and licked his blisters. Mr. Overhill squired Miss Vera Jane McCoy back up the hillside just as her sister-in-law was getting hefted up into the sunlight by the critter and the paltry negro and the fat negro along with Benton Lynch and four strands of rope, and the upright and actual McCoy, who seemed to have a certain flair for the preposterous, rushed in through the cemetery gate to her sister-in-law's casket and brushed the remaining dirt off the top of it and said, "Oh hello Ida dear," and then she knocked with her knuckles on the coffinlid and the fat negro and the paltry negro each drew a breath and listened.

The actual and upright McCoy had begun to marshal the pair of Donahoos and the solitary Kemp into a squad of bearers just as the paltry negro and the fat negro and Benton Lynch were helping to snatch the wiry tattooed white boy's Earp up out of the ground, and the Dinkins and the two Earps and the vagrant strain of Jemison did not greet the boxed-up deceased Earp in any particular way, did not even wipe the dirt clean from the coffinlid but just drooled and spat and fidgeted respectively prior to taking up a coffinhandle apiece and carrying the Earps' daddy out the cemetery gate and up the hillside into the woods. They were followed directly by the actual and upright McCoy and the pair of Donahoos along with the solitary Kemp who had commenced to complain of a crooked spine when time came to lift the coffin, had commenced to complain most forlornly and resolutely, and so had been given to carry instead the gilt-framed portrait of the actual and upright McCoy's sister-in-law which Mr. Overhill had prized out of the headstone. So the actual and upright McCoy herself grabbed onto the backend of the casket and the Donahoos took ahold of opposite sides of the middle of it and the solitary and afflicted Kemp led them into the woods out from which there came presently a ponderous thud which was certainly the sound of the dropping of the sister-in-law and which was followed by the clamor of several harsh, strident, and near about outraged voices raised all at once and together which was certainly the sound of the berating of the Kemp.

The Lemlys got some help with their daddy from the fat negro, and the paltry negro and the wiry tattooed white boy carried grandmomma Lemly and granddaddy Lemly while Benton Lynch toted grandmomma Lemly's powdery sister on down the slope to the creek bottom. So as not to go entirely unproductive Mr. Overhill carried as much of the unwanted three bag Lemly as he could manage, which turned out to be two bags' worth, and the critter brought down the paltry negro's Greer by himself on his back. The four dead Lemlys that were departing with the two live Lemlys got loaded into the bed of the Lemly truck, and the two thirds of the three bag Lemly along with the entire of the boxed up Greet got set down on the roadside and left there temporarily. The fat negro had near about completely uncovered the Donahoos' uncle prior to the departure of the Lemlys and so returned to the cemetery and with the assistance of the wiry tattooed white boy and the paltry negro and Benton Lynch hoisted out of the ground this particular deceased Donahoo who the live Donahoos had said they had come to see but had neglected to even visit with, and the fat negro and the paltry negro took up either end of the Donahoos' uncle and carried him down to the roadside followed by Benton Lynch with an armful of the critter's Rawls in a bag followed by the wiry tattooed white boy and the critter himself with Benton Lynch's Dinkins between them and punctuated by Mr. Overhill with the third bag of the three bag Lemly. The fat negro and the paltry negro set their Donahoo next to the Greer and the critter and the wiry tattooed white boy laid down the Dinkins alongside him while Benton Lynch, without considering why he shouldn't put his Rawls in a bag down with two thirds of the Lemly so when Mr. Overhill arrived with the remaining third and commenced to label the various corpses in their various forms, he could not decipher which three of the four bags was Lemly and which one of the four bags was Rawls. He examined the dirt, questioned Benton Lynch, and solicited opinions from both the negroes and the wiry tattooed white boy too, but still was not satisfied that the Rawls was a Rawls and the Lemly all Lemly even once he had labeled them Rawls and Lemly. It seemed far more likely to Mr. Overhill that the Lemly was only mostly Lemly and the Rawls very possibly entirely part Lemly, but he went ahead and tagged and designated them anyway since it did not matter much who was what now that the both of them were compost.

Mr. Overhill drove the red Dodge pickup out of the creekbottom to the block grocery after a carton of cold Pepsi-Colas, and the fat negro and the paltry negro and the wiry tattooed white boy along with Benton Lynch and the critter returned to the cemetery where they selected new and unearthed Donahoos and Dinkinses and McCoys and Rawlses and Lemlys for themselves. Work ceased temporarily when Mr. Overhill came back and passed out the bottles and divvied up a packet of candied corn but it resumed presently to the accompaniment of an irregular but lively melody that Mr. Overhill whistled through his teeth as he wandered about the cemetery dropping the seventeen dollars onto the dirt mounds he had not dropped the seventeen dollars onto previously and pausing to gaze into the five halfdug, halfpicked, halftroweled holes. Towards the end of the afternoon a storm rolled in over the mountaintop preceded by great bursts of thunder and wind that turned the treeleaves backside up and then the rain itself advanced down the mountainside rattling in the treetops and beating the brush and finally arriving at the cemetery clearing in plump, soaking drops, first one and then another and then a half dozen and a dozen and then all of the rest at once staining the granite markers and dripping from the iron fence and running off the necks and faces of the fat negro who dug and the paltry negro who dug and the wiry tattooed white boy who dug and the critter who troweled and Mr. Overhill who grinned and whistled and off of the pointy nose and down into the carved out hollows of Benton Lynch who laid his shovel handle against his chest and looked all around himself.

At 5:30 promptly the paltry negro gathered all of the shovels and the picks and deposited them beneath the least collapsed part of the collapsed Baptist sanctuary. The critter who had succeeded in reaching what was in this case his Dinkins attempted to trowel him up into a sack and thereby close out the day but his Dinkins had become muddy in the rain and would not well lend himself to troweling or bagging or burping, so the critter dumped what little Dinkins he'd collected back into the hole with the rest of the Dinkins he'd yet to collect and pocketed his trowel for the night. Mr. Overhill brought the fixings out of the cab and set about preparing supper. The wiry tattooed white boy and the fat negro stripped naked and carried their towels and a half-empty jug of pink dish detergent down to the creek where they were determined to bathe even after they stuck their toes into the water and drew them out again. The paltry negro was determined to bathe also but was determined as well not to stray from the middle of the gravel road which put him in a considerable dilemma and he had not even begin to puzzle it out when Benton Lynch, who had not previously given much thought to bathing, determined that he would wash after all and started down the slope to the creekbank in the immediate company of the paltry negro who did not much mind underbrush when someone else beat it back. The critter squatted on the tailgate and scratched himself, apparently indifferent to and entirely immune from the attempted hygiene all around him.

The wiry tattooed white boy sat down in a knee-deep eddy after the fat negro dared him to and all of his skin went to gooseflesh even the dragon on his left bicep and the serpent on his right bicep and the Marlene in a red heart on his right forearm. He poured pink dish detergent all over himself and lathered up and then lay back in the water ever so briefly prior to leaping bolt upright and standing all sudsy and thoroughly goosebumped on the creekbed with a tortured little knot of skin where his testicles had been before they crawled up inside his stomach. The mere sight of him convinced the fat negro and the paltry negro too that they did not wish to get as entirely clean as they had thought previously and the both of them ended up washing their hands mostly while Benton Lynch removed his clothes, soaped himself all over, and waded on out into the center of the creek where he vanished with hardly a ripple and stayed vanished for what seemed a lengthy spell to the fat negro and the paltry negro and for what seemed an incredibly lengthy spell to the wiry tattooed white boy who had been vanished briefly himself. And when he at last did resurface he came up soapless but apparently unaffected otherwise and waded out of the creek past the wiry tattooed white boy and the fat negro and the paltry negro who asked him was he a crazy motherfucker or what.

Mr. Overhill had attempted to build a fire, had heaped up some wet sticks anyway, but did not ever strike a match to them and instead started the truck engine and placed the three cans of corned beef hash and the jar of creamed onions on the manifold to heat them up some. He tended to himself with undiluted drafts of Ancient Age which he took direct from a pint bottle which he kept discreetly in a paper sack even in a densely wooded creekbottom in the middle of nowhere with no natives roundabout but for bagged up and boxed up dead ones. However, the manifold did not seem to have much effect on the three cans of corned beef hash and the jar of creamed onions mostly because they fell off it once Mr. Overhill himself got sufficiently heated up and hit the gearshift with his knee, and even though he discovered them on the ground soon thereafter and returned them to the engine he set the onions atop the battery and balanced the cans of corned beef on the tire jack bolted to the wheel well neither of which tended to heat up quite as dramatically as the manifold did. Consequently, aside from Mr. Overhill himself, nothing really got warmed up for supper and Mr. Overhill portioned out the tepid hash and the onions into coffee cups and divided the remaining saltines equally and then joined the fat negro and the paltry negro and the wiry tattooed white boy and Benton Lynch and the critter at the tailgate of the truck where they ate in the company of a Greer and a Dinkins and a Donahoo and a Rawls and a Lemly who lay in a bunch on the roadside. And after they had eaten, and after the fat negro and the paltry negro and the critter had burped and farted the wiry tattooed white boy into a vicious fit, and after Mr. Overhill had told three times a joke about a shoesalesman he had told two times earlier in the day, they all settled in for the night, Mr. Overhill in the cab of the truck with his sack of Ancient Age and the fat negro and the paltry negro and the wiry tattooed white boy and the critter and Benton Lynch in the bed of the truck with the paltry negro's dope which went round between the paltry negro and the fat negro and the wiry tattooed white boy as they lay with their heads on their arms and watched the darkness come into the creekbottom, lay in silence mostly and watched in silence primarily except for the paltry negro who said, "Whus at?" with most every breath he could draw.

In another half a day they had the cemetery by the dilapidated church emptied of its Lemlys and its Greers and its Rawlses and its Dinkinses and its McCoys and its Donahoos and its Earps who lay together in their bags and boxes on the roadside until Mr. Overhill and the fat negro could load them into the truckbed and drive them up the gravel road and out through Lemly past the block store and the trash bins and the shabby ruinous house and up onto a square of sufficiently high and newly sanctified ground where they set them out again in their various bags and their various boxes. And when there were no more Lemlys and no more Greers and no more Rawlses and Dinkinses and McCoys and Donahoos and Earps by the roadside in the creekbottom, Mr. Overhill and the fat negro carried away all the picks and the shovels and even the trowel too along with the paltry negro and Benton Lynch and the wiry tattooed white boy and the critter who had come out the iron gate and away from the markers and the vases and the flags and the mementos, away from the collapsed sanctuary and down the trail between the locust trees. They dug new holes on the high ground, holes not as deep as the original holes but suitable nonetheless for the plastic bags and the wooden and the metal and the laminated caskets, and Mr. Overhill counted out the appropriate number of new tin markers from a five gallon bucket and wrote the names across them with a wax pencil and he stuck one in the ground at the head of each finished grave and dropped onto the red dirt still the ten and the five and the two ones though the holes were not so deep as before and not so broad and not so long. They were finished before 5:30 even and the paltry negro collected the picks and the shovels and packed them away in the truckbed while Mr. Overhill built a fire and successfully heated four cans of Dinty Moore stew. There was no creek to bathe in so there was not any lathering up or rinsing off or even any handwashing to speak of, just another joke from Mr. Overhill about another shoesalesman and more saltines and more Ancient Age and more dope and then treefrogs and darkness and sleep. They left in the night and so were already somewhere else by daylight, beyond Chattanooga this time, just beyond it on a hillside studded with tombstones and carved markers and one ghastly marble mausoleum, and the fat negro rolled out of the truckbed and pointed across the cemetery to first one rise and then another and then another. "Yonder," he said, "and yonder, and yonder too. Condominyums."

Mr. Busick did not consider himself done with his testicles though he had been accused of as much by Mrs. Busick ever since about 1972 or anyway that's what Mr. Tommy Winn said and that's what Mr. C. W. Bobbit nodded over and that's what Mr. Busick himself smirked at while Deputy Mercer apparently made a note about it on his little pad of paper that swung open from the top. Mr. Busick said it did not seem fitting to him his testicles should go to a place he'd never been to himself, did not seem fitting in the least especially since he always took them wherever he went and what he most desired to know from Deputy Mercer or Mr. Tommy Winn or Mr. C. W. Bobbit either one was what in the hell was a Fuquay-Varina anyhow and where in the hell was it in the first place, and Mr. Tommy Winn spoke up straight off and told him it was where all the best testicles go this time of year and Mr. C. W. Bobbit, who hardly ever added or contributed much of anything, this time did in fact add and contribute, "A regular rash of them," which Mr. Busick and Mr. Winn together yipped and howled over and Deputy Mercer made a note about, and Mr. Bobbit recrossed his legs and rolled his cigarette the width of his mouth and said he believed he was itching to go there himself, and Mr. Busick and Mr. Winn near about expired from breathlessness.

Deputy Mercer wanted to know did the alleged gunman, he called him, have any distinguishing features and Mr. Busick told him he had nothing but from the nose out in all directions, so they commenced to work their way down from the top of his head which Mr. Busick and Mr. Winn and Mr. Bobbit all agreed had been fairly distinguishing itself what with its fullblown and glorious pointiness. Mr. Busick estimated a half a foot between the eyebrows and the hairline but Mr. Winn begged to differ and could not see fit to allow for more than four inches while Mr. Bobbit did not recollect any eyebrows straightoff but was presently reminded of them by Mr. Busick. They all agreed his eyes had been of the sunken variety, probably of the extraordinarily sunken variety, and Mr. Busick was convinced they had been black but Mr. Winn was equally convinced they had been brown and Mr. Bobbit was convinced they had been either brown or black, so Deputy Mercer offered up dark as an alternative and it was agreeable to Mr. Winn and agreeable to Mr. Bobbit but was not in the least agreeable to Mr. Busick who insisted on black since it was after all his testicles that had been threatened.

They did not differ much on the nose except in the magnitude of it and Mr. Busick eventually retreated from his initial estimation and threw in with Mr. Winn and Mr. Bobbit who had themselves described to the deputy a nearly implausible organ and so welcomed the assistance of Mr. Busick whose threatened testicles seemed to lend him more credence than they possessed. The mouth was not a matter of much dissension either since they all agreed on the thinness of the lips and fairly completely agreed on the sheer bulk and squareness of the teeth, but they had some difficulty in conveying their impressions to Deputy Mercer who did not know any Holloways personally and had not been raised around horses except for Mr. Ed. So after casting around for a comparable item that was not a Holloway and not a horse either Mr. Winn at last struck upon Chiclets, which the deputy had never even heard of, and Mr. Busick plucked a box of the big ones off the candy rack and laid out a half dozen of them across the top of the drinkbox and Deputy Mercer studied and puzzled over them momentarily prior to announcing that he believed he got the gist of the thing. Talk of the Adam's apple called for several nectarines and a tangelo out from Mr. Busick's meager produce bin and the tangelo eventually took the majority on account of it was the size of a true

and healthy nectarine while Mr. Busick's nectarines had gone un-
bought and were rather slight and withered, and once Mr. Busick and
Mr. Winn and Mr. Bobbit had in fact settled on the nectarine-sized
tangelo for their model, Mr. Winn rolled up his left pantleg and Mr.
Busick held the fruit in question against Mr. Winn's naked shinbone
so as to illustrate the relationship between the Adam's apple and the
neck since none of the actual necks present could even approach the
alleged gunman's neck, at least not in the area of tubularity, Mr. Busick called it, much to the delight of Deputy Mercer who threw open
his pad and set his pencil to scratching.

There was not much fuss or disagreement about those parts of the
alleged gunman underneath the head and neck of him. Mr. Busick
and Mr. Winn and Mr. Bobbit were all convinced he had stood well
over six feet tall and they all recollected he had worn brown shoes and
blue trousers and some sort of dress jacket, some sort of turd-colored
dress jacket, Mr. Busick said, with turd-colored buttons, and now that
Mr. Busick mentioned it Mr. Winn and Mr. Bobbit believed turd-colored was just the thing it was, just precisely the thing it was, and they
rendered themselves emphatic with the deputy who licked the tipend
of his pencil and made out to write turd-colored on his pad but did
not. The gun was the final item to be analyzed and described, and
though Mr. Busick and Mr. Winn and Mr. Bobbit all agreed it had
been a pistol or a revolver or not a rifle anyway, they could not settle
on a caliber between them and Mr. Winn proposed .38 while Mr.
Bobbit insisted on .45 and Mr. Busick wandered around in the fifties
tossing out whatever seemed likely at the moment, so the deputy
suggested high caliber and Mr. Busick, with the thumb and forefinger
of his right hand, described the diameter of the bore and the deputy
suggested very high caliber to which Mr. Busick added a very on his
own.

And that was near about the conclusion of the fact gathering and
the statement taking and the general describing of the culprit except
for a final question on the part of Deputy Mercer who asked Mr. Busick, "You have any idea at all who he was? Any idea?"

And Mr. Busick told him, "My travel agent, I guess," which Mr.
Winn and Mr. Bobbit went into fits over.

They ran the whole story, not just in Draper and Wentworth but in Neely too on the bottom half of the front page of the *Chronicle* under some exceptionally inky headlines, and from his office in the town hall on the square Sheriff Burton creased the paper midway and set it aside on his desk and then took it up again and then set it aside again and then picked at his badge and fidgeted with his whistle prior to laying back against the wall on two legs of his chair prior to setting full onto the floor again and crossing his arms over his chest. Lawlessness generally got quite completely away from him, made him uneasy and agitated, especially serious lawlessness, malicious and dangerous lawlessness of which armed robbery was at the pure pinnacle next to homicide, which the sheriff did not hardly ever get any of, and just after suicide, which the sheriff most usually annually got some of but which was not an appreciable challenge to him since ordinarily the victim was the sole culprit also, and somewhere in the vicinity of mass murder with a garden implement or such, which the sheriff could only hope for and salivate over. So he was understandably edgy what with an actual armed offense in the neighborhood of his jurisdiction, an actual armed offense with a very high caliber revolver, and the sheriff laid his palms flat out on his desktop and said to himself, *"Very high caliber,"* in a deep and ominous sort of way.

It was going on a month since the sheriff had investigated any sort of violence whatsoever and the last episode had been a passionate but not a lethal outburst north on the 29 highway at the home of Mr. Jules Henry Graham, the least son of Mr. Lamont Graham of Ruffin. Mr. Jules Henry had built himself a house back a ways off the road and had taken a wife and raised a family in it all the while making improvements and embellishments in the form of shrubs and saplings and trumpet flowers and pine bark mulch and a two acre kidney-shaped pond out front between the house and the roadside. Mr. Jules Henry had taken care to place a few drooping willow trees here and there around the water and had set out a number of pink and white azaleas and sown some grass and some ivy and had situated two concrete benches in two picturesque and enticing locations and so had generally made for himself a lush and comely garden spot that he could sit on his front porch and admire, and it was equally admirable from the highway, maybe even especially admirable from the highway on account of how little else there was roundabout worth looking at hard except maybe for the Knights of Columbus clubhouse which was situated off the lefthand side of the road in a cedar grove and which the knights themselves had painted pink and green thereby transforming a fairly harmless and unobtrusive frame structure into the sort of thing your eyes went to even if your stomach resisted. But people generally sped up as they looked at the Knights of Columbus clubhouse and they generally slowed down as they looked at Mr. Jules Henry's lush and comely frontyard pond.

Now Mr. Jules Henry Graham's house and grounds lay almost precisely midway between the Texaco station at the outskirts of Neely and the American Tobacco Company's cigarette plant north towards Danville, so three times a day when the shifts changed a great assortment of people set out from Neely going north and an equally great assortment of people set out from the cigarette plant coming south and they all sped up at the Knights of Columbus clubhouse and they all slowed down at Mr. Jules Henry's garden spot but probably nobody slowed down so much as Mr. Sleepy Pitts slowed down since in his years of driving from Neely to the plant and back again he had watched the property before Mr. Graham's house go from a brambly field to a bulldozed out hole in the ground to a seepy puddle to a fullblown pond to a fullblown and comely and lush and verdant pond with grassy banks and decorative azaleas roundabout and thick viny willows on the water's edge and just generally the fishiest aspect of any body of water in any part of the surrounding countryside, and Mr. Sleepy Pitts, who always traveled with his rod and his reel disassembled and hanging behind him in the truck cab, was one to take notice of fishy places, especially exceptionally fishy places, so while everybody else slowed down in the road Sleepy Pitts near about stopped in it and envisioned the bass and the bream and maybe even the crappie too all across the pond bottom and suspended thick and bounteous throughout the depths of the water.

He was not personally acquainted with Mr. Jules Henry Graham but had grown up with one of Mr. Jules Henry's nephews, Mr. Robert Porter Graham, and consequently figured he could introduce himself as a friend of the family and so stopped in early one evening on his way back to Neely and found Mr. Jules Henry on his frontporch swing with the *Chronicle* in his lap and his Dr. Grabow out of the corner of his mouth smoking and spewing and sparking up most successfully. Mr. Jules Henry had never been much of a talker and Sleepy Pitts was not one to flap and carry on himself, so after the initial hellos and an odd word or two from each party on the health and well-being of Mr. Robert Porter Graham, not much got said straight off and Mr. Jules Henry smoked and gazed out over his lush and comely garden spot for himself and made several appreciative noises in his neck prior to telling Mr. Jules Henry outright that he had himself a lovely pond to sit and look at and Mr. Jules Henry said yes he did and nodded in agreement. And that was the end of the lively banter for another spell until Mrs. Jules Henry finished the dishes and came out onto the porch where she got introduced to Sleepy Pitts partly by Mr. Jules Henry who pointed and partly by Sleepy Pitts who spoke. Mrs. Jules Henry set herself down on the porch swing beside her husband and undertook to strike up a conversation which Sleepy Pitts at first had a very small role in, which Mr. Jules Henry never contributed to, and which Mrs. Jules Henry ultimately transformed into an exceedingly aimless recitation commencing with the general humidity and winding round to a local history of the kidney stone including who had got them, who had passed them, and who had had them surgically excised. Mrs. Jules Henry said kidney stones were much on her mind of late; she could not explain why exactly.

It was an exceedingly long way from kidney stones to bass and bream and maybe crappie too. Actually it is an exceedingly long way from kidney stones to most everything else, and it was precisely the sort of exceedingly long way that Sleepy Pitts did not travel well at all, especially since he had to go unassisted by Mr. Jules Henry, who complacently smoked his Dr. Grabow from the porch swing, and unassisted as well by Mrs. Jules Henry, who could be led off the subject of kidney stones specifically but could not seem to be diverted from human suffering in general. So Sleepy Pitts got to where he wanted to go a piece at a time and went by way of drownings and shark attacks and boating accidents and mercury poisoning which all served to introduce water and served to introduce fish and consequently cushioned the blow some when Sleepy Pitts opened his mouth and told Mrs. Jules Henry she had herself a lovely pond to sit and look at to which Mrs. Jules Henry said yes she did and nodded in agreement.

"Truly lovely," Sleepy Pitts added and made a general racket in his neck which somehow reminded Mrs. Jules Henry of a gentleman she knew in Burlington who had a hole in his throat and talked through what appeared to be a flashlight and she was setting herself to elaborate some on his affliction when Sleepy Pitts came straight out and asked Mr. Jules Henry or Mrs. Jules Henry either one if a man might fish in their pond sometime or another, and Mrs. Jules Henry looked at Mr. Jules Henry who removed his pipe from his mouth, tamped the ash and tobacco with the end of his finger, and said, "A man might."

And Mrs. Jules Henry told him, "Jules Henry!" in a stern and altogether displeased sort of way and Mr. Jules Henry waved his open hand at her and returned his pipe to his mouth.

"I'd be willing to pay," Sleepy Pitts, said. "I'd insist on it."

And Mr. Jules Henry replied, "Two dollars," which got him another Jules Henry! from Mrs. Jules Henry who herself got waved off and hushed up all over again.

And Mr. Sleepy Pitts said that was a fair and just price for the privilege of sitting and looking at and fishing from such a lovely pond and he paid the money and made plans to return a week to the day later so as to anticipate the privilege more thoroughly and then he thanked Mr. Jules Henry, who folded the bills and slipped them into his shirtpocket, and thanked Mrs. Jules Henry, who laid the fingers on her right hand against the bottom of her stomach and said she had a pain, said she had a hot shooting pain, said she believed it was appendicitis, said she had known a woman whose appendix had burst wide open on her.

Mrs. Sleepy Pitts was not disposed to fish herself and was not disposed to tolerate fishing in other people, especially not in Mr. Sleepy Pitts, so somehow or another on the day he had set aside to collect his two dollars' worth of fishing Mr. Sleepy Pitts neglected to tell Mrs. Sleepy Pitts that he was not going to the cigarette factory, or was only going partway to the cigarette factory anyhow, and since he got up when he usually got up and did all of what he usually did and departed when he usually departed Mrs. Sleepy Pitts had no call to suspect he was not going where he usually went, but he was not and this time pulled off the road instead of stopping in it and got his tackle out from the glove compartment and his dissassembled fishing rod off the window rack and proceeded down the roadbank to Mr. Jules Henry Graham's lush and comely garden spot. Sleepy Pitts had pondered and considered and scrutinized and hypothesized for a week now and had at last concluded he would commence with his purple worm followed by the black one and then the red one and would cap off the morning with his green speckled Jitterbug just prior to lunch which Sleepy Pitts had brought in his usual box and had decided he would enjoy from Mr. Jules Henry's furthest concrete bench. He planned to concentrate chiefly on bream throughout the early afternoon and so intended to change over to a cork float and a sinker and a number six hook baited with lightly salted fried dough from a batch he had mixed up at great peril, a batch Mrs. Sleepy Pitts had smelled cooking and had got told was an omelette. He figured he would dispense with the float in the shank of the afternoon and fish for whatever might be on the bottom until the shift changed and then maybe he would keep a bass or a bream or two or possibly a crappie and carry them home to Mrs. Sleepy Pitts who would get told something or another.

But after the purple worm and well into the black one Sleepy Pitts had not hooked anything but part of a treestump and throughout the red worm and on into the Jitterbug he did not attract even a detectable nip and so sat down to lunch perplexed and somewhat agitated. Mr. Jules Henry came around the house and into the frontyard where he piddled with his nandinas while Sleepy Pitts ate his lunch and Sleepy Pitts hooted and waved at him from the concrete bench and held his empty stringer up over his head and in return Mr. Jules Henry saluted with his pruning shears. Sleepy Pitts attached his float and his sinkers from there on the concrete bench and he pinched off a piece of dough and baited his number six hook with it and then laid the whole business out in a shady patch of water underneath the boughs of a willow tree and squatted on the pondbank from where he studied the bobber and held the rod with the tipends of his fingers, but nothing took the bait, nothing took a piece of the bait, nothing even went by and smelled it as far as Sleepy Pitts could tell and he flung the line out of the shade towards the deeper water and adjusted his squat some and watched the bobber and felt of the rod all over again but nothing took the bait or a piece of the bait or sniffed at it there either. So he commenced to circle the pond, pausing to fling his baited hook in what looked to be the fishiest places and he went from the north end to the south end to the north end to the sound end again with the same pinch of unnibbled-at and entirely unthreatened dough wrapped roundabout his hook. Then he raised the float so as to drop the sinkers and the hook some and he recircled and reflung and resquatted at most every place he'd circled to and flung and squatted at previously but with about the same results, or actually with precisely the same results, and so he lowered the hook, lowered it past where it had been lowered to before, and circled and flung and squatted all over again but in the opposite direction this time and so was unsuccessful at last in the very place he had been unsuccessful at first. Eventually he took the float off the line and put it in his shirtpocket and he changed the bait first for a piece off the top of his doughball and then for a piece off the bottom of his doughball and then for a piece direct from the center of his doughball, but the floatless redoughed hook did not seem to attract any more notice than the floated doughed hook or the green speckled Jitterbug or the red worm or the black worm or the purple worm either, and Sleepy Pitts was near about used up with circling and flinging and squatting when the tailend of the second shift going north commenced to meet the frontend of the first shift coming south up the roadbank on the highway and Sleepy Pitts unbaited his hook and cut his tackle loose and took his rod to pieces.

He felt obliged to thank Mr. Jules Henry for the opportunity to fish his pond, even though the two dollars had only bought him considerable risk and aggravation and a slight sunburn on his forearms, and he spied Mr. Jules Henry on his porch swing with his Dr. Grabow and his *Chronicle* and proceeded on up to talk to him. Sleepy Pitts was most grateful, or anyway later he recollected and insisted that he had been most grateful at the outset, and again he held up the stringer for examination, it being as empty and as dry as it had been previously, and he told Mr. Jules Henry, "I tried everywhere, tried every manner of lure and bait I had, but didn't catch a one of them rascals, didn't even get a nibble. I went all roundabout that thing and couldn't even get a bite."

And Mr. Jules Henry, all serene and placid like usual, creased his paper and extracted his Dr. Grabow from his mouth and said, "I didn't think you would. Ain't no fish in it."

They called it a lashing but it wasn't an actual and legitimate lashing, or anyway Sheriff Burton called it a lashing though he himself admitted to being torn between a lashing and a flogging and had even flirted with a flaying before he knew exactly what a flaying was, but it was probably more like a whipping than a lashing or a flogging and was certainly more like a whipping than a flaying, though it would have been a lashing if Sleepy Pitts had selected the little end of the rod which had considerable spring to it and so would have been the ideal device to lash with, and it would have been a flogging if Sleepy Pitts had selected the big end of the rod which was fairly thoroughly stiff and unspringy and so would have been the ideal device to flog with, but Sleepy Pitts selected the middle part of the rod which was not especially springy or especially stiff either and so was the ideal device to do to Mr. Jules Henry what it did to him. Mrs. Jules Henry heard the fuss from the kitchen and came bolting out onto the porch where she attempted to interfere in the proceedings but was delivered a vicious backhanded blow, she called it, and thereby got prevented from succeeding at any serious or useful interfering and so laid idly by as that man, that cruel and mean-hearted man, she called him, raised whelps all about her husband's person. Understandably Mr. Jules Henry had dropped his Dr. Grabow and had let go his *Chronicle* and had drawn himself up into a knot on the porch swing with his arms over his head and he absorbed the majority of the punishment from the elbows out, except for the few stray blows which fell elsewhere every now and again, and probably would have continued to absorb the punishment from the elbows out and otherwise if Mr. Sleepy Pitts had not come to himself and regained his native disposition which usually did not show anything in the way of lashing or flogging or whipping even since they did not call Sleepy Sleepy on account of his quick and violent temper.

He gave himself up, drove directly to the town hall, and took himself and his piece of fishing rod on into the sheriff's office and surrendered which deflated the whole enterprise some for the sheriff who generally liked to go out and fetch his culprits but presently the business took on a new luster when Mr. and Mrs. Jules Henry Graham showed up to discover that Sheriff Burton had gone ahead and caught who they hadn't even turned in yet which was a matter of some amazement especially to Mrs. Jules Henry who had not been whelped and beat up about the forearms and so was not distracted by the discomfort. Of course Mr. Sleepy Pitts had already confessed to the whipping and had already detailed the entire affair to Sheriff Burton and had already apologized for the most of it prior to getting put away in the lockup where Sheriff Burton took Mrs. Jules Henry for purposes of identification and where Mr. Sleepy Pitts apologized all over again but apparently with little effect on Mrs. Jules Henry who would not speak directly to him and would not look directly at him but instead expressed her profound displeasure to Sheriff Burton who in turn expressed it to Sleepy Pitts.

Mr. Jules Henry was probably about as profoundly displeased as Mrs. Jules Henry was but he could not keep his mind on his displeasure on account of the whelps and the bruises and the various abrasions primarily on his forearms but to some degree about his person in general and he sat alone and untended to in a hard-back chair against the wall of the sheriff's office until the mayor's secretary discovered him there and hunted up some salve which she spread roundabout all but the most private places where Mr. Jules Henry figured he had a whelp or two as well but had not really looked to see. The sheriff called Mrs. Sleepy Pitts who was verily astounded to find out her husband was in the lockup and was even more verily astounded to find out why and she came over to the town hall straightaway while her surprise still had most of its edge to it and she apologized to and commiserated with Mr. Jules Henry, who was all greased up and somewhat more comfortable than he had been previously, and then she followed the sheriff and followed Mrs. Jules Henry back to the lockup where she vilified Mr. Sleepy Pitts and allowed Mrs. Jules Henry to vilify him also, and Mr. Sleepy Pitts himself, who was extraordinarily sorry and repentant, brought his stooped shoulders and his bowed head just a tad too close to the cell door and Mrs. Sleepy Pitts shot her arm through the bars and grabbed onto a serious handful of Mr. Sleepy Pitts's hair and did some squeezing and some yanking and some vigorous jerking around which had the effect of rendering Mr. Sleepy Pitts even more extraordinarily sorry and repentant than he had been previously and had the effect of bringing some noticeable delight and pleasure to Mrs. Jules Henry along with some measurable satisfaction to Mrs. Sleepy Pitts and even served to substantially reinvigorate the sheriff who had figured most all the good passion and violence was over and done with.

But after the squeezing and the yanking and the jerking around, most all the good passion and violence was over and done with, and now only a month beyond the actual lashing of Mr. Jules Henry Graham by Mr. Sleepy Pitts, or what was called the actual lashing anyway, the sheriff could not recollect who had got what in the settlement, simply could not recall if Mr. Jules Henry had been awarded his damages or if Mr. Sleepy Pitts had been awarded his two dollar fishing fee or if Mrs. Sleepy Pitts had been awarded her uncontested divorce. He could not remember anything much about the episode except for the brief passion and violence of it, but then it was a theory with the sheriff that the passion and violence of a thing, no matter how brief and fleeting, was about all that mattered anyhow, all that mattered to him anyway since he was in the passion and violence business, or that's what he told the ladies of the Flower Society and of the Sewing Club and of the Daughters of the American Revolution along with the Rotarians and the Knights of Columbus and the members of the Bi-Monthly Book Association, what he told most everybody who invited him out to tell them something prior to hooking his thumbs on his belt and displaying his paraphernalia. So Sheriff Burton could not recollect the justice end of the Graham-Pitts dispute mainly because he was not in the justice business, and he could not recollect much of the violence and passion end of it either mainly because there had not been enough violence and passion to it to suit him which was his primary complaint about law enforcement roundabout. So Sheriff Burton uncrossed his arms and fetched his *Chronicle* up off the desktop and read about the robbery all over again and about the threat to Mr. Busick's private parts and about the very high caliber revolver, and then he packed the paper away by itself in his leather satchel and locked his top drawer and straightened his blotter and excused himself for the afternoon.

Sheriff Burton rented out the upstairs of Mrs. Carrie Alice Dunlop Messick's frame house on Ennis Street behind the Big Apple. Mrs.

Carrie Alice Dunlop Messick had lived well for a time and had never figured she would be reduced to renting out her upstairs, but once Mr. Messick passed away and once Mrs. Messick's colored housekeeper took up with a Greyhound driver from Greensboro Mrs. Messick discovered she did not have anybody to hook her screens and turn her latches at night and since she did not much care for the independence and the solitude she decided to rent out her upstairs even though her upstairs had not been built to be rented out, did not have its own entrance, did not have its own kitchen, did not have anything really but three bedrooms, one bathroom, a little slip of a hallway, and prodigious closet space, but once Sheriff Browner hired on Sheriff Burton as his deputy and once Deputy Burton commenced to cast around for living quarters, Mrs. Messick concluded and determined she would in fact rent out her upstairs since having a lawman under her very own roof seemed near about as good as getting Mr. Messick back and far surpassed the colored housekeeper who turned latches well enough but would not venture into the cellar after sunset and hid under the bedclothes during hard weather.

Sheriff Burton paid Mrs. Messick a nominal monthly fee and kept the yard and carried out the garbage for his board which he took in what had once been a glorious dining room at the center of the house but the plaster had long since cracked open and the paint had mildewed around the windowlights and the carpet had worn down to the matting most everywhere and Mrs. Messick had established her television in one corner and had stacked her magazines in another and had covered the walls with her daughter-in-law's needlepoint samplers and photographs of her grandchildren and one large and colorful and altogether grisly picture of Christ on the cross which hung beside a smaller less colorful and far less grisly picture of him off it, so the dining room was not so glorious any longer but suited the food well enough since it was not so glorious either.

Mrs. Messick could not eat salt on account of her blood pressure and could not eat shortening or any manner of animal fat and was instructed to stay away from butter and eggs and cream sauces and refined sugar and could not effectively digest beef and did not have much fondness for pork which left chicken primarily, lean chicken baked without the assistance of a sauce or seasonings and served with a piece of whitebread alongside a garden salad and a dietetic peach half on a lettuce leaf all of which usually satisfied Mrs. Messick, who was spindly and wiry and altogether insubstantial, and all of which never satisfied Sheriff Burton who generally retired to the upstairs after supper and ate Cheez Doodles in one of his bedrooms, most often in the bedroom with the bed and the television set which he called his den as opposed to the bedroom with the bed and the table and the straight chair which he called his study and the bedroom with the bed and the dresser and the oval mirror which he called his bedroom.

On the evening of the armed robbery article in the *Chronicle* Sheriff Burton carried the newspaper with him to supper which he did not usually make a habit of on account of Mrs. Messick's low opinion of newspapers, elbows, and such on the tabletop at mealtime, but he begged pardon and as Mrs. Messick brought the icewater in from the kitchen the sheriff began reading aloud those parts of the story that did not deal directly with Mr. Busick's privates which somehow seemed less allowable at the supper table than newspapers or elbows either. Occasionally the sheriff interrupted himself to interpolate or surmise or theorize or hypothesize or expand upon and wander from the actual story itself and thereby bring his vast experience to bear on the circumstances, and Mrs. Messick picked at her shortleg and said, Um Hmm, and said, I see, and said, Oh really, and watched the sheriff throw himself carelessly back in his chair and bring himself earnestly forward out of it and wave his arms and point his finger and take up his bottom lip between his teeth.

The sheriff figured the assailant for a product of socio-economic depravity, a father maybe, a husband surely, and likely laid off from the cigarette plant or the brewery outside Eden or the cotton mill or the quarry at Stokesdale. It was the sheriff's opinion that Mr. Busick had not been in much danger of getting shot, he did not mention precisely where Mr. Busick had not been in much danger of getting shot, and the sheriff imagined the money would go for necessities, food, clothing, and such. But, the sheriff said, and this was the part where he shook his finger, a man's got no right to rob and plunder even to clothe and feed his wife and his little ones. A man's got no right to lawlessness, the sheriff said, and this was the part where he took up his lip between his teeth, and Mrs. Messick, who had not Um Hmmed or

I seed or Oh reallyed for a prominent while, left off with her peach half, waved the pointy end of her fork at the sheriff, and told him she had a niece in Stokesdale who made the most exquisite baby blankets and booties and little knit hats, and the sheriff said, "Socio-economic depravity, pure and simple," and Mrs. Messick told him, "And scarves too, fuzzy little scarves with tiny tassels."

The sheriff sat in front of his air circulator and ate his Cheez Doodles and looked at his television set and every now and again picked up the open *Chronicle* and perused the bottom half of the front of it prior to carrying himself to the big sidewindow in his den and peering out into the evening where there was a felon somewhere, somewhere local and close by. And when the sheriff went to bed at last he went to bed with the open *Chronicle* and read the front of it and the back of it and the middle of it and then folded it over and looked at the inky headlines and at the photograph of Mr. Busick, the victim, and at the photograph of Mr. Winn with his chin dangling alongside Mr. Bobbit with his cigarette and the pieces of his arms, the witnesses, and at the little square of roadmap that was Raleigh mostly and Wendell and Garner and Knightdale and Zebulon and down the 401 highway to the south Fuquay-Varina also with a bold black arrow to indicate and distinguish it.

They had circled round through Georgia, crossed east through South Carolina, and come north to a place called Bay Leaf which was not much more of a place than Lemly had been but which was preparing and intending to become a place, preparing and intending to become quite a prominent place when the Neuse River backed up and filled the reservoir which it had not done yet on account of the dam which had not been built yet on account of the general discord between the governor and the congress and the various dirt farmers whose property would become lake bottom. For ten years running there had been talk of a dam and talk of a reservoir and there had even been a settlement once and the shoreline had got surveyed and laid out and the trees had got cut down and a portion of the lake bottom had got bought up but something had happened, some vague and political something, and the dam still did not get built though now everybody expected that it would, even those people who had previously expected that it wouldn't, mostly on account of the laid out shoreline and the cut down trees and the partially bought up lakebottom. The people of Bay Leaf especially expected and anticipated the dam and expected and anticipated the shoreline mostly because they would be on it or actually were on it already though it did not appear much of a shoreline and did not appear much of a lake but must have been a lake and must have been a shoreline because the price of the land along it and around it and all roundabout the vicinity of it tripled and then got bought up in the majority and so what was left quadrupled and got bought up too and little clearings got cut away in the lots and footings got poured and walls got framed out and houses went up, not your regular Bay Leaf houses, your lowslung ranch styles with brick flowerboxes and carports, but wildly geometrical houses, round houses and octagonal houses and square and rectangular houses with triangular outcroppings in the most unexpected places and not a brick to be found anywhere but rough cypress and rough cedar and rough fir and plain old chewed up spruce pine stained and made up to look like cypress and cedar and fir and no grass around the frontyards but just pine mulch and exotic shrubbery and dwarf trees and no grass around the backyards either but just more pine mulch and more shrubbery and generally a redwood deck with some shade to it and a view of the lake which was not a lake yet, not even a marsh but just an expanse of scrub and undergrowth and brambles and treestumps ringed round with houses and ringed round with concrete boatramps and ringed round with narrow wooden floating docks, entirely unbuoyed and thoroughly unfloating floating docks.

The natives of Bay Leaf, both the lowslung red brick fulltime natives and the geometrical roughwood weekend natives were still waiting for the water to rise when Mr. Overhill drove his red Dodge pickup and his load of equipment and his load of manpower into the limits of the township and brought the whole business to a halt in front of a fairly massive marina that the mayor and the firechief and the town clerk and two insurance agents had all invested in together and had constructed a bit prematurely. Initially they stocked boating and fishing supplies and Styrofoam coolers and sunglasses and waterskis but when the dam didn't get built and the river didn't back up they set in to selling sundry unaquatic items like sportsjackets and

neckties and cotton socks and ladies' jewelry and leather tiretread sandals and handbags and openweave sunhats and loafbread and insecti-
cides and window fans and cold beer, and of course candied corn also
which Mr. Overhill bought a half dozen packets of straightaway since
he had been without it in the sack or even between his teeth ever
since Bennetsville which was a whole state away. The town clerk, who
was in charge of the sportsjackets, drew out a map for Mr. Overhill on
a piece of box while Mr. Overhill tried on a 42 long in poplin and
modeled it for himself in front of the mirror on the men's room door
prior to exchanging it for a 44 long in a kind of speckled polyester
which he wore to the back of the store and viewed the lakebed which
was even less of a lakebed than it had been previously on account of
the unmitigated success of the undergrowth, and the sight of the
scrub and the brambles and the treestumps stretching far and away
into the distance prompted Mr. Overhill to snicker and prompted Mr.
Overhill to laugh once outright and prompted Mr. Overhill to holler
across the store to the town clerk and ask him when the tide might be
coming in which the town clerk did not much appreciate and made a
fairly vile reply to which prompted Mr. Overhill to snicker and laugh
outright all over again.

They left Bay Leaf the way they'd come in and headed south back
down the Falls of the Neuse Road until they arrived at a territory
known as the Harricanes which was not on any map and did not have
a sign to announce it like Lemly or Bay Leaf because it was not a legitimate and particular place like Lemly and Bay Leaf were legitimate
and particular places even though just barely. So Mr. Overhill pondered his piece of box with considerable care but nonetheless passed
his turnoff going to the south and turned around and drove on by it
the other way and then stopped in the highway on this third run and
looked at the piece of box and peered down an oiled rural road to his
right and then looked at the piece of box again prior to getting off the
highway at last and heading towards the riverbottom to the strains of
a general and harmonious lament from the paltry negro and the wiry
tattooed white boy who wanted to know where in the fuck they were
going anyway, with the wiry tattooed white boy supplying the where
primarily and the paltry negro supplying the fuck, and Mr. Overhill
told them he'd be goddamned and bound up in hell if he knew him-

self which did not much comfort or satisfy the paltry negro or the wiry tattooed white boy or the fat negro either who threw in with a shit yes whenever there seemed a need for one.

Mr. Overhill proceeded down into the woods at what he considered a prudent velocity which called for liberal and fairly indelicate braking on his part and kicked up some serious nausea in the truckbed thereby choking off and thoroughly stifling the lamentations and complaints and sending the fat negro and the paltry negro and the wiry tattooed white boy to the tailgate to suck air in the company of an additional and equally wiry white boy who was not Benton Lynch and was not the critter either but was Emmet somebody that Mr. Overhill had picked up on the roadside beyond Chattanooga. Emmet chewed his tobacco with Bazooka bubble gum and generally did not clear his chin when he spat. He had no manners to speak of, did not wear socks, and had surrendered the majority of his teeth except for one on the top and six on the bottom all of which were turned and twisted roundabout in his mouth so as to face his earlobes. The paltry negro had despised him straight off but could not decide precisely what sort of motherfucker he was and so called him every sort he could think of, and being proficient and meticulous in his profanity the paltry negro could think of a considerable plenty. The fat negro and the wiry tattooed white boy had despised him at length themselves but not until after the first night in the truckbed when the critter abandoned his fender well so as to squat at Emmet's ear and hiss into it, and Emmet sat up on the blanket and eyed the critter and heard him out and at last opened his own mouth and said, "I got this buddy went to Ve it nahm, cut off a pecker and brought it back with him, hung it on the mirror in his Torino. All dried up now, falling to pieces. Never was no big pecker." And the fat negro drew back his foot and delivered Emmet a wallop across the shoulder which sent him into a wild, impotent rage and he wailed, "Hey! Whud I do?" And the fat negro told him, "Shut up," and the wiry tattooed white boy told him, "Shut up," and the paltry negro announced, "Sick motherfucker," which seemed fitting to the moment.

Not any of them became truly ill though Emmet spat out his lump of bubble gum and tobacco prefatory to an upchuck which never arrived and presently Mr. Overhill turned south off the first oiled road onto a second oiled road that ran parallel to the riverbank and so did not call for the prodigious braking and jerking that had been called for previously. The second oiled road off the first oiled road off the highway curled and turned and wound up and wound out through the very heart of the Harricanes though the heart of the Harricanes was the sort of place you could not know you were in until you were out of it, so Mr. Overhill pondered his piece of box and proceeded ahead slowing at the sideroads he came up on and slowing at the houses he passed, extraordinarily shabby houses with extraordinarily shabby people on the porches of them come out to see just who it was in a red Dodge pickup truck passing through the heart of the Harricanes which Mr. Overhill still did not know he was in since there was not a sign to tell him, not even a bullet-riddled vine-obscured sign laid over in a ditch somewhere, but there was indication enough otherwise just like in niggertown, niggertown most everywhere there is one, which has no signs or markers either but cannot be confused with anywhere else on account of how what lives there lives. There were junked cars in the woods and old appliances and regular trash and garbage strewn down the banks of nearly all the roadside gullies. Chickens ran loose like squirrels and off the road beside the houses the hogs and the pigs were pinned up with planks and wire and most anything else that would take a nail. Where there was washing, it hung out on bushes and treelimbs, and where there were children, they played on the packed dirt with sticks and rocks or just their own ten fingers and like everybody else were diverted and enthralled by the strange and wondrous red Dodge pickup truck with its exotic load of negroes mostly, or so it appeared, and the Gilchrists and the Currins and the Sapps and the Parkers and the Firesheetses of the Harricanes did not see negroes much down in their riverbottom in their woods and so viewed these with measurable attention and curiosity. And the fat negro said to the paltry negro, "These some bad looking whitefolks."

And the paltry negro said to the fat negro, "Stringy motherfuckers, ain't they."

And Emmet told the both of them, "Ain't nothing wrong with these people," and he laid himself partway out over the tailgate and waved his left arm and shouted, "Hey there," up the roadbank to-

wards the worst looking, stringiest bunch of whitefolks even he had
ever seen and nobody not the adults or the children either bothered to
wave back.

"That's right Emmet," the fat negro said, "stir 'em up."

"Stupid motherfucker," the paltry negro told him and pushed him
into the fat negro who pushed him back into the paltry negro and the
two of them together grabbed onto his arms and threw him up towards the truckcab onto the pick and shovel handles and hard against
Benton Lynch and Emmet brought himself upright and wailed, "Hey!
Whud I do?"

Mr. Overhill found the cemetery all by himself, or with his piece
of box only and without call for instructions and directions from any
of the natives who did not seem even to Mr. Overhill much disposed
to instruct or direct. Apparently, plenty of people did plenty of dying
in the Harricanes because surely there was a mass of them buried there
and in a graveyard near about as fine and comely as every other human
undertaking roundabout. There had been a fence once, a wooden
fence, but apparently the primary parts of it had got hauled off and
burnt throughout the winters so there was not much of a fence any
longer but just some pieces of a fence remaining along with the entire
of a gate which was thoroughly wooden also but had not been
knocked down and chopped up likely on account of some sort of localized and collective arrangement which forgave the fence for as long
as the gate stood. The consecrated and sanctified inside of the place
had grown up near about as high as the unconsecrated and unsancti-
fied outside of the place, and the tombstones and the wooden and
granite markers that the freeze had not cracked or pitched about and
the rain and the bugs had not eaten away had got covered up anyhow
with creeping vine and bramble and milkweed and grass of every variety so that nobody in particular got found except by accident and
good fortune which proved altogether troublesome for Mr. Overhill
who got asked by three strappy and duly notified Gilchrists to find
someone in particular, to find someone in particular quick and
straightaway, their mother as it turned out, or two of thems mother
anyway and one of thems aunt, and since these Gilchrists were as bad
looking a bunch of whitefolks as the fat negro and the paltry negro
had ever laid eyes on the two of them together jumped at the oppor-

tunity to make themselves accommodating and commenced to beat the bushes for momma Gilchrist which was not the sort of thing the paltry negro would generally have any part of on account of the prospect of snakes.

They did not find her as quick and straightaway as the two sons and the nephew had desired but they did find her presently off and away under a wateroak and bound up in some prodigious ivy and together they uncovered her and brought her up out of the ground and toted her through the bushes across the cemetery to the two sons and one nephew who as it turned out were not inclined or disposed to haul her off but instead prized open the casket lid and helped themselves to a brooch and a ring and a pendant which had apparently come to momma Gilchrist in a more frivolous day. Two more duly notified Gilchrists arrived from off the road and requested of Mr. Overhill three of their relations, two Gilchrists and a Sapp, which Mr. Overhill dispatched the paltry negro and the fat negro and the wiry tattooed white boy to see after, and the two sons and the nephew of momma Gilchrist, sparked by the literal example of the two new and additional Gilchrists, put in an order for near about the rest of the family, and as best as Mr. Overhill could determine through the weeds and the vines and the variety of grasses the northeast corner of the cemetery was purely littered with Gilchrists, so he got Benton Lynch and Emmet and the critter out from the partly dug holes and sent them off through the brush to join the fat negro and the paltry negro in turning up Gilchrists primarily which they managed with great swiftness and considerable ease on account of the soft, loamy, mole-eaten ground and they kept the three original Gilchrists and the two additional Gilchrists supplied with a steady stream of the boxed up and burped and Ziplocked relations along with a solitary Gilstrap who got turned up by accident but was plundered through and picked over nonetheless.

An assortment of Parkers and Currins and several actual living and breathing Sapps came out from a path in the woods and joined the three original Gilchrists and the two additional Gilchrists along with the ever increasing flow of their dead relations. All four of the Parkers, who were of a sluggish and sedentary stock, lowered themselves onto the casketlids of some previously pilfered Gilchrists while both the

Currins, who were not so sluggish and sedentary as Parkers but near about, squatted on their heels beside the Sapps who as a rule preferred leaning to sitting or squatting and would have most likely tilted themselves against the cemetery fence if the cemetery fence had not been burnt up beforehand. A Sugg who was cousin to the Sapps and uncle to one of the Parkers drove up off the road in a blue Chevrolet Biscayne and wheeled partway on into the cemetery so as to save himself the trouble of getting out of the car, which was generally the way with Suggs, and at his request the Sapps opened up two of the Gilchrists that did not have Parkers on top of them and the Sugg studied the corpses prior to delivering a fairly penetrating assessment of the ravages of death followed by several incisive comments on the noses and chins of Gilchrists, which was a notoriously tender subject with Gilchrists on account of the size of their noses and the shape of their chins, and the Sugg was so extraordinarily incisive, not to say frank and blunt and altogether indelicate, that the Gilchrists got hot and agitated straight off, the three original Gilchrists along with the two additional ones, and the Sugg rolled up his windowglass in self defense and concluded the matter through his side vent much to the open and apparent displeasure of the Gilchrists but much to the delight of the Parkers and the Currins and the Sapps who ever enjoyed discord and agitation especially if they led to a stomping, but the Sugg left off provoking the Gilchrists before he could get himself stomped, which was a particular talent with Suggs, and instead turned his attention to the critter who had crossed the cemetery toting a two-bag Gilchrist and set him down with the rest of his relations.

Like usual the critter's hair was knotted and matted and standing up all over his head and his face and neck were dirt black mostly except for the tracks where the sweat had run through and carried the filth away. His shirt was stiff and gritty and his pants were torn open at the knees and smudged and smeared with fingerprints and crusted food. He was ensconced in his usual bouquet which the flies in particular seemed to adore but which the Gilchrists and the Parkers and the Currins and the Sapps and the solitary Sugg did not appear to think much of judging from how they waved their hands before their faces and wrinkled up the skin around their noseholes, and the solitary Sugg, who had again rolled down his window glass once the Gilchrist threat had passed and dwindled, laid himself partway out the door and said to the critter, "Great God Almighty, what in the shit are you anyway?" And from across the cemetery the paltry negro picked up his head and watched the critter step away from the collection of bagged up and boxed up Gilchrists and step towards the blue Biscayne with the solitary Sugg partway out the window of it and he said to the fat negro, "Oh Jesus, we dead."

The critter looked at the Sugg and the Sugg looked at the critter and when the critter did not make any sort of audible response to the Sugg's previous question the Sugg asked it again and the critter made a noise in his throat followed by several additional similar noises all of which strung together resembled human speech and the Sugg asked his question a third time and then studied and scrutinized the critter's lips so as to possibly decipher and translate the response which came out about as undecipherable and untranslatable as the one before it and just as the Sugg was fixing his mouth to use it again one of the squatting Currins, the nearest squatting Currin who had a proper angle on the whole business, shifted his weight from one heel to the other and told him, "He's pissing on your tire, Walter." And the Sugg looked down over the swell of the door and saw that the critter had loosed himself from his trousers and was sure enough bathing the front left blackwall the sight of which sent the Sugg into an immediate fit of ornate and heathenish swearing and general vilification and the sound of the wild and unrestrained profanity along with the sight of the occasional violent gesture prompted the paltry negro to turn to the fat negro and tell him, "We all dead men." But then the first Gilchrist snickered and the second Gilchrist threw in with him, and pretty soon all of the rest of the Gilchrists were shaking at the shoulders and the Sapps commenced to wheeze and the Currins and the Parkers set in to howling outright and were joined by the critter himself who put his face up snug to the Sugg's face and laughed his most vicious and mean-spirited laugh direct into it so that even the Sapps, who could not generally muster more than a wheeze, hooted and howled and held themselves about the waist as the Sugg squirmed and threatened and swore from the driver's seat of his Biscayne which he did not ever get out of that being the way with Suggs.

Attracted by the great and open display of mirth and levity there among the corpses, Mr. Overhill approached from across the cemetery already laughing somewhat in anticipation of what he would get told had kicked up the great and open display of mirth and the great and open display of levity, and he had not even circled round to the peed on side of the Biscayne and had not hardly Haw Hawed two times in succession when a Currin, three Parkers, and both the Sapps together commenced to run through the episode in all of its glorious circumstances pointing for effect at the blotches on the blackwall and pointing for effect at the departing backside of the critter and pointing for effect at that portion of the solitary Sugg above the doortop after which they shook at the shoulders or wheezed or howled outright or hawhawed depending on their particular disposition. Even the solitary Sugg smirked and shook some at the shoulders and Mr. Overhill observed out loud but to the Sugg primarily, "That Dwight, a little wild and high spirited at times but a fine sort," and he wagged his head and sucked some air through the gaps in his teeth and said, "A fine sort," which prompted the solitary Sugg to eye his blackwall over the doorswell and reply, "Shit," in an entirely unpersuaded tone of voice.

They were three days turning up Parkers and Currins and Sapps and Suggs and a stray, misplaced Gilchrist every now and again before anybody showed up at the cemetery to do something other than pilfer and plunder and pass the afternoon on a coffinlid them being Firesheetses, five Firesheetses all together with a brother and a sister and a momma and a daddy and an old stooped and brittle granddaddy in black hightop sneakers. They had come for the granddaddy's late wife who had been deceased for a dozen years now and they intended to carry her off with them when the water rose because, as the granddaddy put it to Mr. Overhill, she never could swim worth a piddly squat, and then he laughed like a spook and Mr. Overhill threw in with him and clapped him hard between his arthritic shoulder blades and turned to the momma Firesheets and told her, "Your daddy's a regular stitch," and the momma Firesheets lit herself a cigarette and said, "Ain't my daddy."

The daddy Firesheets got him a place atop a Gilchrist and took up with the regular crowd of Parkers and Currins and whatnot and his boy and his girl led Mr. Overhill to their grandmomma's plot and he set the wiry tattooed white boy about the picking and the shoveling of it under the scrutiny of the granddaddy Firesheets and the momma Firesheets and the brother Firesheets, which did not matter much to the wiry tattooed white boy, but under the scrutiny as well of the sister Firesheets and that was another thing entirely. She appeared to be about sixteen years old, or maybe eighteen years old, or possibly twenty-five years old, the wiry tattooed white boy could not tell exactly from over his shoulder which was the only way he could look at her without seeming to look at her and he did not want to seem to look at her or did not want to get caught at seeming to look at her which might suggest an interest on his part and he did not want to appear interested, so he looked at her over his shoulder whenever he felt she was not looking at him and mostly he did not find her looking at him when he turned to look at her because mostly she was not looking at him anyway. She seemed fairly much a vision from heaven as far as the wiry tattooed white boy was concerned. Her hair was the color of wheatstraw and hung kind of thin and wet looking down the sides of her head with a little break on the left and a little break on the right for the white tops of her ears to stick through and she was slender and supple all over and her arms and her legs and the little fleshy recess at the base of her neck were a pure and milky white except for the mosquito bites and the scabs and one tiny plum-colored birthmark on her thigh. The wiry tattooed white boy surveyed from over his shoulder the parts of her covered up by clothes and decided her breasts were supple and probably milky white also with some plum-colored features of their own and he figured her stomach to be flat and likely milky white itself. Her backside did not appear to him overly round or excessive and he featured it a little more snowy than milky along with her frontside which he was just setting himself to garnish with some wheatstraw of its own when she plucked a cigarette out from her momma's vinyl case, lit it, and drew off the smoke slow and sultry prior to exhaling it through her noseholes and the wiry tattooed white boy got caught up in the grace and beauty of the whole business and commenced to ache all over.

He figured they would marry in the spring of the year when the dogwoods were blooming, marry in a chapel in the woods somewhere on a mild and sunny afternoon with just a touch of a breeze, enough anyway to jiggle the blossoms some, and she would wear a long milky dress and he would wear a black suit with shiny lapels, and all the old women would cry on account of her beauty and all the young women would cry on account of his, and they would have a son and then a daughter and then another son and they would live on an expansive farm with a creek running through it and cows and chickens and rail fences and in a two story hewn timber house that he would build himself, and at night he would sit in his favorite chair with his feet on the stone hearth and drink off some sort of iced and civilized drink as he studied his initials in the mortar. The wiry tattooed white boy, still lost somewhat in his reverie, came out of his button up shirt and came out of his undershirt beneath it and then recollected himself sufficiently to flex his dragon and to flex his serpent and to obscure the most of his Marlene and he jerked his sweatrag out from his back pocket and set about wiping his face and wiping his neck and wiping his arms and he nodded at the momma Firesheets and at the grand-daddy Firesheets and at the brother Firesheets and made a general comment about the humidity of the day for their benefit and then he nodded at the sister Firesheets and said to her, "Hey babydoll," and she threw down the buttend of her cigarette and told him ever so sweetly, "Go fuck yourself," which set the wiry tattooed white boy to aching all over afresh. He always did like a woman with some pluck to her.

Mr. Overhill went out and fetched back the Pepsis and the potted meat and the saltines before the wiry tattooed white boy had completely unearthed the grandmomma Firesheets and so him and the fat negro and the paltry negro and Benton Lynch and Emmet and the critter sat in a shady place and watched the sister Firesheets loiter at the graveside as they ate. The wiry tattooed white boy said she was a prime item, said he'd seen her right up tight and figured there weren't any need to put a bag on it even, but the fat negro said he'd put a bag on it and the paltry negro said he'd put a box on it and the wiry tattooed white boy told them he'd eat it with a spoon to which the paltry negro replied, "Jesus," and puckered up his face. Nobody asked him but the critter volunteered that he'd strap her to the bedstead and perform a series of unseemly, unspeakable, and very nearly unimaginable acts upon her person all of which the critter described in his usual excessive detail and the paltry negro said, "Jesus," and puckered up all

over again and the fat negro puckered up with him and the wiry tattooed white boy swung both arms at the critter and kicked at the
critter and chased the critter through the high grass with a stout
length of stick. The fat negro and the paltry negro desired Benton
Lynch's opinion about the matter and they poked at him and jabbed
at him and were generally solicitous of him in a demonstrative sort of
way but Benton Lynch did not even say yes and did not even say no
regardless of the poking and the jabbing and the general demonstra-
tivity. He simply looked down the pointy ridge of his nose at the fat
negro and the paltry negro and ate his share of the fig newtons. The
wiry tattooed white boy returned to his lunch presently without ever
having caught the critter and so without ever having beaten him
either and the critter squatted off out of reach and leered at the wiry
tattooed white boy who still swung the stick when he figured the
critter to be diverted but the critter was never quite diverted enough
to get hit. To cap off the proceedings the fat negro and the paltry
negro and the critter raised their orifices in the thundrous display of
recreational burping and farting, and Emmet, who had finished his
lunch and so could at last pay attention to something else, commenced to chant, "Wham, bang, sweet poontang," in a syncopated
rhythm which the negroes jumped up and danced to.

The wiry tattooed white boy could not find a suitably secluded
place for a purgative urination and so had to return to grandmomma
Firesheets all piqued and agitated and the sight of the sister Firesheets's milky arms and milky legs and bulbous and flat parts too
compounded the pique and the agitation with a thoroughgoing erec-
tion which rode out from the wiry tattooed white boy's trousers like a
piece of Louisville Slugger and the wiry tattooed white boy adjusted
himself and fidgeted and stepped out of the grave and stepped back
into it again and adjusted himself and fidgeted some more but did not
move any appreciable amount of dirt, so when Mr. Overhill, who had
taken his lunch with the Gilchrists and the Parkers and the Currins
and whatnot, stopped by to view the wiry tattooed white boy's
progress there was not any to view and he called in both the negroes
together to see if they couldn't help the wiry tattooed white boy make
some, and they did help him make some or rather they made some
themselves while the wiry tattooed white boy adjusted himself and

fidgeted and stepped out of the grave and stepped back into it again.

The paltry negro told the fat negro he believed now he'd put a crate on it and the fat negro told the paltry negro he believed he'd put a crate on it too and the paltry negro pointed to the front of the wiry tattooed white boy's trousers and figured the wiry tattooed white boy would probably lay that thing to it and the paltry negro stuck his pickhandle into his pants and the fat negro stuck his shovel handle into his pants and the wiry tattooed white boy turned a kind of fruity color and eyed rather slyly the momma Firesheets and the granddaddy Firesheets and the brother Firesheets prior to glancing ever so surreptitiously at the sister Firesheets who fortunately was still not looking at him. And the paltry negro said maybe he'd put a dumpster on it, a big green dumpster, and the fat negro said maybe he would too, and the wiry tattooed white boy lunged at them desperately with the pointy end of his shovel in an attempt to cut off all twenty of their toes.

They had to bring grandmomma Firesheets up with a rope since her box had not given way and the wiry tattooed white boy took off both his shirts all over again and puffed and grunted and flexed his serpent and flexed his dragon and hid his Marlene while Benton Lynch pulled and the fat negro pulled and the paltry negro pulled, and once they'd set her in the high grass the wiry tattooed white boy laid his foot up on the coffinlid, crossed his arms over his knee, and said, "Preeshate it men. Carry on," and the fat negro and the paltry negro and even Benton Lynch too all looked at each other and threw their rope ends down on the ground.

The momma Firesheets and the daddy Firesheets wanted the grandmomma Firesheets in the trunk of their Oldsmobile for the ride back to wherever it was they'd all come from but the granddaddy Firesheets preferred the backseat since the grandmomma Firesheets had always ridden in the backseat previously but the daddy Firesheets explained that with the grandmomma Firesheets in the backseat the brother and the sister Firesheets would have to ride in the trunk which the wiry tattooed white boy objected to most strenuously and Mr. Overhill opened his mouth and began to suggest that they tie the grandmomma Firesheets to the roof of the car but midway through the wiry tattooed white boy broke in and suggested that they tie the grandmomma Firesheets to the roof of the car and he darted off after some rope and darted back with some in time to puff and grunt and flex onto the cartop a little portion of the casket which Mr. Overhill and the daddy Firesheets had already hoisted the biggest portion of. And the wiry tattooed white boy tied his rope secure while Mr. Overhill tied his rope secure and then the wiry tattooed white boy undid Mr. Overhill's rope and tied it secure all over again and he told the Firesheetses he believed it would hold just as Mr. Overhill was telling them he believed it would hold and then the wiry tattooed white boy finagled and sidled his way around the car to where the sister Firesheets was and he gave her his personal assurance that her grandmomma would not fall off in the road and she looked at him full in the face and did not tell him to go fuck himself which encouraged the wiry tattooed white boy some so he asked her, "You live round here?" and though she did not say yes and did not say no she did not tell him to go fuck himself then either which emboldened him still further and so he said to her, "What say me and you go out for a little walk this evening. I'd be grateful for the company," and the sister Firesheets laid her hand direct upon the most prominent part of the wiry tattooed white boy's trousers and told him, "Seems you got all the company you need." The Oldsmobile and the dust from the Oldsmobile and even the sound of the Oldsmobile tires on the gravel had all shrunk and dwindled away before the wiry tattooed white boy could swallow again and he licked his lips and begged pardon of Mr. Overhill and escaped into the bushes where he found some purgation and some relief and did in fact just generally fuck himself after a fashion.

At 5:30 promptly the paltry negro gathered all the shovels and the picks and deposited them in the hollow of a thicket while Mr. Overhill directed a tidying up of the cemetery grounds which had become fairly much littered with boxed up and bagged up Gilchrists and Currins and Parkers and Sapps and Suggs and boxed up and bagged up in-laws of Gilchrists and Currins and Parkers and Sapps and Suggs who lay loose in the high grass and among the scrub and the bushes in a state of random disgorgement. Mr. Overhill had the fat negro and the wiry tattooed white boy and Benton Lynch and Emmet and the critter put all the Gilchrists with the Gilchrists and all the Currins with the Currins and all the Parkers with the Parkers and the Sapps with the Sapps and the Suggs with the Suggs and all the unattached corpses, of which there were no more than eight or ten, he had piled up together under a pecan tree, and once everybody had been properly segregated and relocated Mr. Overhill retreated to the cemetery gateway and observed the little colonies of related corpses and the one slight collection of unrelated corpses who were all just as dead and decomposed as previously but not nearly so random and disgorged and Mr. Overhill announced he was mightily satisfied with the results and clasped his hands together and shook them over his head and the fat negro replied, "Christ almighty," to the wiry tattooed white boy mostly.

They left the riverbottom for the evening just as they had left the riverbottom for the evening the night before on account of the negroes primarily who refused to sleep in a riverbottom where the sort of white folks lived that lived in this riverbottom, and though Mr. Overhill insisted and explained they were all fine sorts of white folks the negroes remained unpersuaded and continued to refuse to sleep in the riverbottom until they were not in it any longer. Like on the night previous Mr. Overhill drove south along the Falls of the Neuse Road to a little shopping center at the north extremity of Raleigh where there was a Burger King at one end and a Bojangles at the other and a drugstore and a Big Star and a pet grooming salon in between, and Mr. Overhill had not hardly parked the truck and climbed out of it when he was greeted by the granddaddy Firesheets who hailed Mr. Overhill from the canopied sidewalk in front of the drugstore. He was still wearing his black sneakers from earlier in the day and was still stooped over and noticeably arthritic but relatively jolly nonetheless and he hollered to Mr. Overhill, "How you?" and Mr. Overhill hollered back at him, "You get the missus home all right?" and the granddaddy Firesheets told him, "Yes it is," and threw up his hand at Mr. Overhill prior to venturing on into the drugstore.

The sound of the granddaddy Firesheets's voice sent a quiver through the wiry tattooed white boy and he leapt out of the truckbed and looked all around the parking lot and along the storefronts for some sign of the wheatstraw or the milky whiteness but could not discovered any and so he set out in the direction of the drugstore and the paltry negro yelled after him, "Put a crate on it," and the fat negro yelled after him, "Or a dumpster," and the paltry negro added, "Or a quonset hut," and the fat negro hollered, "Yea," and then looked at the paltry negro and asked him, "What's a quonset hut?" and Mr. Overhill turned his broad smiling face on the pair of negroes together and said, "Quonset huts. I could tell you tales about them things," and the paltry negro and the fat negro swore each other through the sides of their mouths.

Emmet and the critter and the negroes and Mr. Overhill all settled on the Bojangles and struck out across the parking lot with Emmet in the lead followed by the critter followed by a gesticulating Mr. Overhill in the company of the two sullen negroes who walked with their hands in their pockets and their heads near about buried between their shoulder blades. The wiry tattooed white boy had long since disappeared into the drugstore and Benton Lynch climbed out from the truckbed and headed off alone towards the Big Star where he figured he'd get himself a pudding cup and maybe some pork rinds, but before he'd gotten abreast of the fertilizer and peat moss on the pallets outside the wiry tattooed white boy blew by him in a holy rush and ducked on into the supermarket just the very instant the automatic door had automatically swung open precisely far enough to suit his wiry self, and when Benton Lynch came up on him inside the wiry tattooed white boy was ruminating over a sack of self-rising flour so as to appear oblivious to the sister Firesheets and the momma Firesheets who were comparing potato flakes at the far end of the aisle. Benton Lynch could not find the pudding cups straightaway on account of how there was no sign suspended from the ceiling that said pudding cups on it, not even a sign that said anything suggestive of pudding cups on it, so he cast around through the fruits and the vegetables, searched along the ice cream bin, and picked through an assortment of Twinkies and honey buns but could not discover a pudding cup anywhere he had figured a pudding cup might be and consequently he commenced to cast around and search and pick through a variety of places he figured a pudding cup would not be and eventually he came across two shelves' worth of the item in question in between the disinfectant and the catfood and across from the aluminum foil. He just wanted one vanilla pudding cup but could not buy one vanilla pudding cup without buying three additional vanilla pudding cups or five additional vanilla pudding cups or eleven additional vanilla pudding cups and he just wanted the one by itself and could not say if he would ever desire three more or five more or eleven more and so he had to decide if he should sacrifice the one pudding cup he wanted now for some portion of the nineteen pudding cups he possibly would not want later or accumulate some portion of the nineteen pudding cups he possibly would not want later for the sake of one pudding cup he wanted now. The quandary was considerable and taxing and Benton Lynch took up in his hands the twenty-two pudding cups in their three separate bundles and studied his alternatives, and since the quandary was considerable and was taxing and since the pudding cups in their three separate bundles were cumbersome and difficult to manage Benton Lynch did not have the leisure to notice himself getting approached from the catfood end of the aisle and so he was still thoroughly taxed and emburdened when the sister Firesheets stepped right up under his nose and said to him, "I seen you."

And Benton Lynch turned his usual vacant look on her for a brief moment prior to turning his usual vacant look over his shoulder where he expected to find the wiry tattooed white boy but did not and so he jostled and repositioned the pudding cups in his grasp and pondered over what he would say in return which was a considerable and taxing quandary on its own since Benton Lynch had not got talked at lately by anybody but Mr. Overhill and the negroes who generally did not call for a reply, and he weighed his alternatives and eventually landed upon and came direct out with "Where?"

"I seen you in the graveyard with them other boys," the sister Firesheets told him. "I seen you help pull up my grandmomma and I'm grateful."

"You're welcome," Benton Lynch said, and he looked past the sister Firesheets to the far end of the aisle where the wiry tattooed white boy had stepped into view and picked up a can of flea and tic spray and was perusing the backside of it.

"He's back there ain't he?" she said. "He's back there looking at me, been following me all over this place ever since I come in."

And Benton Lynch looked past her again to the far end of the aisle.

"He ain't nothing to me," she said, "ain't my sort. All his brains in his pants and I don't like them tattoos the least little bit. I mean the human body's a pure and holy thing and there he's painted his all up with pictures of lizards. There's a sickness behind it, I'll tell you that, a genuine sickness." And she whirled around and snapped at the wiry tattooed white boy, "Get on from here. I'm fed up with you, just get on away from me," and the wiry tattooed white boy tried to appear as thoroughly astounded and affronted as he could and he waved the can of flea and tic spray at Benton Lynch and at the sister Firesheets as if that were his genuine article of business and the sister Firesheets told him, "Get on with your mess then. I don't want you trailing me no more," and the wiry tattooed white boy retreated behind a papertowel display and out of sight. "That just sets me off," the sister Firesheets said and laid her milky hands on her hips. "A boy studies your sweet behind so as to get his pecker all stiff and lathered up and then he figures you owe him a place to put it. Well he ain't getting his old lizardy self near me. That just purely sets me off." And Benton Lynch dropped the four pack of vanilla pudding cups and the cans separated from the container and departed in different directions across the linoleum. "What's your name?" the sister Firesheets asked him.

And Benton Lynch told her, "Benton Lynch."

"Mine's Jane Elizabeth Firesheets from my momma and my grandmomma's sister," Jane Elizabeth Firesheets said. "Who you named for?"

"Uncle Benton," Benton Lynch told her.

"On account of what?" Jane Elizabeth Firesheets wanted to know.

"Tires," Benton Lynch told her.

"Well ain't that a thing," Jane Elizabeth Firesheets said. "Where you live?"

"Nowhere much," Benton Lynch told her.

"We got a house out Falls of the Neuse other side of Yates Pond. You know Yates Pond?" Jane Elizabeth Firesheets asked.

And Benton Lynch shook his head yes. He had passed Yates Pond going and coming from the Bojangles the night previous.

"Daddy's going to sell it when the lake comes up," Jane Elizabeth

Firesheets said, "and we all moving to Chalybeate Springs. You know Chalybeate Springs?"

And Benton Lynch shook his head no.

"It's down the road some," Jane Elizabeth Firesheets said. "Daddy's got a brother there and they throwing in together on a farm, going to raise tobacco. Daddy ain't never raised no tobacco. Daddy ain't never done much hardly. What's your daddy do?"

"Eggs," Benton Lynch said.

"Momma don't cook eggs on account of granddaddy can't eat eggs and daddy don't like eggs and Raymond—that's my brother, Raymond. He's an asshole—he don't like eggs either. I'll eat them hard boiled and chopped up on a salad like at the salad bar at the Golden Corral but I don't like them much otherwise myself. You ever eaten at the Golden Corral?" Jane Elizabeth Firesheets wanted to know.

And Benton Lynch shook his head no.

Then Jane Elizabeth Firesheets took a halfstep in Benton Lynch's direction and laid the tipends of her fingers on Benton Lynch's bare forearm. "I can judge people straight off," she said, "I got a gift for it, and I can tell you ain't like the rest of them. I mean you ain't colored but you ain't like them white boys either. Especially him," and she jerked her head at the papertowel display. "I like you," she said and dragged the tipends of her fingers up Benton Lynch's bare forearm almost to the elbow and then back to the wrist. "We live in a little brick house," she said, "a little brick house with green shutters and brown curtains and a yellow buglight on the front porch. Just the other side of Yates Pond," she said. "I'll be home most all night," and she dragged the tipends of her fingers along the back of Benton Lynch's hand and across the tops of the pudding cups prior to turning her back on Benton Lynch and showing him her sweet behind all the way down the aisle.

The wiry tattooed white boy came round the papertowel display at a dead run and did not stop or even slow down noticeably until he had his wild, antic, and thoroughly flushed face full up in Benton Lynch's face which was not wild or antic or thoroughly flushed either but had maintained its usual pointiness and angularity and general vacancy, and the wiry tattooed white boy shook the can of flea and tic spray at the side of Benton Lynch's head in a most threatening and violent manner and said to him, "I'll fucking kill you. Go ahead, lay one finger on her and I'll fucking kill you. I'll chew you up and spit you out. I mean it," and then the wiry tattooed white boy recommenced his dead run and maintained it to the end of the aisle where he paused briefly to whirl around and fire the can of flea and tic spray at Benton Lynch who in jumping sideways to avoid it dropped the twelve pack of vanilla pudding cups onto the floor which made for sixteen cans of pudding scattered across the linoleum.

The critter had already returned to the truckbed by the time Benton Lynch got back to it on account of the manager of the Bojangles had not allowed him into the restaurant proper but had instead sent him around to the drive-thru where he picked up his supper and carried it with him to the fender well, and he had disposed of most everything but for the greasy box and the unopened towelette and the white meatless chicken bones which lay all around and atop his feet, so Benton Lynch offered him one of the four pudding cups he had at last decided to buy and the critter tore off the top and scooped out the most of the pudding with his fingers and licked out the rest of the pudding with his tongue and then proceeded on to the second pudding cup followed by the third one followed by half of the fourth one and the pudding cup tops and empty pudding cup cans piled up with the white meatless chicken bones at the critter's feet. Emmet returned directly with part of a thigh in one hand and part of a biscuit in the other and soon after the ever gesticulating Mr. Overhill crossed the parking lot in the company of the increasingly sullen negroes and he detained them at the fender of the truck with a lengthy explanation of the convective qualities of corrugated metal but did in fact let them loose at last and the fat negro and the paltry negro threw themselves into the truckbed and the fat negro exhaled most profoundly and the paltry negro said, "Jesus, what a windy motherfucker."

The wiry tattooed white boy did not show up directly and Mr. Overhill raced the engine and blew the horn and circled the parking lot but could not seem to lure him out of wherever he was and so Mr. Overhill dispatched the fat negro after him and while the fat negro was searching through the drugstore the wiry tattooed white boy emerged from the Big Star with his arms full of the momma Firesheets's groceries and with the momma Firesheets herself at his left shoulder and the sister Firesheets somewhere in the vicinity of his right shoulder but not at it precisely. The wiry tattooed white boy chatted with the momma Firesheets and showed his teeth all the way to the Oldsmobile and at intervals he attempted to chat with the sister Firesheets and showed his teeth in her direction too, but the sister Firesheets slowed and hung back some and did not appear enchanted with the general palaver. Mr. Overhill eased up behind the Oldsmobile and saluted the momma Firesheets and saluted the sister Firesheets and commented on the sheer airy wondrousness of the evening, he called it, prior to waving the wiry tattooed white boy on into the truckbed, and once the wiry tattooed white boy had shook the momma Firesheets's hand and had nodded at the sister Firesheets ever so imperially he did in fact climb over the tailgate into the truckbed and rode around the parking lot twice before getting dispatched after the fat negro who he found in the drugstore at the magazine rack sharing the anniversary issue of *Penthouse* with the granddaddy Firesheets.

They did not return to the pure heart of the Harricanes but stopped due south at a roadside picnic table where Mr. Overhill intended to pass the evening so as to keep the negroes at ease. However, somebody had deposited the insides of a cantaloupe in the trash barrel chained to a tree next to the picnic table and the seeds and the pulp and the juices had mixed with the rest of the garbage and had stewed in the heat thereby producing a startling and altogether vigorous aroma which not even Mr. Overhill, who could stand almost anything, could stand. So they proceeded a little further into the Harricanes than the negroes had desired they proceed though not nearly so far as the riverbottom and Mr. Overhill pulled off the highway onto a fireroad and parked temporarily under the spreading foliage of a pecan tree until the paltry negro objected on account of how spreading foliage was just the sort of thing a snake was likely to drop out of in the night, and consequently Mr. Overhill pulled on down the road a ways and stopped underneath a white oak which had some spreading foliage of its own though of a far more altitudinous variety and Mr. Overhill asked the paltry negro did the move suit him and the paltry negro said he guessed it would have to.

The fat negro and the paltry negro and the critter commenced the evening's activities by expelling their indigestion all over the wiry tattooed white boy who did not appreciate the gesture much and so grabbed ahold of Emmet and hurled him across the truckbed and Emmet hollered, "Hey! Hey!" and went into his usual impotent rage. Benton Lynch sat on the open tailgate and watched the festivities unoccupied until he picked up his paper sack, which was soft and tissuey at the neck from getting rolled up and rolled back day after day, and he brought out from it not a clean but a rinsed shirt and he returned to it not a clean or a rinsed but a folded shirt and rolled the soft tissuey neck closed again, and not the fat negro or the paltry negro or Emmet or the wiry tattooed white boy either noticed he was gone until he'd already left the fireroad for the highway and only the wiry tattooed white boy got all agitated and irate on account of it and he screamed off into the darkness, "Lynch! Lynch! I'll fucking kill you. One finger on her and you're dead meat. I mean it Lynch. I'll fucking kill you." And the paltry negro said to the fat negro, "That where he off to? Should've took his bag with him, they both gone need one," and the fat negro hooted and the paltry negro hooted himself and Emmet howled once and was setting himself to howl again when he got dragged out of the truckbed by his ears and kicked sharply in the kidneys twice.

Benton Lynch walked a mile and a half along the highway prior to crossing a pasture and circling around Yates Pond to the inhabited side of it and he narrowed down the brick houses with yellow buglights to an even dozen and narrowed down the brick houses with yellow buglights and green shutters to an even half dozen with two additional possibilities that did not have shutters on the actual house but had them instead in the bushes and on the front lawn. However, he could not find but two brick houses with yellow buglights and green shutters and brown window curtains and long sleek Oldsmobiles in the driveway, and when one of the Oldsmobiles turned out to be a Pontiac Benton Lynch stood in the road in front of the Firesheetses' house and wondered to himself what he would do now that he had arrived at where he was going. In fact he dropped off into a kind of funk as he pondered over what he might say to Jane Elizabeth Firesheets and pondered over what she might say to him and as he figured and imagined what him and Jane Elizabeth Firesheets might get worked up enough to do together which was just the sort of thing he had done considerable figuring and imagining about but never truly any of. The whole process remained somewhat vague and mysterious to him though he had seen pictures in magazines and on the backs of his cousin Jerome Lynch's playing cards, pictures of women with tremendous drooping breasts and pictures of gentlemen with tremendous drooping items of their own, but he could not figure precisely how everything got joined up and hooked together and he did not thoroughly understand where the heaping up on the floor came in though he was reasonably certain it came in somewhere. So Benton Lynch stood in the road and puzzled over what went where and puzzled over how it behaved once it got there and consequently did not hear Jane Elizabeth Firesheets call out to him from the screen-in side-porch the first time she did in fact call out and did not hear anything but the noise of it the second time and only realized what the noise was and where it had come from when Jane Elizabeth Firesheets stepped off the porch and into the yard.

She had changed out of her tiny little shorts and her tiny little top and had put on instead a dress with spots on it, and she had pinched her cheeks and colored her lips and her eyelids and had piled her hair up on top of her head where she had twisted it and teased it and just generally annoyed and provoked it into a massy lump. Benton Lynch had never seen such splendor previously, not that he could recollect anyway, and he stood at the end of the driveway and ventilated his molars as he puzzled over what went where with some actual and increasing desperation since he felt himself developing the what of it which rendered the where of it ever more crucial, and Jane Elizabeth Firesheets did not help matters with the tipends of her fingers which she raked lightly along Benton Lynch's forearm. "I knew you'd come," she told him. "I've got a gift."

The grandmomma Firesheets had been laid out along one end of the screened-in porch and the momma Firesheets had bedecked the top of her with a schefflera, two peonies in a pot, and a sickly fern so as to dissipate some of the natural gravity that a casket generally produces. For her part Jane Elizabeth Firesheets had lit a red Christmas candle along about her grandmomma's midsection and had arranged beneath it a plateful of assorted crackers and a plateful of assorted cheese slices and two icy Coca-Colas in the bottle. She set Benton Lynch atop a chaircushion on the floor and took the one beside it for herself and offered up the crackers and the cheese and the Coca-Colas and Benton Lynch ate though he was not particularly hungry and drank though he was not particularly thirsty and squirmed and fidgeted around on his chaircushion though he was not particularly uncomfortable while Jane Elizabeth Firesheets herself did not eat and did not drink and did not squirm or fidget but instead laid on her elbow and with the tipends of her fingers on her free hand agonized and perplexed Benton Lynch still further. She asked him all about himself and where he'd come from and he tried to describe the trailer and the henhouse but could not with much effect and he tried to describe his momma and his daddy but could not with much effect either and he talked somewhat about his brother, Otway Burns, but only slightly somewhat since there was not much he knew about Otway Burns that could be put into words, and once when he had his mouth open for the cause of some utterance or another Jane Elizabeth Firesheets reached out and stuck her finger in it. "You've got the biggest teeth I've ever seen," she said, and she wanted to know did they come from his momma's side or his daddy's side and Benton Lynch closed his mouth to ponder over and work up a reply and got squirmy and fidgety all over again on account of the taste of her.

Jane Elizabeth Firesheets said she had previously intended to become a ballerina but had grown and blossomed appreciably of late and so no longer considered herself flatchested enough for serious dancing, and she sat up on her elbows and arched herself so as to enhance her blessings some and she asked Benton Lynch his opinion on the matter but Benton Lynch said he did not know enough about serious dancing to have an opinion on the matter. Jane Elizabeth Firesheets said she figured she'd simply become a radiologist instead because it was in her nature to assist and administer to people, and if not a radiologist she supposed physical therapy might be in her line and she asked Benton Lynch did he know what a physical therapist did and

Benton Lynch shook his head no he did not. "A physical therapist does this," Jane Elizabeth Firesheets said and worked her fingers over Benton Lynch's calf muscles, "and this," she said and kneaded Benton Lynch's left thigh, "and this," she said and laid her hand on a place where Benton Lynch, aside from his own, had never had a hand laid and though he remained pointy and angular and hollowed out like usual, his eyes rolled back in his head some so as to render him a little less vacant than ordinary.

"Let's me and you go down to the pondbank," Jane Elizabeth Firesheets said and then garnished and punctuated the suggestion with a vigorous therapeutic flurry, and Benton Lynch worked his throat and moved his mouth and attempted to tell her, "All right," and very nearly did.

The wiry tattooed white boy said he would kill him, said he would fucking kill him, said he knew where'd he'd been, said he knew what went on, and said he would fucking kill him for it first chance he got, and as they pulled out of the fireroad and onto the highway the paltry negro said he'd heard her screaming in the night, said he'd heard her wailing and howling and the fat negro asked him what it was she'd been wailing and what it was she'd been howling and the paltry negro shrieked, "Ben Ton oooohh Ben Ton," and the fat negro sucked air and the paltry negro giggled and the critter laughed his low mean laugh and Emmet said, "Wham, bang," and got kicked in the stomach.

All morning the wiry tattooed white boy said he would fucking kill him, said it as he shoveled and as he picked and as he bagged and as he Ziplocked, said it as he rested and took water, and repeated it every time he said it just for emphasis, but as the morning wore on Benton Lynch did not seem any more fucking killed than he had been previously in the day and with the standard assortment of Gilchrists and Parkers and Currins and Sapps and Suggs for an audience he went about his excavation like usual straight up until lunchtime when Jane Elizabeth Firesheets came out from a trail in the woods with a bag lunch and hauled Benton Lynch off into the bushes to eat his share of it. The wiry tattooed white boy took his potted meat and crackers on Mr. Overhill's tailgate and announced to the paltry negro and the fat negro and the critter and Emmet too that he would fucking kill him that he would purely assassinate the son-of-a-bitch, and then he grimly studied the clump of bushes Benton Lynch and Jane Elizabeth Firesheets had disappeared behind and the paltry negro said, "Ben Ton oooohhh Ben Ton," in a high excited voice and the fat negro contributed a series of rhythmic vulgar noises which he persisted in until the wiry tattooed white boy whirled around and hit him full in the face with a handful of saltines. Of course the fat negro came out of the truckbed like a shot and him and the wiry tattooed white boy rolled around on the ground together and the fat negro said, "Sho nuff gone be somebody fucking killed here," and the wiry tattooed white boy responded with a colorful ethnic epithet which served to fire the fat negro still further and he wedged the frontal portion of the wiry tattooed white boy's skull in the crook of his arm and attempted to crack it open. Mr. Overhill asked them why didn't they leave off the fighting and leave off the rolling around but he did not get up from the tailgate to do any active separating primarily on account of the attention the scuffle had aroused among the Parkers and the Currins and the Gilchrists and the Sapps and the Suggs who had got up from their coffinlids and come to watch the proceedings. They were uniformly opposed to the fat negro with the exception of a solitary Currin who had a strong personal aversion to tattoos and he urged on the fat negro in a highly animated and excessively vocal sort of way which one of the Parkers found acutely objectionable and he shoved the Currin from behind and advised him not to be so excessively vocal and not to be so highly animated which prompted the Currin to suggest in return that the Parker stick his finger up his ass like usual so as to keep himself out of trouble. But the Parker, not being pliant and suggestible by nature, did not wait for a second highly animated and excessively vocal outburst but straightaway shoved the Currin again and the Currin turned around and broke the Parker's nose which pained the Parker some but did not deter him much and he reached out with his shoving hand and left the Currin bald on the side of his head. Understandably, the Currin yelped and felt himself which presented the Parker with the opportunity to break the Currin's nose which he promptly took advantage of and the Currin pitched over backwards through his neighbors and relations and landed near about on top of the fat negro and the wiry tattooed white boy who were not at this point doing any considerable rolling around on account of general weariness. The Parker followed the Currin through his neighbors and relations and bent down to pick him up off the ground so as to put him back onto it again but the Currin managed to kick the Parker a clean shot in the groin which the Parker did not appreciate much and had not anticipated whatsoever and he groaned and lamented some and stayed bent over sufficiently long enough to get hit upside the head twice prior to stumbling across the cemetery and falling over a marker. Of course the remaining Parkers and Currins and the Gilchrists and the Sapps and the Suggs followed the dispute as it proceeded on around the cemetery grounds which left the fat negro and the wiry tattooed white boy fairly much alone in each other's arms and between the two of them they decided to break off the hostilities for the time being so as to witness the Parker-Currin disagreement which they joined up with and observed under the hickory tree where the Parker was laying it to the Currin with near about the ferocity that the Currin was laying it to the Parker, and the wiry tattooed white boy got so caught up in the vitality of the proceedings that when Benton Lynch arrived and stuck his angular, pointy, and hollowed out face into the crowd to see what was going on the wiry tattooed white boy turned to him and exclaimed, "These men beating the shit out of each other!" but he remembered himself near about immediately and added, "I'm still going to fucking kill you, you know that."

Benton Lynch and Miss Jane Elizabeth Firesheets engaged in some additional therapy on the west bank of Yates Pond the evening following their initial appointment during the course of which Miss Firesheets had brought her considerable talents to bear upon Benton Lynch's troublesome stiffness and had eradicated and relieved it with measurable success. Consequently, Benton Lynch saw it clear to carry with him on the second night a fairly pure rigidity so as to test Miss Jane Elizabeth Firesheets's powers of eradication and relief and Miss Jane Elizabeth Firesheets welcomed the challenge and rose to it some herself. This time they spread a quilt out on the grass on account of how Jane Elizabeth had laid down on a slugtrail the night before and straightaway she slipped herself out of her print dress and out of her brassiere and out of her gauzy red panties and lay naked and unabashed in the dewy night beside Benton Lynch who had not even taken his shoes off. She was in fact milky white all over just like the wiry tattooed white boy had figured and the breasts which had kept her out of toeshoes did have some plum-colored features, two ample and erect plum-colored features the likes of which Benton Lynch had never seen except possibly in the backside of his cousin Jerome Lynch's four of diamonds, so understandably Benton Lynch paid some profound attention to Jane Elizabeth Firesheets's bosoms, especially to the plum-colored pointy parts of them, and when he talked he talked at them and when he listened he listened towards them and when he felt inclined to reach over and touch some part of Jane Elizabeth Firesheets his hand chiefly ended up on a plum-colored portion of her.

She was full of news about Chalybeate Springs and about her daddy's brother and her daddy's brother's tobacco farm all on account of a phone call her daddy had gotten in the afternoon from a land speculator who was buying up property around the reservoir which was not even a reservoir yet. They had geed and hawed and generally chewed over the matter and the one had rose up some off his price while the other had dropped down some off his and it seemed to Jane Elizabeth Firesheets they might reach some sort of agreement once that part of her daddy that loved to haggle got itself satisfied. So she was commencing to anticipate life in Chalybeate Springs on a tobacco farm and she was commencing to speculate as to when Benton Lynch might join her there and naturally she asked him outright what he considered a favorable month for it and naturally Benton Lynch told the pointy parts of her breasts he didn't know what month might be favorable for it, so she assisted his decision some by naming off the twelve months in succession and allowing Benton Lynch to indicate yes or indicate no and twelve times to the pointy parts of her breasts Benton Lynch indicated no so naturally Jane Elizabeth Firesheets drew on her red gauzy panties and ran her arms through her brassiere straps and had got so much as a solitary foot and ankle into her print dress when Benton Lynch said, "July," which slowed Jane Elizabeth Firesheets some but did not stop her entirely so he tried, "June," instead and she left off dressing but did not set about undressing until he had said, "May," until he had said it twice actually and with some appreciable conviction, conviction enough anyway to bring Jane Elizabeth Firesheets back out of her dress and her brassiere and her gauzy red panties and she rolled her naked self atop Benton Lynch, laid her open hand full upon his stark rigidity, and said to him, "Tell me where it hurts, sweetness."

By the middle of the third day they had dug up and set aside all the Gilchrists and the Parkers and the Currins and the Suggs and the Sapps and the entire allotment of extraneous in-laws, so there was nobody left in the cemetery proper but for the Gilchrists and the Parkers and the Currins and the Suggs and the Sapps who had not ever been buried there, including the Parker with the broken nose and the split lip and the Currin with the broken nose and the bloody scalp who shared the same end of a Gilchrist mausoleum and seemed to have developed a fondness for each other. The fat negro and the paltry negro and the wiry tattooed white boy and the critter and Benton Lynch and Emmet loaded the caskets and bagged-up corpses into the back of the truck and rode on the tailgate to the high ground where they unloaded the caskets and the bagged-up corpses at a level and designated place that had been a homestead once and a cowpasture most recently. Mr. Overhill and the two negroes returned to the riverbottom for a fresh lot while the wiry tattooed white boy and the critter and Benton Lynch and Emmet dug out the snug, shallow holes there were seventeen dollar holes nonetheless, and they deposited and covered over the bagged-up and boxed-up Gilchrists and Parkers and Currins and Suggs and Sapps under the casual scrutiny of no one much, nobody whatsoever really, especially not any living and breathing Gilchrists and Parkers and Currins and Suggs and Sapps who had decided against traveling the mile and a quarter out of the riverbottom to the cowpasture mostly because they were not your uphill sort of people.

By evening they were completely done with the transporting of the bodies and half done with the burying of them and as the paltry negro collected and gathered up the picks and the shovels and hunted a thicket to deposit them in Benton Lynch changed into a rinsed-out shirt and departed for Yates Pond where he had been invited to a regular sit-down supper which he took in the kitchen of the Firesheetses' red brick house with Jane Elizabeth Firesheets at his left elbow and the granddaddy Firesheets at his right elbow. The momma Firesheets had cooked up a potful of chicken and slickers and a batch of biscuits and Jane Elizabeth Firesheets herself had made up a bowlful of her own special potato salad which her brother, Raymond, found a long strand of wheatstraw hair in and got most disgusted and sour on account of. The granddaddy Firesheets recollected one by one every Lynch he'd ever met up with in every place he'd ever been to and quizzed Benton Lynch on his relation to them, which there generally was not any of, and whenever the opportunity presented itself the daddy Firesheets probed and sounded out Benton Lynch's knowledge of tobacco and tobacco farming which there generally was not any of either. The momma Firesheets had bought a cherry cobbler in an aluminum tin for dessert and once she had heated it in the oven she served it up all around and the daddy Firesheets and the granddaddy Firesheets said it tasted good as homemade and Benton Lynch threw in with a yes it did and the brother Firesheets said he didn't give a shit what it tasted like long as there weren't any hair in it and the sister Firesheets told him he was lucky they saw it clear to feed an asshole like him and the brother Firesheets said it weren't ever nothing but slop anyhow and the sister Firesheets got indignant and humphed and huffed and exclaimed, "Stupid little cocksucker," and the brother Firesheets told her, "Cunt," and the momma Firesheets asked the daddy Firesheets was he finished with his plate and the granddaddy Firesheets recollected a whole load of Lynches in Zebulon.

After supper the sister Firesheets took Benton Lynch around the house and showed him the bric-a-brac, especially her own personal and private collection of it in her own personal and private bedroom and in addition she reclined herself full across the bed, laid her tongue out one corner of her mouth, and showed Benton Lynch a thing or two that was not specifically in the line of bric-a-brac but proved interesting nonetheless. They retired to the pondbank with the coming of darkness and tumbled around on the quilt until Benton Lynch's stark rigidity had declined way past troublesome stiffness down to a flaccid and thoroughly invertebrate indifference that not even a gyrating Jane Elizabeth Firesheets in all of her milky and plum-colored splendor could do the least little thing about, so they talked some instead, exchanged addresses, and anticipated May in Chalybeate Springs with Jane Elizabeth Firesheets doing the primary and vocal part of the anticipating and Benton Lynch doing the secondary and silent part of it, and in time Benton Lynch worked up sufficient spine to distract Jane Elizabeth Firesheets and shut her up very nearly completely except for the moaning and the boisterous exhalations which mixed and harmonized somewhat with the crickets and the bullfrogs and the rest of the wildlife roundabout.

They had redeposited the remainder of the Gilchrists and the Parkers and the Currins and the Sapps and the Suggs by the afternoon of the following day and the paltry negro packed up the picks and the shovels in the truckbed and spread out the blanket and Mr. Overhill laid his roadmap across the open tailgate and indicated a route down to one place in Mississippi and down further still to two places in Alabama and then westward into Texas, and the fat negro said, "Sandy dirt," and the paltry negro said, "Easy money," and Emmet said, "Hot damn, hot diggity damn," and the wiry tattooed white boy said, "I'll fucking kill you in Alabama. They won't do nothing to me there. It ain't a civilized place yet. I'll fucking kill you in Alabama for sure." And then they shut themselves up in the truckbed partly atop the blanket and partly atop the pick and shovel handles and Mr. Overhill brought his red Dodge out on the Falls of the Neuse Road heading south away from the Harricanes towards Raleigh. He circled the city on the bypass and exited onto what appeared to be a proper and suitable highway to get him where he was going but which turned out to run more westerly than easterly or southerly and so wasn't nearly so proper and wasn't nearly so suitable as Mr. Overhill had first figured, and consequently he stopped off at a Grocery Boy Jr. for directions and candied corn and while he was still inside jawing with the cashier Benton Lynch caught up his tissuey paper sack in his hands and climbed over the tailgate to the pavement. "Hey!" the wiry tattooed white boy hollered to him, "I'm going to fucking kill you and you ain't running off till I do it, so get back in here," but Benton Lynch just spun his angular, pointy, hollowed out self around and proceeded across the lot and the wiry tattooed white boy hollered, "Hey!" again with about as much effect as previously and then "Hey!" a third time prior to turning to the fat negro and asking him, "Where's he think he's going?" And the fat negro sat up on his elbow and replied, "Who gives a happy shit," and him and the wiry tattooed white boy and the paltry negro and Emmet and the critter too watched Benton

Lynch flag down a red Mustang which took him so far as Durham where he caught a ride to Greensboro and then hitched onto a produce truck straight into downtown Neely or to the back alley at the Big Apple anyway and he walked from there north past the square and down by the icehouse and on out the Danville Road to Oregon Hill. He arrived in the darkness and stood for a time on the rise above his momma and daddy's chickenhouse and his momma and daddy's trailer not listening to anything in particular or looking at anything in particular but just standing on the rise in the darkness listening to and looking at everything in general which was nothing really but ruin and dilapidation and squalor and a little slip of moon that at last lit his way down the slope and direct up to the metal trailer door which he did not tap or knock or beat on but merely opened before himself and shut behind himself and he sat down on the Mediterranean sofa beside his daddy who dropped his mouth open and said, "You're back."

Three

THEY WERE YELLOWHEADED THUMBTACKS and Sheriff Burton said that all together they described a corridor of wanton destruction or if not a corridor of wanton destruction then maybe just an alley of it though at times he did not feel inclined towards a corridor or alley either of destruction wanton or otherwise and instead saw in the trail of tacks a graphic geographical and, in this case, yellowheaded gash in the very fabric of our society, a gash running north to south and then east to west and then sort of south to north and kind of west to east which made it fairly much a rectangular yellowheaded gash though not truly and purely a rectangular yellowheaded gash on account of the stomped in northwest corner in the vicinity of Wentworth. But it was all truly and purely square and geographical enough to suggest to the sheriff some sort of pattern and premeditated design which was why he set aside a portion of his every day to ponder the map on his office wall and especially to ponder the previously thumbtacked parts of it so as to formulate, figure, and speculate as to just what might be the subsequently thumbtacked parts of it.

The accumulation of all the pondering and formulating and figuring and speculating had rendered the sheriff capable of rattling off the placenames and the peoplenames too like a litany and he would sit at his desk with his feet atop one corner of it and his back to the map on his wall and tell himself, "Busick in Draper, McIver in Harrison Crossroads, Barnard in Bethel, Grissom in Locust Hill, Stem in Union Ridge, Troutman in Altamahaw, Ross in Hillsdale, Spencer in Midway," and then he would pinch his bottom lip between his right thumb and forefinger, which was Sheriff Burton's ordinary ponderous and speculative gesture, and he would rattle off the money too telling himself, "$147.00 and $189.00 and $123.00 and $155.00 and $78.00 and $230.00 and $112.00 and $150.00 even," and he would go ahead and ponder and speculate over the money some since he was in the proper posture of it prior to letting loose of his lip, picking himself up out of his chair, and studying the map on the wall outright paying some little attention to the yellowheaded rectangular gash in the very fabric of our society and expending the bulk of his energies on a newly plotted silverheaded gash in the very fabric of our society which was southeast of the yellowheaded gash and not nearly so linear and rectangular but more in the form of a clustery bunch so as to suggest more likely a boil on the buttocks on the very fabric of our society than any sort of gash in it, and since it was in fact a fairly recent boil the sheriff had to look at it as he told himself, "Corinth and Duncan and Wilbon and Angier and Holly Springs and Kipling and Fuquay-Varina," and then off by itself way to the west not like a gash or a boil either but most nearly resembling a wart or maybe a mole or just some slight and almost negligible imperfection in the fabric of our society lay the domed, silvery head of the lone and solitary Lemly tack which even with its detachment and considerable remoteness from the gash and the boil too had some logic to it on account of how the Stem in Union Ridge had not been a Mr. like the Busick and the McIver and the Barnard and the Grissom and the Troutman and the Ross and the Spencer had all been Mr.s but had instead been a Mrs. and so could not have her testicles blown to anywhere that the gentle-men could have their testicles blown to which got her a variant threat to a further region, and the sheriff left off with the boil and the wart together and turned his attention to a scrap of paper he had attached with tape to the top edge of the map, or more precisely to the single word written in blue ink on the scrap of paper attached to the top edge of the map, and twice he mouthed it silently to himself trying out the accent on the frontend of it and on the backend of it, which seemed the more fitting location, and finally drawing off a breath and telling himself out loud, "Poontang," saying it deliberately and with gravity since it seemed somehow extraordinarily significant to him.

Trouble was they weren't any of them his. Trouble was they were all somebody else's—Draper and Harrison Crossroads and Bethel and

Locust Hill and Union Ridge and Altamahaw and Hillsdale and Midway. So while he could advise and hypothesize and theorize and formulate and figure and speculate and tend to his map and his gash and
his boil and his wart, he couldn't do anything much in the way of ex-
amining witnesses and questioning victims and pursuing culprits because they weren't any of them his. They were all somebody else's.
But he was set for the time when they wouldn't be all somebody else's
and it was not long in coming once the yellowheaded rectangular
gash closed in roundabout Neely leaving the sheriff and his territory
ringed round with the corridor of destruction which the sheriff
wanted just a little piece of for himself and which he figured he was
entitled to on account of the general meanness of the times and which
he did in fact get some of not two weeks after Altamahaw had collected a little piece of it for itself.

However, the sheriff did not get his in Neely proper but got it instead on the bypass at Mr. Musselwhite's Citgo station which had not
been a Citgo station for any considerable spell and had been previously Mr. Musselwhite's general grocery and before that Mr. Musselwhite's fruit, vegetable, and snake oil stand and before that the shed
Mr. Musselwhite had kept his mule in. But once the division of roads
and highways bought up the right-of-way and cut the bypass through
and paved it and opened it Mr. Musselwhite's muleshed was sitting
near about on the northbound lane and showed some entrepreneurial
possibilities which was what got the mule evicted and which was
what got the dung shoveled out and which was what got the melons
and the cantaloupes and the peaches and the tomatoes away from the
Big Apple, where Mr. Musselwhite paid something slightly above
wholesale, and out to the bypass where people from all over the place
paid something that did not even resemble retail. And at first it was
just the melons and the cantaloupes and the peaches and the tomatoes
but after a bit it was the melons and the cantaloupes and the peaches
and the tomatoes and the bottled snake oil which Mr. Musselwhite
manufactured himself from melted shortening mostly, and later still it
was the melons and the cantaloupes and the peaches and the tomatoes
and the bottled snake oil along with various grocery items such as
loafbread and crackers and Coca-Colas and cornmeal and sack flour
and cigarettes to which were added pullet eggs and sausage and

smoked ham and tenderloin and pickle and pimento loaf thereby ushering into the muleshed the age of electric refrigeration which called for some general renovation and expansion on the part of Mr. Musselwhite who was not your general renovating and expanding sort and so who himself fashioned an addition from plywood primarily which did not so much improve the muleshed as increase and compound it.

Of course once the pullet eggs and the sausage and the smoked ham and the tenderloin and the pickle and pimento loaf caught on with the people from all over the place just like the melons and the cantaloupes and the peaches and the tomatoes and the snake oil had caught on with them, Mr. Musselwhite felt obliged to introduce a new line of products into his business and decided upon leisurewear, more specifically sunglasses and floppy hats and rubber sandals and floweredy shirts, so he fashioned yet another primarily plywood addition on the opposite end from the previous one and thereby increased and compounded the muleshed still further while maintaining its thoroughly ramshackle and unimproved state which local people did in fact recognize as unimproved and thoroughly ramshackle but which people from all over the place figured for quaint, and once Mr. Musselwhite found out he had a quaint place on his hands he considered there might be some profit for him in antique items on top of the melons and the cantaloupes and the peaches and the tomatoes and the snake oil and the pullet eggs and the sausage and the smoked ham and the tenderloin since antique items generally did turn up in quaint establishments and since, as Mr. Musselwhite understood it, most people—especially people from all over the place—would pay good money for nearly any trifling and incomprehensible geegaw as long a it looked older than they were, and what with two barnfuls and a cellar heaped near about to the floor joists Mr. Musselwhite had no end of geegaws, most particularly crusted and mildewed geegaws which he did not bother to decrust and unmildew but simply transported to the store once he had built a primarily plywood wing for them.

At length the muleshed got purely swallowed up in the additions and though everybody knew it was in there somewhere nobody could tell just where, not even Mr. Musselwhite who had kept track of it for a time but lost it eventually and never could manage to find it again.

The geegaws proved extraordinarily successful for Mr. Musselwhite and he expanded into whatnots and bric-a-brac and rustic dohickeys and carried large, truly perplexing pieces when he could get them, and though the leisurewear and the fruits and vegetables and the pullet eggs and the pork and the pickle and pimento loaf continued to sell briskly Mr. Musselwhite did not believe he was realizing quite the profit he could realize considering what a prodigious lot of bypassing went on around Neely day in and day out. So as Mr. Musselwhite sat on his metal stool behind his cash register and in front of his cigarette rack he studied the range of goods in his inventory and he speculated as to what other retail services he might successfully expand into, and though he considered soft icecream and hot dogs and ladies' cosmetics and hardware he did not do any actual expanding until the notion of gasoline came to him there between his cash register and his cigarettes, gasoline and diesel fuel too, he figured, so as to draw in the truckdrivers who generally would not leave the road for melons and geegaws and assorted pork cuts.

He struck a deal with Citgo and they buried the tanks for him and brought in the pumps and the big orange sign and they assisted and advised Mr. Musselwhite in some thoroughgoing improvements to his quaint structure which they were not nearly so taken with as most everybody else from all over the place, and consequently the thoroughgoing improvements did not get done in plywood but got done in real and actual brick and real and actual mortar by real and actual carpenters and masons who fairly much encased Mr.Musselwhite's quaint structure without closing him down for even a part of a day, and when they got done laying the bricks and hanging the doors and snugging up the windows Mr. Musselwhite could not discover a trace of his plywood wings and nowhere could he detect any degree of palpable quaintness which had pretty much gone the way of his muleshed. So he sat in his new building on his metal stool between his cigarettes and his cash register and sold his fruits and his vegetables and his assorted pork pieces and his leisurewear and his geegaws and his gasoline now too and he opened earlier and closed later and realized near about as much profit as he had previously.

Now Mr. Musselwhite had never been robbed in the true and verifiable and legal sense of the thing though he had once got beat out of some money by a Mrs. Rouse from Lynchburg who had bought from him an old crusted and mildewed porcelain figurine at his usual unreasonable price and had turned around and sold it to a collector in Virginia so as to get back her money and then some which seemed to Mr. Musselwhite as good as thievery, or maybe worse really and appreciably more aggravated than normal thievery on account of the gloating Mrs. Rouse had stopped in to partake of later. But he had never been robbed and threatened and endangered like he got robbed and threatened and endangered on that Thursday morning in late October which would be the October after the summer we lost the bald Jeeter when robbery and threats and endangerment were more prevalent than they had been at any time before. Mr. Musselwhite was alone in the store or very nearly alone anyway with the exception of Mrs. Evander Buffaloe whose company anymore was the same thing as solitude though it had not been so prior to Mr. Evander Buffaloe's departure and probably would not have continued to be if Mr. Evander Buffaloe had simply run off with a woman like the deacon Furches ran off with a woman, which was the sort of thing a wife could recover from and resent eventually, but Mr. Evander Buffaloe had not simply run off with a woman, had not simply run off at all, but had instead departed primarily and there wasn't anything simple about that.

Mr.Evander Buffaloe had kept the books at the Brownlee brothers' slaughterhouse for going on thirty years and him and his wife and his two boys and one girl lived three blocks off the boulevard in what the ladies of the Neely Flower Society called the stately Tucker home though there had not been any Tuckers in it for a full century. They were both from local people, Richardson Road Buffaloes on the one side and Lawsonville Avenue Johnstons on the other, and had got married in the First Baptist Church, which was her persuasion, prior to taking allegiance with the Methodists, which was his. Their boys came near about one right after the other, first Evander Clark Buffaloe II in 1952 and then Vance Johnston Buffaloe in 1953. Martha Porter Buffaloe did not arrive until the winter of 1957 which was after the Buffaloes had vacated their modest brick house behind the grade school and moved into the stately Tucker home that they had bought from some Smiths who had bought it from a Crawford who had bought it from a Moore who had bought it from a Kornegay who might have bought it from a Tucker though possibly not. Mrs. Evander Buffaloe was active in the Women's Christian Circle and worked at the Bargain Box Tuesday afternoons. She was widely well thought of though pitied somewhat on account of her homeliness which is one of the chief features passed from Johnston to Johnston aside from dainty feet. However, Mrs. Evander Buffaloe had learned to dress and carry herself so as to distract from the fullness of her ears and the fleshiness of her nose and the general chinlessness of her chin none of which Mr. Evander Buffaloe had been particularly put off by during their courtship, partially on account of Mrs. Evander Buffaloe's talents and partially on account of the astigmatism Buffaloes pass from one generation to the next instead of homeliness or dainty feet. Otherwise Buffaloes are usually just plain and lean and balding except for the Buffaloe women who are usually not lean, and somehow or another when Mr. Buffaloe coupled his plainness and his leanness and his receding hairline with Mrs. Buffaloe's dainty feet and clandestine homeliness the pair of them together made for what people called a handsome couple and produced between them what people called three handsome children who got some of their momma and some of their daddy in fairly equal shares with the notable exception of Martha Porter Buffaloe who did not get anything from her daddy except his astigmatism and got everything from her momma except her dainty feet and so went around homely and clumsy and thoroughly farsighted until she turned thirteen when she got fat too.

By and large they were your ordinary and normal sort of people. They spent a week every summer at Kitty Hawk and laid flowers at the cemetery every Easter and every Mother's Day. In 1963 Evander Clark II and Vance Johnston played Tiny Tot football in the Wallace E. Abernathy league, or got uniforms anyway and blocked on some kickoffs and blocked on some punts and mostly stood on the sidelines and yelled and chewed their fingernails and spat on ants. In the winter of 1964 Mr. Evander Buffaloe joined a bridge club so as to get out of the house some and in the winter of 1965 Mrs. Evander Buffaloe registered for a political awareness seminar at the Y.W.C.A. so as to get out of the house some without having to play bridge. Throughout the spring of 1966 Mrs. Evander Buffaloe developed some inordinately liberal tendencies, primarily on account of the Y.W.C.A., and in April in the spirit of fairmindedness she purchased from a negro door-to-door salesman a set of encyclopedias which she paid cash money for and which she received twelve volumes of in July, all of them consonants. She did not ever get the vowels, did not ever get the rest of the consonants for that matter, and was forced to withdraw from a summer-long personal introspection workshop at the request of Mr. Evander Buffaloe who found he objected to liberal tendencies. In 1973 Miss Martha Porter Buffaloe became a vegetarian, partly from a sense of pure outrage at the vicious cruelty perpetrated on helpless innocent animals and partly in an attempt to clear up her skin which *Woman's Day* had suggested vegetables might do. In 1974 Miss Martha Porter Buffaloe became a carnivore again and commenced to use a medicated swab in conjunction with vitamin E.

As to their schooling, the Buffaloe children all completed the twelfth grade and Evander Clark II enrolled at the state university in Raleigh where he intended to pursue a business degree but got sidetracked straightaway and set about pursuing the fine art of dissipation instead. He developed a taste for Philip Morris Ovals and Dutch beer and he caught from a girl from Pine Level a wholly unextraordinary and domestic strain of venereal disease which he attempted to make a gift of to a young woman from New Brunswick New Jersey and to her sister also and to her sister's best friend but which he had to keep to himself at last and take a treatment for in the end. He participated in demonstrations against the Asian war and got himself arrested twice, once for failing to disperse and once for setting fire to a sofa in the lobby of the library which the police determined had not been an act of conscience but had instead resulted from the combination of one live and fiery hot Philip Morris Oval, countless Dutch beers, and two little white tablets the size of fertilizer pellets. After two years of steady and earnest extravagance and turpitude Evander Clark II got discharged from the university without any credits to speak of and he returned to the stately Tucker home where he laid around for awhile and complained of ennui which Mrs. Evander Buffaloe took him to Dr. Shackleford to get some medication for but which Dr. Shackleford could not even begin to medicate away and so Evander Clark II continued to lay around and continued to languish and ever increasingly believed that in his two years of college he had done everything there was to do and seen everything there was to see, except maybe for the inside of a barbershop. He felt weary and unmotivated and was in fact tiresome and useless which prompted his daddy to arrange employment for him at the slaughterhouse but Evander Clark II declined to be employed in a bourgeois institution run by philistines, and when his momma attempted to explain to him that the Brownlee brothers had only come from Moncure, Evander Clark II laid his head back and laughed in a most vicious and merciless way. Consequently Mr. Buffaloe cut off his son's association with the Brownlee brothers' philistine meat along with Mr. Wyatt Big Apple Benbow's fruits and vegetables and canned and bottled goods and so provided Evander Clark II the opportunity to lay around and languish straight through the day without any worrisome meals to interrupt him, and on the Sunday the fasting commenced he found it novel and measurably heightening to his awareness, but the novelty wore off some on Monday and by midmorning Tuesday Evander Clark II's awareness, though still heightened, had turned its attention primarily to his stomach cavity. Wednesday he found a quarter in the bottom of a hutch drawer and bought himself a Three Musketeers bar. Thursday he got strapped into a battery-charged prod and encouraged cattle along a chute with it.

Vance Johnston Buffaloe did not prove nearly so unruly and troublesome as his brother. He did not get dissipated or arrested or venereal diseased and successfully earned a certificate in electrical wiring at the Rockingham Technical Institute. He failed to fast any or measurably heighten his awareness but instead took a job straight off with Purdy Electric and bored holes and pulled wire and slid around on his backside under houses. Martha Porter Buffaloe did not pursue a formal education after high school and did not pursue any technical training either but went directly to work at the Rexall in cosmetics which she was not nearly so artful with as her mother but which she could manipulate nonetheless so as to reduce her nose and increase her chin and hide her blemishes and disguise her ears which left only the feet and the fatness for people to openly regard, lament to each other about, and be genuinely sorry for. Like her brother Vance Johnston the electrician and her brother Evander Clark II the cattle prod-der, Martha Porter Buffaloe did not trouble herself to move out of the stately Tucker home into her own residence once she had earned and accumulated the money to do so, and consequently the Buffaloes lived fairly much as they had lived previously except they were bigger now, or at least three of them were anyway, and did not like each other near as much as they had before, especially at supper when the sheer proximity of Buffaloe to Buffaloe made for some noticeable friction.

In the Buffaloe household, time was when opinions had been a thing peculiar to Mr. Buffaloe like his high forehead or his brown front tooth, and when he would lay the tines of his fork on the lip of his plate and dab at his mouth with his napkin and then deliver himself of a viewpoint, Mrs. Buffaloe generally agreed with him straight off and the children, who likely had not been listening anyhow, would not comment and so there was an end to the matter. But when the children grew up their mouths grew up with the rest of them and their attention span drew out some and they became opinionated, or what Mr. Buffaloe considered counter-opinionated since he did not seem to look at anything from one side that they did not see from the other. Of course Evander Clark II was the worst of the bunch because he had been to a university, had actually attended several classes, and so considered himself educated, or worse than educated really, considered himself naturally intuitive and highly intelligent and figured Neely for a vast stagnant pool of ignorance and wrongheadedness that he had miraculously sprung out of and risen above. He had been sufficiently intolerable in his laying around and languishing stage but got worse once he commenced to prod cattle, got actively political and attempted to organize his fellow stockyard employees into a socialist workers' party but they were not much intrigued with socialism and instead chased Evander Clark II throughout the corral and singed and jolted his backside with their own battery-charged prods which was the leading amusement at the slaughterhouse.

Vance Johnston Buffaloe, who had not ever possessed much of a personality in the course of his youth, had begun to become somebody in particular under the guidance and instruction of his fellow electricians and their carpenter friends and mason friends and Sheetrocker friends and painter friends who had reduced their primary needs in life to beer and money and snatch, only the other way around, and most every evening they all collected at the integrated club and pool hall out the Burlington road past the cemetery where the beer got drunk and the money got spent and the snatch got talked about, and if there was anything Vance Johnston Buffaloe and his friends liked better than getting snatch it was talking about getting snatch and if there was anything they liked better than talking about getting snatch it was fighting over what snatch they had gotten, or what snatch they had said they'd gotten anyway, and they would knock each other out of their chairs and beat each other and kick each other and brawl all throughout the pool hall for the sake of some young woman none of them were truly acquainted with and who probably would not have given a happy shit for the whole bunch of them together. Consequently, Vance Johnston Buffaloe, who had not been anybody much prior to his course of study at Rockingham Technical Institute and his subsequent employment at Purdy Electric, developed into a fairly rough and vulgar individual and where he had not possessed much of any opinion on any matter previously he now believed every dilemma could be suitably and satisfyingly resolved if him or one of his friends or somebody like him or one of his friends could get his hands on the responsible individual and whipass, he called it.

Understandably, Martha Porter Buffaloe could not abide either of her brothers on account of how the one bored her and the other offended her, and for less understandable but equally acute reasons, Martha Porter Buffaloe could not abide her parents either. They criticized her weight and criticized her hair and criticized her makeup and criticized her clothes and criticized her friends and just generally picked at her and persecuted her and did not even begin to comprehend her, or that's how she saw it anyhow. She did not venture out in public with them when she could help it on account of how dull and ordinary they were, and though she had attempted on innumerable occasions to instruct them in the ways of stylishness and inform them as to the most burning issues of the modern day, they seemed reluctant to be improved upon if not outright opposed to it, and so Martha Porter Buffaloe eventually washed her hands of her momma and her daddy and decided she would just have to be stylish and informed on her own. Consequently, she wore what clothes she wanted to wear, had her hair cut just precisely how she wanted to have it cut, spread the rouge to her cheeks and the shadow to her eyelids exactly how she wanted to spread the rouge and the shadow, and generally packaged and presented herself to the world like she felt she should be packaged and presented notwithstanding the strident objections of her momma and her daddy who picked at her and persecuted her and did not even begin to comprehend her.

There was not much pleasing talk around the Buffaloe supper table any longer. Every human utterance came under fire from somewhere and so there was not much plain human utterance around the Buffaloe supper table any longer either with the exception of regular utilitarian requests for the meat and the vegetables and the biscuits and whatnot and even they got nasty sometimes on account of Evander Clark II primarily who had completely ceased to refer to Martha Porter Buffaloe as Martha Porter Buffaloe but had commenced instead to call her you and yours, the you being the most of herself and the yours being her thighs which were threatening to become the most of herself. Naturally, Martha Porter Buffaloe did not appreciate the title much and always objected to it straightaway and violently insisted she was on a diet, and she was on a diet though it was one of your superficial mealtime diets that did not have anything to do with losing weight, and insisting as well she was big-boned and possibly suffering from a glandular affliction to all of which her brother would smirk, and he was quite an accomplished and effective smirker, and so Martha Porter Buffaloe would call on her momma and her daddy for support and her daddy would lay the tines of his fork on the lip of his plate and dab at his mouth with his napkin and tell her it appeared to him she could stand to whittle herself down some and her momma would suggest a change in clothes or hairstyle to disguise the fullness of her figure which was usually when Martha Porter Buffaloe departed from the table in exasperation and retired to her bedroom where she took consolation in her record player and her assortment of 45's and soothed herself with the sheer racket and volume the two of them made together.

Undoubtedly the 1970's were strenuous and troublesome years for Mr. Buffaloe in particular on account of how his life had changed so little on the one hand but so greatly on the other. The one child that left home had come back and the two children that hadn't left home still didn't, and though Mrs. Buffaloe told Mr. Buffaloe it was nice to have the family all together it wasn't nice really and he knew it and she knew it too which did not prevent her from expressing the contrary but full well kept her from believing it. Obviously there was not anything at all nice about five fullgrown Buffaloes under the roof of the stately Tucker home, especially since not any of the five fullgrown Buffaloes liked each other, including the Mr. and Mrs. who had liked each other once, had liked each other well enough anyway to concoct the remaining three Buffaloes, but who did not seem to share a special fondness any longer, only a bed and a bathroom and a clothescloset and the general habit of each other roundabout the house. So life inside the stately Tucker home had soured noticeably for Mr. Buffaloe, and commencing with April, 1971, life outside the stately Tucker home soured noticeably for him as well because it was in April of 1971 that Mr. Buffaloe lost his mother who had been laid up and disoriented since November of 1969 and who Mr. Buffaloe had considered all along would be better off dead until she died when he changed his mind. And he had not completely forgiven himself for wishing his mother away and had not completely forgiven his mother for leaving when the United States of America proceeded to withdraw from southeast Asia which Mr. Buffaloe considered to be a pure moral cataclysm, and he was just getting to the point where he could live down his little part of it when the honorable Governor George Corley Wallace was shot to pieces by a crazed white man at some yankee gathering where he should have known better than to go anyway. So there was Mr. Buffaloe with his grief and his disgrace and his solitary vote which torture and the threat of death could not induce him to squander upon a Republican but which he did not much care to spend on an incomprehensible and farfetched Democrat either, and consequently he did not use it at all and got accused of apathy on national television by Dr. Eric Sevareid and he could hardly bear up under the humiliation of it. Then when it did not seem things could become worse they became worse: Mr. Buffaloe's Pontiac stock fell off to nothing, Evander Clark II bought a pair of sneakers, a Coca-Cola, and two hot dogs with Mr. Buffaloe's entire collection of Kennedy half dollars, and on the first Sunday in August of 1977 the Neely

Chronicle ran a graphic and utterly devastating photograph on the bottom front page of the fashion section—Elizabeth Taylor had gotten fat.

It was all Mr. Buffaloe could do to carry on. He had no measurable will or desire remaining to him and of a morning could barely muster the velocity and momentum sufficient to propel him through the day. He took little interest in national events and left off watching the 6:30 news once talk got out of Walter Cronkite's retirement. Anymore he read only the frivolous parts of the *Chronicle,* which was the bulk of it, and rarely did that once the editors dropped Gasoline Alley and Gil Thorp to make room for encapsulated soap opera plots. He could not devote himself to his work because he had always been and surely would always be quite thoroughly indifferent to the Brownlee brothers' debits and credits and general expenses and anymore he could not ignore his work either and meditate with any success on account of his son who was ever getting pursued and electrocuted and so kept the slaughterhouse in an ongoing uproar. Plain and simple, Mr. Buffaloe could not find anything to live for and could not work up the courage and passion to do himself in and so just went along with the flow of the day and the flow of the week and the flow of the month and the flow of the year and did not experience but the usual unpleasantness and disappointment for such a long spell that his attitude ceased to decline and actually leveled off some. He had even laid down his fork and dabbed at his mouth and ventured an opinion or two as late as February of 1979 and he might have been all right, might have stayed leveled off and undeclining if not for the deacon Furches who committed an atrocity symptomatic of the moral degeneration inherent in a capitalistic society, Evander Clark II called it, and his daddy could not find reason to disagree with him.

The deacon Furches ran off with a woman, a Lamont Circle Bailey or actually a Stout by birth who had married a Lamont Circle Bailey and who had lived with him for twenty-six years and shared her bed with him and raised his children and who had even appeared and made out to like him some right up until the first Saturday in March of 1979 when the Lamont Circle Bailey himself drove his wife, the Lamont Circle Stout Bailey, to the depot so as to put her on the train for Rocky Mount where her sister lived but where she was not truly going so far as, and the Lamont Circle Stout Bailey gave her cheek to her husband and he kissed it and the Lamont Circle Bailey gave his cheek to his wife and she kissed it and they held each other's fingers briefly and then departed, the Bailey for Lamont Circle and the Stout Bailey for Greensboro where she was met at the station by the deacon Furches who had packed his things and had left his house in the early morning and driven his blue Le Sabre out of Neely and down 29 south. There was not a Mrs. deacon Furches except for the one in the cemetery, so while the Stout Bailey had given up her home and her husband and her two daughters along with, of course, the primary part of her respectability, the deacon Furches had chiefly surrendered his sofabed, his daddy's General Electric floor circulator, and his $175.00 cleaning deposit, not to mention the good graces of the Baptist church which he lost also but which he was not much concerned over on account of what scant few worldly items the Baptist church held in its good graces anyhow and as the deacon Furches figured it, with such a considerable lot of reviling and disparaging to do the church would likely not be inclined to squander any severe damnation on the solitary escapade of a solitary deacon.

Nobody suspected the deacon Furches and the Lamont Circle Stout Bailey had run off together, though everybody knew they had left on the same morning and had gone off in the same direction, but nobody actually suspected they had been in romantic collusion each with the other because did not either of them seem the passionate and scheming type. The deacon Furches had turned sixty-four and retired from the cigarette plant in November of 1978 and since then had passed his time sitting around at the coalyard and sitting around at the Gulf station and sitting around in the basement of the armory where him and Emmet Dabb and Dennis Tuttle and Colonel J. Richmond Morrison ret. talked about most every bland and unprovocative thing they could think of and they could think of plenty between them. The deacon Furches was a tall man, well over six feet, and he wore his trousers near about up to his mammaries and had coarse black hair growing out the ridge of his nose. He was not at all comely and did not possess one of your scintillating wits and dynamic personalities that most uncomely people develop so as to offset their uncomeliness, and he appeared to merely expect that his life would wind out in its own bland and unprovocative and uncomely way until his friends would find him one day stretched out on his sofabed expired and they would collect around him and wonder if he was.

However, the Lamont Circle Stout Bailey changed all that for the deacon Furches even though she was just as bland and unprovocative and uncomely as he was, maybe even more bland and unprovocative and probably a degree or two less comely. She did not have a figure any longer just some drooping places and some bulging places which she covered up but could not disguise with stretch pants and stretch blouses and stretch jackets and plain flat shoes. She had brown hair that was cut to swirl around close to her head and she had brown eyes too and thin lips and a long pointy chin and a regular stalk of a neck all of which together had worked to remind the deacon Furches of General Douglas MacArthur and so he never could help but get patriotic urges in her presence. However, it is unlikely that the Stout Bailey primarily suggested General MacArthur to the deacon Furches since the most of his urges did not have much of a nationalistic tendency to them and instead were more along the lines of your fiery and savagely passionate urges though probably not your full fiery and savagely passionate urges but more likely just your partly fiery and moderately savagely passionate urges since it is difficult to imagine pure fire and thoroughgoing savagery in a man who buckles his belt across his ribcage. But nonetheless somehow or another her exceedingly inert qualities and his exceedingly inert qualities mixed and mingled together to form a combustible entity, the whole business probably commencing with a few furtive glances from the deacon's pew followed by several warm handshakes at the sanctuary door and complicated further with some apparently accidental encounters along the boulevard and on the square before picking up in fiery and passionate earnest, if even just partly fiery and somewhat passionate earnest, with a series of entirely secret and unaccidental encounters where the affections got announced and the plans got made and the urges got exercised.

They had intended to go as far as Pago Pago which the deacon Furches had measured out and figured to be sufficiently removed from Neely to prevent the primary Lamont Street Bailey or any of his Lamont Street Bailey relations from coming to fetch back the runaway

Lamont Street Stout Bailey since as the deacon Furches had calculated it there was surely no man alive who would travel full across a continent and partway across an ocean to hunt up a frumpy, middleaged bagging and bulging woman, especially one that favored a four star general. But in actuality they did not get so far as Pago Pago on account of the deacon Furches's blue Le Sabre which became ill and troubled in Scottsbluff Nebraska and expired in Pocatello Idaho where it would not even have been if the deacon Furches had not got on the wrong road in Salina Kansas, and when the deacon Furches wired for his pension money and provided his Idaho address he was to a degree fearful and concerned that a Lamont Street Bailey that would not travel full across a continent and partway across an ocean to fetch back a woman that looked like a four star general might travel merely to Idaho to fetch one back, but the deacon Furches and the Lamont Street Stout Bailey stayed on at the Pocatello Motor Hotel for a month and a half apparently undiscovered and unsoughtafter and when they had relocated to a rental house just beyond the city limits the Lamont Street Stout Bailey wrote to her husband a dear Lamont Street Bailey kiss-off letter on pilfered Pocatello Motor Hotel stationery and sent along two insured and registered silver potato pendants for her daughters but still not the primary Lamont Street Bailey or any of his relations either came looking even once they knew precisely where to look.

The news did not break in Neely all at once but broke slowly and in snatches commencing with the destination of the deacon Furches's pension check followed by an announcement of the disappearance of the Lamont Street Stout Bailey who was not in Rocky Mount and was not in Neely and could not be discovered anywhere in between. Then there followed a period of several weeks with no additional news and so most everybody occupied themselves in speculating as to just what the deacon Furches might be doing in Idaho and just what brand of mischief might have befallen the Lamont Street Stout Bailey, and nobody really worked up or even flirted with the theory that the Lamont Street Stout Bailey might be in Idaho herself and that the deacon Furches himself might be her brand of mischief so everybody was equally shocked and surprised when the gist of the dear Lamont Street Bailey kiss-off letter got printed up in the *Chronicle* where not the gist or any other part of it was supposed to get printed up and where not the gist or any other part of it would have gotten printed up if not for the Lamont Street Bailey's sister, a Loop Road Bailey Myrick, who got called in by her distraught brother to read the letter and soon thereafter let out the contents of it to the senior editor of the *Chronicle,* the full-blooded Loop Road Myrick's sister's husband, who felt an especially acute obligation to print the matter at hand, partly on account of the matter itself and partly on account of Mr. Zeno Stiers who was supposed to have passed away and so had been eulogized and tributized for roundabout a quarter page but who continued to linger at the hospital despite his doctor's assurances that he would not. So there was the full-blooded Loop Road Myrick's sister's husband with a quarter page of *Chronicle* to fill and there was the Loop Road Bailey Myrick with the majority of poignant kiss-off letter committed to memory and the rest of it fabricated straight out and naturally the two of them got together so as to broadcast the Lamont Street Bailey's misfortune throughout the county.

Now Mr. Evander Buffaloe, as was the way of things in the stately Tucker home, got ahold of this particular *Chronicle* after work of a Wednesday once Evander Clark II and Vance Johnston had finished taking it apart and turning it all inside out prior to putting it back together anyhow they could. It was Mr. Buffaloe's habit to check on his Pontiac stock at the outset followed by a quick perusal of the boxscores when the season called for it and then a look at the television listings and the weather and Ira Corn on bridge after which he generally read and ingested an actual news item or two, and on this particular Wednesday that Mr. Zeno Stiers lingered at the hospital and so did not get eulogized and tributized Mr. Buffaloe found his attention fully captured by the headline "Deacon Absconds with Local Woman" which was a most strange extraordinary thing to see in the *Chronicle* since year in and year out there was usually not much local absconding, not even any regional absconding to speak of. Consequently, Mr. Buffaloe read the article with the greatest of care and then read it through a second time with near about the greatest of care then too after which he folded the paper ever so carefully, laid it across his lap, and ruminated in profound silence right up until suppertime.

He was likely still ruminating over the deacon and the woman and the absconding at the supper table but not any of the Buffaloes could tell really on account of how Mr. Buffaloe seemed naturally disposed towards ponderous silence whether for the cause of legitimate rumination or not, and he did not partake of the general talk and speculation which was concerned chiefly with the deacon and the woman and the absconding and was concerned slightly with the husband and the daughters and the sister and the lingering Mr. Zeno Stiers for whom little could be expressed except grief and considerable wonderment. Martha Porter Buffaloe could not understand exactly why a woman would desert her husband and her children and go off to Idaho in the company of a man with coarse black hairs growing out of the ridge of his nose, and her mother attempted to explain to her how such a thing could come about but decided midway through her explanation that she did not exactly understand why a woman would desert her husband and her children and go off to Idaho in the company of a man with coarse black hairs growing out of the ridge of his nose either. As Vance Johnston Buffaloe saw it the deacon and the woman too should both have the shit kicked out of them and maybe the husband should have some of the shit kicked out of him for being so spineless as to let his wife get away in the first place, but Evander Clark II insisted it was not a matter of coarse black noseridge hairs or shitkicking either but was instead purely an atrocity symptomatic of the moral degeneration inherent in a capitalistic society and he crossed his arms over himself and let his observation lay there on the table with the meatloaf and the potatoes and the butterbeans and not Mrs. Evander Buffaloe or Martha Porter Buffaloe or Vance Johnston Buffaloe either attempted any sort of reply to lay and wallow there with it so Evander Clark II availed himself of the opportunity to expand some on the degenerative qualities inherent in a capitalistic society of which this particular atrocity was merely symptomatic and when he had blown and expanded so as to render himself sufficiently tiresome he drew off a breath and showed every sign of soaring to new and untried heights of tediousness when his daddy, who had not appeared even remotely interested in the nosehairs or the shitkicking or any little pompous fragment of the moral degeneration, did not lay down his fork on the lip of his plate and did not dab at his mouth with his napkin but opened it anyway and said, "I do wish I could find somebody somewhere worth a great big goddamn," and Mrs. Buffaloe dropped her chin some and got herself all set to agree with him until she heard what she was all set to agree with and then she dropped her chin some more and exclaimed, "Why Evander!" and Martha Porter Buffaloe and Evander Clark II pondered Mr. Buffaloe with some Why Evander! looks of their own but left the additional commenting to their brother, Vance Johnston Buffaloe, who left off grazing on his hunk of meatloaf, picked up his head, and said, "Fucking A, Daddy."

He was not a profane man, not a blasphemous or violent natured man, simply not a man who regularly traded in great big goddamns and so at the introduction of one, especially in the middle of a wholesome meal, Mrs. Evander Buffaloe grew concerned and somewhat agitated and once she had reproved Vance Johnston for his fucking A she turned her entire attention to the great big goddamn and had commenced to cast around for a gentle reproach to Mr. Buffaloe when Mr. Buffaloe himself interrupted her direct in the middle of her hemming and her hawing and said, "There must be somebody somewhere, somewhere out of the way maybe, but somewhere anyhow," and then he dabbed at his mouth and laid his fork against the lip of his plate and gazed out over Mrs. Buffaloe's head to the far dining room wall and Mrs. Buffaloe attempted to reproach him and attempted to reprove him and attempted to make him sorry and apologetic for having uttered a vulgarism at the supper table, but Mr. Buffaloe would not be suitably reproached and reproved or sorry and apologetic either and persisted in gazing out over Mrs. Buffaloe's head to the far dining room wall which he pondered with the hollow and near about haunted expression of a man who fully understands just how exceedingly rare and elusive a great big goddamn might be.

Some people said later it was the woman but it was not the woman because he had not even met the woman yet, and some people said later it was the menopause and the deacon Furches in combination that brought it on but it was not the menopause and was only some little part of the deacon Furches. Mostly it was everything, everything maybe ending with and touched off by the local absconding but everything anyway and not just one or two or three things

T. R. PEARSON

but all of it accumulated and heaped together. The middle block and
mortar McKinney said the footings and foundations of Mr. Buffaloe's
existence had given way beneath him which was just the sort of comment the middle block and mortar McKinney made about most every
affair and happenstance there was to make a comment about but
which he was direct on target with this time on account of how the
footings and foundations of Mr. Buffaloe's existence had given way
beneath him or anyway had sunk and settled appreciably. It seems
nothing much had turned out quite like Mr. Buffaloe had figured it
would. He had figured his children would grow up and move somewhere else, which they didn't, and he had figured his momma could
not make him feel lowly and disappointing once she was dead, which
she could, and he had figured American democracy would handily
persuade and overcome a negligible assortment of misguided savage
orientals, which it wasn't able to, and he had figured the honorable
Governor George Corley Wallace for the thirty-eighth president of
these United States, which he never was, and he figured Pontiac for a
shrewd and perceptive investment, which it did not turn out to be,
and he had figured Elizabeth Taylor would somehow avoid getting
plump and girthsome, which she eventually got, and he had figured
he would become contented and satisfied with employment at the
slaughterhouse, which he hadn't yet, and he had figured the Baptist
church and its clergy and laymen and the most of its regular associates
and attachments to be at least near about as stiffly and earnestly forth-
right and upstanding as they claimed to be, which they weren't not
locally anyway any longer, and so now at last after all his previous figuring and all his subsequent thwarted expectations Mr. Buffaloe
went ahead and decided there was not much left in the world worth a
great big goddamn except maybe for somebody somewhere.

Mrs. Buffaloe gave it out as a vacation, gave it out as a fishing trip
up on the Blue Ridge but when he departed from the depot he was
not in the company of a pole, was not in fact in the company of any
identifiable fishing paraphernalia but just a little canvas grip and ten
navel oranges in a plastic mesh bag. Mrs. Buffaloe went with him to
the station, went with him right up onto the bus, mostly because he
could not keep her from it, and she pleaded with him and begged him
not to go or if he had to go to come home in a week or if he would

not come home in a week to come home in two weeks anyhow and then she laughed ever so lightly and smiled some for the benefit of everybody else who was not to know she was pleading and begging and distraught and finally at length she got run off the bus by the driver and from the pavement waved at Mr. Buffaloe who did not even raise his fingers. And so he was gone and though most everybody knew he had departed nobody knew he was gone really, not even Mrs. Buffaloe who only feared he might be gone and who had in fact been fearing he might up and make off to somewhere ever since the vulgarism at the supper table which seemed to mark Mr. Buffaloe's precipitous abandonment of healthful psychological attitude, or anyway that's what Mrs. Buffaloe's analyst in Greensboro called it once Evander Clark II had persuaded her to visit an analyst in Greensboro on account of her general bafflement and disorientation in the wake of Mr. Buffaloe's fishing trip which nobody much in Neely believed to be a fishing trip any longer and which most everybody had developed ideas and theories about, ideas and theories which covered nearly the entire range of possibilities for a trip on a bus with a grip and a mesh bag full of navel oranges, and wherever people collected and talked they generally set aside some portion of the conversation for serious Buffaloe speculation and while there were those that believed Mr. Buffaloe had run off with a woman or had left to dodge a dark and maybe unlawful past or had embezzled funds from the slaughterhouse or was away taking the cure for tuberculosis or alcoholism or drug addiction not any small group together or even any one person by himself ventured to suppose that Mr. Buffaloe had gone aquesting for that somebody somewhere worth a great big goddamn. That was simply not the sort of thing people figured on from Mr. Buffaloe, not the sort of thing people figured on from anybody really.

Mrs. Buffaloe certainly had not figured on it, had not expected or anticipated it and with some reason since Mr. Buffaloe, along with not being profane and not being blasphemous and not being violent natured, had never been impetuous either, but the supper table vulgarism had apparently changed all that because Mr. Buffaloe had surely uttered it and had just as surely up and gone on account of it, and they did not hear from him for one week and then two weeks and then three weeks and the fourth week was near about spent when at last there arrived at the Buffaloe household a postcard from Winston-Salem with the picture of a Moravian on it, but there was not any message except for the printed message which told what a Moravian was doing on the front of the postcard anyway, so there was not any indication if Mr. Buffaloe was fine or if he was not fine except for the handwritten address which itself was not much any indication really. Then three weeks later the Buffaloes received a second postcard from Statesville, this one with a picture of a Quality Inn on the front of it and still no message on the back of it, and on the basis of the pair of postcards alone Evander Clark II applied his refined powers of reasoning and perception and announced that his father was heading on a direct line towards the westering sun which struck Evander Clark II as highly metaphorical, and he speculated that a third postcard would arrive from somewhere along about Marion or maybe even Asheville and a third postcard did arrive but from Carowinds instead which was a little left of the westering sun and so deflated the metaphor somewhat.

The postcards did not soothe Mrs. Buffaloe much and after the fourth one had come from Spartanburg South Carolina and the fifth one had arrived from Dahlonega Georgia she went ahead and became distracted and disoriented and most mornings and afternoons too retired to her tiny sewing room up near the peak of the mansard and her wailing and sobbing and moaning carried through the gable window and down to the street where people heard her and so figured they could entirely rule out fishing as a possibility. Of course it was the distraction and the disorientation, manifested primarily in the wailing and the sobbing and the moaning, that prompted Evander Clark II to carry his momma to the analyst in Greensboro and the analyst listened to her and nodded at her and though he could not cure and relieve Mrs. Buffaloe he did impoverish her successfully which returned her to the sewing room to wail and sob and moan without the professional listening and without the professional nodding, and after a spell it seemed to curious pedestrians and to neighbors roundabout the stately Tucker home that the noisome laments had diminished appreciably but this was primarily a false impression due to chill weather which had caused the sewing room window to get shut. The actual distraction and disorientation, not to mention the wailing and

the sobbing and the moaning, did not fall off any because Mrs. Buffaloe found she grew increasingly fond of Mr. Buffaloe the longer he
stayed gone to wherever it was he was gone to and nobody knew
where he was gone to any longer or even where he'd been to lately on
account of how the postcards stopped coming seven months after
they'd started coming, so Mrs. Buffaloe could not ask herself why Mr.
Buffaloe was in Winston-Salem or Statesville or at Carowinds or in
Spartanburg or Dahlonega but instead had to settle for some general,
undirected blubbering which she had a talent for and carried out in a
most successful and pathetic sort of way and thereby struck up considerable sympathy and pity among her neighbors and acquaintances
who by that time had ruled out tuberculosis and alcoholism and drug
addiction along with the fishing.

The Buffaloes got by a little more than passably well on the income from the Rexall and the income from Purdy Electric and the
income from the slaughterhouse which had been a paltry income but
got elevated to a respectable income once Evander Clark II assumed
his daddy's bookkeeping position which he assured the Brownlee
brothers he was entirely capable of since he had in fact resided upon a
college campus for the best part of two years and had in fact received
several documented hours of college credit. So the majority of the
Buffaloes got by after Mr. Buffaloe's departure just about like they had
gotten by before it except for the absence of the mouthdabbing and
the forklaying and the opiniongiving which they had not ever paid
much attention to anyhow, and it was only the solitary Buffaloe that
remained affected and even she left off the wailing and the sobbing
and the moaning and the most of the undirected blubbering after Mr.
Buffaloe had been gone for a year and she got numb instead and suffered spells of catatonia which was still affliction enough but wasn't
nearly so noisome and aggravating as the wailing and the sobbing and
the moaning had been.

They did not any of them ever hear direct from Mr. Buffaloe again
after the postcard from Dahlonega, and they did not any of them hear
indirect from Mr. Buffaloe either for nearly two years and probably
would not have ever heard tell of him anymore if Mr. Phillip J. King
had not gone off in the fall of the year to visit his sister's son in Copperhill Tennessee and there in the broadest part of the afternoon di-

rect in front of the Copperhill Legion hall, or actually direct in front of the iron cannon and pile of welded cannonballs in front of the Copperhill Legion hall, Mr. Phillip J. King met on the sidewalk Mr. Evander Buffaloe in the company of a large yellowhaired woman in a clingy, silky sort of dress who had ahold of Mr. Buffaloe's right bicep, and Mr. Phillip J. King said he did not openly greet Mr. Buffaloe but did incline his head some and Mr. Buffaloe parted his lips and showed his brown tooth. "Bottled blonde," Mr. Phillip J. King told it, told it to Mr. Emmet Dabb and Tiny Aaron and Mr. Wyatt Benbow and Mr. Louis Benfield and Coley Britt, "and Lord God Almighty pure melons out to here and I do mean pure melons," and Tiny Aaron spat and said, "Shitfire," and everybody else agreed with the spirit of the observation. They decided to tell a Buffaloe, decided it was their obligation to tell a Buffaloe, and they selected Vance Johnston on account of how a yellowhaired, purely meloned woman was right in his line and he answered the news with some sort of shitfire of his own, though not precisely a shitfire exactly, and then went off to the stately Tucker home where Mr. Phillip J. King and Mr. Emmet Dabb and Tiny Aaron and Mr. Wyatt Benbow and Mr. Louis Benfield and Coley Britt all figured he would disperse and distribute the news, and maybe he did disperse and distribute it to his brother and sister who never let on that they knew though likely they did know, but his momma remained numb and silent and so probably did not ever get told and did not ever find out that Mr. Evander Buffaloe had eventually and actually hunted up somebody somewhere worth a great big goddamn or some little piece of one anyway.

Of course come the October after the summer we lost the bald Jeeter Mrs. Evander Buffaloe was still relatively numb and still relatively silent and prior to gassing up the car Evander Clark II had turned her loose in Mr. Musselwhite's converted muleshed at the chance she might find some pleasure and distraction in the snake oil or the leisurewear or the fruits and vegetables or the assorted pork cuts or the crusted and mildewed geegaws or any of the other accumulated refuse Mr. Musselwhite called his inventory, but Mrs. Evander Buffaloe did not seem to find any pleasure and did not seem to find any distraction, did not even seem to look for any really, and stayed precisely where Evander Clark II had put her there direct in front of Mr. Musselwhite and his cigarette rack. Being relatively numb and relatively silent, Mrs. Evander Buffaloe had not lately produced much in the way of conversation but Mr. Musselwhite talked at length with her anyhow because she was upright and drew breath which was about all he ever required. He told her most everything he told everybody else commencing with a comment on the general seasonableness of the weather which happened to be the case on that particular day of that particular October after the summer we lost the bald Jeeter, but Mr. Musselwhite was certainly as capable and adept with observations on the unseasonableness of the weather also if conditions called for them. Being a man of methodical and organized faculties, Mr. Musselwhite followed up his specific comments with a rambling local history of the annual rainfall, or more truly a rambling local history of the lack of appreciable annual rainfall which was the general and ordinary case roundabout, but even talk of the rain that did not fall prompted Mr. Musselwhite to a word or two on the ache that set into his joints when the rain that did not usually fall actually fell and the topic of aching joints regularly put Mr. Musselwhite in mind of Mrs. Musselwhite's hernia which she would not go under the knife for on account of her fear of modern medicine, and Mr. Musselwhite said he did not think much of modern medicine himself and he asked Mrs. Buffaloe had she ever gotten operated on to which she did not reply but simply looked at Mr. Musselwhite precisely how she'd looked at him all along and if Mr. Musselwhite had known what a lobotomy was he might have figured she'd had one.

Mr. Musselwhite was just getting onto the topic of healthful eating habits which would lead him to a comment or two on the virtues of fruits and fresh vegetables which would in turn put him onto the subject of gardening and so carry him back at last to the local annual rainfall, but he was only partway through his disquisition on chewing when the glass doors swung open and a tall, lean, pointy, hollowed out, angular, and otherwise unremarkable figure passed in through them and did not go to the drinkbox or the Nab and peanut rack and did not even attempt to appear interested in the great glut of merchandise all around him but straightaway stepped up abreast of Mrs. Buffaloe and asked Mr. Musselwhite across the counter, "You know who I am?" to which Mr. Musselwhite did not have a suitable reply on account of how the chewing disquisition had at the moment monopolized his powers of thought, which is just the sort of thing a disquisition will do, so Mr. Musselwhite got shown barrelfirst a Harrington and Richardson Buntline revolver of extraordinarily high caliber and almost simultaneously had his testicles threatened with a place called Merry Oaks which they were not in the vicinity of at the present moment but which Mr. Musselwhite was made to understand they could readily be dispatched to.

Now Mr. Musselwhite had been waiting to get robbed ever since the actual muleshed, had been anticipating and preparing for it, and so once the demand for the contents of the cash drawer was made outright Mr. Musselwhite immediately reached his arm in the general direction of the register but not to the register precisely and instead more directly to a shelf underneath the register where Mr. Musselwhite kept his single-action .22-caliber Savage revolver loaded with six long rifle hollowpoint shells which he figured would be near about as thoroughly damaging and destructive as any solid high caliber bullet, even an extraordinarily high caliber one, and which in fact turned out to be as thoroughly damaging and destructive judging from the hole Mr. Musselwhite made in the cash register which was the first thing he shot. It was probably the adrenaline part of it and the frightening part of it and the double-thumbed cocking action part of it along with the anticipation of the ducking and squatting part of it which caused Mr. Musselwhite to neglect the aiming part of it and consequently he hit direct between the three dollar button and the thirty cent button prior to dropping into a pile on the floor and he had both thumbs on the hammer and was commencing to draw it back again when the tall, lean, pointy, hollowed out, angular, and otherwise unremarkable culprit squeezed off a retaliatory round and the Harrington and Richardson Buntline revolver of extraordinarily high caliber discharged like a thunderclap while the bullet which had been intended for Mr. Musselwhite's testicles flew high and wide into a flint display. Mr. Musselwhite answered with a shot of his own which he managed to put past the cash register and send clean across the store into a Pepsi-Cola wall clock and he had just successfully piled up on the floor again when the Harrington and Richardson Buntline revolver exploded a second time and opened up a large jagged hole in a one pound can of Flying Dutchman aromatic tobacco which was just above the cigarette rack which was just beyond Mrs. Evander Buffaloe who had blinked three times now on account of the pistol reports but had not gone anywhere really, had not even drawn herself in noticeably so as to make a smaller target and in the heat of the moment Mr. Musselwhite decided he would use her for cover and so rose up behind Mrs. Evander Buffaloe to squeeze off his third round which hit dead onto an assortment of carnival glass and got answered straightaway by an additional thunderclap from the Buntline revolver and an additional jagged hole in the one pound can of Flying Dutchman aromatic tobacco. Rounds four and five from Mr. Musselwhite's .22-caliber single-action Savage found out a two liter Truade and a slab of salt pork respectively and the Buntline revolver responded with some wholesale destruction to the cigarette rack which left two bullets altogether and Mr. Musselwhite squandered his on a cantaloupe while the tall, lean, pointy, hollowed out, angular, and otherwise unremarkable culprit fled with his to the door before discharging it full into Mr. Musselwhite's gasoline pump control box which did not please Mr. Musselwhite much and he returned fire with an indelicate and near about searing obscenity that was the closest thing he had to a bullet.

Evander Clark II had heard the shots but had not known they were shots since he had not ever been exposed to any real-life gunfire previously, and he had seen the culprit but had not actually looked at the culprit on account of how he was not in the habit of studying and looking at people but preferred to allow them to ponder and contemplate him without the worry of getting caught at it. Consequently Evander Clark II was vaguely aware of some noise and was vaguely aware of some activity roundabout the doorway but had not become truly and clearly aware of anything really until the gaspump shut down which he went ahead and noticed outright just as Mr. Musselwhite stepped out from the converted muleshed in a fit of wild and frantic profanation directed first around the left front corner of the building and then around the right front corner and finally on up among the hillocks and creases of the pasture which the tall, lean, pointy, hollowed out, angular, and otherwise unremarkable culprit apparently had escaped into. Of course Evander Clark II, who had paid cash money for seventeen dollars' worth of Citgo regular, wanted to know straight off just precisely why the pump had shut down at only thirteen dollars and twenty-eight cents and so he set out around the converted muleshed and hunted up Mr. Musselwhite who was still venting himself towards the hillside when Evander Clark II caught up with him and quizzed him on the gaspump and quizzed him on the remaining three dollars and seventy-two cents' worth of Citgo regular and generally made himself suitably impertinent and intolerable about the entire business until Mr. Musselwhite turned full around to look at him and so revealed in his hand the .22-caliber single-action Savage revolver which captured a goodly portion of Evander Clark II's attention.

"You get a look at him?" Mr. Musselwhite wanted to know.

"At who?" Evander Clark II said somewhat to Mr. Musselwhite but primarily to his pistol.

"That shitass come running out the door," Mr. Musselwhite told him. "You saw him didn't you?"

"I saw somebody," Evander Clark II said, "but I wasn't paying much attention."

"Didn't you hear the gunfire, boy?"

"Is that what that was?"

"Christ Almighty son, me and your momma near about got shot to pieces."

"Shot to pieces!" Evander Clark II said and grew somewhat wild and frantic himself.

"Don't worry, she's all right," Mr. Musselwhite told him. "I mean she ain't exactly all right but she's like she was when she come in, don't you know. I mean it weren't no harm but it weren't no cure either."

Mr. Musselwhite called the sheriff's office but the sheriff was out on official business which likely meant parking violations or some such so Mr. Musselwhite left word of the attempted robbery with Miss Hawkes who worked the switchboard and he made a point to tell her, "Shots were fired," which was how they said it on television whenever shots were fired and consequently the sheriff arrived presently, or probably more shortly than presently and maybe even straightaway propelled as he was by the prospect of gunfire and bodily injury, and he came squealing and skidding to a halt before the converted muleshed and rushed on inside where he did not greet anybody exactly but approached Mr. Musselwhite right off and said, "Square teeth? Pointy nose? Sunk-in eyes? Tall?"

"Tall what?" Mr. Musselwhite asked him.

"Just plain tall, six foot something or another."

And Mr. Musselwhite nodded yes sir.

"That's our boy," the sheriff told him and he turned to Mrs. Buffaloe off his right shoulder and said, "I knew he'd show up. I had it all mapped and figured."

And Mrs. Buffaloe blinked her eyes and dropped her chin some and asked him, "Evander?"

And the sheriff took ahold of Evander Clark II by the sleeve and said to him, "Son, do something with this woman."

Sheriff Burton got most of the pertinent facts himself from Mr. Musselwhite and collected a slight bit of trifling and vague information from Evander Clark II prior to turning the scene of the crime over to his deputy Mr. Larson who fished around for some facts himself and dug in the walls with his knife after the bullets and drank a Pepsi and drank a root beer and ate a peach dumpling and then lamented with Mr. Musselwhite on the hole in his cash register and the holes in his tobacco tin and the holes in his cigarette rack and in his cantaloupe and his slab of fatback and together they collected by the milky fragments of carnival glass and tried to make them into the serving bowl that they had been previously but could not. Sheriff Burton rode the perimeters of Mr. Musselwhite's pasture in his patrol car and stopped at whatever houses or solitary individuals he came up on to ask information which he did not get much of any of except from a Carothers who had been grubbing rocks in a potato field the most of the day who had possibly seen somebody, maybe even a square toothed, pointy nosed, sunken eyed, just plain tall somebody though he could not be certain and maybe it was in the pine thicket along the northern border of his field though he could not be certain of that either but the sheriff crept and snuck and generally stepped lightly into the undergrowth anyway with the heel of his right hand on the simulated pearl handle of his nickel-plated .357 service revolver, and when he got into the midsts of the pine grove where there was not any undergrowth but just needles and pine treetrunks and some bright and some shadowy places he drew his gun and cocked it which he did not get to do much except in the evenings in Mrs. Messick's upstairs, and once he'd stayed in the pine thicket long enough to satisfy himself that he had stayed in the pine thicket long enough he backed out around the treetrunks and through the undergrowth and into the potato field again convinced that the somebody the Carothers had possibly seen possibly in the pine thicket was not there any longer if he'd ever been there in the first place, and the Sheriff rode the perimeters of Mr. Musselwhite's property all over again and rode the perimeters of Mr. Musselwhite's neighbors' property also and struck out in a generally northwest direction for a ways but did not discover anything of significance and so at last returned along the boulevard to the square and to his office and to the map on his back office wall which he stuck a new yellowheaded thumbtack in and a new silverheaded thumbtack in prior to laying back in his office chair, throwing his feet across one corner of his desktop, and telling himself, "Busick in Draper, McIver in Harrison Crossroads, Barnard in Bethel, Grissom in Locust Hill, Stem in Union Ridge, Troutman in Altamahaw, Ross in Hillsdale, Spencer in Midway, Musselwhite in Neely," and then he pinched his bottom lip between his thumb and forefinger and pondered and speculated and eventually told himself, "$147.00 and $189.00 and $123.00 and $155.00 and $78.00 and $230.00 and $112.00 and $150.00 and no dollars at all," and then without setting his feet to the floor or raising himself from his chair on account of he had learned and memorized them too he went ahead and told himself, "Corinth and Duncan and Wilbon and Angier and Holly Springs and Kipling and Fuquay-Varina and Lemly and Merry Oaks," and he let loose of his lip which he had continued to pinch all throughout his pondering and his speculating and he raised his lip holding hand up above his head and then smacked it down on the desktop and told himself, "Hotdamn."

The first one arrived along about October in a pink envelope and the fat Jeeter carried it from the trailer down to the chickenhouse where she gave it over to Mr. Raeford Lynch who sniffed at it and yipped once or twice and then sniffed at it again prior to giving it over to Benton Lynch who did not sniff at it or even look at it really but put it direct in his jacket pocket over the protests of his momma and the protests of his daddy who wanted to know was it a serious affection and who wanted to know did she come from nice people and who wanted to know when did it start up in the first place and who wanted to know could they meet her sometime presently to all of which Benton Lynch responded with a couple of yeses and a couple of noes and nothing much else of any utility to the fat Jeeter and nothing much else of any utility to Mr. Raeford either who chiefly was desirous to learn did Benton Lynch get some and so asked him straightaway once the fat Jeeter had struck out up the hillside and he was all set to wonder how if it was yes and to wonder why not if it was no, but it was not yes or no, was not anything but the usual vacant expression, and Mr. Raeford grew anxious and restless on account of having pondered the topic in the first place and so spat on a chicken to distract and relieve himself some.

Benton Lynch carried the pink envelope off into the woods to open it and sat down under a sweetgum tree where he extracted the pages but did not study them straight off on account of how Jane Elizabeth Firesheets had enclosed a dose of her personal scent along with them and the aroma took hold of Benton Lynch and caused him to recollect in considerable detail the milky whiteness and the plum-colored parts also, particularly the plum-colored parts, and he remembered the funny little way she had to gyrating and squirming and bouncing about and consequently he had to stand up and adjust himself in his trousers before proceeding with the actual words on the actual pages which did not convey much in the way of news or ordinary information either but took the form of questions primarily, questions about himself and about what he was doing and about who he was doing it with and about what sort of weather they were doing it in. There was some little passing reference to Chalybeate Springs and the daddy Firesheets's prospects as a tobacco farmer and slight scandalous mention of the brother Firesheets, who Jane Elizabeth did not seem to have developed a fondness for, followed by a sweltering conclusion which dealt in rather specific detail with precisely what Jane Elizabeth Firesheets would do to Benton Lynch if she could get her fingers on the parts of him she would do it to, and though Benton

Lynch had experienced precisely that sort of therapy on several previous occasions and had seen any number of photographs of the undertaking in progress on the backs of his cousin Jerome Lynch's playing cards, he had never read it in words before and was prompted to stand up all over again and adjust himself once he realized how mighty the pen could be.

Benton Lynch did not write back straightaway mostly because he did not have any idea of exactly what to write since there was not anything he wanted to know and there was not anything he wanted to tell and since there was not anything at all he desired of Jane Elizabeth Firesheets that could be satisfied in a correspondence. And once he did not write back straightaway and once he continued to not write back he received a second pink envelope which contained a heavily scented letter of its own which itself was as thoroughly inquisitive as the previous one though perhaps more pointedly so. Jane Elizabeth Firesheets wanted to know who he was seeing and what he was doing with her and she wished to inform him that if he was in fact doing something with somebody she would go ahead and end it all, meaning herself primarily. Consequently, Benton Lynch decided he'd best sit down and write a letter anyhow even though there still was not anything he wanted to know and not much of anything he wanted to say except for a denial of the something he was accused of doing with somebody and only that so as to keep the milky parts and the plum-colored parts also from any sort of untimely ruin. He did not have much practice at letter writing since he had not ever written but one and that not an actual and verifiable letter really but more towards your note variety to his Aunt Vergie Lynch Newcombe, wife of the jackleg pentecostal preacher, thanking her for the argyle socks she sent to him on his fourteenth birthday, and the fat Jeeter had dictated the whole business to him so in truth he had not ever conceived and executed even a note which rendered the prospect of an actual and verifiable letter all the more overpowering. He sat down to write it a variety of times and locations, first of a morning in the chickenhouse but his daddy and the chickens would not give him the peace to accomplish much, and then of an afternoon at the dinette but he found himself distracted by the television and the crackle and rattle of the graham cracker wrapper along with the inquiries of the fat Jeeter at the commercials when she'd want to know was it a serious affection and did she come from nice people and when did it start up in the first place and could she meet her sometime presently. He made some slight headway of an evening after supper under the sweetgum tree where he laid his solitary leaf of paper across his thigh and single-handedly constructed the salutation which was not precisely in the spirit of the Dear Sweetheart that came in the pink envelopes but was more along the lines of a plain Dear Jane Elizabeth Firesheets which still had some warmth to it and about as much outright treacle as Benton Lynch could muster. He managed an opening few lines in the how are you I am fine vein of personal correspondence and surprised himself with an extended flurry of weather talk and speculation prior to running dry which gave him the occasion to chew on his pencil and gnaw on a stick and suck on a weed and toss a sweetgum ball in the air.

He finished the letter four days after he'd started the letter and even then it barely surpassed the argyle socks note in overall length and hardly approached it in substance but somehow or another Benton Lynch did manage to suggest and imply while attempting to state outright that he was not doing anything with anybody, that he did not know anybody to do anything with, and that even if he did know somebody who was willing to do something the something they would do likely could not even begin to measure up with the something him and Jane Elizabeth Firesheets had done previously the pleasant recollection of which prevented Benton Lynch from attempting the same something with anybody else, that is if he could find anybody else to attempt the same something with him, on account of how he was satisfied in his own mind that nobody anywhere could do anything the way Jane Elizabeth Firesheets could do it.

Jane Elizabeth Firesheets herself shot back a pink-enveloped reply to Benton Lynch's argyle-socks-note-length letter bearing the news that she had decided not to end it all since Benton Lynch had made his feelings for her more plain and open and as a token of her undying passion and regard she enclosed in a piece of Saran Wrap a lock of wheatstraw hair she'd clipped herself and Benton Lynch held it up between his fingers and studied it all over but could not determine from where exactly. The correspondence proceeded thereafter somewhat briskly on the pink-enveloped end of it and a little less briskly but with considerable regularity on the note-length end of it and carried on throughout the fall of the year and into winter when Benton Lynch received, along with his usual pink envelope, a tin of Christmas cookies which Jane Elizabeth Firesheets had baked herself and which he did not discover even a solitary strand of stray wheatstraw hair in. His momma bought for him at the drugstore a plastic hairclip that he stuck in his subsequent note-length letter and in her reply Jane Elizabeth Firesheets managed to pass into pure raptures over it like maybe Benton Lynch had not merely mailed it but had possibly conceived of a necessity and an application for the thing and so had gone ahead and invented it himself. But not the sight of the pink envelope or the Dear Sweetheart or the pure raptures or even the somewhat sultry and provocative talk at the close, which had become a regular feature of Jane Elizabeth Firesheets's correspondence, stirred Benton Lynch much by the time January came around on account of how his lengthy separation from the milky white contours and the plum-colored features also had caused his affections to fade considerably which he realized foremost in his trousers where there was not much cause for adjustment any longer. When an oversized pink envelope arrived the second weekend in February, Benton Lynch did not bother to open it for two days and when he did bother to open it at last he just read the first of it and the end of it and did not ever read the middle of it since by the second weekend in February there was not cause for any adjustment any longer and Benton Lynch recollected the milky contours and the plum-colored features only dimly when he attempted to recollect them at all.

The first week in March all the Firesheetses together picked up and moved to Chalybeate Springs where they took up residence in what Jane Elizabeth Firesheets called a cottage, and she provided in a pink envelope an extended description of the area roundabout that Benton Lynch read half of since by the first week in March he did not have any affection at all for Jane Elizabeth Firesheets, at least not any that he could discover, so he did not send off an argyle-socks-note-length reply to the Chalybeate Springs travelogue letter, and when the second pink envelope of March showed up on the dinette with the premium notice and the pizza coupons Benton Lynch was not excited like he had been excited previously and was not embarrassed like he had been embarrassed previously but was just plain annoyed like he had not been annoyed before. He could not comprehend, could not even begin to fathom, why he had ever felt at all strongly about the milky whiteness and the plum-colored parts also and at a distance of some months he could not say truly just what had made the pond-bank therapeutics so savory and attractive to him. He had trouble rec-ollecting what Jane Elizabeth Firesheets even looked like exactly and he did not think of her at all for days at a time and so had fairly com-pletely returned to his natural pointy, gangly, toothsome, and pri-marily vacant state and likely Benton Lynch, who mostly simply was not previously, would have become entirely unblatant and completely unoutright all over again if not for Jimmy, just plain Jimmy, who showed up in the third pink envelope of March right there at the outset of a sentence. "Jimmy," it said, "helped Daddy shore up the porch floor," and since Jimmy was not the brother Firesheets and was not the granddaddy Firesheets and was not the uncle Firesheets as far as Benton Lynch could tell, that left him to be somebody else, some-body else who had not gotten mentioned previously on the page and did not get explained subsequently on the page and so was construed to be a mysterious somebody else, maybe a neighbor and perhaps even a relation, but surely a male somebody else and so naturally equipped for therapeutics and modest acrobatics and any other activity per-formable on a pondbank in addition to watching a cork bobber.

In the fourth pink envelope of March, which was the last pink en-velope of March, Jimmy cut a dead limb off a hickory tree with his chainsaw and got asked to supper, which was somewhat of an ad-vancement from shoring up porch flooring, but he still did not get explained sufficiently, or not sufficiently anyway to entirely satisfy Benton Lynch who had figured for a while he was entirely satisfied but then discovered that he wasn't, so the fourth pink envelope of March, which was the last pink envelope of March, got answered with a letter that in sheer bulk and magnitude far outstripped anything Benton Lynch had ever before accomplished with a pencil. He made some trifling statements, asked several dull and harmless questions, ventured on a serious observation or two, and threw in a couple of veiled inquiries as to the identity and motives of the Jimmy in question, highly veiled inquiries, so highly veiled in fact as to be senseless and impenetrable, and consequently the first pink envelope of April did not supply Benton Lynch with any satisfying information about the Jimmy in question except that he tarred around the cottage chimney and made the granddaddy Firesheets a walking stick from a portion of rhododendron stalk which was pertinent maybe and illuminating to a degree but not at all satisfying to Benton Lynch who was only just coming to realize how extremely dissatisfied he was.

Mostly he hadn't ever been anything previously, not dissatisfied or satisfied either and certainly not troubled and impassioned on account of a woman, or on account of those parts of a woman that men generally get troubled and impassioned on account of which is not usually the intellect or the sense of humor or any little portion of the rest of the temperment but most generally falls in the category of milky white parts and plum-colored parts also. And in his particular case Benton Lynch had not had the occasion to anticipate and desire and long for free run over Jane Elizabeth Firesheets's milky white and plum-colored parts since he had gotten it even before he knew he wanted it and so was pressed to work up an appetite after the meal had already commenced which somehow he accomplished with measurable and thoroughgoing success. But ever since January when the recollection of Jane Elizabeth Firesheets's chief attributes—which would be the pointy and prominent portions of her upper torso and the flexible and gyrating portions of her lower torso—had commenced to fade from Benton Lynch's consciousness and from his trousers also he had not been much troubled and impassioned and not much dissatisfied either, and likely he would have remained untroubled and unimpassioned and undissatisfied if not for the Jimmy of Chalybeate Springs who shored up porch flooring and cut hickory limbs and ate supper and tarred chimneys and made rhododendron walking sticks and who possibly as well got some access to those parts of Jane Elizabeth Firesheets that Benton Lynch himself had touched with his own fingers and who possibly got some access also to those parts that Benton Lynch himself had examined otherwise. Consequently, it was not really his absence from Jane Elizabeth Firesheets's chief attributes that troubled Benton Lynch so but was more truly the likelihood or the suspicion or maybe just the vague and bothersome notion that the milky white and plum-colored parts, which had been his entirely, were not his entirely any longer, so naturally Benton Lynch, who had never been much of anything before, began to be a jackass.

The first week in April he wrote Jane Elizabeth Firesheets the second in what would be a series of fairly massive and magnitudinous letters, and unlike the first of the massive and magnitudinous letters in which Benton Lynch exhausted a sizable piece of being trifling and dull and harmless, he went direct to inquisitive in the second one, or direct to inquisitive following the Dear Sweetheart anyway, and he came straight out with some questions and some accusations and a palpable threat or two and then dispatched the thing and waited in an agitated state for a reply, which was extraordinary and novel for Benton Lynch since he had never been in an agitated state previously, but he did not get soothed much when the first pink envelope of April did at last arrive on account of how Jane Elizabeth Firesheets failed to confirm much of anything and failed to deny much of anything and failed to say much of anything substantial except for "Jimmy" when she told how he'd clipped the bushes and glazed a window and puttied up a hole in the wall, and even though clipping and glazing and puttying aren't your usual intimate activities the idea of Jimmy in the shrubbery and Jimmy at the windowlight and Jimmy in the very bowels of the cottage with his spackling and his knife seared and agonized Benton Lynch like so many firecoals and so it was in a wounded and tormented state that he sent out the third in the series of fairly massive and magnitudinous letters, and since he was not accustomed to being wounded and was not accustomed to being tormented he failed to stir any sympathy to speak of in Jane Elizabeth Firesheets who did not reply immediately to the third massive and magnitudinous letter and so got a fourth one straightaway since Benton Lynch figured the third one had got misplaced or misrouted or had maybe got read and misinterpreted, and though he commenced the fourth massive and magnitudinous letter in the same wounded and tormented state that had carried him through the third one he managed to become purely frantic along about the midway point prior to lapsing into a truly pathetic lament that culminated in the love and kisses and the jagged indecipherable scrawl beneath it.

Jane Elizabeth Firesheets did in fact answer the fourth massive and magnitudinous letter, or actually did in fact answer the third massive and magnitudinous letter but not until she'd already received the fourth one, and in her reply she admitted to harboring an affection for the Jimmy of Chalybeate Springs, and though for the sake of Benton Lynch's wounded and tormented feelings she did not cleanly admit to having harbored anything else for him, be it on a pondbank or in a grassy clearing or maybe even in a bed somewhere, Benton Lynch well enough comprehended the implications and well enough comprehended the open admission and while he managed to persevere through Jane Elizabeth Firesheet's explanation of natural juices and savage passionate urges, he was not comforted by it much and felt instead like he'd been sliced open with a handscythe and left to die. The fat Jeeter and Mr. Raeford Lynch, especially Mr. Raeford Lynch, could not fully understand how their boy could be hollowed out and pointy and angular and vacant like usual one week and then agitated and tormented and wounded and frantic and pathetic and plainly agonized the next, and they were beginning to grow concerned, or actually it was the fat Jeeter who was beginning to grow concerned and who had suggested to Mr. Raeford Lynch that he'd best begin to grow concerned also, which he had himself begun to do on account of the general sway the fat Jeeter's suggestions held with him, when Benton Lynch up and departed in the first week of the month of May, which would have been the May of the spring before the summer we lost the bald Jeeter, and not even with a sack this time or any shirts except for the one on him and with hardly any notion of just where he was going aside from the name of the place which he told to the man that picked him up on the highway who threw his car in gear and asked him, "What?"

Likely he would have arrived at Chalybeate Springs sooner than he did arrive there if he'd had any idea where it was, which he didn't, or if anybody that picked him up had had any idea where it was, which they didn't either, so he toured several southeastern counties in an assortment of vehicles and with a great variety of people and almost entirely without incident except for the marine from Fayetteville who desired Benton Lynch to render him a service which Benton Lynch was neither inclined nor oriented to render nor could even accurately imagine for that matter. He did not actually get to the cottage until nightfall and only then after some exhaustive inquiring which Benton Lynch was not much accomplished at since he preferred yeses and noes to all other forms of human communication, and by the time he did arrive at the cottage it had already stopped being a cottage or maybe had not yet become a cottage entirely because it appeared a shack instead that maybe had been a cottage once or maybe would be a cottage presently but would have to stop being a hovel first which it truly was but got flattered and elevated by the darkness.

He did not knock on the door straightaway but lingered under an ivy-laden chinaberry tree in the corner of the frontyard for a while and looked in the windows where he could see the granddaddy Firesheets talking at the daddy Firesheets and on occasion getting talked at back and where he could every now and again get a glimpse of the momma Firesheets and the brother Firesheets and for one fleeting moment a piece of Jane Elizabeth Firesheets's wheatstraw hair which gave him the nervous stomach and so instead of stepping up onto the cottage porch and knocking on the cottage door, Benton Lynch circled round to the backyard and hunted up the outhouse which he got caught making use of by the brother Firesheets who near about sat down on top of him. They were pleased to see him in the majority; even the brother Firesheets himself gave Benton Lynch a suitable greeting once he'd recovered from his own case of the nervous stomach which he had contracted at the outhouse and remedied there also. The momma Firesheets offered him a hunk of spongecake and the daddy Firesheets offered him a chair and the granddaddy Firesheets offered him an opinion as to the perils of hitchhiking in the modern day and the brother Firesheets offered him an apology for having near about sat his bare bottom down on Benton Lynch's bare topside.

As for Jane Elizabeth Firesheets, she hung back noticeably from the conversation in general and hung back noticeably from Benton Lynch's person in particular and could not be encouraged to be sociable by her mother who attempted to encourage her and by her daddy who attempted to encourage her and by her granddaddy who attempted to encourage her and even by her brother who endeavored to badger and insult her into an outburst. She simply would not have anything much to do with Benton Lynch and did not appear at all pleased to see him and exhibited her displeasure in a dark corner of the room where she sulked and brooded and just generally failed to enliven to talk any. The granddaddy Firesheets recollected one by one every Lynch he'd ever met up with in every place he'd ever been to and quizzed Benton Lynch on his relation to them, and when he was able to in between Lynches, the daddy Firesheets probed and sounded out Benton Lynch's knowledge of tobacco and tobacco farming. The momma Firesheets hoped out loud that Benton Lynch was enjoying the spongecake which Benton Lynch told her yes ma'm he was and the brother Firesheets called his sister a twatheaded moron in an attempt to fire her up some which judging from the sudden separation of her bottom lip for her top lip he succeeded at and likely she would have offered up some sort of utterance or another if not for her granddaddy who recollected a whole load of Lynches in Zebulon and wanted to know from Benton Lynch where they his Lynches or not.

They could not offer him a place to sleep in the house on account of it was a cottage-sized house or a shack-sized hovel, depending on the light, and so instead they offered him a place to sleep in the barn which was a regular barn-sized barn with the usual haysmell and manurestink and ammonia pockets, and he stepped off the backporch and struck out across the yard in the company of Jane Elizabeth Firesheets who carried a blanket over one arm and a quilt over the other and who had not been much enthused at the prospect of leading Benton Lynch across the yard to the regular barn-sized barn but had been encouraged to do so by her granddaddy and her momma and flat out directed to do so by her daddy and so did so, or was in the process of doing so anyhow midway between the porch and the barn when Benton Lynch snatcher her by the elbow and spun her around to face him and probably would have said some sort of fiery thing to her if he had not used up the best part of his passion and agitation in the snatching and the spinning and so could only ponder her in a helpless and pathetic sort of way and got pondered back briefly prior to getting snapped and hissed at.

"What are you doing here?" Jane Elizabeth Firesheets wanted to know.

"It's May," Benton Lynch told her. "We said May. You said May."

"Well it's all different now," she said. "That was then and this is now, and it's all different," and she tried to turn around and set back out towards the barn but Benton Lynch snatched her by the elbow again and spun her to him.

"Why's it all different?" he asked her.

"It just is."

And Jane Elizabeth Firesheets did spin around successfully and did set back out towards the barn and would have gone ahead and arrived there if Benton Lynch had not said, "Jimmy?" just plain Jimmy in a flatout spiteful sort of way which stopped Jane Elizabeth Firesheets where she was and very nearly spun her around all over again but not quite, so instead she addressed Benton Lynch with her backside primarily and advised him against any hasty and ill-considered judgments on account of how he would be talking about the man she loved.

"Him?" Benton Lynch said.

"He is my soulmate," Jane Elizabeth Firesheets told him.

"Your soulmate?" Benton Lynch said, openly perplexed.

And regardless of just who she was telling it to, Jane Elizabeth Firesheets turned around with her face all opened up in a grin and said, "He's a regular prince," and she closed up the gap between herself and Benton Lynch that she had only recently opened up and with her mouth still laid full out she told him, "Jimmy says me and him's like gears in a machine, not neither one of us any good without the other. Appears to me he's got the poet in his blood, don't you think?" And though it had not seemed physically possible for Jane Elizabeth Firesheets to grin any more completely than she was grinning already, the points of her mouth went ahead and disappeared around her jawbones.

Benton Lynch could not rein in his agitation and torment straightaway, but that did not matter much on account of how Jane Elizabeth Firesheets's personal euphoria kept her from noticing the agitation and kept her from noticing the torment, near about kept her from noticing any little part of Benton Lynch or big part either, so he had the leisure to collect and gather up his composure and when the fit had passed and he felt reasonably unagitated and untormented again, he said to Jane Elizabeth Firesheets, "I figured me and you was like gears in a machine. I figured we wasn't not neither one of us any good without the other."

"Oh, Benton," Jane Elizabeth Firesheets said and freed her right arm from the blanket so as to touch Benton Lynch with the tipends of her fingers, "we didn't have nothing much but a night or two and now it's all a fond recollection that will fade and dwindle like all rec-ollections do. Jimmy says that," Jane Elizabeth Firesheets added and very gently drew her fingers along Benton Lynch's forearm which did not serve to aid the fading any and certainly not the dwindling. "We should be grateful," she said, "we should be grateful and satisfied that such a lovely thing happened between us."

And Benton Lynch reached out with his hand and laid it on a par-ticular part of Jane Elizabeth Firesheets thereby indicating he'd be even more grateful and more satisfied if the lovely thing that had happened between them previously would happen between them again, at least once anyhow, but Jane Elizabeth Firesheets backed out from under his fingers and out from under his palm and told him it would be a dangerous and most likely lethal activity from Benton Lynch on account of how Jimmy simply adored her and would most undoubtedly commit murder if he only found out Benton Lynch had put his hand where he had put it.

"Well, if he adores you so much, where is he then?" Benton Lynch asked her, and Jane Elizabeth Firesheets said something low and indecipherable so Benton Lynch asked her, "Huh?" and waited with his arms crossed over himself.

"He's occupied," Jane Elizabeth Firesheets told him.

"Occupied where?" Benton Lynch wanted to know.

And Jane Elizabeth Firesheets blew out a breath and said, "Jimmy's thirty days in the lockup. Mr. Merit down the road here, Jimmy hit him with a prybar. Weren't no fault of Jimmy's, they was both drinking and got to bickering about some money Mr. Merit said he'd let out to Jimmy that he never did and Jimmy told him he never did and Mr. Merit said he was a damned liar and well Jimmy just don't have a tolerance when it comes to getting told he's one damned thing or another damned thing and so he hit him with a prybar which was handy at the time but didn't even hit him flush, just kind of bounced the flat part of it off Mr. Merit's left ear and he says he's got damage and his doctor at the clinic, who's likely in with him, says he got damage too and so Jimmy's in the lockup thirty days."

"Don't sound no count to me," Benton Lynch observed.

"He's a saint," Jane Elizabeth Firesheets said and grew huffy of a sudden.

And Benton Lynch told her, "Ha!" which he'd never had the occasion to tell anybody before but which he found gave him a pleasant and satisfying feeling when he told it to Jane Elizabeth Firesheets.

"Well then," she replied, "if you're going to be nasty I just won't have a thing to do with you."

"Don't then," Benton Lynch told her.

"I won't," she said and flailed at Benton Lynch with the blanket just prior to flailing at him with the quilt. "Make your own bed and lie in it your own self," she told him and fired out towards the house in what had all the trappings of a wiry tattooed white boy fit of pique, and Benton Lynch hurled a second "Ha!" behind her and then a third one and stood in the middle of the yard and watched the door slam shut and the porchlight go out.

They offered him his sleeping place in the barn and what the granddaddy called three squares and a toddy in exchange for general labor, or anyhow the granddaddy Firesheets and the daddy Firesheets and the momma Firesheets and the brother Firesheets offered him the sleeping place and offered him the three squares and the toddy while Jane Elizabeth Firesheets offered him little of anything or more truly nothing whatsoever except for the hard looks and the exasperated exhalations. Straightoff the general labor turned out to be singular and specific labor at least for a week or two when Benton Lynch and the granddaddy Firesheets and the daddy Firesheets and the brother Firesheets along with the uncle Firesheets, who would be W. P. Firesheets, and the uncle Firesheets's boy, who would be W. P. Firesheets also but did not get called W.P., did not actually get called anything in particular, all worked together setting out the tobacco by hand on account of how W. P. Firesheets, the one that got called it, did not own a mechanized setter, was not about to rent one out for money, and could not fine one to borrow either. So they strung gunnysacks over their shoulders and carried sticks to poke with and bent over and raised up what seemed five or six hundred times a day for at least a week or two, or anyhow for as long as it took to plant the twelve acre patch down in the W. P. Firesheets's rocky bottom and the five acre patch between his house and the hedgerow on the north boundary. Then of course there was the wheatstraw to cut and bale and get in before the rain came which they wished on the tobacco but wished off the wheatstraw at the same time, so the W. P. Firesheets paid actual rent money for a mower and a baler and his boy towed the first one and he towed the second one and the daddy Firesheets followed up the both of them with the flatbed trailer that the brother Firesheets and Benton Lynch tossed the bales onto where the granddaddy Firesheets stacked them when he was not pitching about and falling over from the swells and dips in the hayfield.

The women cooked the lunch every day and served it out back of the uncle Firesheets's house on the concrete welltop and every once and again Jane Elizabeth Firesheets would put together a batch of her potato salad which Benton Lynch would attempt to praise extravagantly although he had no background to speak of in extravagant praising or even moderate or negligible praising either, so the ain't this simply delicious that showed up every time the potato salad did had no favorable effect on Jane Elizabeth Firesheets who was preoccupied in counting down the days of the month to the twenty-seventh when what was in the lockup would get turned loose on Chalybeate Springs again, and probably Jane Eliabeth Firesheets would have continued to be preoccupied and would have continued to shun and ignore Benton Lynch, no matter how much potato salad he could choke down, if she had not got sent out with the garbage on the early evening of the twenty-second which was just a scant five days from the twenty-seventh or four days really if you went ahead and counted the evening of the twenty-second as the twenty-third, which Jane Elizabeth Firesheets went ahead and did. She was on her way to the garbage can and was not intending to go anywhere after the garbage can but back to the house. However, in the normal course of looking around the yard she happened to spy on Benton Lynch between the slats in the barnwall and it appeared to her he was either taking off some clothes that he had on or putting on some clothes that he didn't and naturally she found herself interested in the proceedings in an idle and curious sort of way so she stepped on over to the barn, which was a trifle northeast of the house but not so far northeast of the house as to be out of the way back to it, and lingered at the middle of the barnwall where the slats did not meet so well as they met at the corners.

Benton Lynch was just coming out of his underwear when Jane Elizabeth Firesheets got her eyes focused sufficiently to see what was what and he threw his briefs on the floor atop his shirt and his pants and his socks and stretched and scratched himself prior to fetching off a nail on the wall the trousers he'd borrowed from the brother Firesheets which he shook the dust out of and put one foot in before he decided he'd not quite had his spate of scratching or stretching either but scratching mostly and so he took himself up in his fingers all over again. Jane Elizabeth Firesheets watched the whole business with what she told herself was strictly a clinical fascination and she paid particular attention to Benton Lynch's equipment which she had never before observed when it was not at least somewhat agitated and astir. She studied the way it hung ever so loosely and flopped and laid about in Benton Lynch's hand and the sad and sorry spectacle of Benton Lynch's virility drooping between his fingers roused up the therapist in her and she slipped along the barnwall to the barndoor and stuck her head around the jamb of it and said, "Hey."

Naturally out of reflex Benton Lynch attempted to cover himself with the brother Firesheets's trousers and he succeeded temporarily, succeeded anyway until Jane Elizabeth Firesheets crossed the planking and stopped herself directly in front of him where he could smell the smell of her and even in the dimness could see enough of the milky white parts to remind him of the plum-colored parts, and it was likely the recollection of the plum-colored parts in combination with the sight of the milky white parts and the smell of the smell that caused what had been hanging ever so loosely and flopping and laying about to raise up and salute and thereby become the kind of animal that a pair of trousers could not hide but certainly could have hung from. Of course once the brother Firesheets's pants commenced to levitate, the merciful and therapeutic side of Jane Elizabeth Firesheets more truly asserted itself since Benton Lynch's equipment had assumed what was to her mind its native condition and she took the trousers in hand prior to taking in hand the equipment itself while Benton Lynch, who had never before fainted or been especially prone to queasiness, got all pale and goose-pimply at the touch of her finger and figured he would surely drop into a pile on the barnfloor. But he managed not to somehow and instead reached out his hand and laid it on a particular part of Jane Elizabeth Firesheets and this time she did not back out from under his fingers and out from under his palm but ooohed a little and aaahed some and exhaled in an entirely unexasperated sort of way.

They laid down side by side on top of the quilt and on top of the blanket and Benton Lynch helped Jane Elizabeth Firesheets out of her shirt and out of her gauzy brassiere and out of her tiny shorts and her scant red panties and then studied and examined her actual plum-colored parts with some considerable intensity, and anyhow studied and examined them until Jane Elizabeth Firesheets removed herself to the lower reaches of Benton Lynch's person so as to have a word with his equipment, and the confab which transpired probably would have dropped Benton Lynch into a pile on the floor if he had not been in a pile on the floor already. At the earnest insistence of Jane Elizabeth Firesheets, Benton Lynch presently took his turn communicating with her lower reaches, after which she and him together allowed their lower reaches to mingle and chat with each other prior to striking up what appeared to be a a fairly frantic debate with equally gracious amounts of give and take. Benton Lynch got satisfied straightaway, got satisfied entirely too straightaway as far as Jane Elizabeth Firesheets was concerned and she demanded that she have the opportunity to get satisfied herself and consequently Benton Lynch rolled over and played dead on his backside while Jane Elizabeth Firesheets bounced and gyrated on his frontside until she did in fact get satisfied or anyway until she did in fact hoot once and fall over in a sweaty heap.

So then they laid there together all hot and winded with Jane Elizabeth Firesheets stretched out frontupwards looking at the barnloft and Benton Lynch stretched out side upwards looking at the plum-colored parts, which he had not been able to contemplate lately, and the mere sight of the plum-colored parts all dilated and upright commenced to stir and agitate Benton Lynch afresh and so put him in favor of reopening the channels of communication and he was on his way to becoming truly fossilized all over again when Jane Elizabeth Firesheets blew out a breath and said she guessed she would have to tell Jimmy just exactly what went on, guessed it would be the fair and proper thing to do, guessed she would not ever rest easy again until he knew all about it. Now this was not the sort of news to aid Benton Lynch's stark rigidity much, or fairly stark rigidity anyway, and it fell off to nothing directly once Benton Lynch had begun to imagine just what it might feel like to get hit with a prybar, even if only the flat side of a prybar bounced off his ear, and he went ahead and wondered out loud why Jane Elizabeth Firesheets felt compelled to mention their little dialogue to her Jimmy in the lockup since he surely would not ever find out about it otherwise.

"Because," she told him, "truth is the very cornerstone of Romance. Jimmy says that."

And Benton Lynch suggested that maybe she could not tell him anything, which would be very much like telling the truth, or anyway would not be same as lying, but Jane Elizabeth Firesheets sat up on her elbow and told him again that truth was the very cornerstone of Romance, "the whole truth and nothing but the truth," she added in a grave and sanctimonious sort of way, and so Benton Lynch suggested that maybe she could go ahead and tell him just what she'd done and just when she'd done it but not exactly who she'd done it with, and Jane Elizabeth Firesheets did not say anything grave or sanctimonious but shook her head ever so slightly from side to side and thereby set Benton Lynch to wondering just what he might get for having laid his equipment where he'd laid it and so he asked Jane Elizabeth Firesheets, "What's gone happen to me?"

"Likely get killed," she told him. "Jimmy takes a hard view of this kind of thing."

"Then what's gone happen to you?" he asked her.

"Well," she said and laid her head back some, "I got charms can soothe the beast in him," and she dangled her tongue out one side of her mouth and raked her fingers across the flattest whitest part of her stomach prior to wrapping them clean around the noticeably faded and dwindled flower of Benton Lynch's manhood which got rejuvenated somewhat straightoff but not rejuvenated entirely.

"You mean nothing's gone happen to you but I'm gone get my head broke open?" Benton Lynch said.

And Jane Elizabeth Firesheets told him, "Likely he'll purely rip you all to pieces, but that's just his way. I mean Jimmy says you got to take life by the throat, can't just lay back and wait cause nothing comes to him that lays back and him that waits. So Jimmy says you got to take life by the throat and shake it hard, that's what Jimmy says. He says the world's his oyster. Jimmy don't bend to nobody, don't give way to nothing. Jimmy's a regular electrified dynamo, that what he says, and likely he'll purely rip you all to pieces, and likely he'd just as purely rip me all to pieces too except for what I can do for him that you can't hardly do for him, not that you ain't got your own charms sugarbunch," and Jane Elizabeth Firesheets struck in with some vigorous finger exercises which Benton Lynch appreciated but could not bring himself to truly enjoy on account of his predicament, and he told Jane Elizabeth Firesheets, "This ain't no time for that. I'm gone get killed."

And Jane Elizabeth Firesheets told him back, "It's likely," and once he'd rolled over so as to withdraw his participation Jane Elizabeth Firesheets said, "If that's how you want to be," and laid down flush on her backside.

Of course once Benton Lynch had withdrawn his participation and once Jane Elizabeth Firesheets had laid down flush on her backside Benton Lynch decided that if he was going to get ripped all to pieces anyhow he might as well be as guilty as he could manage to be and so he told Jane Elizabeth Firesheets he'd changed his mind and naturally she told him she'd changed hers too and he laid his private parts up next to her private parts and commenced to make some friction but Jane Elizabeth Firesheets told him, "No, this ain't no proper time for it," and Benton Lynch dropped the pointiest part of his face square down on the flattest whitest part of Jane Elizabeth Firesheets's stomach but Jane Elizabeth Firesheets told him, "No, I can't," and Benton Lynch reached out and took up the tipend of a plum-colored part between his thumb and forefinger and Jane Elizabeth Firesheets opened her mouth so as to say no she couldn't once more but nothing ever came out but plain air until the moaning and the hooting set in in earnest.

So they got together on the barnfloor the evening of the twenty-second, which Jane Elizabeth Firesheets was not so eager to count as the twenty-third any longer, and then they went ahead and got together on the evening of the actual twenty-third prior to the evening of the twenty-fourth when Jane Elizabeth Firesheets insisted they try it in the barnloft on account of how the altitude might have a stimulating effect and it did have a stimulating effect as far as Benton Lynch could tell or maybe it was just an exhausting effect due to the climbing up and the climbing down along with the burrowing around in the wheatstraw in between. On the afternoon of the twenty-fifth Jane Elizabeth Firesheets laid her nimble fingers on Benton Lynch's private parts in a blueberry thicket and the two of them got somewhat pricked and scored over in the ensuing scuffle but recovered by nightfall and hauled Benton Lynch's quilt and Benton Lynch's blanket out into the dewy grass under the starlight and whoever happened to be on the bottom at the time studied the constellations and the little sliver of moon in the southeast.

On the afternoon of the twenty-sixth Benton Lynch moved out of Jane Elizabeth Firesheets's daddy's barn and moved into Jane Elizabeth Firesheets's daddy's brother's barn so as to be out from under Jimmy in the lockup when he got turned out of the lockup at last, and he got turned out of the lockup at last on the morning of the twenty-seventh but by the early afternoon Benton Lynch still had not been purely ripped all to pieces and had not been purely ripped all to pieces by nightfall either and so half expected to wake up in little pulpy bits come morningtime but woke up unpulpy and unripped-up and fairly regular except for the apprehension and except for the dread which he carried around with him throughout the morning, on into the afternoon, and all the way to twilight when Jane Elizabeth Firesheets visited him in her daddy's brother's barn and confessed that maybe the whole truth and nothing but the truth was not exactly the cornerstone of romance when the health and well-being of such an organ as Benton Lynch possessed hung in the balance, and so she had not told Jimmy just what went on on the barnfloor and in the barnloft and in the blueberry thicket and on the dewy grass but had told him instead all about her pointy and angular and hollowed out and square toothed momma's sister's child since she figured Jimmy would not suspect that cousins would do with each other what Benton Lynch and Jane Elizabeth Firesheets had been doing with each other. And Benton Lynch was so excessively pleased at having the apprehension and the dread lifted from him that he offered to show Jane Elizabeth Firesheets the organ he possessed so as to demonstrate how openly grateful it was, but Jane Elizabeth Firesheets got testy straight off and said she had some scruples and principles if you please and so she settled for laying her fingers ever so briefly atop Benton Lynch's pantsleg.

He got introduced to Jimmy on the afternoon of the twenty-ninth while he was cutting brush with the daddy Firesheets and the brother Firesheets and the daddy Firesheets's brother along with the daddy Firesheets's brother's boy. Jimmy came round from his momma's house on the Fayetteville highway so as to lend some assistance, not any actual and helpful assistance really but mainly some verbal and fairly antagonizing assistance in the form of a Cut that bush yonder or Hack it higher or Hack it lower or Don't that just eat shit which seemed to be Jimmy's favorite expression probably on account of its far reaching and general application. He was not as tall as Benton Lynch, but then hardly anybody was so tall as Benton Lynch, and he was considerably thicker, but then most everybody was considerably thicker too. He breathed through his mouth primarily probably because his nose was flat where it had got caved in by something or another and his eyebrows joined together in the middle of his forehead and so ran uninterrupted from temple to temple which lent Jimmy a kind of prehistoric demeanor especially when he squatted on his heels which he had a tendency for. The daddy Firesheets introduced Jimmy to Benton Lynch and introduced Benton Lynch to Jimmy, and though he did not say anything in the line of nephew or relation either, it did not seem to matter any since Jimmy had not paid much attention to the introduction and had not paid much attention to Benton Lynch either which was about as natural and ordinary for him as his eyebrow or his squat.

Jane Elizabeth Firesheets stopped by on her way to setting the lunch out on the welltop and she laid her arm across Jimmy's shoulders and stooped down to nibble at his ear the sight of which drew Benton Lynch's stomach up in a little knotty ball and he swung his bushax somewhat blindly and near about separated the brother Firesheets from his left foot and the brother Firesheets grew hot and abusive straightaway since his left foot was an object of some utility to him. At lunchtime Jimmy made several pronouncements about life in general, that would be aside from the shiteating which is a sort of pronouncement about life, and he ate three or four shares of everything and smoked a half dozen of the daddy Firesheets's brother's Pall Malls as he had not been what he called on the outside long enough to buy any himself. After lunch Jimmy dragged off a pile of brush, or a piece of a pile of brush anyway, and squatted some more and advised Benton Lynch and the brother Firesheets and the daddy Firesheets's brother's boy on bushax technique without laying his hands or any of his fingers either on a real and actual bushax. Jane Elizabeth Firesheets showed up again as the afternoon commenced to wane and wrapped her arms about Jimmy's shoulders and laid her face up next to his face and Jimmy reached round and grabbed up a handful of her sweet behind right there in front of her daddy and in front of her brother and in front of her daddy's brother and her daddy's brother's boy and in front of her momma's sister's child too who watched the handful of sweet behind right when it first got grabbed and held and studied it as it proceeded on down the road towards the daddy Firesheets's cottage and the daddy Firesheets's barnfloor and barnloft also, and then the brother Firesheets backed clear across the stubble as Benton Lynch wound up with the bushax and laid the blade of it into a melon-sized hunk of quartzstone which caused the sparks to fly and did not please any of the Firesheetses much.

Jane Elizabeth Firesheets did not have hardly anything to do with Benton Lynch all throughout the month of June. Of course she said hello to him when he was around to say hello to and she passed the time of day with him when she was so inclined and every once and again of an evening she dropped by the daddy Firesheets's brother's barn and laid her hand on Benton Lynch's pantsleg but would not allow Benton Lynch to lay his hand on any piece of herself due to her scruples and her principles if you please. Sometimes when he could not help it otherwise Benton Lynch passed near the daddy Firesheets's

barn when the hooting and the moaning was in progress, which was
where all the hooting and the moaning took place anymore, and the
ruckus generally dried his mouth out and tied his stomach up too,
and he figured the ruckus itself and the idea of the ruckus would not
continue to do that for long but the ruckus itself as well as the idea
and recollection of the ruckus did continue to dry his mouth out and
did continue to tie his stomach up all throughout the month of June
and he discovered that the less of Jane Elizabeth Firesheets he had the
more of her he wanted and the more of her he wanted the less of her
he got. He found it painful to even imagine Jimmy of the lockup laying his thick self and his flat nose and his solitary eyebrow atop the
milky white portions and the plum-colored parts too so as to have his
way with them, and it was a matter of pure wonder and bafflement to
him that he'd ever grown weary of even the least little insignificant
piece of Jane Elizabeth Firesheets who did not seem to him capable of
insignificance any longer whenever he took the time to ponder the
various parts and portions of her which was the thing he did the most
of next to breathing.

Benton Lynch had come to Chalybeate Springs to relieve himself
of his torment and his agitation and for a spell in the shank of May he
had got shed of the both of them but they had come back, had come
back more potent for having departed, and they lingeed with him all
throughout the brushcutting and the beanpicking and the tobacco-
topping but he got to where he could hide them fairly well from most
everybody except Jane Elizabeth Firesheets who he could hide them
almost completely from partly on account of his pure effort and labor
in the matter and partly on account of her indifference. So what little
traces of torment and agitation he did display did not get noticed by
Jane Elizabeth Firesheets and whenever she had a thing to say about
Jimmy and her affection for him she went ahead and said it to Benton
Lynch and could not see his stomach knot up or his mouth go dry.
Jane Elizabeth Firesheets was desirous that Benton Lynch think
highly of her Jimmy and consequently was ever asking him wasn't
Jimmy just the wisest thing or wasn't Jimmy just the handsomest
thing or wasn't Jimmy just a regular stitch, and all throughout June
Benton Lynch told her yes, he guessed so since he figured a yes, he
guessed so was his only chance of laying his hands on the milky white

parts and plum-colored parts ever again, and partway through July he was still guessing that Jimmy was wise and handsome and lively and was still figuring he'd get rewarded sometime or another with the seeing and the touching and the general partaking of the milky white parts and the plum-colored parts too, but he had not got rewarded all throughout June and had not got rewarded partway through July and so eventually just got fed up with the yesing and the guessing so primarily because Jimmy was not wise and was not handsome and was not at all lively to the least little degree, so finally of an evening outside the daddy Firesheets's brother's barn when Benton Lynch got asked about the wisdom and the good looks and the purely refined sense of humor he up and told Jane Elizabeth Firesheets, "I ain't real taken with him."

"Why Benton Lynch," Jane Elizabeth Firesheets said back, "I do believe you're jealous," and she attempted to lay the tipends of her fingers on Benton Lynch's pantsleg like she had so many times previously, but Benton Lynch knocked her hand away and said, "Ha!" hard and spiteful and this time without any pleasure or satisfaction to speak of.

"No call to get nasty," Jane Elizabeth Firesheets said. "You don't have to like him. I like him good enough for both of us."

"Well that's fine with me," Benton Lynch told her, "cause I got no use for him. He squats all day like a toadfrog and ain't worth a shit for nothing."

"I beg your pardon, sir," Jane Elizabeth Firesheets shot back in her purest scruples and principles if you please tone of voice. "Let's you and me get straight just who it is that's not worth a shit. Look at you, you ain't worth anything and Jimmy, well Jimmy's set to be something sometime but you ain't anything and won't never be."

"Ha!" Benton Lynch said again just as hard and just as spiteful as before.

"Well tell me then, what prospects you got? Just what is it you got a talent for?"

And Benton Lynch, who had never considered he possessed a talent and who did not figure he had much in the way of prospects decided against admitting anything of the sort to Jane Elizabeth

Firesheets and so told her instead, "I ain't sorry and I ain't lazy and you don't know I won't be somebody sometime. You can't know it."

"Don't seem likely, Benton," Jane Elizabeth Firesheets said. "You just don't strike me as the sort that'll ever mount up to anything. But Jimmy, now you can look at Jimmy and just know something will come of him. I mean it sort of hangs all over him, don't you know." And Jane Elizabeth Firesheets got all wistful and gazed off into the treetops. "He's the wisest and handsomest thing," she said, "and just a regular stitch."

"Well, I ain't real taken with him," Benton Lynch told her.

"You don't have to be," Jane Elizabeth Firesheets said.

"It's a good thing, cause I ain't, and I ain't real taken with you either," Benton Lynch said and then jabbed his hands into his pockets and stalked off away from Jane Elizabeth Firesheets and away from her daddy's brother's barn and towards nowhere in particular.

"Benton Lynch where are you going?" Jane Elizabeth Firesheets demanded. "I got a right to know." But Benton Lynch did not stop and did not open his mouth either. "You answer me. Benton Lynch where are you going?"

And still Benton Lynch did not stop but he did open his mouth and in his flattest, emptiest, most thoroughly vacant voice he told her, "Somewhere else."

He slept in a ditch outside Apex which was all he could get a ride to, but it was a dry ditch and the evening was not particularly sweltering so he slept well enough when the bugs did not crawl over him, and early on in the morning he caught a ride with a dirt farmer clear to Roxboro where he bought a stack of flapjacks and a cup of coffee in a grill downtown and got talked at by a retired dentist who had given up his office and had given up his patients but had not got completely shed of his occupation and so still discussed teeth primarily, specifically Benton Lynch's teeth which fairly much got away with him on account of how especially big they were and how especially square they were. Benton Lynch could not seem to get out of Roxboro except by walking and so he did walk west on the 158 highway clear out of the town limits and on into the county before he got picked up by a woman who thought he was a Montague which she explained was why she picked him up in the first place since she generally did not stop for just anybody on the highway and she carried Benton Lynch for a mile or two prior to letting him out at a body shop which she said was where she was turning off but she did not turn off and so Benton Lynch walked a ways further west and got picked up shortly by a half dozen negroes in a 1971 Buick Electra, all of them a little drunk and wild on stump liquor except for the driver who was near about done in with it and so took the load of them clean to Yancey-ville on both sides of the road and every now and again in the ditches too. And then it was a truck and a Pinto and he was on the rise once more above his momma and daddy's chickenhouse and his momma and daddy's trailer with the ruin and the dilapidation and the squalor laid out full before him.

Of course there were not any pink envelopes throughout the rest of July and there were not any pink envelopes throughout the entire of August, only the agitation and the torment and then the bald Jeeter stretched out dead on her bedlinen which led to the sofa and atop it Mr. Tiny Aaron who dropped his chin and said revolver and who dropped his chin and said some dollars and some cents too, and it was like life opened up its collar and showed Benton Lynch its throat, or anyway that's what he might have figured if he'd been at all poetical instead of just vacant and just hollowed out aside from somewhat agitated and somewhat tormented too, and so he paid the dollars and paid the cents and carried home the revolver hid in the folds of his jacket and late in the afternoons for a week running while his momma napped on the couch and his daddy napped in the henhouse Benton Lynch stood before the mirror on the back of the bathroom door in his good brown jacket and his good brown trousers and said to himself, "You know who I am?"

Four

THE SHERIFF CALLED IT MAYHEM, called it pure and undiluted mayhem once Bambi Kinch had stuck the microphone direct under his nose and asked him what he might call it if he could call it some one thing or another and the sheriff took ahold of his chin for a spell prior to settling on mayhem pure and undiluted which satisfied him sufficiently and near about set Bambi Kinch to tingling since she did not cover much mayhem but generally just your usual violence and savagery. The sheriff had been all for posing in front of his map with its yellowheaded gash to the north and its silverheaded boil to the southeast and its little Lemly fleck off to the west, but Bambi Kinch who held the microphone decided the map did not suit and Larry who pointed the camera agreed that the map did not suit and Bub who had dragged a cable briefly but did not seem to perform a function otherwise failed to object when Miss Bambi Kinch led Sheriff Burton out from his office, down the courthouse steps and partway across the square. They set up so as to put Colonel Blalock off the sheriff's right shoulder and off Bambi Kinch's left one, or rather they set up so as to put Colonel Blalock's bronze scowl and the pointy end of Colonel Blalock's bronze sword direct in between the sheriff and Miss Kinch who had figured and conjectured that the face and the saber too would give her segment what she called local identity and Larry told her it was a sterling notion and the sheriff told her guessed it was too and Bub, who did not say exactly what sort of notion he figured it to be, left off with the bunch of them at the Action News 5 van where he sat sideways in the driver's seat and ate shelled peanuts out of a sack.

Sheriff Burton told Miss Bambi Kinch ahead of time he would answer pure and undiluted mayhem if she would ask him something he could answer it to, and so together they formulated a question with suggestions from Larry who was near about as thrilled and over-whelmed with the idea of mayhem as anybody on account of what it rendered up for him, or that's what he said it was on account of any-way, and Bambi Kinch said it rendered up a thing or two for her also, and the both of them together congratulated the sheriff for rendering up what it was he rendered up with his pure and undiluted mayhem and Sheriff Burton poked the toe of his right shoe down into the ground and told them it wasn't anything really but they insisted it was evocative, most highly evocative, and the sheriff said he guessed it might be. So Bub sat sideways and ate shelled peanuts and Larry pointed the camera and Miss Bambi Kinch held the microphone as Sheriff Burton told most of the rest of the state what his particular part of the state was in the throes of and he traveled all the way to Leaksville to watch himself tell it on his ladyfriend's color console and his ladyfriend, who was a Sugg, brought home barbecue and coleslaw and hushpuppies and served them on the coffee table. The sheriff spilt hotsauce down his shirtfront during a motor oil commercial and his ladyfriend Sugg licked her napkin and set about cleaning it off him but was only half done when Bambi Kinch showed up on the screen and so got interrupted by Sheriff Burton and together him and her watched the sheriff say mayhem pure and undiluted.

It had not got to be mayhem until the second week in November when it rose up from corridors and gashes and shots fired all at once and of a sudden and so did get to be mayhem after all, mayhem pure and undiluted they said on the television and in the papers, but it was not actually pure and was hardly undiluted though likely it was may-hem mostly on account of who got killed from it which would be Vernon Littlejohn of Spray first cousin to the coach Littlejohn Little-johns and Vernon Littlejohn's condition kept him from getting just plain killed and murdered and fairly much dictated the mayhem, fairly much insisted on it. Vernon Littlejohn's arteries had commenced to harden when he reached sixty-seven and he had not been able to think straight ever since which would be tribulation enough for most peo-ple but was compounded in Vernon Littlejohn's particular instance by the grocery he had run on the 87 highway for as long as anybody could recollect and certainly for longer than Vernon Littlejohn could recollect since he could not recollect hardly anything anymore that had happened two minutes previous from the point he tried to recollect it, or anyhow two minutes previous on a good day and more towards one minute previous those times when his arteries were particularly stiff and rigid which had been rare times once but had steadily become fairly usual and ordinary right up to the afternoon Vernon Littlejohn did not have to bother to recollect anything any longer.

Mrs. Vernon Littlejohn helped out in the grocery when she could but she suffered from the phlebitis in both legs and so generally took to her bed early on in the afternoon for the most of the year and hardly ever got out of it in the summer of the year due to the heat and humidity in combination with her rubber stockings all of which together served to break her legs out in a rash. Consequently, Mr. Vernon Littlejohn ran his grocery almost entirely by himself for the most of the year and absolutely entirely by himself for the rest of the year although Mrs. Littlejohn encouraged him to hire help which Mr. Littlejohn saw the advantage in but somehow could not ever recollect to do, so it was just him and his arteries all the summer and just him and his arteries the afternoons throughout the winter and he got on well enough as long as it was mostly him and partly his arteries but gradually it slid in the other direction and became mostly his arteries and only partly him and he did not get along so well from there on out. The trouble was primarily that Mr. Vernon Littlejohn could not make change, or rather could not make anything but the wrong change and so not only gave back a lot of money to people who had a little coming and gave back a little money to people who had a lot coming but regularly returned an assortment of bills and silver too to people who had nothing coming whatsoever, and the problem reached a kind of a head when Mrs. Jack Foster's boy, little Jack, bought three Sweet Tarts and a Tic Tac with a dollar and got $283.46 change which seemed considerably fortunate to him and he carried the money to the Western Auto in downtown Spray so as to shop for a bicycle but he could not decide between a red one with a ten speed sprocket and a yellow one with a spider seat and consequently he bought the red one and the yellow one and paid a little colored boy

$22.00 to ride the yellow one home for him which was the only one the little colored boy could sit on and pedal.

Fosters being Fosters and Pendergasts, which was what Mrs. Foster had been prior to becoming what she was, being Pendergasts little Jack did not get made to take back but one of the bicycles and did not get made to take that back really but did anyhow on his own which was how he did most everything he ended up doing since he was the one that ran the show and big Jack and Mrs. Pendergast Foster were just the ones that let him. So accordingly Mr. Littlejohn did not get back but what Little Jack decided he should get back which turned out to be the price of the returned bicycle, which would be the red bicycle that little Jack could not hardly reach the pedals on himself, and even then it was not the full and entire price of the bicycle but only that part of the price of the bicycle left over from little Jack's share of it and little Jack took a sizable share of it, as was little Jack's way in most things. However, Mr. Vernon Litlejohn accepted the money as a kind of windfall since he did not recollect that any money was missing although Mrs. Littlejohn had told him it was, and consequently Mrs. Littlejohn was the one to do the majority of the worrying over Mr. Littlejohn's earnings and how they came to go where they went, and just as consequently Mrs. Littlejohn was the one, stretched out there on her bed with her rubber hose draped over the bedstead, to do the devising and the formulating too so as to prevent Mr. Littlejohn's earnings from going where they generally went and channel them instead to where they did not usually end up which turned out to be a Tampa Jewel box once Mrs. Littlejohn had successfully devised and formulated the new Littlejohn method of changemaking.

Mr. Littlejohn kept the Tampa Jewel box on a shelf under the cash register and every morning Mrs. Littlejohn put inside it $50.00 in tens and fives and ones and silver and pennies. The new Littlejohn method of changemaking was intended to keep Mr. Littlejohn out of the register in the majority so as to reduce his losses to just some sizable or middling or maybe even scant portion of the tens and the fives and the ones and the silver and the pennies. So Mr. Littlejohn did not have to make change any better than he had been making change and mostly did not have to make change at all but instead simply snatched the Tampa Jewel box off the shelf and opened it up for the customer to make his own change out of, which Mr. Littlejohn did not have any qualms about since he had always believed that people were basically honest and trustworthy and since he still believed it whenever he could recollect that he always had. And Mr. Littlejohn's experience showed him in fact that people were basically honest and trustworthy since his regular customers who traded near about daily at his grocery did not ever take from him but a little more than they were entitled to while even his irregular customers did not even lift much in addition to that, so Mr. Littlejohn even accumulated some money in the course of a day and even realized a profit every once and again and even made back the $283.46, or had made back the most of it anyhow by the second week of November when of a sudden Mr. Littlejohn ceased to accumulate and realize and make back anything any longer.

They printed two pictures of him up towards the top of the front page of the *Chronicle,* one from Mrs. Littlejohn's silver frame on the nightstand taken back when Mr. Littlejohn's arteries had been as soft and ordinary as everybody else's and another taken about as late as it could be taken of Mr. Vernon Littlejohn strapped and buckled onto a gurney under a taut bedsheet that showed off the tip of his nose and the upright ends of his feet. According to Mr. H. Monroe Aycock, who wrote the article that filled up the space all around Mr. Littlejohn with his ordinary arteries and Mr. Littlejohn with his buckle and his bedsheet, the events of the day transpired beneath a leaden sky and in particularly brisk and gusty weather which seemed somehow notable and significant to Mr. H. Monroe Aycock who let the sky go to ashen in the bottom of column one and then to tufted and gray midway through column two while the wind picked up some and whipped and tore and screeched and whatnot and the temperature fell off to bracing or maybe rose up to it since Mr. Aycock did not clearly explain if bracing was colder than brisk or brisk was colder than bracing. He built towards and concluded with a paragraph on the sheer and general oppressiveness of the afternoon and seemed to indicate that maybe it had caused some little piece of the calamity, or actually seemed to indicate that maybe it had caused some major piece of the calamity, but between the leaden sky and leaden bullet public opinion tended to ride with the latter though most everybody agreed that Mr.

H. Monroe Aycock was to be congratulated on his vivid and fairly lyrical rendering of what most everybody agreed was in fact a true and verifiable calamity.

However, as Mr. H. Monroe Aycock's passions and sensibilities kept to the lyrical end of things he did not truly get around to the hard facts and circumstances of the calamity and consequently the full-blooded Loop Road Myrick's sister's husband felt compelled to supplement Mr. H. Monroe Aycock's account of the calamity with one of his own devising which was not nearly so stirring and dramatic as Mr. H. Monroe Aycock's but proved to be appreciably more informative. The full-blooded Loop Road Myrick's sister's husband, with the aid of material evidence and eyewitness accounts and the usual guesses and assumptions, reconstructed and reconstituted the crime as best he could which turned out to be accurate in the majority except for the ferocious struggle which the full-blooded Loop Road Myrick's sister's husband decided there had been one of on account of the ointments and pouches of loose chew and cigarette packs that lay strewn all about the stiffening corpse which Mr. Vernon Littlejohn had decided he did not want to get made into just prior to getting made into one, or anyway that was the theory formulated by the full-blooded Loop Road Myrick's sister's huband who judged the evidence and figured there had been a struggle of some considerable ferocity, a wild and frantic battle near about that had caused the ointments and the pouches and the cigarette packs to get strewn like they did get strewn and had caused Mr. Vernon Littlejohn to get shot and murdered and killed like he did get shot and murdered and killed.

But there had not been an actual struggle really, had not been anything much wild and frantic about it except for the dying which Mr. Littlejohn pulled off with appreciable vigor. Otherwise this time was just the same as the other times. He stayed outside off behind a honeysuckle hedgerow until the lady in the green Plymouth came out with her loafbread and her Coca-Colas and the man in the farmtruck got his five gallons of fuel oil and departed. Then he stepped on around the corner and in through the door and looked to see was it just him and was it just the clerk and it was just him and the clerk, or actually just him primarily since the clerk had propped his feet up by the gas heater and dozed off. So he said, "Hey," in his usual flat and vacant voice and when the clerk ran his tongue out his mouth and chewed the air he said, "Hey," again and slapped the counter with the flat of his hand. Of course Mr. Littlejohn, who stayed somewhat perplexed and confused on account of his affliction, generally woke up in a pure quandary and he stretched himself and dragged over to the register and rubbed the top of his head and yawned and was just about to close his mouth when he got asked, "You know who I am?" and so did not close his mouth entirely but replied straightway, "Why surely," and since the Harrington and Richardson Buntline revolver was already too far out from the folds of the jacket to get put back it got brought on out the rest of its length and got aimed and pointed and then the question got asked all over again and Mr. Littlejohn said he guessed he knew though maybe he didn't know after all and so he found himself informed shortly in a most straightforward and demonstrative sort of way and he eyed the pistol barrel afresh and eyed his privates, or rather eyed the part of his trousers where he recollected his privates to be, and he recollected fairly accurately in this instance, and he said, "I guess you'll be wanting this then," and he reached his arm in the general direction of the register but not to the register precisely and instead more directly to a shelf underneath the register.

The bullet did not hit him in the testicles exactly, did not even hit him in the stomach, but entered direct through his chest and exited square between his shoulders and it wasn't even the hole in himself that snared his attention initially but was instead the thundrous bang from the pistol which he jumped from and which he figured was all he jumped from until he saw where the angular, pointy, and hollowed out face was looking and looked there for himself. It was a big ragged pulpy wound and the blood sluiced out from it soaking Mr. Littlejohn's shirtfront and splattering somewhat onto his hands and the top of his Tampa Jewel box, and it had even stung him the least little bit until he saw it when it commenced to ache and burn and torment him and thereby caused him to raise his fingers up and touch it and he drew them away all bloodied over and looked at them with his mouth hanging loose and open. Then he commenced to sink, commenced to sink straight down into the floorboards it appeared like a man in a quagmire and he seemed contented with sinking initially and just watched himself get shorter until he decided he was not contented with sinking after all and so scratched and grabbed at anything he could scratch and grab at which turned out to be ointments and loose chew and cigarettes and they came down all around him and atop him and joined him on the floorboards from where he gazed up at the ceiling primarily, gazed up at the ceiling exclusively really until the angular, pointy, and hollowed out face showed itself over the counter and so he gazed up at it instead and it gazed down at him and watched him blow out the last of his breath and watched his eyelids flutter and go still.

And Sheriff Burton called it mayhem pure and undiluted and called it willful and called it vicious and called it heinous too when he'd had time to think of heinous which he did not get much occasion to throw around and so threw around now that he could, and most everybody else called it heinous once the sheriff did and called it vicious and willful and called it mayhem pure and undiluted in addition to just plain meanness which the most of them had called it straight off and continued to call it primarily except for the sheriff and except of course for the bulk of old ladies roundabout who did not find plain meanness lurid enough to suit them and so insisted on the heinous and the vicious and the willful and the mayhem pure and undiluted along with most every other thing that would scare and terrify them and palpitate their hearts at night, but it got to be mayhem alone, solely mayhem pure and undiluted once the sheriff said it to Miss Bambi Kinch, said it there in the middle of town with the pointy bronze sword and the bronze scowl over his shoulder and got broadcast and circulated saying it all across the piedmont and partway into Virginia, and he asked his ladyfriend the Leaksville Sugg her true opinion once Bambi Kinch had said it was Bambi Kinch and had sent things on back to the studio, and the Leaksville Sugg licked her napkin again and told him she did not believe it would come out altogether on account of the vinegar and the tomato juice in combination.

He folded it up and mailed it in an envelope without even an argyle-socks-length note to explain what it was since he figured it would explain what it was by itself and Jane Elizabeth Firesheets took it out

from the envelope and unfolded it and looked for a note or just some
trace of handwriting somewhere but did not discover any and so
looked at the inky headlines and at the photograph of Mr. Busick, the
victim, and at the photograph of Mr. Winn with his chin dangling
alongside Mr. Bobbit with his cigarette and the pieces of his arms, the
witnesses, and at the little square of roadmap that was Raleigh mostly
and Wendell and Garner and Knightdale and Zebulon and down the
401 highway to the south Fuquay-Varina also with a bold black arrow
to indicate and distinguish it, and she sat down on the front cottage
steps with the unfolded paper in her fingers and she looked away from
it and then looked back at it again and her mouth commenced to lay
out across her face and wrap partly around her jawbones. He sent her
the McIver one too and then the Barnard one and the Grissom one
and the Stem one also and still not even an argyle-socks-length note to
explain what they were since he figured they would explain what they
were by themselves, and they did explain what they were by themselves and got pressed all together in a *Glamour* magazine where they
stayed when they were not getting looked at.

The first pink envelope did not contain anything of much consequence as far as Benton Lynch was concerned, not anything anyway
worth adjusting himself in his trousers over but just your polite talk
and your general inquiry and some passing mention of Jimmy who
had gotten himself into a difficulty that remained vague and unspeci-
fied but still thrilled Benton Lynch near about as much as a sweltering
conclusion would have thrilled him though not precisely as much exactly, and it was not until the second pink envelope that Benton
Lynch learned the true nature of Jimmy's predicament which had
something to do with a social security check and something to do
with his endorsement on the back of it and something to do with the
pocketbook he had pilfered it from and considerable to do with the
three to five in Caledonia he was very likely to get on account of all of
it. Of course, Jane Elizabeth Firesheets could not hide her agitation
and her dismay and wondered out loud along about the bottom of the
back of the first page just what she would do for three to five years
without anybody to see to her needs and to see to her desires and
Benton Lynch, who had been sitting down, stood up as he commenced to wonder about her desires some himself.

She did not get to any purely sultry and provocative talk until the third pink envelope which was shot full of purely sultry and provocative talk from the Dear Sugarbunch straight through to the p.s. and the whole business kept Benton Lynch on his feet for a solid day and likely would have kept him upright for the majority of the day after but he could not stand up on the bus which was what he took out from the depot in Neely south to Greensboro and then east clear to Raleigh where he changed over to a local and made the twenty-seven miles to Chalybeate Springs in just under two hours and at last descended onto the roadside where he stretched and adjusted and scratched himself prior to walking the twenty-eighth mile and the twenty-ninth mile too clear out to the cottage that was still a hovel there in the afternoon light but was preparing to become a shack once the evening set in, was preparing to become a shack with some suggestion of a cottage to it.

Right off he ran up on the granddaddy Firesheets who was in the sideyard tending to the grandmomma Firesheets's marker and he greeted Benton Lynch enthusiastically which was the way the granddaddy Firesheets did most everything he bothered to do and then he led him on into the cottage proper so as to let him get greeted by everybody else and the momma Firesheets said Hey and the daddy Firesheets said Hey and the brother Firesheets asked him where in the hell he'd run off to and on account of what and Benton Lynch said Hey back. Jane Elizabeth Firesheets was out behind the barn throwing seed to the chickens and Benton Lynch excused himself from the momma and the daddy and the brother and the granddaddy Firesheets and slipped out the door, across the backyard, and direct up behind Jane Elizabeth Firesheets who felt his long pointy fingers on the flattest whitest part of her stomach and so instinctively yipped and howled and flung the seed bucket prior to whirling around so as to discover just whose long pointy fingers it was on the flattest whitest part of her stomach, though she had figured they were attached to who they were attached to, and she put her face up in his face and asked her, "What are you doing here?" but not much at all like she had asked him that previously.

They retired to the barnfloor almost straightaway, or actually as immediately straightaway as they could encourage their legs to take them, and they rolled around on the wood planking and grappled with each other for a spell until Jane Elizabeth Firesheets suggested and then insisted on the hayloft, not so much for the loft part of it this time but more for the hay part of it, and naturally Benton Lynch agreed with her emphatically almost before she could finish suggesting it as he was in a state which had rendered him acutely agreeable and thoroughly emphatic, and he laid his head back and watched Jane Elizabeth Firesheets's sweet behind ascend towards the barnroof after which he endeavored to ascend some himself and even succeeded at it but without any grace to speak of. They rolled around in the hay some and grappled some like they had rolled around and grappled on the wood planking and then Jane Elizabeth Firesheets took the liberty of separating Benton Lynch from his trousers and from cotton briefs, or anyway she had commenced to take the liberty of separating Benton Lynch from his trousers and his briefs when she discovered she had to separate him as well from his Harrington and Richardson Buntline revolver of extraordinarily high caliber which she had taken for something long and steely from the outset but not a gun exactly, and she held it and looked at it and cocked it and uncocked it and pointed it and ran her tongue out her mouth and back in her mouth again and said, "Oooohhh," in a tone Benton Lynch had never heard used on a revolver before.

He got invited to undo the buttons down Jane Elizabeth Firesheets's blousefront but could not synchronize and coordinate his fingers sufficiently to undo them like they were meant to be undone and so tugged at the buttonhole side of the blouse with one hand and yanked at the button side of if with the other and thereby laid the thing open with the kind of passion and vigor that prompted Jane Elizabeth Firesheets to oooohhh all over again and Benton Lynch could tell it was genuine and legitimate oooohhhing once he'd unhooked and opened Jane Elizabeth Firesheets's brassiere so as to see for himself the plum-colored parts which had blossomed and spread out like they usually did when the oooohhhing was genuine and when the oooohhhing was legitimate. As a token of her gratitude and appreciation for the open display of passion and of vigor, Jane Elizabeth Firesheets undertook to render Benton Lynch unconscious with some lively fingerplay and general therapy and since Benton Lynch was not one of your natural oooohhhers or one of your natural squirmers too, he just breathed heavy and inadvertently whistled through his nose a time or two before lapsing off into what appeared to be a faint once Jane Elizabeth Firesheets stuck the pointy pink tipend of her tongue direct into his bellybutton.

They got all knotted and tangled up together presently though not exactly after any fashion they had got knotted and tangled up before but a little sideways this time and somewhat upside down which Jane Elizabeth Firesheets said she picked up from Jimmy who Benton Lynch of a sudden discovered an appreciation for that he had not previously been aware of. Of course they got knotted and tangled together rightside up too and backwards for a spell and with him on for the ride and her on for the ride and then a little sideways and somewhat upside down again prior to getting unknotted and untangled up and just laying together in the hay so as to recuperate. Jane Elizabeth Firesheets fetched a squashed and flattened pack of cigarettes out from her back pantspocket and rounded one up some and lit it while Benton Lynch engaged himself in the observation of the plum-colored parts which had commenced to shrink in ever so slightly. Jane Elizabeth Firesheets said it was the best she'd had, said it was the best she'd had ever, and she asked Benton Lynch was it the best he'd had ever too and Benton Lynch grunted like he usually grunted when Jane Elizabeth Firesheets asked him was it the best he'd had which she always asked him. But she insisted this time it was really the best she'd had, the best she'd had ever, probably on account of she'd never done it with a true culprit before, hadn't ever had the occasion to get all knotted and tangled up with an actual outlaw, she called it.

"I thought Jimmy was a culprit," Benton Lynch said still eying the plum-colored parts which appeared to contract acutely.

"Jimmy was a hoodlum," Jane Elizabeth Firesheets told him in a sharp and spiteful sort of way. "Oh he had his wit and he had his charm and he had his regular good looks but he didn't ever do nothing but little old piddly mess. I mean he didn't have no class and didn't have no style much and wasn't never anything going to come of him. I guess I just got took in."

"I guess," Benton Lynch said.

And Jane Elizabeth Firesheets rolled onto her side and reached her arm across Benton Lynch's midsection and told him, "But you, you got this," and she ran her fingers down the long slender barrel of the Harrington and Richardson Buntline revolver and wrapped them around the grip of it. "I ain't never seen a gun so big as this one," she said and picked it up and cocked it and uncocked it and held it in front of herself in both her hands. "What do they do when you point it at them? What do they say to you?" she wanted to know.

"They don't say nothing much," Benton Lynch told her, "don't do nothing much either."

"They do what you say do, don't they?"

"I guess," Benton Lynch told her.

"I bet they do just exactly what you say do. I bet they don't hardly breathe or move or nothing less you say breathe or less you say move. I bet they don't never stop looking at this thing here." And Jane Elizabeth Firesheets cocked the hammer with both her thumbs and drew onto the ridge beam overhead. "Lord, don't you know that feels good," she said, "don't you just know it."

"I guess," Benton Lynch told her, addressing almost exclusively her plum-colored parts which had shrunk in and shriveled so as to be only a portion of what they had been previously.

"And I suppose they just throw the money at you," Jane Elizabeth Firesheets said. "I mean I don't figure they'd be anxious to get shot on account of it. Probably ain't even their money anyhow."

"Likely not," Benton Lynch told her.

"And it's a bunch of money, I imagine. I imagine it's a pure load of money, isn't it?"

"What's that?"

"The money, Benton. I said I imagine whenever you make off with some it's a load of it."

"Ain't no regular load," Benton Lynch said, "just whatever's around in the cash drawer and that ain't been no regular load so far."

"But it's something anyhow," Jane Elizabeth Firesheets told him, "and you get the thrill of sticking somebody up for it. I mean it must make you tingly all over."

"I could go to prison," Benton Lynch said.

And Jane Elizabeth Firesheets cocked and pointed the gun all over again. "Yea," she told him, "ain't that exciting."

Jane Elizabeth Firesheets wanted to see firsthand Benton Lynch's technique and wanted to get stuck up doing it, but Benton Lynch was reluctant and a little embarrassed to show off his technique straightaway and flatout refused to do it until Jane Elizabeth Firesheets suggested that she might flatout refuse to do a few things herself, and so Benton Lynch got up out of the hay and played like the culprit and Jane Elizabeth Firesheets got up out of the hay and played like the clerk. As he did not have any pants to stick his gun into, Benton Lynch held his pistol behind his back and stepped up square in front of Jane Elizabeth Firesheets who was making out to dust the countertop. "May I help you?" she said, and Benton Lynch asked her did she know who he was and she told him of course she did, but Benton Lynch told her back she didn't and explained why and so they started all over again with the May I help you? followed by the You know who I am? which immediately preceded the arrival of the Buntline revolver that got brought into view but did not get aimed at Jane Elizabeth Firesheets exactly, or anyway did not get aimed at Jane Elizabeth Firesheets exactly until Jane Elizabeth Firesheets insisted it get aimed at her exactly and so it did get aimed at her exactly eventually but did not get cocked straightaway until Jane Elizabeth Firesheets insisted it get cocked too if cocking was what Benton Lynch usually did to it once he had aimed it, so it got aimed at Jane Elizabeth Firesheets and got cocked as well after which Jane Elizabeth Firesheets had her testicles threatened with Walnut Cove which was the first place to pop into Benton Lynch's head.

And Jane Elizabeth Firesheets said, "Hold on here. You see any balls to blow to Walnut Cove or anywhere else?"

And since he could not discover any but his own, Benton Lynch shook his head no.

"Well what is it you're going to say if it's a woman?" Jane Elizabeth Firesheets wanted to know.

And as the Stem in Union Ridge already had been a woman unlike the Busick and the McIver and the Barnard and the Grissom, Benton Lynch told Jane Elizabeth Firesheets what it was he would say since he had already said it.

And Jane Elizabeth Firesheets asked him, "Poontang?" to which Benton Lynch shook his head yes.

She wanted to take it from the outset one time through and so Benton Lynch uncocked the pistol and stuck it behind his back and Jane Elizabeth Firesheets commenced to dust the countertop and she stayed at it until she got talked to and then aimed and cocked at, and likely it was the sight of the bore along with the threat of the bullet that thrilled and excited her and caused her plum-colored parts to swell and expand appreciably the sight of which distracted Benton Lynch from his thievery and thrilled and excited him to where it was a pure toss up as to which of his weapons would go off first. Naturally when she saw that both barrels were trained on her, Jane Elizabeth Firesheets got even more thrilled and even more excited which led to some additional swelling and some additional expanding and thereby set Benton Lynch into a pure frenzy and he near about threw himself at Jane Elizabeth Firesheets and knocked her down into a haypile where him and her did some serious wrestling and tumbling around and gyrating and oooohhhing and groaning and grunting and nose-whistling and not a shabby lot of perspiring until at last they both gave out almost simultaneously and laid back free of each other panting towards the rafters. Jane Elizabeth Firesheets said it was the best she'd had, said it was the best she'd had ever, and she asked Benton Lynch was it the best he'd had ever too and Benton Lynch told her he believed it actually was.

They planned to make off together, planned to rent out a modest little house off and away somewhere and loot and plunder the countryside roundabout it until they had massed and accumulated sufficient money to buy a ragtop and take it south to Daytona so as to drive it on the beach which Jane Elizabeth Firesheets admitted had always been a particular ambition of hers ever since she gave up the ballet, and though it had not ever been a particular ambition of Benton Lynch's he said he would be pleased to own a ragtop and drive it on the beach, insisted he would be pleased to own a ragtop and drive it on the beach, insisted upon it most strenuously and with considerable passion so as to be permitted to go back to looking at and touching those parts of Jane Elizabeth Firesheets he had been looking at and touching when they got onto the subject of the ragtop in the first place. And it had to be a brick house, Jane Elizabeth Firesheets said, a modest little brick house off and away somewhere to loot and plunder from primarily on account of the insulating qualities of brick which Jane Elizabeth Firesheets had developed a refined appreciation of especially since her move to Chalybeate Springs as your cottages and your shacks and your hovels generally do not display much in the way of insulating qualities, and Jane Elizabeth Firesheets complained that her feet had not known a warm moment since Labor Day which she said was a particular problem in chesty women like herself whose blood did not circulate like it did in everybody else. And Benton Lynch, who appreciated at least half of the dilemma, nodded his head sympathetically.

The momma Firesheets and the daddy Firesheets and the granddaddy Firesheets and the brother Firesheets all got told it was a visit northwest to the trailer and the dilapidated henhouse so as to acquaint the Jeeter Lynch and the pure Lynch with Miss Jane Elizabeth Firesheets and it was a visit to the northwest and even to the trailer and the dilapidated henhouse eventually, but straightaway it was just a visit to the northwest alone up through Raleigh, west on to Graham, and then north on 87 as far as Altamahaw where Jane Elizabeth Firesheets insisted her and Benton Lynch get off the bus and do some casting around, she called it. Naturally Benton Lynch wanted to know some casting around for what and Jane Elizabeth Firesheets told him Action and Benton Lynch asked her what sort of Action exactly and Jane Elizabeth Firesheets pointed at the front of Benton Lynch's trousers where the pistol was which Benton Lynch had been afraid she would point at. He was not so anxious for Action himself and he followed Jane Elizabeth Firesheets out from the bus station and along the street all the while attempting to convince her that she was not so anxious for Action either, but Jane Elizabeth Firesheets told him she knew what she was anxious for, told him she'd figured he'd be anxious for it too unless of course he was too scared to be anxious, unless of course it hadn't been him doing any of it all along, and then she struck on out ahead of him and Benton Lynch watched her sweet behind ever so briefly prior to blowing out a breath and saying, "Where then?" which spun her around and brought her on back to him. "Out this way," she said and hooked her fingers in the crook of his elbow. "There's bound to be something out this way."

And there was something out that way in the form of big Robroy

Troutman's Grocery Boy Jr. on the right side of 87 just past the city limit. It was chiefly operated by big Robroy himself who was known as big Robroy not because there was a little Robroy anywhere but mostly because big Robroy was just too plain big to stay regular Robroy, was too plain tall and too plain wide to be anything else but big Robroy. Mrs. big Robroy, who was not especially dainty herself, generally sat behind the counter with Mr. big Robroy weekday afternoons and Jane Elizabeth Firesheets could see the both of them from the corner of the parking lot, Mrs. big Robroy reading a beauty magazine and Mr. big Robroy cleaning under his fingernails with the edge of a laminated pocket calendar. Jane Elizabeth Firesheets desired to do the casing herself, insisted upon doing the casing actually even though Benton Lynch told her she'd done quite enough with the casing around, told her he usually did not do much casing anyhow but just some sneaking and some lurking and whatnot, and Jane Elizabeth Firesheets wanted to know what in the world he thought casing was if not sneaking and lurking and whatnot, and so Benton Lynch admitted to having cased previously but was still reluctant to let Jane Elizabeth Firesheets partake of the least little bit of the sneaking and the lurking and the whatnot on account of the risks to her person and to those parts of her person which Benton Lynch so adored. However, once Jane Elizabeth Firesheets got so far as desiring and insisting on a thing there ordinarily was not any beating her back from it and consequently she got to case after all once she'd outlined the alternatives for Benton Lynch who developed a new appreciation of her stand on the matter and watched her cross the parking lot past the gaspumps and step on into the store proper where she browsed all throughout the premises, lingered some at the breadrack, and then bought a pack of Winstons from Mr. big Robroy who she chatted with and grinned at and even touched ever so briefly with the tipends of her fingers until Mrs. big Robroy looked up from her beauty magazine and commenced to glare in a venomous sort of way.

Jane Elizabeth Firesheets reported that there weren't nobody but them two and they didn't strike her as troublesome since the man was too fat to get anywhere in a hurry and the woman couldn't kill with her ugly which was what she seemed to have the most of, and though not intending to tell Benton Lynch his business, Jane Elizabeth Firesheets went on to suggest that maybe he ought to squeeze off a round in between the two of them just to get the blood going but Benton Lynch told her he did not believe he would and Jane Elizabeth Firesheets suggested that maybe he should consider it and Benton Lynch said he would consider it but did not believe the considering would change his mind any and Jane Elizabeth Firesheets asked him what in the world he had the gun for then and Benton Lynch told her to point primarily and Jane Elizabeth Firesheets asked him why didn't he go ahead and shoot it every once in a while just to stir things up a little and Benton Lynch did not say anything directly and so Jane Elizabeth Firesheets asked him again and Benton Lynch did not say anything directly the second time either and so Jane Elizabeth Firesheets demanded to know how come and Benton Lynch told her, "I ain't got no bullets," which seemed to hit Jane Elizabeth Firesheets all wrong and she crossed her arms over herself and exclaimed, "Sweet Jesus Christ!"

Benton Lynch attempted to explain to her the economics of his predicament, attempted to explain to her how the sizable lead bullet and the sizable brass casing and the hot powder load all together ran into some money not to mention his general reluctance to shoot anybody in the first place, but Jane Elizabeth Firesheets just turned her backside on him and he walked around to her frontside but she just turned her backside on him again and so Benton Lynch told her backside he'd buy some bullets, told her backside he'd buy some bullets first chance he got, but Jane Elizabeth Firesheets said that wouldn't cure it, and said it wasn't even the bullets anyway, it was just that she'd figured he was mean and vicious and she guessed he wasn't after all. Then she exhaled, drew in her shoulders some, and said she supposed she'd get over it. And although Benton Lynch insisted he was mean and insisted he was vicious, Jane Elizabeth Firesheets did not unstoop her shoulders or show him her frontside or generally seem at all convinced that he had any savagery to him, so Benton Lynch stomped on the asphalt and said he'd just let her see for herself exactly what sort of nasty motherfucker he could be and Jane Elizabeth Firesheets stiffened some on account of how talk like that generally had a way with her.

He crossed the parking lot at near about a dead run with his long skinny arms slashing the air, and he did not even pull up at the door but kicked it open and ran straight to the counter where Mr. big Robroy had stood up to see what the commotion was and Mrs. big Robroy had laid down her magazine and turned her lips inside out in utter annoyance. And Jane Elizabeth Firesheets watched Benton Lynch holler something at Mr. big Robroy, holler something she could not hear exactly but could understand well enough, and Jane Elizabeth Firesheets watched Mr. big Robroy shake his head no. So he drew it out from his trousers and cocked it and did not just aim it this time but laid the bore of it flush against Mr. big Robroy's pantsfront and with his free hand grabbed up a portion of Mr. big Robroy's shirt and apparently a portion of Mr. big Robroy's chesthairs as well, and he brought his pointy hollowed out face up tight into Mr. big Robroy's face and he communicated some with Mr. big Robroy who in turn communicated some with Mrs. big Robroy who let her mouth go rightside in and made some considerable use of it as she crossed behind Mr. big Robroy to the cash register, opened the drawer of it, and emptied out what money there was into a brown paper bag which she rolled down the neck of and set on the countertop. With his left hand still full of shirtfront and chesthairs, Benton Lynch raised up his pistol and pushed on the tipend of Mr. big Robroy's nose with it so as to bring home a point he was at the time making to Mr. big Robroy, and when Mr. big Robroy seemed to comprehend just exactly what it was he was meant to comprehend, Benton Lynch opened his mouth and bared his big square teeth first at Mr. big Robroy and then at Mrs. big Robroy who got called something unseemly on top of it.

He recrossed the parking lot at a full and thorough dead run with his long skinny arms slashing the air and the rolled up paper sack bulging out from his jacket pocket, and Jane Elizabeth Firesheets turned her full frontside to him and set herself to tell him how wrong and sorry she was, set herself to tell him how mean and vicious he'd turned out to be after all, but before she could even get started good she got snatched up like a mailsack and carried along with some immediate velocity and Jane Elizabeth Firesheets wanted to know the why of it, demanded to know the why of it, and Benton Lynch told her they generally called it making off which he explained was the prudent thing to do once you'd separated a man from his money, and

Jane Elizabeth Firesheets admitted she had not considered the getting away part of it quite as carefully as she might have. They crossed the road and ducked off around a brick house but could not pass through the backyard on account of a Cyclone fence and the dog it had been put up for, and when they came back out towards the road again Mrs. big Robroy Troutman commenced to scream at them from the parking lot of the Grocery Boy Jr., commenced to scream at them in a general and hysterical sort of way, and wailed and waved her arms and pointed every now and again, and Benton Lynch and Jane Elizabeth Firesheets tore out to the south towards town and ducked off this time behind a little white frame house without a fence and without a dog either but just a green Nova parked beside it and a shriveled up white-haired lady in the kitchen window, and Jane Elizabeth Firesheets grinned and said Hey to her and jerked at Benton Lynch's arm and told him to grin and say Hey to her too, and Benton Lynch wanted to know exactly what for until Jane Elizabeth Firesheets pinched up some of his armskin and squeezed it and Benton Lynch grinned and said Hey.

The shriveled up white-haired lady said Hey back but did not truly grin in the course of it and Jane Elizabeth Firesheets stepped a little closer to the window than she had been previously and asked her, "Have you seen our cat, ma'm?" and Benton Lynch and the shriveled up white-haired lady near about harmonized with "Cat?" which got some more armskin pinched up and squeezed and Jane Elizabeth Firesheets said, "Yes ma'm. He's a big yellow cat and he run off. Raymond here thought he seen him come up this way, didn't you Raymond," and once Jane Elizabeth Firesheets had showed Benton Lynch her two fingers he said, "Yes ma'm," and fairly smirked. The shriveled up white-haired lady could not recollect having seen a big yellow cat, and could not recollect having seen a cat of any description roundabout the house anytime lately which she said suited her just fine on account of her allergy to cats which caused her eyes to water and her nose to run and her glands to get puffy, and Jane Elizabeth Firesheets asked what was it she said as her voice did not carry especially well through the windowglass, so the shriveled up white-haired lady stepped on around to the sidedoor and opened up the six light

wooden one and the aluminum storm one and said she could not recollect having seen a big yellow cat, could not recollect having seen a
cat of any description roundabout the house lately which suited her
just fine on account of her allergy to cats which caused her eyes to
water and her nose to run and her glands to get puffy. And Jane Elizabeth Firesheets said, "Yes ma'm," and stepped up onto the stoop and
then pushed her way on into the house taking with her the shriveled
up white-haired lady who insisted she had not seen a big yellow cat,
insisted she had not seen any cat whatsoever.

"Shut up," Jane Elizabeth Firesheets told her. "We want the keys
to that car yonder."

"He'll turn up on his own," the shriveled up white-haired lady
said. "You needn't go out scouring the countryside."

"Just you shut up," Jane Elizabeth Firesheets told her and she
turned around to Benton Lynch, who was still outside standing where
he'd been standing and was still wondering about most everything in
general, and she said to him, "Get in here and do something with this
woman," and so he stepped on into the house himself and asked her,
"What?"

"Show it to her," Jane Elizabeth Firesheets told him. "Go on and
show it to her," and she pointed her finger at Benton Lynch's pantsfront and the shriveled up white-haired lady sucked air.

So he went ahead and drew it on out and cocked it and pointed it
and Jane Elizabeth Firesheets said, "We want the keys to that car yonder. Now where are they?"

And the shriveled up white-haired lady addressed the bore of the
Harrington and Richardson Buntline revolver primarily and told it,
"In my pocketbook," and pointed backwards over her shoulder fairly
much towards the ceiling.

Jane Elizabeth Firesheets emptied the thing out on the kitchen
table and took the keys and the credit cards and what money there
was along with a little round tortoiseshell compact that she said she'd
always wanted one of, and she searched through the refrigerator after
some cheese but there was not any cheese in the refrigerator or anywhere else in the house that she could discover and Jane Elizabeth
Firesheets wanted to know why not and the shriveled up white-haired

lady told her she could not pass cheese, and Jane Elizabeth Firesheets said that was the sorriest reason she'd ever heard of and she told Benton Lynch, "Knock her on the head."

"What?"

"Knock her on the head," Jane Elizabeth Firesheets insisted. "Go on. They always knock them on the head."

"I don't like cheese much myself," Benton Lynch observed.

And Jane Elizabeth Firesheets said, "Christ Almighty. Gimme that thing," and she took hold of the gun by the handle and swung it for practice once but did not find the grip suited her. "We can't leave this woman running loose," Jane Elizabeth Firesheets said.

"We could tie her up. We could lock her in a closet."

"Nope," Jane Elizabeth Firesheets said. "We gone knock her on the head. They always knock them on the head," and she took the gun by the barrel and made a swing with it that way which proved far more satisfactory and so she backed the shriveled up white-haired lady against the corner cupboard and swung the pistol one time at the crown of her head striking her flush on the topnotch with the butt-end of the handle, and the shriveled up white-haired lady said, "Ouch!" and reached her fingers up to touch herself as Jane Elizabeth Firesheets swung the pistol a second time and chiefly struck her fingers but some of her topnotch too and the shriveled up white-haired lady said, "Stop!" and Jane Elizabeth Firesheets swung the gun again and hit pure scalp causing the shriveled up white-haired lady to slide down the face of the corner cupboard in a shriveled up white-haired heap on the floor, and Jane Elizabeth Firesheets gave the pistol back to Benton Lynch and told him, "Ain't nothing to it."

She drove and he lay curled and knotted up on the floorboard so as to not be seen traveling south through Altamahaw, and he heard the one siren off behind them and they met the other on the highway and Jane Elizabeth Firesheets told him, "State trooper," and asked him wasn't it just thrilling, wasn't it just absolutely thrilling. Once she got to Graham she took the 85 highway to the west but only traveled the little ways to Burlington where she stopped at the outlet mall on account of how she'd always wanted to stop at the outlet mall but had never before had the opportunity to, and Benton Lynch asked her couldn't they come back to the outlet mall some other time but Jane

Elizabeth Firesheets told him as long as she was there already she might as well go on ahead and buy a thing or two and she reached over and helped herself to the rolled up paper sack in Benton Lynch's jacket pocket and took out a handful of money from it. Benton Lynch couldn't judge time with much accuracy on the floorboard on account of how everything seemed to take forever so he figured Jane Elizabeth Firesheets stayed gone from twenty minutes to two and a half hours before she came back with two paper bags and a big Styrofoam cup that did not have any of the Coke left in it but did have some of the ice which she gave Benton Lynch and then showed him the pair of nylons she'd bought and the two pair of sheer black underpanties and the shortsleeve pink sweater with padded shoulders that she was particularly fond of and she held it up in front of herself and wanted to know from Benton Lynch did the pink set off the highlights in her hair and soften up her milky white skintone, and Benton Lynch studied the pink sweater and the milky white skin and the wheatstraw hair all at once and together and told Jane Elizabeth Firesheets pink was just the thing for her and she said she thought so too and decided it would not suit her to do anything but wear her pink sweater straightaway so she came out of her blouse right there in the front seat of the Nova and Benton Lynch watched the new pink sweater go on overtop the brassiere, or actually watched the brassiere disappear beneath the new pink sweater, and got agitated there on the floorboard and commenced to fidget and squirm and slide around until he managed to wedge himself up under the glove compartment.

They decided to keep west as far as Greensboro, or anyhow Jane Elizabeth Firesheets decided to keep west as far as Greensboro and a little bit past it to the Albert Pick Motor Hotel at the airport exit where she took a room as Mrs. Roosevelt and parked the Nova around at the backside of the lot and collected up her nylons and her panties and her discarded blouse and offered some little assistance in the unbending of Benton Lynch's various joints. She wanted to count the money first thing, insisted on counting the money first thing, and spilled it from the sack all over the bed where she spread it out with her hands and picked it up and dropped it and generally threw it around some and guessed it was probably a thousand dollars or probably eight hundred dollars or probably six hundred dollars anyway and then actually counted it and totaled it up and figured it was likely upwards of $230.00 before the nylons and the underpanties and the pink shortsleeve sweater, and she told Benton Lynch it was a right fair haul but Benton Lynch, who had laid himself out on the part of the bed where the money wasn't told her back, "It ain't hardly worth knocking an old lady on the head for."

Naturally that touched off Jane Elizabeth Firesheets as she herself had done what knocking on the head had gotten done and in her best scruples and principles if you please voice she wanted to know from Benton Lynch just why he'd set out in a line of work he didn't have the stomach for.

"It ain't my line of work to beat up on old women," Benton Lynch said.

And Jane Elizabeth Firesheets laid her hands on her hips and told him back, "I didn't see you jump in to keep me from it."

"Well we were in a predicament, we were in a pure fix and wouldn't never been in one if you hadn't wanted some Action."

"It's my fault then is it," Jane Elizabeth Firesheets said, "and here I've run off from home and left my momma and daddy and my brother and my granddaddy and give up a man that loved me truly, just give up everything for you and you a criminal getting tracked down everywhere. Ain't this some gratitude."

And Benton Lynch crossed his arms over himself and told her, "Nobody made you come and nobody keeping you here."

"That's right, use me up, violate my holy temple, and then just throw me off somewhere. You just a sorry little cocksucker like all the rest of them."

And Benton Lynch, who was not one to usually move in a quick and snakelike sort of way, moved in a quick and snakelike sort of way this time, rising up from the bed and taking Jane Elizabeth Firesheets by the shoulders in one motion and flinging her down onto the mattress in another. "I ain't taking that off you," he told her.

And Jane Elizabeth Firesheets said, "Shitass," and kicked at him and punched at him and tried to get up but he pushed her back down onto the bed and so she tried to get up again but he pushed her back down again and so she held her wrist and moaned until he leaned over to see what the trouble was when she raised up of a sudden and butted him square in the nose with her forehead. Naturally the tears blinded Benton Lynch straightaway and Jane Elizabeth Firesheets slipped off the bed to his right side and punched him in the ear prior to clench-ing her hands together so as to hammer him in the stomach one time, and even though he was part blinded and part deaf and near about fully stooped over, Benton Lynch managed to hook his fingers into some little piece of Jane Elizabeth Firesheets's new shortsleeve pink sweater and though it was not much of a little piece it was enough of one for Benton Lynch to hurl Jane Elizabeth Firesheets against the headboard with and of course the hooking and the hurling caused the fabric to give and stretch some which Jane Elizabeth Firesheets took notice of immediately and she grabbed up the little stretched and bulging portion between her fingers and shrieked, "You've ruint it! You sorry son-of-bitch you," and then she went fairly berserk and flailed with her arms and kicked with her legs and hollered and swore and spat once or twice and was just generally all over Benton Lynch from everywhere at once and so he threw himself at her to cover her up and smother her some and she tried to flail and tried to kick and still hollered and swore and spat, but with the weight and bulk of Benton Lynch atop her Jane Elizabeth Firesheets could not draw breath with much effect and so did not do anything after a spell but lay stretched out on the bed beneath Benton Lynch's cumbersome weight and bulk and with her private parts in close proximity to his private parts, and likely it was somewhat the proximity and somewhat the weight and bulk and somewhat the agitation and exasperation all mixed up together with the actual bedstead and the actual mattress and pillows and the actual bedlinens that stirred and excited Jane Eliz-abeth Firesheets who wiggled her hips just enough to get detected at it and got answered with the best part of a gyration which led to some true grinding and some oooohhhing and some groaning and some grunting and some nosewhistling and directly the articles of clothing were sailing all about the room except for the pink shortsleeve sweater, which got folded up and put in a drawer, and except for the two pair of socks, which did not get separated from the two pair of feet as the bedsheets were noticeably chilly.

They had not ever gyrated and oooohhhed and groaned and grunted and nosewhistled atop a proper mattress before and so found the whole business novel and exotic which intensified the gyrating and the oooohhhing and the groaning and the grunting and even the nosewhistling too and thereby hastened the exhaustion some and while they recovered they told each other how sorry they were about what they had said and what they had done and then they talked about the little brick house and the ragtop, or anyhow Jane Elizabeth Firesheets talked about the little brick house and the ragtop and Benton Lynch watched her naked parts and let her until he'd had enough of the talking and had enough of the recovering and reinstigated the gyrating and the oooohhhing and the groaning and the grunting and the nosewhistling and persevered with it near about courageously but ultimately gave out all over again. Jane Elizabeth Firesheets suggested they should take a shower to get shed of the perspiration and the various by-products of the undertaking, but Benton Lynch, who had never washed himself in front of a woman before, did not take to the idea right off and consequently got dragged into the bathroom and pushed up under the showerhead and Jane Elizabeth Firesheets unwrapped the Ivory and lathered Benton Lynch with it prior to handing the cake over to Benton Lynch who returned the favor and then they rinsed and dried each other and got back into their socks and got back into the bed, but even after all the soaping and the lathering and the rinsing and the drying off somehow Benton Lynch did not feel much cleaner than he had previously and laid on his back thinking about the plum-colored parts and the milky white parts and the wheatstraw parts until he could not stand to just think about them any longer and rolled over to find Jane Elizabeth Firesheets curled up asleep with her mouth open and her every breath clicking in her throat.

They continued to the west as far as Winston-Salem since it was Jane Elizabeth Firesheets's opinion that they should go to the trailer and the dilapidated henhouse by the most undirect and roundabout way they could go there, which Jane Elizabeth Firesheets said was how it always got done everywhere she'd ever seen it get done. So they did not head north exactly until the 158 highway and even then they did not proceed direct to Neely and on to Oregon Hill but instead went a little west at Stokesdale and then northeast a spell and then a little west some more and finally pure east to Pelham and south down

29 to the gravel road that led up and over the rise to the trailer and the henhouse and the general ruin. They had not been expected or anticipated by the fat Jeeter or Mr. Raeford either and so did not get greeted exactly, or anyway did not get greeted perceptibly by the fat Jeeter, who they caught in the middle of her favorite story and partway through a graham cracker, and only got purely leered at by Mr. Raeford who did not see much milky whiteness from day to day except for feathers and except for eggs.

The fat Jeeter thawed out and heated six chicken fried beef patties and served them along with some canned succotash and a dozen Hungry Jack biscuits, and once she'd fixed it all and got it on the table the fat Jeeter ate the primary part of it as well and Benton Lynch watched her and chewed his ice while Mr. Raeford fairly much interviewed Jane Elizabeth Firesheets and patted her near hand some and rubbed her near arm some and pinched her near cheek some and grinned a whole hell of a lot and just generally made a jackass out of himself which he persisted in after supper and on throughout the evening there on the Mediterranean sofa in front of the television where he patted and rubbed and pinched those parts he had patted and rubbed and pinched previously and ventured off into some bold new territory as the evening wore on and the beer cans got crushed and discarded. However, Mr. Raeford did not truly get anything for all his patting and rubbing and pinching except unduly agitated or anyway did not get anything from Jane Elizabeth Firesheets, but later in the night he did manage to slide down the paneling and pile up on the trailer floor a number of times, the first occasion being far and away the most violent one, and Jane Elizabeth Firesheets sat bolt upright in bed and said, "Whut's at?"

"Daddy," Benton Lynch told her.

"Doing what?" Jane Elizabeth Firesheets wanted to know.

"Hardly anything," Benton Lynch told her and he showed his big square teeth which Jane Elizabeth Firesheets could not see in the darkness.

And Jane Elizabeth Firesheets laid back down and clasped her hands under her head. "Your daddy must not ever get none," she said. "Looked at me like he could smell it."

"Momma and him don't get on much," Benton Lynch told her.

"I guess not," she said, "and don't seem to me like he'd want none even if he could get it. Your momma's a hog. I ain't seen her yet when she wasn't chewing something."

"Momma's all right," Benton Lynch told her. "Daddy's all right too. They just don't get on much anymore."

And Jane Elizabeth Firesheets sat up sideways on her elbow and said, "I'll tell you one thing Benton Lynch, they can get on as little as they please but I ain't staying around here to listen to it. Can't hardly turn around in this place, your daddy's done touched every touchable thing I got, and your momma don't care for nothing won't fit in her mouth. I ain't staying around here."

"It ain't so bad as that."

"I'm telling you this thing Benton Lynch, I ain't staying around here. Don't no robber I ever heard tell of live in a trailer with his momma and daddy. This just ain't no way to do it and me and you gone go out and find us a place to rent, gone find us a place tomorrow."

"It ain't so bad as that."

"Tomorrow Benton Lynch," Jane Elizabeth Firesheets said and then she added, "or me and you ain't gone get on at all," and Jane Elizabeth Firesheets rolled over and showed Benton Lynch her backside but not hardly like she'd shown him her backside previous times.

They had not eaten the waffles the fat Jeeter heated in the toaster and Jane Elizabeth Firesheets had only been patted on the forearm once when they left in the Nova to look for a place to live which Benton Lynch did not feel it proper to tell his parents they were leaving in the Nova to do and so told them they were just going to drive roundabout for a spell and they did drive roundabout for a spell but did not find anything to suit Jane Elizabeth Firesheets, actually did not find anything for rent until Benton Lynch suggested they buy a *Chronicle* which they bought and studied the classified section of where a woman in Stacy had taken out an advertisement for a Christian couple to fill her bungalow, and Jane Elizabeth Firesheets said she'd always wanted to live in a bungalow so they called the woman and did in fact get up with her before midday, but the woman in Stacy looked at Jane Elizabeth Firesheets and Benton Lynch one time hard and decided they were likely not the Christian couple she was after and she told them as much which prompted Jane Elizabeth Fire-sheets to call the woman a snotty old bag and so she went ahead and decided they were certainly not the Christian couple she was after.

They looked at two apartments in Neely proper and a tenant house out the Burlington road which had been advertised as well ventilated but turned out near about windy, and as Jane Elizabeth Firesheets and Benton Lynch could not see that ventilation was much of an asset they declined the tenant house partly on account of the draft throughout it and partly on account of the general look of the place which Jane Elizabeth Firesheets said was altogether too niggery for decent white folks, and likely it was somewhat the draft and somewhat the niggery that discouraged Jane Elizabeth Firesheets but surely it was mostly the bungalow or anyhow the idea of the bungalow that she could not shake loose of since she had always wanted to live in a bungalow, had decided she had been meant to live in a bungalow ever since earlier in the day when she saw what a bungalow was, but no matter how she held her head or squinted or shaded her eyes she could not see even the least little hint of bungalow in the tenant house and had failed to discover a trace of it in the pair of Neely proper apartments and so was understandably downcast and discouraged since she could not find anything with that bungalow quaintness and that bungalow charm to it except for the actual Stacy bungalow that she had not been Christian enough to move into.

There were not any promising advertisements after the well ventilated tenant house which had not itself truly been a promising advertisement but had got read and taken as one by Jane Elizabeth Firesheets who had figured there might be some hidden charm and might be some hidden quaintness where there had only turned out to be a preponderance of ventilation. So they did not know where they would go to find what it was they were looking to find though Jane Elizabeth Firesheets insisted she knew where they would not go to find what it was she knew they would find if they went back there, and consequently Benton Lynch felt pressed to make something in the way of a suggestion and so he made something in the way of one and directed Jane Elizabeth Firesheets who directed the stolen green Nova down the boulevard to Lawsonville Avenue and then east four blocks to the second Mrs. Cummings's house. Benton Lynch had vis-

ited Otway Burns once previously and so let himself and Jane Elizabeth Firesheets in through Mrs. Cummings's side door and up the
back stairway to the third floor where Benton Lynch knocked three
times hard on what had been Otway Burns Lynch's door but was not
Otway Burns Lynch's door any longer and so got answered by Miss
Alma Sue Frazier of the Roxboro Fraziers whose door it had become
and who was still in her housecoat and had not yet tended to herself
and so did not have any face to show them but the one she had woke
up with. Benton Lynch looked at Miss Alma Sue Frazier like she'd
been dredged up off a riverbottom with a grappling hook and did not
offer to speak to her until she asked him, "What is it?" which
prompted him to ask her back, "Otway Burns Lynch?" and Miss
Alma Sue Frazier pointed at the floor and thereby sent Benton Lynch
and Jane Elizabeth Firesheets down a flight to the second floor hallway which Otway Burns Lynch had moved onto once Mr. Etlington
had relocated to the first floor after Mrs. Hinton got sent to the Ma-
sonic Eastern Star Home in Greensboro as it was the way of things
among Mrs. Cummings's boarders to precipitate ever downward and
so drop lower and lower in the house and closer and closer to the
kitchen and to the dining room, or as low and as close as ground level
anyhow but not quite so low as the basement where the Ling brothers
lived in a little concrete room with a lavatory in the corner of it and
two tiny dirty windows near about on the ceiling. They were very
quiet and very clean and extraordinarily yellow and blinked an awful
lot even for Chinamen.

Benton Lynch knocked three times all over again and did in fact
rouse up Otway Burns who was between shifts at the cigarette plant
where he had got promoted from pushing cigarettes around on a cart
and now organized and directed and orchestrated the general pushing
around of cigarettes on carts all throughout the plant which did not
call for any actual pushing on his own part but just the organizing
and directing and orchestrating, and as he did not do anything to get
dirty any longer he had left off wearing the green poplin trousers and
the green poplin shirt and the leather Red Wing boots and instead
wore suits primarily, some that he owned and some that he'd paid on
and every now and again a sportcoat from the Johnny Miller collection when he felt lively and bold enough for it. But it was just a plain

gray flannel suit with a plain gray vest overtop and a powderblue shirt and a skinny maroon tie that he opened the door in and Benton Lynch said to him, "Hey," and Otway Burns pondered Jane Elizabeth Firesheets and pondered Benton Lynch again before his eyebrows rose up and he said, "Oh," and then said Hey back.

Benton Lynch made the necessary introduction, or anyhow pointed at Jane Elizabeth Firesheets and worked his mouth and pointed at Otway Burns Lynch and worked his mouth and then stepped aside so Jane Elizabeth Firesheets and Otway Burns Lynch could introduce themselves to each other which they succeeded at more completely and Otway Burns stuck his arm out to Jane Elizabeth Firesheets with his hand hanging off the end of it like a rag on a peg and Jane Elizabeth Firesheets took ahold of his fingers and near about curtsied which was not the sort of thing Jane Elizabeth Firesheets had much history of but her knees could not seem to help themselves in the presence of Otway Burns Lynch who was not fat like his momma or vile like his daddy or pointy and angular and hollowed out like his brother but was fairly regular or even better than regular really partly on account of his gray flannel suit that he owned the most of and partly on account of his broad foreign accent that he had contrived, cultivated, and mastered on his own. With one regal sweeping gesture he invited Jane Elizabeth Firesheets and Benton Lynch on into his room which he did not call his room but called his quarters when he was not calling it his digs, and he asked them wouldn't they like some herbal tea from southeast Asia and showed them his cupful which was almost precisely the color of urine and Benton Lynch, who had said straightaway he would have some herbal tea before he saw what the herbal tea looked like, decided he would not have some herbal tea after all while Jane Elizabeth Firesheets got purely rapturous over it and clasped her hands together and could not seem to control her delight at the prospect of southeast Asian herbal tea which she said she'd been in the mood for since she didn't know when, and from his little hotplate by the window Otway Burns observed, "How extraordinary," and Jane Elizabeth Firesheets told him, "Yes, quite."

Otway Burns Lynch asked after his momma and his daddy, who he did not call Momma and Daddy but called Mother and Father instead, as he had not had occasion to drop by the trailer lately, which he did not call the trailer but called the homeplace where he would not drop by to exactly but rather would pop in at, and he said he had been meaning to call, which he did not call call but called telephone, in lieu of popping in, which was what he said precisely, but had not gotten round to it and so was curious to know were his momma and daddy getting along all right, which he called carrying on, and Jane Elizabeth Firesheets, who had not been asked any of it, answered all of it. "I'll say," she told him.

Benton Lynch sat on the couch with the fronts of his knees against the edge of the coffee table, and Jane Elizabeth Firesheets wandered roundabout Otway Burns Lynch's quarters picking up and perusing various of Otway Burns Lynch's personal items when they seemed worth troubling herself to pick up and peruse and eventually she parked in front of a framed picture of a woman dying in an opera and she asked Otway Burns Lynch what she was doing and who was she anyhow and Otway Burns Lynch told her who she was in Italian and said she was dying in an opera and told what it was in Italian, and Jane Elizabeth Firesheets said she'd almost gone into the theater herself, said she'd almost gone into the ballet, and Otway Burns Lynch bobbed his teaball in his pot of water and said, "Oh?" and Benton Lynch looked at that portion of Jane Elizabeth Firesheets where he knew the plum-colored parts to be. She said she'd always had a natural talent for the dance, she called it, said she'd always had an instinct for rhythms and melodies, and she asked Benton Lynch didn't she have an instinct and Benton Lynch said yes she did. And Otway Burns Lynch asked her why had she not pursued her endemic urges to which Jane Elizabeth Firesheets replied that personal family matters had kept her from it, though she insisted she could still cut a figure with the best of them and of a sudden Jane Elizabeth Firesheets lit out towards the center of the room, leapt into the air, and managed about a quartertwist prior to landing firm on the hardwood causing every loose item in the place to jump up and settle again. "Brava!" Otway Burns Lynch exclaimed, and from the sofa with his knees against the coffee table Benton Lynch said, "Christ," but to himself mostly.

Jane Elizabeth Firesheets told Otway Burns Lynch the southeast Asian herbal tea was simply divine, though that was after Jane Eliza-

beth Firesheets had spooned in a few sugars and added a touch of
honey since the southeast Asian herbal tea in its natural naked yellow
state had not struck Jane Elizabeth Firesheets as simply divine exactly,
but she insisted the sugar and the honey too brought out the oriental
subtleties of the blend and she offered her cup to Otway Burns Lynch
who sipped from it and rolled the tea around in his mouth and looked
off towards the ceiling. He said he did believe the sugar and the honey
noticeably enhanced the tea, he said he believed they enhanced it noticeably, and Jane Elizabeth Firesheets offered her cup to Benton
Lynch so as to allow him to taste the oriental subtleties and appreciate
the noticeable enhancement for himself, but since the sugar and the
honey together had not rendered the southeast Asian herbal tea any
less urine colored than it had been previously, Benton Lynch declined
to drink any, and so Jane Elizabeth Firesheets asked him why didn't
he take just one tiny little taste, and Benton French said he did not
believe he wanted a tiny little taste, and so Jane Elizabeth Firesheets
insisted he just sip at it one time, but Benton Lynch said he did not
want to sip at it, and so Jane Elizabeth Firesheets turned her face so as
to show it to Benton Lynch exclusively and stretched it and twisted it
and just generally worked it up into an indisputable and fairly ferocious goddamn-well-better-drink-this-fucking-tea expression and she
said to him, "Please," and Benton Lynch said he guessed he'd have
just one tiny little taste and so sipped at the tea for himself and got
asked wasn't it subtle and wasn't it enhanced and said Yes, wasn't it.

They got around to the bungalow presently, or anyhow got
around to the bungalow once Otway Burns Lynch had pointed out a
few of his more precious possessions and had explained what they
were and where they'd come from and how much he'd given for
them, all of which Jane Elizabeth Firesheets announced she was purely
intrigued with and every now and again she'd turn to Benton Lynch
and ask him wasn't he intrigued too, at the same time indicating to
him that he should be, and he would shake his head Yes he was. But
they did in fact get around to the bungalow presently and Jane Elizabeth Firesheets told Otway Burns Lynch what had happened to them
earlier in the day with the woman from Stacy, or anyway related to
him an episode loosely based on what had happened to them earlier in
the day with the woman from Stacy who Jane Elizabeth Firesheets de-

scribed as surly once Otway Burns Lynch told her surly was the word she was looking for, and she asked Benton Lynch wasn't it surly that the lady had been after all and Benton Lynch shook his head yes. She told Otway Burns she was after a bungalow chiefly but would take most any quaint and charming place she could come up on and she said Benton Lynch had suggested, and she pointed at Benton Lynch for effect, that maybe Otway Burns Lynch could help them find some quaint and charming place, perhaps even an actual bungalow, on account of his numerous acquaintances and contacts roundabout, and Otway Burns Lynch set his teacup down and took his chin in his hand and admitted he did have numerous acquaintances and numerous contacts too. Then he pondered for a spell and chewed his bottom lip and at last snapped his fingers one time and announced he believed he had a line on just the thing, not a bungalow exactly but the sort of place that could be construed as quaint and could be made charming, and Jane Elizabeth Firesheets got all agitated and excited and wanted to know what was it and where was it and how much was it, and Otway Burns told her it belonged to a Mr. Jack Albright and he said to Benton Lynch, "You know Jack Albright, don't you?" but Benton Lynch, who did not have numerous acquaintances and numerous contacts, shook his head no.

Otway Burns Lynch said it was a five room painted block house with a wood before it and a tobacco field behind it and a hedgerow to the left of it and a garden plot to the right of it, and he said it had been empty for a while on account of Mr. Jack Albright could not find anybody to let it out to that suited him, not that he was courting Christians—Otway Burns said Mr. Jack Albright did not show any particular enthusiasm for Christianity—but just that he did not want any niggers and did not want any trash, though Otway Burns did not call them niggers and did not call them trash. And then Otway Burns held his chin again and thoroughly chewed his lip prior to announcing that he believed he could get what he called an inside line on the Jack Albright painted block bungalow if an inside line was what Benton Lynch and Jane Elizabeth Firesheets wanted gotten, and Jane Elizabeth Firesheets said most emphatically Yes it was what she wanted gotten and said most emphatically Yes it was what he wanted gotten too, and then she asked Benton Lynch wasn't it just exactly what he wanted gotten after she'd already said most emphatically it was and Benton Lynch told her he supposed so, and Otway Burns Lynch said, "Done then," and gave his fingers to Jane Elizabeth Firesheets who shook them and said Done then herself after glancing inquiringly at Benton Lynch who did not seem to find the finger shaking in any way objectionable or stirring either.

They slept another night at the trailer even though Jane Elizabeth Firesheets had announced and swore she would not sleep another night at the trailer, and the morning after the night they slept at the trailer that Jane Elizabeth Firesheets had swore she wouldn't she in- sisted Benton Lynch get up with his brother but Benton Lynch told her Otway Burns would call or Otway Burns would drop by though Jane Elizabeth Firesheets feared he would not telephone and would not pop in either and kept after Benton Lynch until Otway Burns did in fact ring up which was what he told the fat Jeeter he was doing in lieu of popping in which he did not presently have the leisure for, and as the fat Jeeter and Otway Burns exchanged trifles Jane Elizabeth Firesheets fretted by the dinette until at long last the fat Jeeter handed the phone receiver over to Benton Lynch who exchanged a trifle or two himself and then just listened some which did not soothe Jane Elizabeth Firesheets's fretfulness the least little bit and she pulled at Benton Lynch's arm and wanted to know was it done but just got an- swered with several all rights and a couple of Uh Huhs and so contin- ued to fret and continued to pull and continued to yank until Benton Lynch cradled the receiver, turned full around to Jane Elizabeth Fire- sheets, and told her, "Otway Burns says hey."

They moved in directly even though it wasn't exactly what Jane Elizabeth Firesheets had figured it would be and even though Jane Elizabeth Firesheets and Benton Lynch weren't exactly what Mr. Jack Albright had figured they were, but it all got settled and it all got done anyhow and they moved in directly without hardly a grumble from the fat Jeeter and with somewhat of a stifled grumble from Mr. Raeford Lynch who could not grumble outright in front of the fat Jeeter and so rubbed Jane Elizabeth Firesheets's near arm and patted her near cheek and touched another thing or two as a general sendoff. They piled up what clothes they had in the backseat of the Nova along with an iron frypan that the fat Jeeter hadn't any use for ever since her electric skillet and they stopped off at the 7-Eleven for a bottle of Champale which Jane Elizabeth Firesheets intended to break against the front stoop for luck but Benton Lynch convinced her Champale was not lucky but for boats and so they drank it at supper with their eggs that they had to eat off their fingers direct out of the iron pan as they did not have any dishes or any utensils either except for Benton Lynch's pocket knife. There was, however, some furniture roundabout that Mr. Jack Albright had gone ahead and let out with the house, primarily an iron bedstead with iron springs and a mattress and a kitchen table and two kitchen chairs and several curtain rods and a piece of a drapery and a solitary upholstered settee that smelled like old socks, and once Benton Lynch had licked off his fingers and Jane Elizabeth Firesheets had run water in the pan they toured the house together and Benton Lynch got told what the kitchen would look like and what the living room would look like and how bright and airy the den and the bathroom would be and then he got taken on into the bedroom which suited him already and he snatched up Jane Elizabeth Firesheets and fell with her onto the mattress which smelled like old socks itself once you got your nose right up to it.

As Jane Elizabeth Firesheets figured it they needed some general repair and renovation money but Benton Lynch insisted they had about as much general repair and renovation money as they would likely require, or anyhow he insisted it for a spell until Jane Elizabeth Firesheets fetched a state roadmap out from the glovebox of the Nova and commenced to cast around for a favorable spot to draw some funds out of which moved Benton Lynch away from insisting and more towards suggesting and Jane Elizabeth Firesheets struck on and decided upon Hillsdale almost straightaway which prompted a little pleading and pathetic moaning on Benton Lynch's part but Jane Elizabeth Firesheets just smoothed out the wrinkles in the brown jacket with the flat of her hand and preceded Benton Lynch out the door to the driveway. She took the 158 highway southwest and then headed due south along route 135 to Hillsdale where there was no scantling amount of puny grocery and convenience stores and she pulled into a couple of lots and aided Benton Lynch in casing a Pantry and a Li'l General but they were both too busy to suit him and he directed her out the city limits a ways on a backroad where they came up on Ross's

Grocery No. 2 which did not have much of a crowd about it, did not even appear open really, and Benton Lynch announced that this was the very place he would knock over, he called it.

Jane Elizabeth Firesheets parked the Nova back a ways behind Ross's Grocery No. 2 just off the blacktop alongside of a curing barn and Benton Lynch glanced at the roadmap and said to himself, "Duncan," prior to getting a goodluck kiss on the cheek and a thera-peutic flurry somewhere else so as to remind him what he had to live for, and then he excused himself to go off and plunder and he did go off and plunder, plundered direct from the proprietary Ross who did not have a No. 1 grocery any longer and so stayed permanent at the No. 2 and who as well had cultivated an endearment for his private parts and did not want them going anywhere without him and so gave up the extent of his riches which Jane Elizabeth Firesheets said, "Shit," at once Benton Lynch had counted it out on the seat. She did not see as $112.00 would go hardly anywhere, did not see as how she could be expected to set up house with $112.00 and she bitched some and moaned some partly out the window and partly at Benton Lynch who had retired to the floorboard and consequently could not see where it was they had stopped until Jane Elizabeth Firesheets told him, "Get on out and do something," and he peeked up over the dashboard at the gaspumps and the glassy storefront and before he could even say, "Uh Uh," before he could even work up the spit to say Uh Uh, Jane Elizabeth Firesheets unfolded the map herself and told him, "Corinth. Now get on out," and she opened the door for him since he did not seem disposed to open the door and she pushed him with her foot since he did not seem disposed to get on out the door once she'd gone to the trouble to open it and she did not give him a kiss or a flurry or a goodluck even but drove on around the store out of sight.

Jane Elizabeth Firesheets said $262.00 would likely be quite a plenty. Jane Elizabeth Firesheets said $262.00 would likely be a suit-able and fitting amount and she reached down underneath the dash and patted Benton Lynch atop his head. Jane Elizabeth Firesheets said she was going to buy some pots and some pans and a knife and a fork and spoon set and some bedlinens and pillows and plastic window-shades and bathtowels and a shower curtain and two or three of those plastic endtables that stack up on each other. Jane Elizabeth Firesheets said she had to have a radio too, maybe even a record player, and one of those tiny Japanese televisions that you can put on your stomach which she told Benton Lynch she'd had a particular yearning for since she'd never looked at anything but a Motorola, and she said she wanted a half dozen houseplants and a doormat with some ducks on it and a hatrack and a picture for over the sofa and a picture for over the bed, and once she had steered into the K-Mart plaza west of Neely and parked the Nova in the lot she asked Benton Lynch was there anything he had a particular yearning for and he laid his head back against the door panel and told her, "Uh Uh."

She got it all but for the television which she did not have the money to get as tiny Japanese stomachtop models were at a premium, so instead she bought a Ricky Skaggs record album for her new radio/phonograph and pushed it all outside in a cart which she left beside the Nova for Benton Lynch to unload while she went in the Food Lion next to the K-Mart and bought potatoes and a pork roast and applesauce in a jar and white wine and lime sherbet and toilet paper and something potent and sweet-smelling for the old socks aroma all of which she carted outside too and all of which she piled into what of the backseat Benton Lynch had not already piled things into. And Jane Elizabeth Firesheets said she guessed they'd live like royalty for a spell, said she guessed they'd live like a duke and a princess, and she asked Benton Lynch didn't he guess that was the truth of it and Benton Lynch said he guessed it was, and so she talked about dukes and she talked about princesses all the way back to the bungalow which Jane Elizabeth Firesheets had decided was not one of your pure and absolute bungalows but had some measurable cottage to it and maybe a touch of hideaway seeing as how it was tucked off behind the hedgerow and the general undergrowth and she stopped just short of the driveway and told Benton Lynch to raise up and look see didn't it have some cottage and some hideaway to it and Benton Lynch brought his face up over the door panel to the windowglass and told her, "Uh Huh."

Jane Elizabeth Firesheets situated her pots and her pans and her flatware and arranged the plastic tables and set out the plants and instructed Benton Lynch to hang the windowshades but Jane Elizabeth

Firesheets neglected to buy any windowshade hardware and so Benton Lynch did not have anything to hang the windowshades from and decided he would hang the shower curtain instead but Jane Elizabeth Firesheets had neglected to buy any shower curtain hooks too and so Benton Lynch figured he would treat the sofa with the potent and sweet-smelling disinfectant and so he treated the sofa with the potent and sweet-smelling disinfectant and then sat down on it and sniffed for the old sock aroma which was just about when Jane Elizabeth Firesheets came out from the bedroom and up the hallway towards the kitchen and she spied Benton Lynch on the sofa where he was midway through his sniffing but she did not truly notice the sniffing and was taken primarily with the sitting instead and she laid her hands on her hips and asked Benton Lynch why in the shit didn't he do something useful for a change and he attempted to explain to her the sniffing part of it that went along with the sitting part of it but Jane Elizabeth Firesheets just turned around and stomped back into the bedroom since she had not asked her question so as to get an answer to it.

Benton Lynch made himself especially useful thereafter and insisted on hanging the picture over the sofa and hanging the picture over the bed and demanded the privilege of connecting the record player and then would not hear of resting himself until he had moved and adjusted most every piece of furniture to Jane Elizabeth Firesheets's satisfaction after which he offered to cook supper and Jane Elizabeth Firesheets told him No, thank you, so he offered to help cook supper and Jane Elizabeth Firesheets told him No, thank you again, and so he offered to set out the dishes and the silverware on the table and Jane Elizabeth Firesheets told him plain No, and so he insisted on setting out the dishes and the silverware on the table and Jane Elizabeth Firesheets asked him why in the shit didn't he get out from under her feet anyhow.

She barbecued the pork roast in the oven and boiled the potatoes and opened the applesauce and as she had not recollected to buy any proper dinner candles she hunted up a pink birthday candle and a white birthday candle in the back of the utensil drawer and stuck them on a shoebox top and set them on the table. Then she got herself done up somewhat for supper, piled her hair up onto the point of her head, slipped into a lacy white dress, and put some color to her cheeks out of the compact she had got in Altamahaw instead of the cheese after which she lit the birthday candles and called Benton Lynch off the sofa where he had been just sitting and hardly sniffing at all. Benton Lynch had not expected birthday candles and so was somewhat surprised by them and had not expected the pile of hair and the lacy white dress and the rouge either and so was somewhat surprised by them and had not truly expected a pork roast but was not very astounded and dumbstruck by it like he was verily astounded and dumbstruck by the shimmer and glisten of the milky white skin and the wheatstraw hair in the birthday candlelight. He lost his appetite almost straightaway but she made him sit down at the table anyhow and she made him unscrew the top off the wine and pour out a portion for herself and a portion for himself and she made him raise up his glass and knock it together with hers in a toast. "Luck," she said.

She had a present for him, told him she had a present for him and brought it up from her lap where she'd kept it hid away. It was near about the slightest of boxes wrapped in a piece of bag and tied up with string and he loosed the string and tore the paper and read the box which he found to contain fifty Remington .45-caliber hollow point cartridges with brass casings and copper tips, and Benton Lynch said, "Oh," and Jane Elizabeth Firesheets told him, "Dump some out," and he dumped some out and they laid there on the tabletop bigger around than a twenty-penny spike and generally meaner looking, or anyhow they laid there on the tabletop but for the one Jane Elizabeth Firesheets took up between her fingers and held in the birthday-candlelight and the sight of it there with the orange glow dancing roundabout the casing made Jane Elizabeth Firesheets all tingly and she told Benton Lynch as much and showed him a scant piece of her tongue which straightaway rendered Benton Lynch a little worse than tingly himself and he came near about direct across the tabletop after Jane Elizabeth Firesheets and reached around behind her and commenced to take her dress off right there in the kitchen and the idea of getting her dress took off her in the kitchen made Jane Elizabeth Firesheets even more tingly than she'd been at the outset and once her dress had dropped off her to the floor she helped Benton

Lynch out of his shirt and loosened his pants for him and they both slipped down onto the linoleum and rolled around until they got chilled enough to retire to the bedroom. Jane Elizabeth Firesheets sat up high and gyrated and laid down low and let Benton Lynch gyrate some and then the both of them slammed together for a while and Benton Lynch panted hard and grunted once and Jane Elizabeth Firesheets groaned prior to whimpering prior to passing out what looked like dead away. She did not revive for a considerable while, but naturally when she did revive she told Benton Lynch it was the best she'd had ever and asked him wasn't it the best he'd had ever too and he made some kind of affirmative noise or another and laid his head on the soft fleshy part of Jane Elizabeth Firesheet's frontside. She raked her fingers through his hair and asked him was he happy and asked him was he contented and he told her Yes and she told him back she was happy and she was contented too. "But," she said and then played with Benton Lynch's hair momentarily until she said again, "But," and then proceeded with, "me and you we've shared our passion and our love and the very roof over our heads and you've met all my people and I've told you all about them and all about me and I've met your people but you ain't never told me anything about anybody, especially not anything about you. I wish you would tell me something, Benton."

"Ain't nothing to tell," Benton Lynch said.

"Bound to be," Jane Elizabeth Firesheets insisted.

"Ain't," Benton Lynch said.

And Jane Elizabeth Firesheets told him, "All right then," and lifted her fingers up from Benton Lynch's scalp and removed the fleshy part of her frontside out from under Benton Lynch's right ear and once his face hit the bedlinen he decided there was likely something to tell after all and he said, "Hold it."

"What for?" Jane Elizabeth Firesheets asked him.

"I thought of something," Benton Lynch said. "I thought of something about me." And he lifted his head so as to make room for the fleshy part of Jane Elizabeth Firesheets's frontside which got put back where it had been. "Go on," she told him and he adjusted himself until his ear was just where he wanted his ear to be and was as

unfolded and as uncrimped as he could get it and he waited to feel the
fingertips on his scalp after which he did in fact open his mouth and
begin to speak. "We stepped in some shit," he said, "stepped in some
big, big shit."

They didn't none of them want to end up like Mr. Vernon Littlejohn had ended up all stretched out dead in his own puddle, didn't
none of them want to get even the least little piece of what Mr. Vernon Littlejohn had got the whole of and so they did not struggle, did
not breathe hardly, especially Mr. Radford whose store it was anyhow
but not Mr. Burke or Mr. Mountcastle either who had only stopped
in to jaw and then got reason to wish they never had. They said he did
not seem anything but agitated and agitated was the last thing in the
world they wanted him to seem what with his right hand wrapped
around what it was wrapped around and his foremost finger flush up
against what it was flush up against. And straightaway the sheriff
wanted to know, "Square teeth?" and Mr. Radford and Mr. Burke and
Mr. Mountcastle told him, "Yes sir." And the sheriff wanted to know,
"Pointy nose?" and Mr. Radford and Mr. Burke and Mr. Mountcastle
told him, "Yes sir" again. And the sheriff wanted to know, "Tall of
stature?" and Mr. Radford and Mr. Burke told him plain "Yes sir" a
third time while Mr. Mountcastle of Eden told him just exactly and
precisely how tall of stature right down to the quarter inch.

The sheriff asked after the manner of dress and got a jacket from
Mr. Radford and some trousers from Mr. Burke and the entire ensem-
ble from the Eden Mountcastle who recollected a missing button on
the top jacketpocket and a greasy smudge on the left trouserknee and
seemed to recall that one of the brown brogans had a black shoelace
and one of them didn't but he could not recollect which was what
and apologized for it. The sheriff wanted to know were there distinguishing marks, scars and moles and warts and such, and Mr. Radford
took up his chin in his hand and Mr. Burke crossed his arms over
himself and together they considered the matter and decided there
had not been any detectable scars or moles or warts and such, except
for the scar on his left thumbjoint, Mr. Mountcastle said, and the
mole on his forehead and the piece of wart just at the hairline on the

back of his neck. And the sheriff asked them did he cock the gun and did he point it and if he did cock it and point it what did he cock it and point it at, and Mr. Radford said it was his jewels which the Burke did not object to and the Mountcastle did not elaborate upon, and the sheriff asked Mr. Radford, "Where was it this time?" and Mr. Radford told him, "Lillington," and Mr. Burke agreed, "Lillington," and Mr. Mountcastle said, "Down 401 south, don't you know, twenty-six, maybe twenty-seven miles outside Raleigh."

The sheriff was anxious to identify the weapon precisely and he asked Mr. Radford if he could precisely identify the weapon and Mr. Radford told him, "Sure enough. It was a pistol," and he looked at Mr. Burke who agreed with him that most definitely it was a pistol, and Mr. Radford held his hands apart in front of him what he judged to be the length of the barrel and then looked to Mr. Burke again who said, "Longer," and then looked to Mr. Mountcastle who said, "Whatever's nine inches."

"Nine inches?" the sheriff asked him.

And Mr. Mountcastle said, "Yes sir. Standard bore length on a Harrington and Richardson Buntline revolver."

"A Harrington and Richardson Buntline revolver?" the sheriff asked him.

"Yes sir," Mr. Mountcastle said. "Forty-five caliber."

"You're certain?" the sheriff asked him.

"Yes sir," Mr. Mountcastle said.

"It had a wood grip," Mr. Radford added.

"Surely did," Mr. Burke said.

And Mr. Mountcastle told the sheriff, "Walnut."

Sheriff Burton had rode to Greensboro with his eyewitness account from Mr. Musselwhite and had got the police artist there to draw him a picture which he took out from his front shirtpocket, unfolded, and showed to Mr. Radford. "This the man that robbed you?" he wanted to know, and Mr. Radford told him, "Well I do guess it is," and the picture got stuck in the face of Mr. Burke who said, "Yes sir, the very one," and then got shown to Mr. Mountcastle who asked could he hold it and carried it direct under an incandescent bulb where he found himself in possession of a rude line drawing of a face that, except for the freckles, was the very image of Mortimer Snerd.

And the sheriff asked Mr. Mountcastle, "That the man?" and got told, "Lord no."

"Ain't nobody looks like that," Mr. Mountcastle said. "I mean the teeth was big but they wasn't sitting out in the horizontal and the nose was pointy but you couldn't hardly bore a hole with it and if a man's eyes was that far back in his head he could see out his ears. That ain't him, favors him some but it just ain't him."

"All right then," the sheriff told him, "we gone make it him, you and me," and he took Mr. Mountcastle in what appeared to be custody and drove him off in the squad car not so far as Greensboro since Mr. Mountcastle flatout refused to ride so far as Greensboro but so far anyhow as Mrs. Alice Covington's house on Russell Avenue. Mrs. Alice Covington painted snow scenes on rocks at Christmas and bunnies on rocks at Easter and turkeys on rocks at Thanksgiving and just sundry items on rocks the rest of the time, and though it was just rocks and just Santas and bunnies and turkeys and flowers and butterflies and whatnot Mrs. Alice Covington was considered quite the artist roundabout and was measurably pleased and gratified to find herself called upon by the sheriff and the Mountcastle, was measurably pleased and gratified to find herself privy to even some little piece of the mayhem pure and undiluted and she studied the police artist's rough drawing of Mortimer Snerd and aired out her appreciation for the general texture of the thing. She told the sheriff she found it a primitive piece but moving and satisfying nonetheless and she asked him didn't he think it had a dash of the Fauves to it and the sheriff told her it was a plain Beasley, likely some strain of Beasley indigenous to Greensboro, and the sheriff said it might be primitive and it might be moving and satisfying too but it wasn't who they wanted it to be, and Mrs. Covington chewed on her top lip ever so briefly prior to suggesting to the sheriff, "Matisse?" and the sheriff told her, "No ma'm. Beasley."

Mr. Mountcastle said the teeth were what was wrong primarily but the nose was what was wrong too and the eyes were what was wrong on top of it and he took in hand the primitive and moving and satisfying Beasley and pointed out to Mrs. Covington what she might do to the teeth and what she might do to the nose and the eyes as well but Mrs. Covington would not lay her pencil point to any part of the

Greensboro Beasley's paper on account of the pure sanctity of the artistic endeavor, she called it, and so she fetched a broad hunk of shale out from under her worktable and set to sketching on it with the assistance of the Eden Mountcastle who suggested how she might draw one thing and indicated how she might draw another, and once she'd sketched out the face to suit the Mountcastle she touched it up here and there so as to suit herself and then set about the painting of it with acrylic paint and tiny little pig bristle brushes and when she got done she held the thing away from herself and eyed it at arm's length prior to turning it around to Sheriff Burton and the Eden Mountcastle who found themselves perusing what looked to be Howdy Doody but for the checked shirt and neckerchief, and though Howdy Doody was closer than Mortimer Snerd Howdy Doody was not right on it exactly and the Eden Mountcastle suggested and indicated that Mrs. Covington hollow out the eyes some and get shed of the freckles and get shed of the grin all of which Mrs. Covington obliged him in prior to turning the thing roundabout to the sheriff and the Eden Mountcastle all over again and the sheriff said, "Well?" and the Eden Mountcastle told him, "Yes sir, the very one."

The full-blooded Loop Road Myrick's sister's husband had not ever reproduced a picture from a rock before but said he would attempt to, and the sheriff asked him would he keep Mr. H. Monroe Aycock otherwise occupied and write the copy himself on account of how it was the sort of thing which called for a fact or two to leak in with the general palaver, and the full-blooded Loop Road Myrick's sister's husband nodded and then studied the hunk of shale and said, "Alice Covington?" and the sheriff nodded and the Loop Road Myrick's sister's husband said he had one of her Christmas rocks holding his backhall door open.

They printed the picture in color at the top of the front page of the morning *Chronicle* which did not from year to year come out with much but your seasonal color picture of a pumpkin in autumn and a flower in springtime and such as that, so an unseasonal color picture especially an unseasonal color picture of a man painted on a rock captured the attention of most everybody in general and captured the attention of Mr. Tiny Aaron quite specifically. He had got up in the dark when he usually got up and had put on his striped robe and his

socks and had dunked his head in the sink and plugged in the percu-
lator and then had got the paper in and carried it to the breakfast
room with the rubberband still on it. He did not open it up to look at
it until he'd poured himself a cup of coffee and creamed it and sugared
it and dumped a little of it in the saucer so as to blow on it and slurp
it out, but when he did unroll the paper at last he got attracted
straightaway to the color photograph and he looked at it with his
mouth open a little and then read the print all roundabout it with his
mouth moving a little and then looked at it again with his lips still
parted and swallowed once and slurped some coffee and finally told
himself aloud, "Uh Oh."

Five

Mr. Raeford Lynch said it weren't him, said it weren't no way it could be him, said it just plain weren't him and kicked at the ground and swore and spat a time or two. The fat Jeeter said it weren't him too but without the enthusiasm that Mr. Raeford said it weren't him and then she put something in her mouth and chewed it and swallowed it. Mr. Raeford said it weren't in a Lynch to kill and pilfer, said it weren't in a Lynch to do but the decent and righteous thing and he swore and spat and kicked at the ground all over again. "It weren't him," Mr. Raeford said. "That boy's good as gold," and the fat Jeeter said it weren't him too and put something in her mouth and chewed it and swallowed it.

The full-blooded Loop Road Myrick's sister's husband ran the picture of the rock once in the morning of a Thursday and once in the evening of a Thursday and it was not until Saturday late that he got ahold of an actual snapshot which Mr. Raeford and the fat Jeeter had to be excised from along with a piece of the trailer and assorted chickens. It was a grainy black and white picture that Otway Burns had taken with his Instamatic the summer he had decided a photographer was what he intended to be which was the summer he wore the skyblue seersucker jacket, even in August, and tied the silk handkerchief around his neck. He had posed the fat Jeeter and had posed Mr. Raeford and Benton, had even posed the chickens to the extent that the chickens would let themselves get posed, and had turned the Instamatic at a tilt for effect which the full-blooded Loop Road Myrick's sister's husband did not seem to appreciate much, which nobody at the *Chronicle* seemed to appreciate much really except for Mr. H. Monroe Aycock who could see the art in the thing, who could sense the aura of the latent creative juices, he called them, and who objected to the razor blade and the general excising because of the art and because of the juices, and consequently so as to shut Mr. H. Monroe Aycock up the full-blooded Loop Road Myrick's sister's husband let him write the accompanying copy, and Mr. H. Monroe Aycock said it would be a contemplative piece with ramifications and got asked if maybe he couldn't throw in a fact or two every now and again when the mood hit him.

Mr. H. Monroe Aycock followed his usual method of composition which called for several feverish bursts of torrid scribbling interrupted by spells of pure and unproductive reflection when he would mostly marvel at what he had been torrid over just previously and then anticipate just what he might say once he got to feeling torrid again, but he was not torrid much in the afternoon at the office and did not get truly frantic until after supper when he retired to his study, which was the paymaster's desk in the northwest corner of the dining room, where he worked himself up into a comtemplative fit with ramifications and then reflected and marveled and even doodled some in the margin of the page. He was awfully pleased and awfully satisfied once he got done scribbling and marveling and doodling and so as to share and distribute his pleasure and his satisfaction he stepped into the living room and read aloud his contemplative piece with ramifications to Mrs. H. Monroe Aycock while she quilted a pillow cover and watched The Love Boat on television which she would not let Mr. H. Monroe Aycock turn off, which she would not let Mr. H. Monroe Aycock even turn down entirely on account of how the girl off The Brady Bunch and the girl off Petticoat Junction had both gotten themselves infatuated over the boy off The Partridge Family who had a romantic fondness for Betty White as he did not know she was his aunt. Mr. H. Monroe Aycock read the contemplative parts and read the ramifications too in a loud theatrical voice that fairly completely drowned out the television except when Captain Steuben and Gopher got into a heated discussion over Gopher's mother, as played by Ethel Merman, and except when the man from Burlington came on to sell his Datsuns. Otherwise Mr. H. Monroe Aycock made himself heard almost exclusively and he finished out with a boisterous flourish followed by a lingering poetical silence after which he asked Mrs. H. Monroe Aycock, "Well?" and Mrs. H. Monroe Aycock told him, "That's very nice dear," and Mr. H. Monroe Aycock told her back he had figured it was.

Most people found it even more inspiring and even more vivid and lyrical than the ode to Vernon Littlejohn or anyhow that was the general consensus among the guests at Mrs. Estelle Singletary's annual autumn harvest brunch which everybody with an opinion worth airing usually attended. Mrs. Estelle Singletary herself was particularly fond of the part about breaking the bonds of degradation and the shackles of penury. She said it stirred her, said it stirred her profoundly, and while Miss Bernice Fay Frazier found herself stirred by the bonds and the shackles as well she argued that the part about striking out at the myriad inequities of this our existence was likely the most moving and agitating piece of prose she had ever had the pleasure to peruse, and the widow Mrs. Jennings W. Hayes wanted to know just how many was a myriad anyhow but she never did find out as Miss Bernice Fay Frazier got short and peevish straightaway and insulted the widow Mrs. Jennings W. Hayes's poetical sensibilities. Mr. H. Monroe Aycock himself arrived shortly thereafter and accepted the congratulations of the hostess and of the hostess's sister and of the general assortment of guests as well and he got asked almost right off did he have a favorite part and what was it and as he liked so very much of the thing he had to think a minute before he could decide and at last he selected the part where the chickenhouse and the chickens served as a metaphor for the hectic, troubled, and fateful lives we lead on our speck of swirling dust in the vast darkness of space, and he repeated the speck-of-swirling-dust-in-the-vast-darkness-of-space part of it as he found that phrase particularly apt, he called it.

Mrs. Estelle Singletary directed Mr. H. Monroe Aycock to the only comfortable chair in the house and assorted guests collected roundabout him once he had sat himself down so as to congratulate him all over again on the article as a whole and especially on the swirling-speck-of-dust portion since the particular aptness of it had hit most everybody once Mr. H. Monroe Aycock had pointed it out to them. Mrs. Estelle Singletary brought him his coffee with his cream and his sugar already in it and as she handed it to him she happened to mention how profoundly stirred she'd been by the bonds and the shackles which Miss Bernice Fay Frazier got wind of and so felt compelled to say a word or two on the myriad inequities of this our existence and felt compelled to tell how she'd been moved and how she'd been agitated which the widow Mrs. Jennings W. Hayes happened to be near enough to hear and so got reminded of what it was she wanted to find out and she slipped up on Mr. H. Monroe Aycock when he was otherwise unengaged and asked him just how many was a myriad anyhow.

"Scores and scores," he told her.

"How many's that?" she wanted to know.

"Very many," he said.

And the widow Mrs. Jennings W. Hayes told him back, "Ah."

The widow Mrs. Askew, who had been strangely silent and reflective all throughout the proceedings, set her untouched waldorf salad and her nibbled at sliver of breakfast steak down on the coffee table and wondered out loud how it was that a man who would plunder and kill could have risen out of Jeeter stock and Mr. H. Monroe Aycock commenced to put forth his theory and his hypothesis on the influences of deviant brain cells in conjunction with socio-economic considerations but the widow Mrs. Askew had not wondered what she had wondered so as to get a theory and a hypothesis but had instead wondered what she had wondered so as to proceed on to wondering something else which she did in fact wonder once Mr. H. Monroe Aycock had played out on his brain cells and his considerations and she asked out loud why it was that the bald Jeeter had not seemed larcenous or murderous or even a little criminal which she had not asked out loud so as to get answered out loud but which did get answered out loud by Mr. H. Monroe Aycock who had a theory and a hypothesis on that part of the thing too as he had studied the whole business from every end and the middle also, and the widow Mrs. Askew heard the theory and heard the hypothesis and once Mr. H. Monroe Aycock had spent himself on them and closed his mouth at last the widow Mrs. Askew recollected aloud the peculiar way the bald Jeeter had of stooping over so as not to dump her wig off and she dabbed at the underside of her nose with her napkin and said, "Three months, almost three months to the very day."

"Hardly seems it," Miss Bernice Fay Frazier observed.

"Surely doesn't," the widow Mrs. Jennings W. Hayes added.

"We were near about sisters," Mrs. Askew said, "near about kin," and began to blubber genuinely. "We were like this."

And Miss Bernice Fay Frazier said, "So were we."

"We were too," the widow Mrs. Jennings W. Hayes added, "we surely were," and she raised her fingers up into the air and joined in the general waving.

They could not hunt him up anywhere, not Sheriff Burton or his fulltime deputy Mr. Larson or his parttime deputy Mr. Warner, they did not even know where to start to look as they could not get anything out of the fat Jeeter but for the chewing and the swallowing or out of Mr. Raeford Lynch either but for the swearing and the spitting and the stomping around. So they did not find him straight off as they did not know where to look to find him exactly though they had thought they had found him a week to the very day after Mrs. Alice Covington's picture on the shalestone when Mr. Newsome ran up the courthouse steps and direct into the sheriff's office all blanched and winded. "I seen him," he wheezed. "I seen him just now," and the sheriff got especially stern and earnest of a sudden and leapt to his feet in that purposeful sort of way people will leap to their feet when they are stern and earnest and he asked Mr. Newsome, "Where?"

"Out 29 a ways on the roadside," Mr. Newsome told him.

"Doing what?"

"Just sitting," Mr. Newsome said.

"Just sitting on the roadside?"

"In a truck," Mr. Newsome said, "in that pickup truck of his."

"Alone?" the sheriff wanted to know.

"Naw. Had that crew in the back."

"Lynch ain't got no crew," the sheriff said.

And Mr. Newsome studied the sheriff like maybe part of his face had puffed up and turned colors of a sudden. "Lynch?" he said.

"Lynch ain't got no crew," the sheriff told him.

"Overhill," Mr. Newsome said back.

"Overhill who?" the sheriff asked him.

"Overhill the gravedigger," Mr. Newsome said. "Overhill the gravedigger what Benton Lynch used to work for."

"Sometime lately?" the sheriff wanted to know.

"Not real lately," Mr. Newsome told him, "but sometime."

"Well what is it you want me to do with him?"

"Round him up," Mr. Newsome said. "Round him up and ask him a thing or two."

"Such as?"

"Well how in the hell should I know. You the law and if you can't see a hot tip when it comes up and slaps you in the face then ain't nothing I can tell you." And Mr. Newsome whirled around and attempted to storm on out the door but he had whirled around a little too vigorously and overshot the door and stormed off towards the wall instead and so had to stop and adjust his course some which gave Sheriff Burton the opportunity to catch up with him and lay his thick mealy hand on Mr. Newsome's shoulder and tell Mr. Newsome, "All right now, no call to get hot. Take me to him," and he followed Mr. Newsome out the office door and into the hallway where he attempted to tell the mayor's secretary, who was his secretary too sometimes, just where he was going and just why he was going there but the mayor's secretary was not behind her desk in her little alcove and there was no sign of her anywhere in the hallway but for the remote clack clack clacking of her heels on the courthouse steps as she descended towards the square on her way to the offices of the *Chronicle* so as to tell whoever might listen about the Overhill and about the truck and about the crew in the back of it.

They were right where Mr. Newsome had said they would be and they were doing just precisely what Mr. Newsome had said they were doing which was not anything really or not much of anything really as most of the boys in the back were poking and kicking and generally beating up on one of the boys in the back while Mr. Overhill laid up against the cab door sucking on the neck of his Ancient Age bottle. The poking and the kicking and the general beating along with the sucking too did not even let up any when the sheriff and Mr. Newsome eased off the pavement in the squad car and as the sheriff situated in the ring on his belt the long black club he fetched out from under the carseat some variant form of humanity crawled out from the bed onto the tailgate and attempted to urinate over the edge of it which he very nearly succeeded at. Sheriff Burton asked for Mr. Overhill's registration and asked for Mr. Overhill's license, and though Mr.

Overhill scratched around in the glove compartment and come up with the registration soon enough he could not find his license straightaway on account of how it was in his wallet and on account of how his wallet was in his gray pants and he did not have any idea where his gray pants were and commenced to cast around for them underneath the maps and the general rubbish in the truck cab and continued to cast around for them until Mr. Newsome pointed out to him that he was wearing his gray pants which, after some gaping and some gawking, Mr. Overhill learned to be the truth of the thing and he did in fact fish his wallet out from the right back pocket of his gray pants where he said it had been all along.

Sheriff Burton studied the license just like he had studied the registration and asked Mr. Overhill if he was in fact Mr. Claud Elwyn Overhill of Altoona Pennsylvania, and the poking and the kicking and the general beating up broke off of a sudden in the truckbed and five or six voices raised up at once saying, "Claude Elwyn!" and Mr. Overhill said, "Shit," and snatched back his license and snatched back his registration. "C.E." he told the sheriff and then turned around and told "C.E." to the back cab window and got answered with "Right, Claude," from two people at once followed by some florid profanity of which a solitary motherfucker was the only truly distinguishable item.

The sheriff wanted to know from Mr. Claude Elwyn Overhill just why he'd come to park himself and his truck and his crew out 29 on the roadside and Mr. Claude Elwyn Overhill told him, "We just come straight up from Louisiana and we're recuperating from it afore continuing on through Virginia and into Ohio."

"Recuperating?" the sheriff said.

"That's right."

"Seems to me you're just plain drunk," the sheriff said.

"Well that's a part of the cure," Mr. Overhill told him, "and anyhow I ain't doing nothing in this truck but sitting."

"Just sitting," the sheriff said.

"That's right."

"You not here to meet anybody?"

"Now who would I meet in this shithole?" Mr. Overhill wanted to know.

"A Lynch maybe," the sheriff told him.

"A Lynch what?"

And Mr. Newsome piped in with, "Benton Lynch, Benton Lynch. You picked him up in my store, put your stinking feet all over my chairseat."

"Who's he?" Mr. Overhill asked Sheriff Burton, "and what's his trouble?"

"Mr. Newsome here says you picked up Benton Lynch at his store a while back and carried him off with you wherever it was you went."

"Gangly?" Mr. Overhill said. "Horsefaced?"

"That's the one."

"Well hell," Mr. Overhill said, "I ain't see him since, I ain't seen him since uh. Hey," and he turned around to the back cab window, "where is it we ain't seen Benton Lynch since?"

"Benton Lynch!" the wiry tatooed white boy said back and stuck his face between two of the side louvers. "I'll fucking kill him. Where is he?"

"That's what I said, I said where is it we ain't seen Benton Lynch since?"

And the wiry tattooed white boy with his face still between the side louvers told Mr. Newsome primarily, "I will, I'll fucking kill him."

And Mr. Overhill laughed some and shook his head some and told Sheriff Burton primarily, "He don't mean nothing by it."

"You got no love for Benton Lynch then," the sheriff said to the wiry tattooed white boy and got told back, "Hell no."

"So you'd tell me where to find him if you knew where he was."

"I'd hunt him up my own self and I'd fucking kill him," the wiry tattooed white boy said between the louvers, "but I ain't got no idea where to look."

"We ain't seen him," Mr. Overhill said, "we ain't none of us seen him since somewhere or another. What is it he done anyway?"

"Well," the sheriff said and hooked his thumbs behind his belt so as to show off his paraphernalia some, "we figure he's robbed some people, we figure he's shot at one man, we figure he's killed another one. We figure he's armed and dangerous and likely a little desperate round about now.

"Benton Lynch?" Mr. Overhill said.

"That's the one," the sheriff told him.

And Mr. Overhill exclaimed, "Well I'll be goddamned!" and when the crew in the back heard Mr. Overhill being goddamned so enthusiastically they decided they would be goddamned too and so they were all goddamned together, were all moved and astounded, and did not say anything aside from the sporadic goddamns until the paltry negro piped in with "that ugly motherfucker" in a warm and affectionate sort of way.

The shock and amazement had not worn off but partly when Mr. H. Monroe Aycock eased up behind the sheriff's patrol car in his green Ford Galaxy and he got out the door with his pad and his pencil and his plastic camera and beat it on up to the truckcab like there might be some advantage gained from beating it on up to the truckcab but he did not get anything aside from a pair of hard looks and a "Who's he?" which was not even directed at him anyhow, and Sheriff Burton attempted to explain Mr. H. Monroe Aycock to Mr. Overhill but as there was really no explaining Mr. H. Monroe Aycock the sheriff let Mr. Aycock ask his questions and make his observations and air out his theories and thereby exhibit his various characteristics and his various qualities all of which Mr. Overhill paid some appreciable attention to right up until Mr. H. Monroe Aycock paused to draw breath when Mr. Overhill asked the sheriff, "Who is this asshole anyhow," which seemed to indicate to Sheriff Burton that Mr. H. Monroe Aycock had fairly well given himself away and so he went ahead and said, "Mr. H. Monroe Aycock," to Mr. Overhill and went ahead and said, "Mr. C. E. Overhill," to Mr. Aycock and did not further embellish the introduction himself though it got a Claude Elwyn or two added to it from the truckbed.

Mr. H. Monroe Aycock generally conducted curious interviews in that he usually did the primary part of the talking and wrote down the most of what he said and only every now and again asked a question, ordinarily a question that could be answered with a plain yes or a plain no, but the trouble was that Mr. H. Monroe Aycock, aside from doing the primary part of the talking, ordinarily did the primary part of the listening too since there was nobody much that cared to follow him where it was he seemed to regularly go, so when Mr. Overhill said his plain yeses and said his plain noes he never truly knew what he was saying plain yes or plain no to but just said one or the other anyhow and then rested his ears for a spell. Mr. Overhill did manage to squeeze in an actual and solitary comment just prior to the picture taking and did manage to get his own picture taken separate from the crew, even managed to get it taken twice as he was sure his eyes had been closed the first time, after which he got the fat negro and the paltry negro and the wiry tatooed white boy and Emmett and the critter along with somebody else they had picked up somewhere out onto the tailgate together and Mr. H. Monroe Aycock backed up with his plastic camera until he could get everybody just where he wanted to get them and he snapped one picture and was set to snap a second one when Mr. Overhill said to him, "Hey buddy, your camera's a little cattywumpus," and Mr. H. Monroe Aycock looked at him in that cold steely way he had practiced looking at people and let loose with a plain yes himself.

They did not run the picture cattywumpus exactly, actually they did not run the picture cattywumpus at all on account of the full-blooded Loop Road Myrick's sister's husband who was not the sort to tolerate much foolishness and looked just once at the photograph all crooked and sideways and then looked just once at Mr. H. Monroe Aycock and told him, "This ain't Batman," and so they ran the picture of the crew all square and proper and ran the picture of Mr. Overhill, the one with his eyes open, right next to it and filled up the rest of the top of the page with the story of the thing which was a dense and highly intricate piece of journalistic writing that had some plain yeses and some plain noes to it along with an ample dose of your speck-of-swirling-dust-in-the-vast-darkness-of-space talk which Mr. Overhill seemed to agree with, seemed to even have said some of, though he had not actually listened to much of it and had not uttered any of it except for the yeses and except for the noes and except for the "fine sort" which got printed underneath his name and underneath his picture.

S. A. Knox picked it up off the sheriff's desk and unfolded it and looked at the picture of Mr. Overhill and at the picture of Mr. Overhill's crew and ran the tipend of his tongue up and down the grooves in his teeth as he looked at some of the words and some of the paragraphs though did not truly read any of them prior to refolding the

Chronicle and handing it over to S. A. Billingham who unfolded it and looked at the picture of Mr. Overhill and at the picture of Mr. Overhill's crew and did not even bother with the words and the paragraphs at all but went ahead and announced, "Raggedy-assed bunch," which S. A. Knox said, "Surenough," to and Sheriff Burton nodded at. They had come in from Raleigh at the request of no one in particular but had just got wind of things, they called it, had just got wind of things at the bureau and so had dropped on by to aid in the apprehension of the suspect, they called it, though Sheriff Burton insisted he was just before apprehending the suspect entirely unaided and he suggested that maybe S. A. Knox and S. A. Billingham ought to get on back to entrapping public officials or whatever it was they'd been up to, and S. A. Billingham haled one time loud and sharp and S. A. Knox honked in his throat and said to Sheriff Burton, "I like you," and S. A. Billingham said he did too. The sheriff, however, did not have much use for either one of them and decided it straightaway, had decided it primarily on account of how S. A. Knox was ever drawing back his coatflaps so as to show off his oiled leather shoulder holster and the buttend of his automatic revolver, drawing them back even in public places or actually especially in public places, and even going as far as to take his entire coat off in Mr. Castleberry's Gold Leaf Dinette where Mr. Castleberry's girl, June, wanted to touch the shank of the thing and was allowed to. The sheriff simply did not hold with that sort of behavior in an enforcement officer and so did not have much regard for S. A. Knox from the outset and went ahead and did not have much regard for S. A. Billingham either as he was in with him and the sheriff told them to go on back to wherever it was they'd come from and get on back to whatever it was they'd been doing but they just haled at him and honked at him and went most everywhere he went so as to be available for consultation and advice though they did not ever get consulted and did not ever get advised.

It seemed to the sheriff they did not ever do anything fruitful and constructive really except for once and it was the sort of fruitful and constructive thing he was getting around to himself but just had not gotten around to yet and S. A. Billingham simply beat him to it when he got up from the Mediterranean sofa and commenced to wander roundabout the tiny paneled living room as Mr. Raeford Lynch swore and spewed on account of one thing or on account of another and the fat Jeeter chewed something and swallowed it. S. A. Billingham looked at the pictures on the walls and looked at the geegaws on the tabletops and flipped through a magazine or two prior to snatching up a photograph off the t.v. and asking the fat Jeeter, "What one's this?" and asking the fat Jeeter, "Well where is he then?" And the sheriff said he had been getting around to it himself but just had not gotten around to it yet, insisted he had been getting around to it himself, said it was the very next thing he was going to do anyhow, and S. A. Billingham held the sidedoor open for him and said, "Uh Huh," to him as the sheriff passed on into the hallway and commenced to climb the stairs with the two S. A.'s just behind him, and he knocked on the door on account of how he was local and they weren't which indicated to him that he should do the knocking and they should just do the standing around and they did just the standing around until a voice from inside asked, "Who is it?" to which the sheriff answered, "Sheriff Burton," and to which the S.A.'s answered, "Billingham, S.B.I." and "Knox, S.B.I." and then fetched their badges and their picture identification cards out from their inside jacket pockets and showed them to the door panels initially though eventually showed them to Miss Alma Sue Frazier who got told what it was once she asked, "What is it?" and then pointed to the floorboards in reply.

Jane Elizabeth Firesheets bought four pink azaleas that did not look much in the cans and did not look much along the front banister either but got planted there anyhow by Benton Lynch who dug the holes and fertilized the dirt and set the bushes while Jane Elizabeth Firesheets looked on from the ditch so as to get the wide view of the thing, she called it, so as to coordinate the various components into their proper spatial relationships which she had been told she could do best from the ditch by the nurseryman Mr. Jimmy Oakley's only boy, little Jimmy Oakley, who'd attended horticulture school and so had a grasp of coordinated spatial relationships and such though he could not grow azaleas worth a piddle. She'd brought home a half dozen hydrangeas for the sideyard and had to back on up into the hedgerow to get the wide view of them and as she was not much taken with standing in the hedgerow she asked Benton Lynch would he stop dragging ass if you please and plant the goddamn things and Benton Lynch grunted a little louder than he had been grunting and waggled his elbows a little faster than he had been waggling his elbows and so created the illusion of accelerated labor which satisfied Jane Elizabeth Firesheets for near about five full minutes after which she asked Benton Lynch would he stop dragging ass if you please and plant the goddamn things.

She decided she wanted to root some ivy around the trunk of the chinaberry tree in the sideyard and she figured a camellia bush would suit the front right corner of the house as well as anything and so she went after the ivy and went after the camellia bush in the green Nova but had got only partway to Mr. Oakley's nursery when the engine commenced to rumble and sputter and at last cut off altogether leaving Jane Elizabeth Firesheets just halfway where she was going and just halfway from where she'd come and not near anything really but for a solitary house down off the roadbank a ways with a kidney shaped pond before it and some shrubs and bushes and ornamental plant beds and such all throughout the grounds. She admired the general prospect some from up along the pavement and paid particular attention to the various spatial relationships which clearly exhibited themselves even though autumn had set in in earnest and the most of the leaves had dropped off the bushes and the shrubs and the willow trees and were getting themselves raked into a pile by Mr. Lamont Graham's least son, Jules Henry, who had his pipe going and had his rake going and had turned his thoughts loose as well and so did not hear Jane Elizabeth Firesheets call to him and whistle at him and did not see her until she was close enough to him to reach out and touch his sleeve with the tipends of her fingers which she did in fact reach out and touch his sleeve with and Mr. Jules Henry lurched backwards and snatched his pipe from his mouth and said, "Ain't no fishing here," and Jane Elizabeth Firesheets told him, "All right," and reached out all over again with the tipends of her fingers so as to soothe Mr. Jules Henry whose agitation was quite apparent and undisguised.

Of course he settled down presently as Mr. Jules Henry appre-

ciated milky whiteness as much as the next fellow and Jane Elizabeth
Firesheets asked him all about his spatial relationships prior to quiz-
zing him on his flora in general, and Mr. Jules Henry offered up his
elbow and squired Jane Elizabeth Firesheets along the kidney shaped
pondbank indicating what was what and just why it had ended up
where it had ended up. Jane Elizabeth Firesheets said it was plain to
her that Mr. Jules Henry had a way with spatial relationships and Mr.
Jules Henry admitted he had always figured he did, and they were ap-
proaching the bulbous northwest end of the pond admiring Mr. Jules
Henry's azaleas and the dying stalks of Mr. Jules Henry's trumpet
flowers along with Mr. Jules Henry's nandinas, or anyway admiring
how the azaleas did not cramp and stifle the trumpet flowers which
did not cramp and stifle the nandinas, when Jane Elizabeth Firesheets
shrieked and let loose of Mr. Jules Henry's elbow so as to dash over to
one of Mr. Jules Henry's concrete benches and sit herself down on it.
"Oh I do like this," she said and rubbed the benchtop with the flat of
both hands and Mr. Jules Henry, who had got caught up in the dash-
ing and the activity it had generated all about Jane Elizabeth Firesheets's person, found himself struck speechless temporarily and so
could not tell her straight off just where he'd got the concrete bench
from and just how much he'd given for it though he did tell her presently as Jane Elizabeth Firesheets insisted she had to know on account
of how she had to have one just precisely exactly like it.

Naturally it was only once Jane Elizabeth Firesheets decided she
had to have a concrete bench just precisely exactly like Mr. Jules
Henry's concrete bench that she recollected how the backseat of the
green Nova could not possibly accommodate one which led her to
recollect how the backseat and the frontseat and all the rest of the
Nova too was dead and broken on the roadside and so she got pitiful
straightaway and explained her predicament to Mr. Jules Henry with
her lips turned inside out. Fortunately Mr. Jules Henry possessed a fair
degree of mechanical aptitude along with a hammer and some
wrenches and screwdrivers and a drill press and he fetched his socket
set and a flathead and a phillipshead and accompanied Jane Elizabeth
Firesheets up the roadbank where he listened to her turn the key and
listened to the starter click and peered in the brake fluid container and

then proceeded to take various parts of the Nova engine all to pieces prior to blowing on them and putting them back together again which was Mr. Jules Henry's chief talent where automobiles were concerned. And after he'd gotten sufficiently greasy from the ratcheting and the screwing and unscrewing and after he'd gotten noticeably dizzy and lightheaded from all the blowing, Mr. Jules Henry determined and decided that Jane Elizabeth Firesheets's green Nova was dead and broken and so he told her it was dead and told her it was broken and suggested she get it towed off to a proper garage and Jane Elizabeth Firesheets got pitiful all over again. She turned her lips inside out and sucked up air through her nose a time or two and said she did not know what she would do, did not know anybody who would carry her where she needed to be carried as she was from somewhere else altogether and did not make friends easy like some people made friends easy and she dropped her head and commenced to snort and shake at the shoulders and Mr. Jules Henry said, "Now darling," and reached out with the tipends of his fingers.

He called the garage up the road and arranged for the towing and then started his gold Chevrolet pickup and let it run in the sideyard while him and Mrs. Jules Henry and Jane Elizabeth Firesheets drank hot tea in the breakfast room and talked about the ballet and told what ailments they'd suffered through and strayed off on spatial relationships ever so briefly prior to concluding with a catalog of the terminal cases roundabout as rendered by Mrs. Jules Henry who had the sort of flare for gravity that Jane Elizabeth Firesheets said she'd never seen the likes of previously and Mrs. Jules Henry told her back, "Well thank you." Mr. Jules Henry drove Jane Elizabeth Firesheets out to Mr. Oakley's straight off where she got her ivy, which was green and hardy, and where she got her camellia bush, which was primarily just sticks in a pot, and then they proceeded northwest a spell to the place where Mr. Jules Henry had bought his concrete bench, which was not exclusively a concrete bench outlet but sold ceramic flowerpots too and flagstones and birdbaths and a general assortment of yard ornaments. They did not have but two benches to pick from as there had been a kind of a run on benches, or anyhow as they had sold the other two in the course of the summer, and Mr. Jules Henry and an old colored man who could not raise the bench between them but could drag it well enough did drag it across the lot to Mr. Jules Henry's truckbed and then stood together at the tailgate and speculated as to how they might get it from the ground up into the truck without actually lifting the thing while Jane Elizabeth Firesheets for her part wandered in amongst the ornaments and selected two cement babies to carry home with her, one of them a cupid for the ivy bed and the other just a regular cement baby which showed a remarkable resemblance to Jane Elizabeth Firesheets's daddy's brother's boy except for the baby part of it. She carried one under each arm and secured them behind the fender wells of Mr. Jules Henry's truckbed which Mr. Jules Henry and the old colored man had not managed to speculate and hypothesize and just plain wish the bench up into yet and likely they would have left off with the speculating and the hypothesizing and the wishing too and thereby quit the whole business if Jane Elizabeth Firesheets had not picked up one end of the thing herself and so shamed the two of them into picking up the other end.

Benton Lynch slipped around the house and in through the backdoor when he heard the truck coming and he peeked out the little square window in the frontdoor and watched the gold pickup pull on into the yard and stop there and he watched Jane Elizabeth Firesheets get out one side of it and Mr. Jules Henry get out the other side of it, who he did not know was Mr. Jules Henry, and he listened to Jane Elizabeth Firesheets call out for him in the pleasant way she had of calling out for him when there was somebody aside from just him and just her to hear it, and then he listened to Jane Elizabeth Firesheets call out for him in the way she called out for him when it was just him and when it was just her, and then he listened to Jane Elizabeth Firesheets call out for him in that if-you-ever-want-to-see-any-naked-part-of-me-again way she had of calling out for him, and Benton Lynch opened the door just enough to stick his head outside and said, "What is it?"

Mr. Jules Henry wanted to know just what sort of Lynch he was since Mr. Jules Henry himself was acquainted with an assortment of Lynches, and Benton Lynch told him he was just a regular Lynch. "Tobacco Lynch or Chickenhouse Lynch?" Mr. Jules Henry asked.

"Chickenhouse," Benton Lynch told him.

"I know your daddy," Mr. Jules Henry said. "Been knowing him for years. Never seen a man could quite spit to match him."

And Benton Lynch could not recollect ever seeing a man that could quite spit to match him either.

Jane Elizabeth Firesheets got the ivy and the camellia bush out from the truckbed and removed the cement babies from behind the wheel wells one at a time commencing with the plain cement baby which she held up to Benton Lynch as she asked him, "Now who does this look just exactly like?"

"Nobody I ever seen," Benton Lynch told her.

"Ain't I got a cousin it favors?"

And Benton Lynch said, "Maybe. Somewhere."

"Ain't I got a cousin you seen it favors?" Jane Elizabeth Firesheets asked him.

"I didn't ever see him when he was little," Benton Lynch said.

And Jane Elizabeth Firesheets let the cement baby down some so as to put her own face up into Benton Lynch's face and tell him, "Christ AllMighty!"

She did not pick up either end of the bench this time but let Mr. Jules Henry and Benton Lynch struggle with it their own selves while she directed and orchestrated them to the pear tree in the sideyard straightoff but decided she did not much care for the bench beneath the pear tree once it was beneath it as there would ever be the threat of shock and discomfort from falling pears so she directed and orchestrated the thing around the house to the chinaberry tree which the ivy would get planted at the base of and so make for a suitable backdrop and Jane Elizabeth Firesheets sat down on the flat concrete top and surveyed the vista, she called it, which was only a moderate success as far as vistas go, and she decided maybe the vista would be improved from under the dogwood tree in the frontyard but once she sat beneath it she discovered the vista was not improved much, likely was not improved any, so it was back to the chinaberry tree where Mr. Jules Henry finally dropped his end of the bench and clutched at his shirtfront some and panted prior to making a wry and altogether pointed comment about women as a general form of humanity and though Benton Lynch did not laugh at it outright and did not agree with it outright Jane Elizabeth Firesheets sensed he approved of it anyhow and so she showed him one of her faces which did not seem to mean any solitary sharp and sour thing in particular but just all of them in general.

Once Mr. Jules Henry had wiped his forehead and regulated his breathing he sat himself down on the concrete bench beside Jane Elizabeth Firesheets and surveyed the vista with her. She told him it was not the best vista she'd ever seen but she guessed it would have to do, and Mr. Jules Henry told her back the vista did not matter much anyway. "A man don't so much look out from a bench," he said, "as he looks in from it," and Jane Elizabeth Firesheets slapped her hands together and told Mr. Jules Henry that was the finest and truest thing she'd heard anytime lately and she asked Benton Lynch wasn't it the finest and truest thing he'd heard anytime lately too but Benton Lynch had not been listening exactly and so said, "What's that?" instead of Yes and instead of No, and Jane Elizabeth Firesheets told Mr. Jules Henry, "Don't matter. Ain't nothing for him to see." And Benton Lynch said, "What's that?" all over again.

After Mr. Jules Henry had got thanked and departed Jane Elizabeth Firesheets told Benton Lynch all about the green Nova like maybe he'd been responsible for it somehow, and she told him it would cost money to get it back and she told him they did not have any money much on account of the shrubbery and the bench and the cement babies and whatnot and that seemed to be fairly much his fault too. So they had to make a withdrawal, Jane Elizabeth Firesheets said, had to make a sizable one, and Benton Lynch wanted to know how exactly with no green Nova to get to a place in and no green Nova to get away from it in either and she told him he'd do it like he done it at the outset, do it like he done it at the start. Naturally Benton Lynch resisted for a spell as he was not particularly fond of plundering any longer, and Jane Elizabeth Firesheets put the bullets in the gun and fetched the brown jacket out from the closet but Benton Lynch would not take the jacket and would not take the gun straightaway and attempted to have an opinion on the matter but Jane Elizabeth Firesheets showed him a face he could decipher well enough and so the gun got stuck in his pants and the jacket got buttoned across his stomach and Jane Elizabeth Firesheets laid her mouth right up alongside Benton Lynch's head and told him, "Merry Oaks," prior to nibbling on his earlobe.

He decided on the bypass, which was not so remote as other places, and he crossed the gravel road and struck out through the underbrush and on into the woods which was an oak and hickory woods primarily and then a pine grove and then a power company right-of-way and then a pine grove again and then the north border of a potato field which Benton Lynch at last spilled out into and crossed direct through the middle of prior to resting himself atop a rise at the far end where he could look down across the hillocks and creases of a pasture to the bypass and to the Citgo station alongside it which did not seem to have much in the way of business except for a Pontiac at the pumps. He ran most all the way back, sprinted actually, sprinted up the hillocks and along the creases and then due north into the pine thicket and across the right-of-way and into the pine thicket again and straight through to the oak and hickory woods where sprinting became somewhat of a treacherous undertaking but got persisted in nonetheless. He even sprinted through the underbrush and tore his trousers and his kneecaps and fairly darted across the gravel road and around the house to the backdoor which he opened with his shoulder primarily and shut with his entire backside. He could not get a breath straight off, could not swallow either, and tried to grab his knees but could not bend over on account of the pistol barrel, so he just leaned against the door and panted while Jane Elizabeth Firesheets asked him, "Well?" and then asked him, "Well?" again and then patted his left jacket pocket with her hand and his right jacket pocket with her hand prior to crossing her arms over her chest and asking him, "Well?" a third time, but he still could not get up spit or get up air either and so instead drew the Harrington and Richardson Buntline revolver out from his pants, tilted it barrel upwards, and rotated the chamber so as to drop the empty casings one after another onto the linoleum.

She said it was like riding a horse, or anyhow at first she said it was like riding a horse and then she changed it to falling off a horse since she could not seem to make riding a horse work for her like she wanted it to work for her, and she insisted he had to strike out again as straightaway as he could manage to strike out again, but even after she'd soothed him and held him and laid his ear against the fleshy part of her frontside he would not commit himself to striking out anytime soon, would not commit himself to striking out anytime later, would not do anything really but watch the ceiling and blow long forlorn breaths out his mouth and so she continued to soothe him and continued to talk at him and desired to know chiefly just what it was like to shoot at somebody and Benton Lynch set out to tell her but realized early on that he could not tell her really since it was not the shooting but the getting shot at part of it that had made the most serious impression upon him and so she asked what was it like to get shot at anyhow and he set out to tell her but realized early on it was not the sort of thing he could render into words so he did not tell her anything afterall but just watched the ceiling and blew long forlorn breaths out his mouth.

She stayed on him, stayed right atop him maybe not every hour of the twenty-four but in a pure and pervasive sort of way, and she told him to pick himself up off the ground and get back on that thing, told him there weren't no other way to it and likely he'd get put off again but he'd just have to pick himself up one more time as that was how things operated in a general way, but Benton Lynch just watched the ceilings and watched the walls some and ventilated himself and every once and again got soothed though Jane Elizabeth Firesheets gave out of sympathy and compassion a goodly while before Benton Lynch had exhausted his forlorn exhalations so he just laid around breathing hard and Jane Elizabeth Firesheets attempted to impress upon him how food cost money and rent cost money and electricity cost money and how the green Nova would cost a few dollars itself, and though Benton Lynch persisted in watching the ceilings and watching the walls too his forlorn exhalations gradually got transformed into resigned ones.

Jane Elizabeth Firesheets put the bullets in the gun and fetched the brown jacket out from the closet and Benton Lynch did not venture an opinion on the matter this time but just stuck the pistol in his pants and just buttoned the jacket shut over it and got his ear nibbled and got his privates caressed prior to getting shown out the front door. He walked a ways, walked a considerable ways west primarily but south some too and did not ever attempt to get a lift but got one anyhow from a Ruffin Jasper who was out with his brother-in-law and stopped in the road long enough to direct Benton Lynch on up into the truckbed with the Ruffin Jasper's hound which was pleased at the company and stuck its nose direct into Benton Lynch's crotch like dogs will usually insist on doing in a public place. He did not know where he would end up but just sat on the Ruffin Jasper's toolbox and took the air and watched the scenery down 14 to the south and then north on 87 towards Stacy and when he spied the frame grocery and the gaspumps just shy of the town limits he figured he knew where he'd end up after all and slapped the cabroof twice prior to jumping out onto the roadside. And he did not come back and did not come back and Jane Elizabeth Firesheets fretted straightoff and then lapsed into some peevishness which itself turned into a thoroughgoing surly fit and the surliness persisted and even got pitched up some when he still did not come back and did not come back and things had rose up to a wild and venomous head by the time Benton Lynch finally tapped on the front doorglass with his pointy first knuckle.

"Where in the shit you been that's what I'd like to know?" Jane Elizabeth Firesheets asked him once she had succeeded in opening the frontdoor which she had wanted to jerk and yank open for the effect of the thing and which she attempted to jerk and yank open but got thwarted at on account of the chainlatch and so only managed the jerking and the yanking but could not manage the actual opening part of it until she'd shut the door and unfastened the chain but by then the most of her anger had dwindled away to pure exasperation which did not lend itself to anything but hysteria really and so she blubbered and screeched and attempted to say an intelligible thing or two but couldn't seem to until Benton Lynch had stepped into the house and had shut the door behind him when Jane Elizabeth Firesheets caught a glimpse of the Tampa Jewel box under his arm and snatched it away for herself, and she prized open the top with her fingernail and found the two twenties and the singles and the dimes and quarters which was actually more that it looked like though not much more, anyhow not hardly enough to suit Jane Elizabeth Firesheets who slapped the boxtop shut and said she would just be goddamned, just be purely goddamned, and she shook the box at Benton

Lynch and defied him to tell her what would buy the groceries and pay the rent and pay the lights and get the green Nova back.

He could not tell her even after she'd asked him three or four times could he tell her. He did not even attempt to work his mouth but just leaned against the front door and at length drew the Harrington and Richardson Buntline revolver out from his trousers, tilted it barrel upwards, and let drop a lone empty casing onto the planking. "I killed a man," he said.

And Jane Elizabeth Firesheets, who had finally got surly all over again, deflated straightaway and asked him, "What for?"

"That."

"This ain't hardly nothing," Jane Elizabeth Firesheets told him and shook the box so as to demonstrate how close to nothing it truly was.

"I figured," Benton Lynch began, "I mean he just stooped over and well I figured that, I mean I just shot him."

"Dead?"

"Lord," Benton Lynch said, "stone dead," and he laid the pistol on the stacked up plastic tabletop and dropped himself onto the sofa without any grace or restraint to speak of.

"In the balls?" Jane Elizabeth Firesheets wanted to know, "killed a man in his balls? Don't seem likely somehow."

And Benton Lynch laid his long first finger direct across the center of his chest. "Near about here," he said.

"Well I guess that did punch his ticket," Jane Elizabeth Firesheets observed. "I mean this thing don't shoot peas."

And Benton Lynch told her, "Yea," which was a yea it punched his ticket primarily but somewhat of a yea this thing don't shoot peas as well.

"And I guess he dropped over dead straightaway," Jane Elizabeth Firesheets said, "I mean I don't guess he lurched and stumbled around much, did he?"

"Some," Benton Lynch told her, "sort of spun and pitched off backwards a little."

"And I don't guess they was blood all over," Jane Elizabeth Firesheets said, "I mean I don't guess they was blood all over like at the movie show."

"Come out a foot seemed like."

"A pure foot?"

"Seemed like."

And Jane Elizabeth Firesheets said, "Christ Almighty," and set herself next to Benton Lynch on the sofa with some grace and some restraint too. "It ain't like it's your fault," she said. "I mean there's some things people shouldn't never do when they're getting robbed and stooping and reaching is one of them. So it ain't truly like it's your fault, I mean you did the shooting and the killing but he did the stooping and the reaching and so there's some blame for you but there's some blame for him too."

"Hell, I just killed him," Benton Lynch said, "ain't hardly his fault."

"But he did something," Jane Elizabeth Firesheets told him.

"Not nothing but get shot," Benton Lynch said, "and it don't matter no how."

"Does matter," Jane Elizabeth Firesheets insisted, "does matter too on account of you can't go round feeling like the blame's all to be laid on you cause that ain't the kind of thing a man can bear up under."

"It don't matter," Benton Lynch said. "It don't feel like anything anyhow."

"Not anything?" Jane Elizabeth Firesheets asked him.

"Nothing."

"Might feel like something tomorrow," Jane Elizabeth Firesheets said, "might feel like something altogether entirely different tomorrow," and she drew Benton Lynch's head down to her and set about dragging her fingers across his scalp.

"Maybe," Benton Lynch told her and uncrimped his ear so as to let it lie flat.

And Jane Elizabeth Firesheets said aloud but not to Benton Lynch exactly, "A killer, a mean and vicious killer. Well Jesus Christ."

Jane Elizabeth Firesheets liked it best in the morning as it tended to get her blood going and rouse up her various senses while Benton Lynch generally liked it best most anytime and so was usually ready to accommodate Jane Elizabeth Firesheets once he'd got the crust out of his eyes, but the morning following the afternoon Benton Lynch had shot Mr. Vernon Littlejohn stone dead Jane Elizabeth Firesheets could not seem to muster him into a thoroughgoing rigidity no matter where she laid her fingers and no matter what she probed with the pointy pink tip of her tongue and naturally it was an item of some concern with her that she could near about double it over well into the gyrating and the grinding which did not get contributed to by even the slightest little snatch of nosewhistling. She knew it wasn't the best she'd had ever, knew it wasn't the best he'd had ever either and so did not bother to tell him it was for her and ask him if it was for him but instead she sat up on her elbow and wanted to know was it altogether entirely different in the daylight like she said it might be. Benton Lynch did not answer right off but just studied Jane Elizabeth Firesheets's frontside for a spell commencing with the wheatstraw part and working his way up past the milky white part to the plum-colored parts which were somewhat swelled out but somewhat shrunk in too and drooping and sagging as well off to the low side, and there in the morning sunlight he studied how they drooped and sagged and considered the freckles and the moles on them and the place the bed-spread had made along with the hairs that sprouted all roundabout the plum-colored parts, most of them tiny little hairs but some of them not and none of them anything he'd ever bothered to notice much before.

"I bet it's worrisome," Jane Elizabeth Firesheets said. "I bet it's worrisome this morning when it wasn't any worrisome last night. That's it. That's it right there, ain't it?"

And Benton Lynch told her, "Uh Huh," told her he supposed it was.

"Well the blame ain't hardly all yours," Jane Elizabeth Firesheets said and she commenced to refresh him on the stooping and the reaching aspect of the thing and reminded him just how the blame was to get portioned out after which she had a thing or two to say on horses and the riding of them, or actually the falling off of them primarily along with the getting back up on them again, but as Benton Lynch had heard all about the falling off them and the getting back up on them previously he got up from the bed and went out the bed-room door and down the hallway to the bathroom and Jane Elizabeth Firesheets continued to talk about the blame and continued to talk about the guilt and the impact of the whole business only louder now, loud enough to be heard over the watertaps anyway, and Benton Lynch splashed his face and looked at himself in the mirror, looked at the pointy places some and the hollowed out and angular places too, but looked at the two vacant and sunk-in places primarily, and heard the talking from the bedroom, persistent and steady and concluding with a pair of isn't its that did not get answered straightaway and so got contributed to once Jane Elizabeth Firesheets had sat up in the bed so as to increase her volume some. "Isn't it?" she said a third time and Benton Lynch, who figured it probably was or likely could be, splashed his face and told her, "All right."

She counted it out and totaled it up two times over and got somewhere around $64.00 the first time and somewhere around $67.00 the second and so figured it at just about $65.50 which was not enough to pay the rent or the lights and the fuel oil together but was just barely enough to get the green Nova back from the garage on 29 where the engine of it had got taken to pieces and blown on by a certified mechanic who knew just where to be windy and so had got the thing running again. Of course they did not have any way to fetch it back but to walk over and get it and Benton Lynch volunteered to do the walking over and the fetching back as the garage was such an appreciable ways from the hideaway-bungalow and as Benton Lynch wanted to get out and wanted to walk anyhow, but Jane Elizabeth Firesheets seemed to feel that he did not have much business out in public since he had, if he would pardon her for mentioning it, killed a man just the day before which was precisely the sort of thing to stir up people, and so she walked the appreciable ways to the garage on 29 or anyhow set out with the intention of walking the entire appreciable ways but had only walked a small portion of it when she got a ride with a passing Dunleavy who had been quite taken with her backside and so stopped for her. She bought some eggs on the way home and bought some milk and bought some Champale and picked up a *Chronicle* as well which she opened in her lap in the green Nova and studied the front page of, especially the part all roundabout the photographs of Mr. Vernon Littlejohn with his ordinary arteries and Mr. Vernon Littlejohn with his buckle and his bedsheet, and she took in the leaden sky portion of it and the brisk and gusty portion of it along with the ashen and the tufted and gray and the bracing portions too and of a sudden she found herself altogether struck with the lyrical beauty of the thing, taken with the poetry and the drama of it, and somewhat caught up in the tragedy though not caught up in the tragedy entirely. Mostly she just felt significant, significant primarily on account of Benton Lynch who had been significant himself for a spell but had cocked his hammer and pulled his trigger and thereby had become something beyond significant, something bigger than significant really, something rare and desperate and utterly fearful which naturally enhanced the angularity and the pointiness and the vacancy to a considerable degree, and so Jane Elizabeth Firesheets felt not only significant but began to feel a little sweltery too and she got herself home in a ferocious hurry and burst on in through the frontdoor with her eggs and her milk and her Champale and her *Chronicle* as well.

Benton Lynch had not moved from the sofa, or anyhow was on it when she got back just like he'd been on it when she left, and she deposited the eggs and the milk and the Champale on the stacked up plastic table and threw herself down beside him without much grace or restraint to speak of. "You're famous," she said, "top of the front page where all the big news goes," and she dropped the open *Chronicle* onto his lap for him to peruse and study it but he did not peruse and study it really, did not hardly glance at it, so she took it back up and commenced to read it out loud to him leaving one hand free to gesture with when she got to the dramatic and the lyrical and the poetical parts of the thing, and she did wave her hand and move her fingers and change her voice up and down and generally performed the entire article in a sterling and impeccable sort of way but Benton Lynch did not appear much moved by any part of the business and just sat like he'd been sitting and watched the wall before him some and the ceiling above him some. As for Jane Elizabeth Firesheets, however, she was considerably moved by the dramatic and the lyrical and the poetical parts of the thing and she got sweltery all over again and took her gesturing hand and set it to rubbing and massaging herself about the neck and shoulders prior to migrating south a ways, and she told Benton Lynch there was something about a famous, something about a dangerous and mean and vicious man that set her blood to boiling, and Benton Lynch left off watching the wall and watching the ceiling too and got a little interested in the workout Jane Elizabeth Firesheets was inflicting upon herself, and she opened up her shirtfront and maneuvered her fingers even more vigorously still and Benton Lynch stuck his pointy nose between the shirtflaps so as to see the process up close and once Jane Elizabeth Firesheets had detected the first little piece of whistling she grabbed Benton Lynch's head from behind and mashed his face direct into her frontside.

It was all considerably savage and brutal even if it did take place on a sofa mostly. The clothes got tore some and balled up and thrown all roundabout the room and in the throes of passion Benton Lynch bucked up of a sudden and loosened Jane Elizabeth Firesheet's front teeth with the back of his head. But there was not much lasting harm done otherwise and they banged together and gyrated and even fell off the sofa and onto the hardwood without missing a beat, and for a spell Benton Lynch nosewhistled like he had not nosewhistled anytime lately and Jane Elizabeth Firesheets oooohhhed and squealed and bounced and jiggled and generally made such a spectacle of herself that Benton Lynch began to figure maybe the gyrating and the oooohhhing and the nosewhistling and the milky white parts and the plum-colored parts too were all in fact the best things to partake of and have in this life, were maybe even the only things worth partaking of and worth having, but before he could decide and conclude outright that there was not anything better, that there was not anything more really, he commenced to tingle and commenced to pant and flush and felt himself surge and discharge and knew of a sudden that there was actually not anything worth partaking of and worth having, especially not the milky white parts and the plum-colored parts and the wheatstraw parts too. And Jane Elizabeth Firesheets exhaled most profoundly and laid the back of her hand across her forehead and said it was the best she'd had ever, and she asked him wasn't it the best he'd had ever too, wasn't it just absolutely the best he'd ever had and Benton Lynch grunted prior to blowing out a breath himself and contemplating the ceiling.

She said she would not ask him to but for the rent money and the light money and the fuel oil money as well as the grocery money which she hated to even bother him with as he'd shot at one clerk lately and killed another, but it did not seem to Jane Elizabeth Firesheets that the time was right for them to get evicted or disconnected or frozen or go hungry either and so she had to suggest and felt compelled to insist that Benton Lynch do what it was he generally did when things got tight and do it just like he generally did it so as to maintain the rhythm and habit of things and keep his nerve up where he usually kept it, and though he was not perceptibly enthusiastic Benton Lynch didn't object or argue and instead just sat around on or about the sofa and laid around on or about the bed and watched all the walls and watched all the ceilings for three or four days which Jane Elizabeth Firesheets called cooling off but which did not seem to be anything really to Benton Lynch. And when they did at last go out Jane Elizabeth Firesheets decided when and decided where and fetched the map out from the glove compartment and decided that too. For his part Benton Lynch only did the actual plundering while Jane Elizabeth Firesheets parked off a ways and left the engine to run, and he felt fairly usual and fairly normal when he asked his question and when he showed his revolver and when he gave his answer too, but once Mr. Radford lowered his arms some so as to reach for the cash drawer Benton Lynch got agitated of a sudden and commenced to feel all tight and quivery inside and he shook his gun close by Mr. Radford's upper lip and threatened him afresh and turned partway around to Mr. Burke and Mr. Mountcastle and made some overtures to them as well prior to returning his attention to Mr. Radford and addressing him all over again with the breech of the revolver mostly, so Mr. Radford reached down to the cash drawer without seeming to move his hand or his arm either and brought out just regular money which he put into a sack.

Jane Elizabeth Firesheets said it was a pure haul, said she could tell just by the bulk of the thing, and she lifted the sack up off the carseat and set it down again and said she figured it for $400.00 anyway and maybe $450.00 and even after she'd spilled it out on the bedspread she still figured it for $375.00 and thought it might hit $300.00 while she was partway through the counting of it, but it did not ever approach $300.00 really, did not ever get past $238.00 which it did not even get up to until the third time through, but Jane Elizabeth Firesheets still insisted it was a pure haul coming as it did just after the $65.50 which had not struck her as any sort of haul at all. And she commenced to spend it straightaway like maybe it was $400.00 after all, and she paid the rent and paid the lights and paid the fuel oil and took the Nova out to the K-Mart Plaza where she went into the Food Lion straight-off and bought a family pack of ribeye steaks and chopped mushrooms in a jar and large grade A eggs instead of the medium ones and real butter and a bottle of sparkling water and beer imported from Canada and spinach quiche in a milk carton and the pie shells to go with it along with four rolls of the powderblue toilet paper that smelled so sweet and she figured she was done once she got to the checkout but she decided she'd have herself a magazine and as she could not choose between the *People* and the *Us* and the *Star* and the *Life* and the *Cosmopolitan* and the *Glamour* and the *Enquirer* and the *Family Circle* and the diet book and the horoscope book and the word puzzles she went ahead and bought one of just about everything but the almanac and she said, "Cash," in a loud high voice when they asked how would she pay for it all and she showed off the twenties and the tens and the fives and the ones too. There was not hardly any left after that but there was enough anyhow to carry into the K-Mart where she could not buy outright what she had intended to buy outright but where she could lay it away and did lay away a little Japanese radio/television that would sit on your stomach if you had the muscles for it and she figured she did.

As for Benton Lynch, he just cooled off some on the sofa and cooled off some on the bed and cooled off some at the kitchen table and watched the walls and watched the ceiling and looked at the woman on the *Cosmopolitan* and at the woman on the *Glamour* and tried to work a word puzzle, even wrote down some letters in the boxes, but did not get any of it right and so went back to the walls and the ceiling and the women on the magazines until the Thursday he got to see himself on a rock and he looked at that for a spell. He sat around for near about ten or twelve days altogether and looked at and watched most every item in the house and anything he could spy out the window too, and every morning Jane Elizabeth Firesheets drove down the road to the Easy-Go Mart and brought back a *Chronicle* and she would read the parts about Benton Lynch out loud to him when there were parts about Benton Lynch to read and she read the one about Mr. Overhill with special relish and vigor, the first time through with the vigor so as to get the facts of it and so as to, ever so briefly, vilify the wiry tattooed white boy, and the second time through with the relish so as to savor Mr. H. Monroe Aycock's style and poetical grace which Jane Elizabeth Firesheets did the most of the savoring of though she encouraged Benton Lynch to savor it some himself.

He laid around a week before she even hinted that maybe he would finish cooling off sometime and go out and get hot all over again and it was not until ten days that she said outright he would surely plunder somebody somewhere sometime soon and it was not until twelve days that she told him where and told him when and attempted to persuade him to agree with it, attempted to persuade him with her plum-colored parts primarily which she brought out from her nightgown into the morning light, and as it was a Sunday the plum-colored parts struck Benton Lynch as particularly forbidden and so naturally all the more worth having and he endeavored to have them straightoff and lunged at them nose foremost but got intercepted and interfered with and just generally thwarted until he agreed to the where and agreed to the when after which he was given the free run he had been burning to get until he got it when he decided he did not want it much after all. She did what she did to him like she usually did it and he did what he normally did to her and they got tangled and locked up together like they most always got tangled and locked up and in the regular sequence and then there was some oooohhhing and groaning on her part followed by a smattering of nosewhistling on his, all of it concluding and terminating in a general disengagement and she laid on her side of the bed and whimpered some and perspired and he laid on his side of the bed and sweated and just laid still and just sweated until he got up of a sudden and carried himself off to the bathroom where he splashed his face and looked in the mirror at his pointy places and at his angular and hollowed out places prior to glaring down between his legs at something else entirely and he said, "You," which came out loud and firm and primarily in the way of an accusation, and from the bed Jane Elizabeth was just set to ask him, "You who?" had her mouth all open and

ready for it but did not get to ask it after all on account of the squealing and the screeching and the brief spell of honking that came from
outside somewhere, somewhere close by, and Jane Elizabeth Firesheets
said, "What in the shit is that?" instead which was not what she had
opened and readied her mouth to say but which seemed to suit better
to the moment.

The sheriff beat the bullhorn one time with the fleshy part of his
palm, which was the most of his palm, and said, "Goddamn this
thing," without pulling the trigger as that was not what he had a
mind to broadcast. But once he did in fact pull the trigger after the
solitary lick the bullhorn honked again and squealed again and about
half screeched and so Sheriff Burton beat it one more time with his
open hand and pummeled it with some additional abuse. Deputy Larson told him it was the batteries likely but the sheriff snapped back
that he had put in new ones just lately and he wondered out loud why
it was Deputy Larson couldn't watch the crowd like he'd been instructed to do and Deputy Larson said, "Yes sir," and hung his head
and turned back around to the crowd which was not much of a crowd
really but just Mr. H. Monroe Aycock and Mr. Jack Albright and Mr.
Jack Albright's negro tenant who was a Stone and Mr. Jack Albright's negro tenant's dog who was a plain assortment of most
everything possible.
S. A. Knox said he had his mouth too close to it and S. A. Billingham said he had the trigger pulled in too far and so he drew his
mouth back some and let the trigger out some and it did not screech
and did not squeal and did not honk but a little and so the sheriff
went ahead and drew a breath and said, "We know you're in there,"
which the sheriff had always wanted to say, especially through a bullhorn, and it came out and filled the air almost exactly like he'd imagined it would except for the squealing which punctuated it. "Don't
make any trouble now," he added. "You'd best give yourself up," and
that came out plain and clear without any squealing whatsoever but
without any volume much either as the sheriff had inadvertently let
loose of the trigger. So he squeezed the trigger again and the bullhorn
screeched and honked and squealed and he beat it twice this time

prior to throwing it onto the ground and using just his cupped hands and just his lungs instead. "Don't make any trouble now," he hollered. "You'd best give yourself up," and him and S. A. Knox and S. A. Billingham and the crowd and Deputy Larson over his shoulder studied the frontdoor of the hideaway-bungalow, which was the only door they could see of it, but nobody saw it swing open, nobody saw it get set ajar even the least little bit as it did not get swung open or set ajar either but just got looked out ever so briefly by Benton Lynch and by Benton Lynch only as Jane Elizabeth Firesheets was not tall enough to see out the little square windows.

S. A. Billingham picked the bullhorn up off the ground and laid his mouth next to the little end of it and squeezed the trigger and identified himself and identified his partner and identified their agency and did not get preceded by any squealing or screeching or honking, did not get interrupted by any, and did not get punctuated by any either which prompted Deputy Larson to wonder if maybe it wasn't the batteries after all, to wonder if maybe throwing it on the ground hadn't done it some good, and he asked Sheriff Burton if maybe he didn't figure that was the case of it and while Sheriff Burton had a few things to say to Deputy Larson in reply they did not any of them have much at all to do with the bullhorn or the batteries either. S. A. Billingham said he knew they were in there and he said they'd be smart not to make any trouble and go ahead and give themselves up, and when the sheriff told S. A. Billingham he'd just finished saying the same thing himself, S. A. Billingham told him it was the sort of thing that bore repeating especially without the squealing and the screeching and the honking to distract from it, and Deputy Larson figured it was a bad connection, a bad connection that maybe the impact had healed up, and he set out to tell how he'd beat his lawnmower with a stick of redoak once but got sent around to the back of the house by Sheriff Burton who was not much interested in the deputy's mechanical aptitude.

The mayor's secretary had been fairly much touring the city ever since she heard where they were going and why which she found out from Mrs. Deputy Larson who did not get occasion to tell the mayor's secretary hardly anything she did not know already, and as it was a Sunday morning people did not have much to do but worship and since a desperate criminal holed up in a farmhouse and surrounded by the law seemed a degree or two more inviting than an oak pew most people figured they'd worship later. So the crowd, which had started out as two white men, a negro, and a dog, expanded in size and complexity and came to encompass all manner of people who were as a group anxious to see justice done and a little bloodthirsty too. Naturally Sheriff Burton recognized the bloodthirstiness right off as he was trained to and so he called on the radio for his auxiliary deputies which was the loan officer at the First Union, Mr. Fontain, along with Mr. Demitt the pharmacist, but he had not needed a radio really since Mr. Fontain and Mr. Demitt were as bloodthirsty as the next fellow and came out from the crowd so as to control it and marshal it as best they could, and they did control it and did marshal it on their own for a while but got assisted eventually by Miss Bambi Kinch who stepped out from the Action News 5 van and marshaled and controlled the crowd herself without even attempting to.

She offered Sheriff Burton her fingers and Sheriff Burton took ahold of them and shook them ever so slightly and got told what a pleasure it was to be seen again and said near about the same thing himself and was set to make a comment or two on the general predicament when S. A. Knox S.B.I. stuck out his fingers to Bambi Kinch and told her, "S. A. Knox S.B.I." prior to pondering Bambi Kinch's yellow hair which was S. A. Knox's favorite kind of hair to find on a woman. Bambi Kinch shook S. A. Billingham's fingers too and Mr. Fontain and Mr. Demitt wanted their fingers shook as well but had a crowd to control and marshal and so had to settle for nods and grins and such. Larry got the camera out from the back of the van and carried it over to where Bambi Kinch wanted it which was four different places altogether before he struck on one with a backdrop to suit her, and Bub switched on the switches and plugged in the plugs and set up the antenna and then carried the camera cable over to Larry when he was good and ready to. She talked to the sheriff first and was careful to put the bungalow door just between him and her, and the sheriff told her this and told her that and speculated and wondered and then got cut off while he still had some theorizing left to do and he told Bambi Kinch he had some theorizing left but she told him back she wanted a few words from an S.A. on account of their general

credibility, she called it, and S. A. Knox volunteered to give her whatever few words she wanted and he told her armed robbery and told her
attempted armed robbery and told her assault and told her murder
one and then he rattled off the names near about as fluently as the
sheriff himself, commencing with the Busick and concluding not
with the Radford exactly but with a widowwoman Smallwood instead, a widowwoman Smallwood from Altamahaw who had got all
fractured and scrambled and could not recall how. And Bambi Kinch
said, "Him?" and S. A. Knox directed her attention around to the
green Nova and told her, "Him for sure," and then laid his hands on
his hips so as to show off his straps and his holster and pistolbutt
which launched Sheriff Burton into a regular paroxysm but not extended regular paroxysm on account of the scream that came out
from the bungalow-hideaway or anyhow came out from the entrails of
it, Bambi Kinch called it, and she asked S. A. Knox what it was anyhow and S. A. Knox told her, "Duress likely," which satisfied Bambi
Kinch well enough and satisfied S. A. Knox too but did not much
suit the sheriff who wondered out loud, "What in the hell was that?"
and Jane Elizabeth Firesheets said it had been intended for a plaintive
cry.

"Well what's the good of it?" Benton Lynch wanted to know, and
Jane Elizabeth Firesheets explained how they would not storm a place
that had a threatened woman in it and it seemed to her she could not
suggest and hint at a threatened woman any better than with a plaintive cry so she cut loose with a second one and then peeked out from
behind the front windowshade to see the effect of it which was not
entirely apparent straightaway as Jane Elizabeth Firesheets could not
read Duress off S. A. Knox's lips though Sheriff Burton's sentiments
seemed plain enough. And Jane Elizabeth Firesheets said, "I knew it, I
knew it right off. Come here, Benton, come here and look and see if
it's not that woman off the t.v. I figured it was, I'd know that yellow
hair anyplace. Come here. Come here." But Benton Lynch did not go
anywhere really and just stayed on the sofa with his pistol in his hands
and his arms dangling down between his knees and when he was not
watching the ceiling and watching the walls he watched Jane Elizabeth Firesheets's backside ever so briefly and blew out a forlorn exha-
lation.

Sheriff Burton said he did not give a happy shit what they called it as long as they did something on account of it, and then he pardoned himself to Bambi Kinch who excused him.

"Like what?" S. A. Knox wanted to know, and Sheriff Burton told him as he was the S.A. seemed he could come up with something on his own, or anyhow him and S. A. Billingham together might be able to generate a solitary idea between them, just some tiny little useful notion, which Sheriff Burton said it seemed to him they should be able to do somehow.

"All right then," S. A. Knox said, and S. A. Billingham said, "All right then," for himself, and they did get together and did discuss the matter and at length did decide on some tiny little useful notion which S. A. Knox got the privilege of announcing as he was the most maligned S. A. of the two. "We'll fan out," he said.

"What for?" the sheriff asked him.

"So as to surround the place," S. A. Billingham told him.

"And then?"

"Why then we'll tell him to come out," S. A. Knox said.

"And he'll come out?" the sheriff wanted to know.

"That's right."

"The boy's killed one man, shot at another, cracked an old woman's head open, and plundered near about the entire countryside and he's gone come out just because you tell him he'd better?"

"That's right."

"What about the girl?" the sheriff said. "What about the DU-RESS?"

"Might be she's in with him," S. A. Knox said back. "Might be she's in with him and he's just gone mean on her."

"Might be she's not."

"Well, she likely was once anyhow and maybe still is. I got my suspicions."

"Oh you do?"

"Yes sir."

"Well what's it gone be then?" the sheriff wanted to know.

"We'll fan out." S. A. Knox told him. "We'll fan out and take him when he comes to us."

And Sheriff Burton said, "All right," and S. A. Billingham said,

"Agreed," and S. A. Knox said, "Agreed," too just to finish the thing.

The sheriff circled off to the right and the S. A.'s circled off to the left which put the sheriff in the backyard and the S. A.'s in the front-yard and forced Deputy Larson over into the sideyard, and as they had not agreed beforehand just who would do the shouting, Sheriff Burton and the two S. A.'s together commenced to shout almost in unison very nearly the same request but not the same request exactly and so they all three decided independently they would shout again and thereby clear up any lingering confusion as to the coming out and the surrendering, and they all three did shout again, almost harmoniously this time.

Jane Elizabeth Firesheets said she'd never been so worked up over a thing before, said she'd never felt the blood pump and surge in her like it was pumping and like it was surging and she stepped round from window to window and snuck a look out at the crowd and at the S.A.'s and at the deputy and at the sheriff himself and her blood pumped and surged and got her generally worked up like she'd never been worked up over a thing before. She told Benton Lynch they'd insist on a helicopter and insist on a jet and insist on getting carried wherever it was they wanted to get carried like Daytona or maybe even so far as Miami where they had brick houses too, and she said they'd hide and lay low for a spell and Benton Lynch would grow a mustache and she'd have her hair trimmed away and maybe they'd get some legitimate work somewhere after a bit and so just blend in and mesh and whatnot, and she asked Benton Lynch wasn't that the way it should go, wasn't that the way it could happen, but from his place on the sofa Benton Lynch just breathed hard and watched the ceiling and watched the walls and said he couldn't grow a mustache, said he didn't have the follicles for it.

Sheriff Burton told Deputy Larson, "Pssssst," and Deputy Larson thought it was a groundsnake and jerked his feet out from under himself and jigged briefly prior to getting Pssssssted at again and then just plain called to and so he left his post in the sideyard and held a brief confab in the back of the house with Sheriff Burton who sent him off to the trunk of the squad car after the gun and after the tear gas which he had not consulted the S.A.'s on but which he figured would be a little more persuasive than all the hollering and yelling he could muster. And though Jane Elizabeth Firesheets did not know what the deputy was off to fetch exactly she saw for herself he was off to fetch something anyhow and she called to Benton Lynch from the backdoor and told him to come look how the deputy was off to fetch something and Benton Lynch came to the backdoor to look out the windows of it and see for himself but the deputy was already gone from sight by the time he got there and the sheriff moved around to the sideyard and so got gone from sight presently himself which left nothing to look at really, or nothing anyhow to hold Jane Elizabeth Firesheets's attention and she hurried off to the frontwindow so as to see what it was the deputy had gone off to fetch while Benton Lynch lingered at the backdoor and looked out the little square windows of it across the yard to the tobacco field, where the stalks had been cut and plowed under, and on beyond that to the pine grove and the water hole amidst it and the scantling dogwoods that had managed to take root and flourish somehow or another and above it all to the sky which was not especially tufted or gray but plain blue mostly clear out to where it disappeared over the pine tree tops which was where Benton Lynch looked primarily once he had looked most everywhere else and which was what he exhaled and sighed at prior to throwing the barrel bolt and turning the knob.

Jane Elizabeth Firesheets did not hear the bolt and did not hear the knob and did not hear the thing open but heard it shut plain enough and so ran to it and looked out the little square windows of it at Benton Lynch's backside as it receded from her across the yard and on into the field, and while Sheriff Burton did not hear the bolt or the knob and did not hear the thing open either he heard it shut plain enough his own self and ducked around the corner of the house in time to see the profile of the pointy nose and one hollowed out cheek and a solitary vacant eye along with the Harrington and Richardson Buntline revolver dangling at the end of the near arm. He cocked his own nickel-plated pistol and hollered, "Hold it, buddy," with about as much authority as he could manage but the nose and the cheek and the eye and the gun along with everything else beat it on out of the backyard and into the dirt field where the feet went from furrow to furrow and generated some velocity. The sheriff hollered, "Hold it, buddy," a second time as loud and earnestly as before and fired a shot into the air but the feet did not stop or even slow any and so he aimed this time and hollered with his arms out before him and his left eye shut and then he squeezed off the first one and the whole angular pointy and hollowed out body flinched but proceeded nonetheless, or anyhow proceeded until he squeezed off the next one which took the feet away and put Benton Lynch on his knees atop a furrow where he bobbed back and forth until the third one hit him and knocked him over on his face. And Sheriff Burton opened his left eye and trotted some himself out across the backyard and into the field while Jane Elizabeth Firesheets took up a dishtowel off the kitchen countertop and commenced to rip it into long slender pieces.

They all came round the house presently, the S. A.'s in somewhat of a squat and with their guns drawn, but everybody else stark upright and at a dead run with Deputy Larson in the front followed hard up by Mr. Fontain and Mr. Demitt and the unmarshaled and uncontrolled crowd behind them, or anyhow that part of the unmarshaled and uncontrolled crowd that still had some run in them which included Bambi Kinch who always wore her flats just in case and had included the cameraman Larry until his cable got wrapped around a treestump and stopped him of a sudden. The sheriff had come up cautious and ready but there had not been anything to be cautious and ready about really as did not anything move but the plume of dust his nostril stirred up and then there was not that even, so he loosed the pistol from the fingers and eyed the empty chambers of it and then got run up on and surrounded and just generally washed over by the S.A.'s and the deputies and Miss Bambi Kinch and everybody else too who all wanted to see a dead man up close and saw one. And Sheriff Burton said to S. A. Knox and S. A. Billingham, "He wouldn't stop," and he said to Deputy Larson and Deputies Fontain and Demitt and Bambi Kinch and everybody else too, "He wouldn't stop," and S. A. Billingham poked the pointy tip of his shoe into Benton Lynch's ribcage and thereby satisfied himself that the culprit was in fact deceased before stepping across the body so as to grab up a piece of Sheriff Burton's shoulder with his fingers and tell him, "Outstanding," which was followed by what congratulations and salutations seemed appropriate to the moment and the sheriff got his hand shook and got his back pounded and even took ahold of Bambi Kinch's fingers for the second time in an hour before anybody recollected Jane Elizabeth Firesheets who Deputy Larson recollected first off and he said to the sheriff, "What about her?" and jerked his head at the house which reminded the S.A.'s primarily and they both exclaimed, "Her!" all at once and to each other prior to making off in a squat with their guns drawn.

They took up positions on either side of the backdoor and S. A. Billingham kicked the thing in with his left foot as somehow that seemed to him more expedient than turning the knob and S. A. Knox plunged on into the kitchen with S. A. Billingham right up tight behind him. They snuck up the hallway to the front room where S. A. Knox peeked behind the sofa and S. A. Billingham yanked open the coat closet door without discovering anything between them really except for an ever so insubstantial stale sock aroma, and then they snuck back down the hallway into the bathroom and S. A. Billingham snatched up a handful of shower curtain and jerked the thing down off the hooks but did not find anything in the tub except for the green spot the drip had made, and as it was S. A. Knox that went into the bedroom first it was S. A. Knox that truly found her when she was at last found though S. A. Billingham came in just behind him and found her himself and together they stood fairly much in the doorway and holstered their pistols and dropped their chins some and just generally contemplated Jane Elizabeth Firesheets who lay all naked and goose pimply atop the mattress with her ankles tied to the iron bedposts on one end and her wrists tied to the iron bedposts on the other. She humphed and harumphed and attempted to speak but she had a pair of gauzy underpanties stuffed in her mouth and so could not make much in the way of conversation and instead she jerked and squirmed and rolled on the bedlinen revealing the back of her milky whiteness as well as the front of it and setting her plum-colored parts into fairly violent motion and they accelerated to a constant and near about mesmerizing speed and maintained it until S. A. Knox sat himself down on the mattress and relieved Jane Elizabeth Firesheets of the balled up gauzy underpanties while S. A. Billingham loosed the rags from her ankles and the rags from her wrists. "Praise

God!" she wailed. "Praise God!" and as S. A. Knox endeavored to wrap his coat around her she laid her bare frontside against him and whimpered.

Mr. Emmett Dabb had mixed the punch in a bucket and would not tell what it was but for the gingerale that the Leaksville Lassiter deciphered and arrived at once she'd separated the various components in her mouth and smacked them between her lips, and though Mrs. Estelle Singletary insisted it was Hi-C too Mr. Dabb would not admit to anything but the gingerale and thereby touched off and peeved Mrs. Estelle Singletary who had a great native capacity for irritation and she snapped at and bickered with Miss Bernice Fay Frazier for a spell to relieve herself some. The food got put all roundabout the trailer on most everything that had a top to it, and as there was not any considerable room inside, the men got to stand outside chiefly except to get the chicken and the deviled eggs and the bean salad and the sponge cake when they felt a need to. The fat Jeeter and little Ivy Jeeter Throckmorton Lanier sat together on the Mediterranean sofa and held each other in their arms and every now and again the fat Jeeter would dab at her eyes with Mr. Raeford Lynch's yellow bandanna and wonder aloud, "Why, oh why?" and when his mouth and his throat were otherwise unoccupied the Reverend Mr. Lynwood Wilkerson would attempt to tell her straightoff just exactly precisely why, oh why, but mostly he would hold up his open hand and chew fast for a spell. For his part Mr. Raeford Lynch was intensely profane and made some extraordinarily vile comments on the outside of the trailer and every now and again stepped through the doorway and made a vile comment or two on the inside as well prior to excusing himself to the reverend and to the ladies and especially to Miss Jane Elizabeth Firesheets who was in the care of the widow Mrs. Askew and the widow Mrs. Hayes in the far corner of the den and who found herself from time to time in the care of Mr. Raeford too which got her knee touched and her arm rubbed and her general self leered at. And it was while Mr. Raeford was touching and rubbing and leering that the men on the outside did their most earnest conversing under the guidance of Mr. H. Monroe Aycock who had come as just a regular human being and did not take notes or snapshots but nonetheless could not help but observe how apt it all was, dramatically speaking, and the consensus among the men fell with Mr. H. Monroe Aycock who set his left foot up on the trailer step, laid his forearm across his knee and said dramatically it was likely the aptest thing he'd ever seen.

Commander Avery selected the casket himself as not the fat Jeeter or Mr. Raeford or Otway Burns either were much disposed to pick one, and he decided upon the plain pine box with the iron fittings which seemed to him to make an altogether appropriate statement and he said as much to the fat Jeeter and Mr. Raeford and Otway Burns too but did not any of them seem taken with the aura of the thing except maybe for Jane Elizabeth Firesheets who had not got consulted exactly but went ahead and observed that the pine casket was rough and rugged like he'd been rough and rugged, and she attempted to observe an additional something but her lips turned all inside out on her and she put her face against Otway Burns's coatfront and touched his arm with the tipends of her fingers. The people who viewed him were most generally the people who had gorged themselves in his honor the night previous, or not in his honor exactly but somewhat in his honor anyhow, and they arrived at the Heavenly Rest curious to see what he looked like up close since not anybody of them had known him much but for his likeness on a rock. The fat Jeeter received sympathy on the Duncan Phyfe couch with little Ivy Jeeter Throckmorton Lanier on her left side and Mr. Raeford's sister Vergie on her right side and with Jane Elizabeth Firesheets off just a slight ways in a chair where she got some sympathy too and hard looks every now and again on top of it. But sympathy was not primarily what people had come on account of and instead they gathered all roundabout Benton Lynch's half-open casket and viewed him with noticeable intensity as he had been mean and vicious and savage and considerably sought after and finally shot to pieces though he did not look it really, did not look anything really but pointy and sunk in and hollowed out and just generally deceased.

The men malingered outside in the cold on Commander Avery's frontporch and smoked and spat and listened to Mr. Fontain and Mr. Demitt who raised up their arms like the sheriff had raised up his arms and said, "Hold it, buddy," like the sheriff had said Hold it, buddy, and closed their left eyes like the sheriff had closed his left eye and made pistol shots with their breath, and then they talked about the sheriff, not just Mr. Fontain and Mr. Demitt, but all of them talked about the sheriff in a way he'd have been pleased to hear if he'd been there to do it, but he was not there to do it as it had not seemed the fitting and just place for him to be and so he took supper with Mrs. Messick and got talked at and congratulated and fawned over and was even offered seconds once but not in a voice that seemed at all sincere and he wasn't hungry anyhow and just drank his water and picked at his greenbeans and tore his piece of loafbread in half.

He led the procession himself though Deputy Larson said he'd do it, insisted he'd be pleased to, and he used the lights primarily but let loose with the siren every now and again at crossings and he took the route by the hospital and then left across the boulevard to the Burlington road and out to the cemetery. The afternoon was cold and likely tufted and gray to the trained eye though just cloudy to most everybody else and sunless and windy too out in the memorial park part of the cemetery where they had bulldozed the trees but only breezy every now and again up on the hillside where there were some elms and some oaks and some cedars of Lebanon and even some shrubbery here and there to break the monotony of pure headstones. Mr. Raeford's brothers Benton, Jip, and Harland Lynch carried one side of the casket and Mr. Raeford himself along with Otway Burns and William Petworth carried the other side of it and they set the whole business down over the hole atop the belts of the commander's shiny chrome casket lowering contraption which freed Mr. Raeford to fetch the fat Jeeter out from one side of the limousine and freed Otway Burns to fetch Jane Elizabeth Firesheets out from the other. And all the Lynches and the Jeeter-Lynch and the Firesheetses sat in the folding metal chairs under the canopy, that is it was only Lynches and the Jeeter-Lynch and the Firesheetses until Mrs. Phillip J. King fell over a guy wire and got put in Mr. Harland Lynch's chair to collect and tend to herself.

The Reverend Wilkerson said pretty much what he usually said but with some embellishments as it was a special case, and the tenor Mr. Tupperman sang The Lord's Prayer without any accompaniment or much success to speak of, after which the proceedings got benedicted by the reverend and at last finalized by Mrs. Jack Vestal who did not sound out with her "Farewell, brave soul" all shrill and firm like usual but said it anyhow and flung her good linen handkerchief which settled on the very lip of the grave and got kicked on in by Mr. Raeford. And that was fairly much the end of it though people loitered and smoked like people will and the widow Mrs. Askew and Mrs. Hayes corralled little Ivy Jeeter Throckmorton Lanier's husband down the hillside and waved their fingers at him for a spell. And then there was not anybody left but for the pair of men from the vault company, who sealed up the casket and covered it over, and but for Sheriff Burton, who stood off a ways and watched the canopy come down and the chairs get folded and the grave get filled up, and then there was not anybody but him and he still stood off a ways and still watched until a gust of wind came ripping down from the hillcrest and blew the solitary wreath over backwards when Sheriff Burton turned of a sudden and very nearly fled.

Mrs. Messick had prepared an actual beefroast and dirt grown chunked potatoes with butter in them as opposed to the flaked and reconstituted variety she was usually partial to, and she called up the stairway and hollered up the stairway and screeched up the stairway and then dialed the phone but she did not get an answer and did not get an explanation and did not get an apology, did not get anything but agitated and disgusted and so called and hollered and screeched up the stairway to tell Sheriff Burton as much and when he did not answer and did not explain and did not apologize again she got more agitated and more disgusted. He had not turned on the lights when he came in as it had not been dark when he came in but just gray and murky and he sat in the bedroom with the table and the straight chair in it chewing his foremost finger and watching the afternoon give way to the evening, and though he heard the calling and the hollering and the screeching and the ringing of the telephone he just sat in the darkness and breathed in and breathed out and figured and pondered and wondered until late in the night.

Fuquay-Varina
1983

About the Author

T. R. Pearson was born in Winston-Salem, North Carolina, in 1956. He is the author of a previous novel, *A Short History of a Small Place.*